MASTER of MEN !

THE SPIDER®

The DOOM LEGION

by WILL MURRAY

cover by JOE DeVITO

Altus Press • 2018

ACKNOWLEDGEMENTS

Argosy Communications, Inc., Elizabeth Carter Bissette, Gary A. Buckingham, Kendra Crossen Burroughs, Frederick C. Davis, Jeff Deischer, Dafydd Neal Dyar, Joel Frieman, Shlomo Frieman, John Fleming Gould, Robert J. Hogan, Tim King, Dave McDonnell, Matthew Moring, Don O'Malley, Norvell W. Page, Ray Riethmeier, Emile C. Tepperman, Matt Terrio, Harry Steeger, and Robert Weinberg.

FRONT COVER ILLUSTRATION COMMISSIONED BY

Dave Smith

To Joel Frieman,

The Fan Who Owned The Spider...

Chapter 1

HALLOWEEN BALL

SOME PRESENTIMENT of danger caused Richard Wentworth to turn his head toward the new arrival to the Halloween masquerade ball being held at the Metropolitan Museum of Art.

Other heads turned as well. How could they not?

For the man striding boldly through the wide entranceway stood nearly seven feet tall. A leather hood concealed his head entirely, save for a narrow horizontal slot permitting vision. He wore a medieval outfit—cotton tunic, laced breeches and buccaneer boots—suggesting a medieval executioner. One black-gloved hand clutched the oaken handle of the double-headed axe belonging to the grisly trade.

Nita van Sloan turned, and her violet eyes widened like twin explosions of wonder.

"Dick! That man is almost a—"

"—a giant?" finished Wentworth, intense grey-blue eyes tracking the imposing individual. His gaze fell to the fellow's boots and he saw that they were elevator boots, the soles unusually thick.

"Not quite a colossus, my dear," Wentworth murmured pleasantly. "His boots are built to increase his height. Yet, even without them, he must stand at least six feet, four."

"I wonder who he might be?" breathed Nita.

"It's a puzzle," admitted Wentworth, scion of the Wentworth millions. "I do not recall anyone on the social register standing quite so tall, although there are several six-footers among the Four Hundred."

Suspicion threaded his tones. Those piercing eyes narrowed slightly, almost imperceptibly.

Nita gasped. "Do you suspect—?"

Wentworth's bantering tone darkened. "I always suspect strangers. Even at a Halloween gala. Crime takes no holidays. Surely you know that."

Wentworth strode forward, his proud black-haired head showing a slightly arrogant tilt. An aristocrat among men; his forebears had bequeathed to him certain innate mannerisms that made him stand out among all others.

Gathering up his forest-green great cloak, Wentworth accosted the tall fellow with a pleasant smile.

"Welcome!" he greeted laughingly. "Since I am attired as Robin Hood, and you are a headsman from approximately the same era, I said to myself I must meet that fellow. Perhaps we knew each other in a past life."

The voice muffled by the leather helmet was thick with an accent that Wentworth recognized from his fighting days in the World War.

"I am pleased to make your acquaintance, *Herr* Robin. Or is it properly *Herr* Hood?"

Wentworth laughed lightly. "No one living knows the true name of the famous outlaw of Sherwood Forest. So I imagine your guess is as good as mine. Do I detect the flavor of Wiesbaden in your voice?"

The tall man hesitated before replying in his deep, guttural intonations.

"You are very astute, *Herr*— You have me at a disadvantage. For I do not know your true name."

Nita drew up, and at this remark she laughed as well. "It isn't every day that a visitor to New York fails to recognize the notorious Richard Wentworth."

"*Ach!* Now I place you. Richard Wentworth, a man of means

and a criminologist of some note. Many tales are told about you—not all of them pleasant."

Wentworth let that comment pass. Retaining his pleasant smile, he said, "Permit me to introduce my fiancée, Maid Marian—otherwise Miss Nita van Sloan. Whom do I have the pleasure of addressing?"

"You may call me Friedrich von Maur. And you are correct about Wiesbaden. My people hail from the Taunus Mountains. Perhaps you have heard of them."

Again, Wentworth laughed. "Your people, or your mountains? I am confused."

The lower portion of the leather helmet belled out with the headsman's laughter. "You have a sense of humor, I see. *Gut, gut.* Very good. It is wonderful to have a sense of humor. You possess a handsome face, and therefore you have much to feel good about."

There was an edge to the man's voice at that last. Wentworth frowned slightly. The guttural tone seemed to verge on jealousy. This caused Wentworth to wonder what sort of face the leather helmet concealed. Perhaps not one that was very favorably disposed. The lines of the thick leather were rather unpleasant, without being repulsive....

Removing a silver cigarette case from his green tunic, Wentworth extracted a slim cigarette, offering the open case to the other, who declined with an upraised palm.

"I do not indulge, thank you."

Shrugging nonchalantly, Wentworth pocketed the case, lighting the cigarette with an elegant platinum lighter.

Exhaling a long plume that spread into a greyish web of smoke, Wentworth inquired dryly, "What brings you to New York, von Maur?"

"I was in the war."

"As was I," returned Wentworth. "My rank was major. And yours?"

"Alas, I never rose very high in the Kaiser's army. I achieved no special rank. But all that was long ago. I have come to take in the Art of War exhibit. I understand there are many unique items to be viewed here."

"Indeed," said Wentworth. "I myself am anxious to look them over, once the conversational opportunities die down."

"Speaking for myself," declared von Maur, "a close study of the exhibit summons me more than any conversational interludes." Realizing the inadvertent slight of his statement, the tall man caught himself. He bowed slightly. "Not that I have not found our exchange most pleasant. Perhaps we will continue once I have satisfied my curiosity."

The tall headsman clicked his heels rather smartly, and Wentworth returned the favor. It was as if two aristocrats had encountered one another after a long lapse of acquaintance.

"Good to meet you, Wentworth," said von Maur.

"I look forward to hearing your appraisal of the exhibits," returned Wentworth, nodding his head.

Slinging his headsman's axe over his burly shoulder, the tall German strode off, boot heels clicking.

Nita van Sloan leaned in to ask, "Does that satisfy your curiosity?"

A tight smile dribbled smoke which formed an obscuring mask before Wentworth's handsome features. "On the contrary. It rather exacerbates it. I have the distinct feeling that I have encountered that individual in the past."

"During the war… or since the Armistice?"

"I do not know, but I fail to place the name von Maur."

"If I recall my German correctly," said Nita, watching the man's broad back disappear through the arch leading to the exhibit hall, "Maur means 'dark.' "

"Quite so. He is 'Friedrich of the Dark.' In all but his name. But a legitimate one. And yet…."

Wentworth's eyes became reflective and his brow furrowed deeply. Nita could tell that Dick was searching his memory for the face behind that muffled voice.

When he appeared to have drifted off too far, Nita wondered, "I wonder what could be keeping the commissioner?"

"Kirkpatrick is often late," Wentworth said shortly. "You know that. Some vital police business, no doubt."

Suddenly, Nita was tugging at his forest-green cloak, pointing across the room.

"Dick! Look who just walked in."

"Who?"

"Nothing less than the notorious Spider. In the flesh."

THE MAN who entered from the side was garbed in a flowing black cloak which shuddered and shook with each step. A wide-brimmed slouch hat covered his head. Beneath that bent brim was a domino mask of rich black velvet, to which was attached a skirt of dark muslin, which served to conceal the wearer's lower face.

His shoulders were twisted, and he walked as if his back was broken. Instinctively, the milling crowd, who were attired as witches, goblins and other fanciful figures of old, gave way before him. There was an aura of the sinister about him.

"Passable, passable," murmured Wentworth. "I might almost believe he was The Spider."

"His cape is incorrect," pointed out Nita.

"No doubt. I am unfamiliar with The Spider's gait, never having encountered the gentleman."

"Hush, Dick. Do not speak ill of the dead."

Wentworth's eyes grew steely. "The Spider has been believed dead many times. I have never believed it before, nor do I believe it now. He always manages to come back from the dead, rather like a vampire who emerges from his casket at midnight."

The couple were watching The Spider as he promenaded around the crowd, accepting a drink from a nervous waiter, and sampling the hors d'oeuvres.

Behind the velvet mask, glittering eyes surveyed the room. And when he turned suddenly, his cloak caught the light of ceiling chandeliers, revealing a thin stitching of silver thread in the patten of a spider's web that might have been woven by a demented arachnid. For it was broken in places and not symmetrical. It had the appearance of a cobweb created by agitated spiders.

"Clever touch," quipped Wentworth.

"Too bad The Spider himself never thought of that," agreed Nita.

Wentworth was studying the man's curtained profile. It appeared to be a rough face, with a nose that was discernibly flat. Nature had not been kind to it. Or perhaps it was a face that had been pummeled by horny-knuckled fists in the past.

"I do not place the gentleman's rather blunt profile," Wentworth decided.

"This is a Halloween ball. You're not supposed to…."

"I do not place it," snapped Wentworth, "and I do not like it. There is something about that fellow that raises my hackles."

Nita lowered her voice conspiratorially. "Your hackles… or *The Spider's?*"

"The Spider, my dear, does not have hackles," Wentworth returned smoothly. "He does, however, possess intuition. And at this precise moment, that intuition is making his scalp tingle."

"Shall we attempt an introduction?"

Wentworth shook his head carefully. "No, I prefer to observe this imposter first. To see if my suspicions are borne out."

"Oh, Dick! Is there anyone present who doesn't raise your suspicions?"

Richard Wentworth did not reply to the exasperated question.

He was studying the guest dressed as The Spider. Of all the people present, Wentworth knew that this apparition was not in fact the feared Master of Men. For Dick Wentworth himself was The Spider... lone wolf avenger of justice who operated outside of the Law....

Someone dressed as Frankenstein's monster sidled up and, through gristle-grey lips in a greenish face, drawled, "It looks as if someone is stealing your thunder, eh, Wentworth?"

Wentworth turned scornful eyes in the fellow's direction.

"Are you insinuating that I am The Spider himself?"

"Not at all, not at all." The man laughed nervously. Wentworth's stern tone had deflated the other's jocular demeanor. "It's only, well... you know what the tabloids say."

"I know only that the tabloids are sensationalistic trash and rarely print the unadorned truth," snapped Wentworth. "Only what serves their circulation."

"You have to admit that he's a creepy sort."

"That much, I do admit. Perhaps he is the real Spider, here to steal some rare artworks. I think we should all keep an eye on him. Don't you?"

The nervous laugh returned. "I will leave that to you, old boy. You are the criminologist. I am merely a—"

"Merely the head of the largest textile concern in greater Manhattan."

"You recognize me even in this getup?"

"I do, McAllister. So nice to see you again. You should drop by my club sometime."

"I will look you up," said McAllister, clumping off in his clumsy thick-soled boots.

Wentworth's gaze had returned to the figure of The Spider. The deformed figure was moving about the room again, and the unnerving manner with which he inspected those he met caused revelers to shrink and retreat before him.

They were in the museum's uppermost floor, milling about beneath the skylight. The night was clear, the air was crisp, and there was a moon that looked as if it was fashioned for floating through the Halloween sky. It was a slim ghostly crescent that shed little lunar light, its full glory shrouded in darkness—as if masked.

Stars spangled the sky with their lesser lights twinkling like winking eyes.

Nita looked up and shivered.

Noticing this, Wentworth asked solicitously, "Are you cold, my darling?"

"It's not that, Dick. But for a moment those stars made me think of the myriad eyes of wicked spiders."

"Since when are you afraid of spiders?" laughed Wentworth.

"Since The Spider first walked," Nita replied with a slight shudder.

Richard Wentworth fell silent. A sternness came over the impassive shield that was his face.

Well did he know what his beloved fiancée meant. Ever since first Wentworth picked up the twin automatics of The Spider, this paladin of the people could know no rest, enjoy no normalcy so long as the criminal element ran unchecked. Long ago, they had come to the realization that they could never enjoy the pleasures of marriage or parenthood, or a future unblemished by scandal. It was the price they paid for their shared secret… however unwillingly….

As his thoughts ruminated upon their unconsummated fate, Wentworth spied a streak of emerald raking the night sky. It described a parabola as it passed overhead.

"Look, Dick!" Nita said excitedly. "A shooting star!"

Shortly after the green streak faded, there came a loud bang that was muffled by the grey walls of the museum. The floor under their feet actually shook briefly. The night sky turned greenish for a flash of a moment.

"That sounded close!" someone called out.

"I wonder what it was?" exclaimed another.

A few—but very few—of the costumed attendees went out into the night to see what had happened. Most remained, displaying the unconcern of the very wealthy toward what did not directly affect them.

Nita looked to Dick imploringly.

"Unless I am very much mistaken," stated Wentworth. "A meteorite has struck nearby. From the dull sound of its thud, I would suspect Central Park."

"How odd," breathed Nita. "Of all the places to land in crowded Manhattan...."

"Perhaps I might break away for a moment and see what is to be seen." Wentworth's steely eyes were upon the skulking Spider figure as he spoke these words. Studying his chiseled profile, Nita realized that her fiancé was torn between his interest in the sinister caped figure and his desire to investigate the source of that unexpected sound.

Bringing her lips close to her lover's ear, Nita whispered a suggestion. "I can keep an eye on that rather fashionable Spider if you would prefer to go out into the night."

"I do, and I would. Thank you, my dear. I shouldn't be long."

Breaking away, Richard Wentworth headed for the marble stairs that led below and struck out into the crisp evening.

The weird figure of The Spider also slipped away at the same time....

Chapter 2

HELL'S HALLOWEEN

BOUNDING DOWN the granite steps of the Metropolitan Museum of Art, Richard Wentworth was conscious of the flapping of his green great cloak around his pumping legs. Slung across his muscular back was a deerskin quiver packed with fletched arrows.

In one hand, he clutched his horn bow strung with catgut.

As he landed in Central Park's Great Lawn—the museum abutted the park at its rear—Wentworth made a short, sharp left. He might have been the actual Robin Hood plunging into Sherwood Forest in a bygone era, for he had drawn the face-concealing rustic hood over his head….

Except that the dusky greenery of Manhattan's magnificent park was lit by an eerie, pulsing glow. If pieces of jade, emerald and chalcedony could be ignited to create a fire, they might glow with such an eerie green luminance as this. It turned the Central Park Reservoir immediately to the north into a chlorophyll-colored pond, and outlined the stark trees in such a way that it smacked of a horror movie director's set.

The weird glow was coming in the direction of the Ramble, a labyrinth of twisting paths containing the folly known as Belvedere Castle.

Wentworth hastened in the direction of that awful radiance. It had a sick quality, one that made his stomach clench.

"What manner of meteorite could produce such a witch-fire?" he muttered to himself.

For a moment he regretted not claiming his waiting limousine, parked on Fifth Avenue. It would have enabled him to reach the heart of the park by one of the transverse roads. So eager had he been to investigate Wentworth did not consider that option.

A sudden sharp woman's scream impelled him to redouble his efforts. On pumping legs, he made his way fearlessly toward the spot where the meteor had made impact.

A tightening of his firm mouth was the only outward sign of his concern....

As he moved through the trees, Wentworth caught sight of a second point of illumination. It was a lambent flame, but soon it turned into a roaring rush of fire.

As the flames climbed in intensity, the woman began screaming over and over again.

"Fire! God, I'm on fire! Please save me!"

"Good Lord," choked Wentworth.

His pounding feet brought him to the woman who was weaving among the stout trees of Central Park, stumbling and careening in her wailing agony.

She was a human torch!

Throwing off his forest-green great cloak, Wentworth fell upon her, threw her to the ground and attempted to smother the leaping flames with the heavy material. Her moans were terrible, ghastly.

"What happened to you?" he demanded.

Her words were halting gasps. "A jack-o'-lantern... did this. His eyes... *green....*"

"Talk sense, woman!" Wentworth urged. He was beating at the green fabric, desperate to quench the last licking tongues. The stench in his nostrils was terrible. Roasted human flesh.... He had smelled it before, in India... Asia... and since....

The writhing, moaning woman managed to say, "His glowing eyes burned me...." before she expired.

Wentworth was reluctant to accept her death. He carefully shook the woman's shoulders, turned her face to the moonlight, but it was not moonlight that painted her agony-twisted features. Rather, it was the hideous green light emanating from the fallen meteor, just yards away.

Respectfully covering her features with the tail of the great cloak, Wentworth stood up and looked around. A cold cosmic anger burned in his grey-blue eyes.

"A jack-o'-lantern did this…" he said coldly.

Impossible as the tale had sounded, Wentworth knew that a dying woman would not lie… understood that people in the last extremity did not waste breath on banalities.

Under the green wool tunic were holstered a pair of .45-caliber automatics. These were the guns of The Spider, but Wentworth did not reach for them. Instead, he picked up his dropped bow and drew a shaft from the quiver across his back.

Nocking the arrow on the bowstring, he slipped through the trees like a stalking hunter of old.

Perhaps Richard Wentworth was not far from being a modern Robin Hood. He did not steal from the rich so as to lift up the poor. Instead, he stood as a human shield for the helpless downtrodden humanity against power-drunk criminals who would squeeze the last ounce of blood from their lives.

Something moved in the greenery ahead, and Wentworth's questing eyes snapped around to fix upon a bizarre figure that walked in a herky-jerky manner. It was almost as if a child's wind-up toy had been brought to life.

The head of the thing was huge and round, as if it was encased in something like a diver's helmet. But the head casing was no construction of steel and glass such as deep-sea divers wear when braving the pressures of the depths.

For the color of the head was a brilliant orange! *Pumpkin* orange.

Wentworth crept up on the creature, his arrow ready for instant release.

Although he was crafty in his avoidance of twigs, the park was blanketed in a profusion of fallen leaves. Wentworth could not help but step on the desiccated membranes, which rustled under his careful tread.

The bulbous-headed thing heard his approach and turned.

There in the moonlight, he beheld its face. The orange visage of a jack-o'-lantern! The mouth was a ragged slash suggestive of drunken laughter. The nose was a mere triangle. But inverted, like the empty nostril cavities of a skull turned upside down.

The eyes were a different matter entirely. They were shaped like five-pointed stars—stars that glared with an emerald light that seemed somehow unearthly.

As the thing swiveled about jerkily, Wentworth saw the beams emanating from those artificial eyes. Whatever they touched, smoked and began to burn: piles of leaves, dried tree bark, common park litter.

Then the terrible radiance of those star-shaped optics turned their full force upon him.

His face instantly felt hot, feverish. Wentworth smelled the smoke of one sleeve as it smoldered before he noticed that it was catching fire.

No time to put out the burning cloth. His hands were full. Drawing back on his bow string, he released the arrow. It flew true.

Whatever that thing was, it had caused a woman to combust into flame and perish horribly. Now it had turned its terrible wrath upon him. There would be no quarter given.

The hardwood shaft whistled in a short flight and it struck the apparition dead center in its chest, no doubt bisecting the beating heart… assuming that the creature had one.

The monster was knocked backward and fell. In falling, its head struck a rock, causing the jack-o'-lantern skull to split open. The travesty of humanity jittered in its death throes, throwing up lean arms as it howled weirdly.

Wentworth ran up to the fallen creature and saw that the greenish rays burning from the eyes were cooking the star-like holes in what was undoubtedly a large pumpkin that had been carved into the form of a Halloween jack-o'-lantern.

With a fierce kick, Wentworth shattered the broken gourd, revealing the face which the head concealed.

He steeled himself for some weird horror, but instead beheld simply a man's thin face. The jaw was undershot, and the planes of the features unremarkable. The man appeared to be in his late thirties, or perhaps older. It was not the face of a criminal or a mad man. The fellow might have been a mere accountant. His clothing was a shapeless assemblage that might have been purchased at a joke shop or novelty store.

To all outward appearances, this was a man dressed for Halloween.

Except for the eyes. The true color could not be discerned. For they glowed eerily. Each one sent out a single coruscating beam of jade light. Cool light, pleasant in its way. Whatever the rays touched inexplicably caught fire as if scorched by a blowtorch.

As Wentworth watched with a kind of curious horror, the glow began to fade. The man's convulsions increased, then subsided. His heaving chest became still. He was dead.

When the emerald glow finally ceased, thin moonlight revealed the actual color of the eyes. They were a faded grey. There was nothing remarkable about them.

Wentworth's attention went to the green radiance emanating from the woodsy pocket of the park called the Ramble. The meteoric glow was an identical shade of green.

That coincidence told Richard Wentworth that it was death to approach the meteorite....

Fading back, he circled the pulsing thing from interstellar space.

On the other side of the point of impact, a police whistle skirled. Three times the officer gave a long blast.

Then his voice raised in a cry, "Get out of here! Get the hell out of the park! Let the law handle this."

The sound of running feet came as the evacuation of the Ramble commenced.

Wentworth recognized the man's voice. Patrolman Riley. He knew him well. Riley had the Central Park beat, had enjoyed it for several years. Whenever Wentworth and Nita van Sloan went for a horseback ride in Central Park, Riley always had a sunny smile and a hearty greeting.

Continuing his circle, Wentworth attempted to rendezvous with the shouting officer. As he worked his way toward the Ramble, he smelled burning hair. Shortly thereafter, he came upon a collie lying on its side, whimpering piteously. Its hair was scorched black. Around its throat was a red collar. A long leash wound blackly like a serpent around its head.

"Poor fellow," murmured Wentworth. The leash warned him to expect a human victim before long. For there could be no doubt that someone walking their dog had encountered the jack-o'-lantern man.

Moving on, Wentworth found what he took to be the dog's owner. The man—if it was a man—had been burned in a manner quite differently from the poor woman.

This individual wore a simple grey suit. It was untouched. The head was something different. It was a charred ball of smoking moat. There was no hair—only a bonfire burning at the top of the smoldering skull. Nor was there any way to recognize the fellow, for his features were entirely obliterated.

Checking his pulse to make sure he was deceased, Wentworth loped onward, jaw clenching in repressed anger, his quiver of arrows rattling softly… what fiendish power was abroad in the night?

Suddenly, a lurid light swept the surroundings. The red head-lights of a police machine! The sound of a powerful engine came muttering up.

SWIFTLY CHANGING direction, Wentworth pelted toward East Drive, stepped challengingly into the path of the oncoming limousine. Lifting his hands, he attempted to flag down the machine.

The heavy auto braked, and the back door fell open. Out popped the familiar gaunt form of Commissioner of Police Stanley Kirkpatrick, eyes frosty in his saturnine face, the waxed points of his military mustaches bristling.

"Dick! What on earth is going on here!"

"I just left the masquerade ball, Kirk. A meteorite has landed in Central Park. But it is no ordinary meteor. People have been consumed in flames."

"I'll summon the fire department by radio."

Wentworth reached the limousine side, bent down and said, "Send for the riot squad. We are not dealing with an ordinary fire. But with something far worse."

Nodding, Kirkpatrick used the shortwave in his passenger compartment to call for help.

"And get the fire department down here as well!" he finished, snapping the microphone back onto its hook.

Stepping fully out of the limousine, Kirkpatrick smoothed the perfect points of his military mustache and his greying brows turned inward as they regarded his longtime friend.

"I notice that you have come as Robin Hood."

"I do not see your costume, Kirk."

The police commissioner vented a short laugh. "Look more closely. These brass buttons have been out of date for thirty years." Reaching behind him, he brought out a constable's helmet of the type popular at the turn of the century.

Wentworth would have smiled ironically—but it was not a night for levity.

Instead, he remarked, "Going as a police constable of your youth?"

Kirkpatrick demanded, "What did you mean by *far worse?*"

Wentworth pointed toward the pulsing glow that filled Central Park with macabre illumination.

"That meteorite is no ordinary one, Kirk. In some manner I cannot understand, its radiations are affecting anyone who wanders too close to it. They become human automatons. But that is not the worst of it. Some insidious force is thrown out. And anything it encounters, or touches, smolders and then bursts into flame."

Noticing for the first time Wentworth's right arm, Kirkpatrick saw the charred wool.

"I might as well confess to you now," said Wentworth solemnly, "I was forced to slay a man so afflicted. I had no choice in the matter. His eye-beams were setting the surroundings alight. And he had already killed at least one woman, if not others. Pierced his heart with my arrow, Kirk."

"There will have to be an inquest. But you know that."

"And I am ready to face it. But first we must get control of the perimeter surrounding the meteorite. I heard Officer Riley attempting to clear the park. I was on my way to warn him about the dangers when I heard your approach."

"Get in!" said the commissioner, dropping back into the limousine. Wentworth slid in after him, slamming the door shut. He had to rearrange his longbow several times to make it fit comfortably across his lap. The quiver made sitting awkward, to say the least.

As the driver got the machine in motion, Wentworth rapidly filled in his old friend.

"I came upon two victims, not counting a collie dog that had been burnt alive. There may be others."

Kirkpatrick nodded heavily. "From what you tell me, it is a virtual certainty. This is ghastly!"

"But the threat can be contained if we act properly."

It was a tribute to the long-standing friendship between

Richard Wentworth and the police commissioner that when a threat arose to the great city, they often worked hand in glove, not exactly as equals but very close to it.

That Wentworth had often been accused of being the dreaded Spider was something of which they seldom spoke. Despite their deep friendship, should the wealthy criminologist ever be brought to book for The Spider's many crimes, Kirkpatrick's sense of duty would not permit him to hesitate in sending his closest friend in the world to Sing Sing Prison and the electric chair....

The limousine whirled around the bend... and a tottering figure reeled into its lurid headlamps!

It was a human scarecrow. That is, a tall thin man dressed as a cornfield scarecrow. He flopped around as if boneless, yet managed to stay on his feet. Dry hay stuffing protruded from throat, wrists and waist. His tattered clothes might have been borrowed from one of the hoboes who camped down by the rail yards.

"That man looks injured!" cried Kirkpatrick.

Wentworth's hand shot out and arrested the commissioner from opening his door.

"Not so fast. I recognize that clumsy gait. That man is a victim of the Green Meteorite. He is not on fire. The poor wretch is *causing* destruction."

The limousine driver tootled his horn, and the scarecrow suddenly pivoted.

Only then did the awful radiance of his eyes glare out.

The windshield glass began to bubble and cloud up. The paint on the hood smoked and smoldered.

"The devil!" cried Kirkpatrick.

"It is one of the Meteorite Monsters. There is no saving the devil, as you call him." Turning to his companion, Wentworth added, "Kirk, one of us will have to shoot him."

Kirkpatrick hesitated. "Very well. I will do it."

Unbuttoning his police officer's tunic, he pulled out a long-barreled .38-caliber revolver, then thrust himself out of the limousine.

As the window glass continued melting, Kirkpatrick lined up a single shot and fired toward the chilly green beams coming from the scarecrow's eyes.

A single bullet shattered the skull of the thing. It flopped about, twisted, and its knees buckled. It fell on its face finally. As it lay there dying, green radiance made a halo around its shapeless sack-encased head. Beneath the fractured face, the melting asphalt gave up a bitter stink.

Clapping the door shut, Kirkpatrick resumed his seat. "Sergeant Carter," he commanded. "Do your best to move us to the other side of the meteor glow."

By this time, the windshield was impenetrable to vision. The driver took up a revolver of his own, reached up and knocked out the glass so that he could drive safely.

Once they were in motion again, Wentworth muttered darkly, "This is a damnable development."

"And for it to happen on Halloween, of all nights," groaned Kirkpatrick.

Chapter 3

ENCOUNTER WITH DOOM

PATROLMAN AUGUSTUS RILEY was cursing as he rushed around the edges of the Ramble, where the hellish thing from outer space had landed.

He soon shouted himself hoarse, by which actions he had succeeded in stampeding some of the late-night strollers out of this part of the park. But that was the least of the task before him….

A weird greenish glow, pulsing like a beating heart, turned the entire park as green as Christmas trees. Muttering to himself, he said, "Orange would've been a more fitting color, if you ask me. This being Halloween night."

But no one had asked Patrolman Riley. He alone had the thankless task of keeping the public out of harm's way. And no sooner had he shooed away those who had been present when the monster rock had landed, than rubberneckers and other gawkers attracted by the unusual glow began infiltrating the park to see what was up.

Turning them back was going to be a challenge.

Riley ran to intercept a gaggle of gawkers. He raised his hands and said, "Turn around and go back. This is a police emergency. Nothing to see here for the public."

"Nothing to see?" one of them yelled back. "It looks like the Martians have landed!"

"No Martians, and begone with you. I'm not going to say it twice." Riley's voice was a croak. He could not make himself understood. There was no volume left in his raw throat.

"Is this a publicity stunt?" another man demanded.

"Not that I know of!" Riley hurled back. "And it doesn't matter. You are ordered out of the park. Turn around and make tracks. Or I'll run you all in."

The gaggle was stubborn. They wanted a look at what was making the greenish glow.

In the distance came the urgent cry of approaching sirens....

Hearing that, Riley broke out in a relieved grin, lifted his steel whistle and blew as strong a blast as his laboring lungs could summon up.

"Here come the paddy wagons," he warned. "If any of you are standing about when they pull up, it's off to the station house with you."

That did the trick. The curious group broke up and retreated from the park.

Riley moved toward one of the transverse roads, so he could meet the arriving police. At least he hoped those were police sirens he heard. For all he knew, the fire department had been summoned.

Reaching the side of the road, Riley stood in a nest of dried leaves and watched for the approaching vehicles. From time to time, he turned his gaze in the direction of the pulsing green light coming from the weird thing that had slammed into Central Park with enough force to cause the surrounding buildings to tremble and shake.

Ambling about on his beat, Riley had been one of the first ones shaken. A greenish flash had accompanied a loud boom. He had thought that a bomb had gone off. Then he saw the eerie cold glow. He knew it was no bomb.

Watching the lambent green light while he waited, Patrolman Riley was struck by the way it ebbed and flowed. He wondered what was making it glow. He knew that most meteors entering the earth's atmosphere were composed of iron, nickel or some common earthly substance. The streaks they made in the sky corresponded to the colors created when such substances were burned. He had read that in a magazine article somewhere.

Taking off his uniform cap and scratching his head, Riley searched his memory for what substance produced a greenish glow. But he could not remember exactly.

In the act of lifting his cap to set it back on his head, his body gave a brief shudder. He seemed to hesitate, as if suddenly forgetful. He stared at the cap in his hand as if no longer recognizing it. Turning his wrist, he examined the policeman's hat from several angles, and did not appear to recognize it any longer.

Fist loosening, he dropped it, looked around and began walking aimlessly.

His burning emerald eyes lifted to a tree branch where a solitary squirrel perched. He stared at the small grey animal, as if not recognizing it, either.

The squirrel stared back with small dark eyes, as if fascinated by the weird greenish luminance of Patrolman Riley's gaze.

The squirrel had been holding an acorn between its tiny paws. The nut grew warm and then hot, and the squirrel suddenly dropped it. Then its smooth fur started to shrivel and smolder. Shrieking, the squirrel shot up into the trees like a furry-tailed comet.

There came a soft sound of bursting flame, a screech, and the squirrel dropped down into a pile of dead leaves, which soon caught fire.

The tiny funeral pyre for the squirrel held Patrolman Riley's attention for several minutes. No comprehension showed on his expressionless green-lit face....

Behind him, the road turned hell-red, painting the surrounding trees and mixing with the greenish glow to produce an atmosphere of dismal chromatic murk.

Stiffly, Riley turned toward the road and the throaty purr of an approaching automobile....

Chapter 4

CONFLAGRATION IN GREEN

COOL NIGHT air was pouring through the empty windshield of the police limousine as it chased its bouncing red headlight beams through Central Park.

At the side of the road, Stanley Kirkpatrick caught sight of a smoking body and shuddered visibly. Leaping flames danced upon the fallen hulk. Lesser bonfires blazed here and there. They could be seen through the trees, which were shedding the first leaves of Autumn.

Kirkpatrick grunted, "The morgue will be busy tonight."

Taking a shallow turn, the driver came upon a figure in blue stepping off the side of the transverse roadway.

"Commissioner, that looks like Riley up ahead."

"Pull up to him," ordered Kirkpatrick.

Then Richard Wentworth noticed the chilly green shine emanating from the officer's eyes, and the absence of a uniform hat. The sixth sense that belonged to The Spider alone began raising an alarm in his subconscious.

"Sergeant Cartor," he rapped out. "Do not approach that police officer. If you value your life!"

"Dick!" Kirkpatrick shouted. "Whatever do you mean?"

"Tell the driver to do as I said, Kirk."

Reluctantly, the Commissioner gave the order and the driver braked expertly.

Only then did Officer Riley turn completely about and the strong luminosity of his eyes flared up, obscuring his blank features with their garish glow.

He started forward, loose fingers forming fists.

Stepping out of the limousine, Richard Wentworth reached in for his bow. Donning the quiver of arrows, he extracted a feathered shaft and nocked the weapon expertly.

On the other side of the stopped machine, Stanley Kirkpatrick emerged with drawn revolver.

The police officer came on with strange intent. His head was hunkered down between his shoulders. At either side of his gun belt, his fists were two mallets of hard bone, the knuckles showing pale white.

Wentworth carefully drew his bow string back as far as the tension would permit. "Give the word, Kirkpatrick, and I will strike him in the shoulder."

Instead of replying, the Commissioner called out, "Officer Riley! This is Kirkpatrick. Halt your advance. Stand at attention. That is an order!"

But Riley did not respond. He did not seem to have a mind anymore. His advance was strange, menacing. Yet he did not go for his revolver.

Then the hood of the police limousine started smoking. Swiftly, its dark paint bubbled ominously….

His face paling, Stanley Kirkpatrick said with heavy reluctance, "Do your best, Dick. You have my official permission. Above all, do not kill him. He is a police officer."

"I do not know what he is anymore," said Wentworth firmly. "But you have my word that I will not harm Riley."

Wentworth had been an expert at archery, going back to his days at Dunherst. He had been holding the bowstring taut, but now he released.

The shaft caught the advancing man in blue on the left shoulder and spun him completely around and then around again. No sound came from the man. Not even a grunt of pain. Only a whirl and splash of fast-moving emerald light.

Completing his turn, Officer Riley continued on, the murderous glare of his eyes coming closer.

At the wheel, the driver began complaining. "Commissioner, I'm feeling awful hot. It's like I'm burning up with fever."

His face and voice ghastly, Kirkpatrick ground out, "Hold your position." To Wentworth, he said, "I appreciate your effort, but that officer will have to be stopped cold."

Wentworth said hotly, "You know I cannot shoot a police officer to death. Not under any circumstances—not even in self-defense."

"I know," said Kirkpatrick thickly. "Upon my shoulders falls that terrible burden."

Now it was Wentworth's voice that shook with strain.

"Try to shatter the kneecap! That should disable him."

Kirkpatrick did. His scorching bullet traversed the space between his steel gun barrel and the advancing officer's knee, riding a brief comet of saffron flame.

The bullet shattered the kneecap. Officer Riley went down, staggering. He fell heavily. Then, to their horror, he proceeded to drag himself by hand, pushing himself along the road with his one good foot, like a maimed crocodile.

Twin emerald beams burned from his eyes. They were like green ice come to life. The right front tire of the police limousine began to give up rubbery smoke and melted. The glass of one headlight broke with a sudden crack.

Undeterred by his shattered kneecap, the man in blue continued his murderous advance.

Desperately Kirkpatrick called, "Riley! Do you recognize my voice? Are you in possession of your faculties?"

Officer Riley did not so much as vocalize an animal growl. He was utterly silent as he crawled along, a veritable living dead man created by a substance from unknown space....

It seemed ridiculous, ludicrous that a man with a broken

kneecap crawling around on the dirt could radiate such a sense of menace, of imminent peril. Officer Riley could no more stand up on his two feet than he could flap his arms and fly off into the night like a bat. Yet the closer he came, the more the front of the limousine reacted to the green glare of his burning orbs.

Police Commissioner Stanley Kirkpatrick choked down a sob of resignation. His eyes turned to Wentworth's, unlocked.

"I no longer have a choice in the matter."

"We can retreat."

"We can retreat, yes," said Kirkpatrick, thick-voiced. "But what we cannot do is abandon our duty. If I do not do it, one of my officers will have to. I must put this man down. I have to slay a fellow officer. I cannot with clear conscience give that order to any of my patrolmen. You understand that, don't you, Dick?"

"Perfectly," said Wentworth. "And if it were in my power to lift that burden off your shoulders, I would do so instantly. But Richard Wentworth cannot slay a police officer. You should not have to. But your duty demands otherwise. No, Police Commissioner Kirkpatrick. You must do your duty as you see fit."

LIFTING A blue sleeve, Stanley Kirkpatrick laid the long revolver barrel atop its surface, sighted carefully, and placed a bullet perfectly in the center of the officer's exposed forehead.

The head rocked back, and behind it appeared a splash of liquid matter, greyish mixed with scarlet.

Then the head fell heavily, and the sound of it striking the ground was awful in their ears.

Dropping his smoking revolver to the ground as if it were an unclean thing, Stanley Kirkpatrick turned away from the horrible sight, his shoulders shaking, mustached mouth moving, but uttering no audible words.

Wentworth slipped around the back of the limousine and to his side.

"Of course," he said solicitously, "I will testify at the inquest as to the righteousness of your course of action. No one in your position could have done otherwise."

Kirkpatrick nodded, and his eyes were full of hot moisture. He looked away, not in shame but in resignation.

"I knew Riley well," he said thickly. "I met his wife on two occasions. If I remember correctly, he has three sons. His greatest wish was to have a daughter someday...."

At that last, Kirkpatrick's voice broke. Wentworth clapped him on the shoulders and said nothing.

Out of the corner of his eyes, Wentworth caught a glimpse of something half familiar. Something floated through the greenish glow, something that intercepted the light of a half-dozen small bonfires that was slowly growing, consuming scattered piles of leaves, climbing the trunks of hearty oaks, and leaping about like imps from Hades.

It was the figure of a hunched man wearing a black cloak, a floppy hat clamped over his head. In the greenish glow mixed with the firelight, the outer cloak showed. Silvery stitchery suggesting the clotted cobweb of a demented spider came to life with moving red and green lights like electric arachnids scuttling along the shifting strands.

"Whatever is he doing?" murmured Wentworth.

Then it became clear. The sinister figure threw up his arms, throwing back the two wings of his cloak, silhouetting his black-clad form in the artificial cobweb of its lining as if to announce his identity.

A single automatic of blue steel glinted in the weird ever-changing light, its muzzle pointed in their direction.

Had it not been for the blue steel surface, Wentworth might not have succeeded in the snap-shot that he was forced to take. The weapon made a perfect target. If one possessed the gun-wisdom to react in time.

The longbow clattered to the asphalt and Wentworth's hands went to the speed holsters under his green tunic. They came up clutching heavy automatics that had been carefully blackened to avoid reflecting telltale light.

Wentworth fired once with the right-hand automatic. The aiming gun flew from the man's gloved fingers, discharging harmlessly into the air. There came a sharp bark of surprise, mingled with vehement cursing.

A second bullet knocked the slouch hat from the man's head, carried it away, disclosing a black domino mask and heavy features half-revealed by the violent jerking of the gauzy skirt hanging from the mask's lower edge.

There had been no time to push Kirkpatrick out of harm's way. Indeed, it was not clear who was the intended target. But the police commissioner reacted with trained precision.

Pivoting, his gaze snapped toward Wentworth's smoking automatics, which were pointed into the trees.

"What is this!"

The alert driver answered that question for his superior.

"It was The Spider, sir. He's up in those trees. Tried to take a shot at us."

"The Spider!" barked Kirkpatrick. "What on earth is he doing here?"

"Why don't we ask him?" said Wentworth. And he was rushing ahead, into the trees.

Kirkpatrick followed, but not before he claimed his driver's Police Positive. The weapon used to put down officer Riley could not be fired again, pending an official inquest.

Together, they plunged into the trees, blundered around, but no trace of The Spider could they find.

Due to the nearness of the Green Meteorite and its transforming radiations, they dared not penetrate the Ramble.

"Did you see him clearly?" demanded Kirkpatrick.

Reluctantly lowering his automatics, but not his vigilance, Wentworth said, "I did. He was dressed as The Spider. Except that his cloak was stitched in the arrangement of a spider web."

"Peculiar," mused Kirkpatrick.

"It may be possible to identify him. A man identically garbed appeared at the Halloween ball, storming about the room in a rather sinister manner. He molested no one, but I observed that those whom he approached, shrank from him as if he were truly The Spider himself."

Kirkpatrick studied his old friend carefully. "From the tone of your voice, Dick, I gather you do not believe him to be the actual Spider."

"I do not," returned Wentworth flatly. "That is not what troubles me the most. If this man were trying to kill me, he could have done it at the ball. Provided he was brave enough and confident in his escape. It is possible he was not. But I cannot shake the nagging feeling that I was not his target."

"Are you saying that this was an assassination attempt?"

"That is not an inescapable conclusion, yet it is one I would take seriously, were I you," said Wentworth.

"The Spider has never before sought my life...."

Wentworth took a cigarette from a silver case, put it in his mouth and applied bright flame from a platinum cigarette lighter. Restoring the lighter to his tunic, he remarked through a gushing plume of cigarette smoke, "Therefore, there is excellent reason to doubt that the blackguard is the actual Spider of infamy."

The keening of police sirens mixed with ambulances and fire apparatus began filling the eerily-lit landscape, and the two men returned to the limousine to join them.

Chapter 5

THE STEEL MASK

A WELTER of converging police vehicles screeched to the edge of Central Park, braking en mass. Fire trucks were jostling through the traffic, seeking places to stop.

Kirkpatrick's limousine jerked to a halt and he stepped out.

"You men!" he shouted hoarsely. "Cordon off the area! It is too dangerous for the public, and whatever you do, do not approach the green glow. Consider it as poisonous to life as radium."

Two police sergeants fell to executing their commander's orders.

Moving heavily, Kirkpatrick accosted the fire marshal, who was stepping out of his own official red sedan.

"Comstock. A word with you, please."

Fire Marshal Comstock was a grizzled veteran. He could see the individual brushfires that were spreading through Central Park, understood keenly that a conflagration was imminent.

"I've got to put those fires out come what may."

"If your men enter the green zone," Kirkpatrick warned, "they are as good as dead and buried."

"Is it that bad?"

"It is far worse than bad."

And as if to underscore that flat statement, the whinnying of a horse in distress pierced the night.

All heads swung toward the sound. From out of the weird-ly-illuminated woods, the animal came charging, tearing about, and acting wildly.

That itself was not astounding. Many rode horses through Central Park, although not often this late in the evening. This was obviously one of the animals stabled nearby for that purpose.

This horse carried no saddle and bore no rider. It was a chestnut mare, sleek of coat and muscular the way thoroughbred horses are.

The eyes of the animal, however, were not ordinary. They burned like green coals. Each fear-widened orb sent out a beam in opposite directions from either side of its long head.

As the horse reared and swung its powerful body about, the opposing beams touched trees, bushes and swirling leaves. These ignited. The leaves simply disappeared as if made of flash paper. The trunks of the trees began to smolder and catch fire.

Horror was in his own eyes when Stanley Kirkpatrick beheld the terrible sight.

He barked, "Someone put that horse down! Quickly!"

A half-dozen police revolvers leapt from holsters, swiftly snapping and spitting fiery tongues.

Whistling slugs hammered the bucking beast, slammed him around, and he crumpled. The elongated head tried to lift off the ground. It faltered as the green radiance began to fade, along with its life force. Evidently, the power of the eye-beams was directly tied to the vitality of the owner's afflicted orbs.

A lone officer stepped up bravely. Taking a marksman's stance, he fired a bullet into the animal's skull from a safe distance. The head subsided, and the uncanny eye radiance dwindled to nothing....

"Beastly business," Wentworth murmured.

"What got into that poor creature!" a sergeant asked of no one in particular.

Commissioner Kirkpatrick responded to that by addressing his men. "If you see any one—man, woman or God forbid, even child—possessed by the green radiation, you must shoot on sight.

Shoot to kill. It is the only way to stop the spread of this hellish contagion."

"How are we going to deal with this meteorite?" Fire Marshal Comstock demanded. "We can't get close enough to spray it with fire hoses. Not if what you say is true, Commissioner."

A heaviness settled upon Kirkpatrick's uniform shoulders. "I do not know, Comstock. But do your best to put out such brushfires as you can without subjecting your men to destruction. For if any of them succumb to the Green Meteorite, my officers will have no choice but to put them down... is that understood?"

"Clearly," answered the fire official. He stalked off to do his duty.

While fire hoses were unloaded and affixed to city water hydrants, Kirkpatrick and Wentworth conferred.

"Dynamite might do the job of destroying that demonic thing," suggested Kirkpatrick.

"Possibly," replied Wentworth. "But consider this: Blowing up the meteorite might simply scatter smaller pieces across a larger area. That would expand the problem, not contain it."

As they spoke, the first high-pressure fire hoses were dragged into the trees; they soon filled, fattened, then gushed water through brass nozzles held steady by burly men.

"Those hoses may be necessary to control the crowds," suggested Wentworth.

"My men will control the crowd," said Kirkpatrick dismissively.

"Not if the crowds infiltrate the forbidden zone and become infected by meteor radiation. Fire hoses could knock them out. Perhaps some of these victims can be saved."

Kirkpatrick rolled his shoulders under his old-fashioned uniform and said, "I will keep that in mind, Dick." His tone lightening, he asked, "Shouldn't you be seeing to Nita?"

"Are you trying to get rid of me, Kirk?"

"This is not a crime scene; more in the nature of a natural disaster. I do not think you are needed here any longer."

"Are you forgetting the assassin Spider?"

"I doubt that he will return, given that I am surrounded by many men. And where The Spider is prowling, it might be wise for Richard Wentworth to make himself scarce."

"Very well then," said Wentworth, executing a polite bow. "I will see to Nita. Perhaps I will return to catch up on your progress anon."

Slipping through the police sawhorses that had already been set in place, Wentworth returned to the Metropolitan Museum of Art.

It rankled him to leave his dear friend to cope with the situation alone, but Stanley Kirkpatrick was a proud man. When he did not need assistance, he would not stand for any. Wentworth understood that about him. There was no need to make a scene, or press the point.

As he strode back into the museum, Wentworth kept his eyes sharp for the strange figure of a Spider who was not *The* Spider. But that fantastic figure did not make himself known.

THE HALLOWEEN masquerade was still going strong when Richard Wentworth returned to the museum.

Entering the main ballroom, he failed to spot Nita van Sloan. That was of no immediate moment. The place was crowded with costumed revelers and many had wandered off into the other rooms to admire the exhibitions.

As he pushed through the crowd, insinuating himself between two dowagers of different ages who were dressed as Marie Antoinette, Wentworth noticed a flash in one corner. Always alert to danger, he stiffened. But it proved to be the flash of a portrait camera.

A couple dressed as blue-faced goblins were posing for the

photographer who was attired in a monk's outfit, although his robes were scarlet red. The hood threw shadows across his face, obscuring but not concealing a celluloid skull mask.

Wentworth recalled that he had read that the fashion photographer Carleton Victor was scheduled to be in attendance. He had never met the man. In fact, Victor had rebuffed all past requests to photograph Wentworth. He had found that odd. Carleton Victor specialized in the Four Hundred, and Richard Wentworth was nothing if not an upright member of that exclusive club.

He walked over to the corner and introduced himself.

"Richard Wentworth. Carleton Victor, I presume?"

The crystal-clear blue eyes in the death's head mask regarded him. "At your service, Mr. Wentworth. I don't believe we have ever met before."

"My secretary has called several times to request a sitting."

Changing the film in his camera, Victor laughed lightly and perhaps a little dismissively.

"I'm sure you know that I have a waiting list composed of celebrities and other notables going back many months."

"I do not doubt it," said Wentworth. "But I find it rather peculiar that I have called you over a period of three years without luck."

"Mr. Huntley Walsh is ahead of you, as is Morton Clegg. Perhaps you might pose for me now. And we could arrange for a more formal portrait sitting when my schedule permits."

Wentworth smoothed his ruffled tunic and remarked, "I am not at my best at present. I've just come from Central Park where there is quite a bit of commotion."

Victor's voice turned serious. "I thought I heard sirens."

"A meteor has landed in Central Park. It has touched off scattered fires, and produced certain other inconveniences for the police commissioner, as well as the New York Fire Department."

As he spoke, Wentworth studied the eyes of the man, but could make little of them. Victor held his head directly under a chandelier and thus kept his bony countenance ever in shadow.

Something about the man's voice seemed familiar. But Wentworth could not place it.

"Perhaps you might want to lug your camera over and capture the tableau."

Victor chuckled lightly, and again there was something dismissive about it. "I am a portrait photographer, not a tabloid cameraman. I bend my artistry to capturing on film notables such as yourself exclusively."

"Of course," said Wentworth smoothly. "By the way, have you seen any sign of my fiancée? She is dressed as Maid Marian."

The hooded death's-head shook from side to side. "I've not taken her portrait, but I would be delighted to do so if you would bring her around."

"Let me do exactly that," said Wentworth, excusing himself.

Taking a promenade around the museum, Richard Wentworth wandered through the Egyptian room and then into the Armor room until he came to the costume exhibit.

Here, he thought, he might most likely find Nita van Sloan.

His deduction proved to be correct. Her familiar figure was going from exhibit to exhibit, studying examples of costumes going back centuries and coming from many points on the globe.

"How are you, my dear?" he asked, approaching her from behind.

But when he drew up to the figure dressed as Maid Marian, she turned and presented an entirely different face than expected. Instead of violet eyes and chestnut curls, this woman was brown-eyed and exceedingly bleached in her hair color.

"I beg your pardon," he said hastily. "I thought for a minute you were Miss van Sloan. You appear to be wearing a costume identical to hers."

The blonde woman smiled. "That is because this *is* her costume. Miss van Sloan suggested that we exchange outfits."

One dark eyebrow shot upward. "Oh?"

"Yes. We are about the same size, and she fancied mine. I am hiding from my husband and she is evidently avoiding you."

"I assume she suggested this imposture by way of a... jest."

The blonde smiled more brightly. "That is what she said. And from the surprised expression on your face, I would say her prank worked well. I'm only sorry she's not here to see it."

"And how were you dressed, Mrs.—?"

"Mrs. McAllister. I was a common witch. If you wish to find your fiancée, look for a black conical hat. She'll be carrying a broomstick. Perhaps you can use your long bow to launch the broomstick in celebration when you find her."

Smiling tightly, Wentworth said, "I will keep your suggestion in mind."

Picking up his pace, he continued his circuit of the museum. It was not like Nita van Sloan to play pranks. No doubt she had good reason for making the exchange. As the fiancée of the notorious Richard Wentworth, Nita obviously wished to disguise her identity.

"But to what purpose?" he murmured. "Was she stalking the imposter Spider? If so, she may no longer be in the museum."

Wentworth frowned as he moved from exhibition room to exhibition room.

Finally, he came to the Art of War exhibit. Here, in tall glass cases, armor from all over the world was arrayed and displayed. Here also were special exhibits from the Great War.

As he stepped between suits of armor, Wentworth came to a single item in a corner. Under glass stood a featureless helmet of steel, painted black. It was large and came to a conical point, like an old stovepipe. Two slits were machined for the eyes. He recognized it as in the style of a "sugarloaf" helm, such as knights of Germany wore into battle centuries back. It appeared to be crude, as if belonging to the High Middle Ages.

But the plaque set inside the glass declared otherwise. It read:

GREAT HELM OF STAHLMASKE

Helmet was discovered in wartime ruin in which its unknown
owner had presumably perished in October, 1918.

Wentworth remembered the tales of Stahlmaske from his days with the American Expeditionary Force. A German war-scientist's face had been terribly disfigured in an aerial battle during an operation in France. This disfigurement was so unnerving that he was forced to wear a steel shell rather than show his features to the world.

The owner of the helmet had been a terror to the Allied side until his reported death late in the war. His actual face and identity had never been disclosed to the public. But he was rumored to have been a member of German nobility.

Finding no trace of Nita in the otherwise deserted room, Wentworth exited, and made a final circuit before concluding that Nita had, in truth, left the museum, possibly to trail The Spider who was not.

AFTER WENTWORTH departed, an imposing figure that had stood concealed behind a hanging tapestry emblazoned with a griffin swept the heavy cloth to one side and stepped into the light.

He lurked for a moment. Nearly seven feet tall and attired like a medieval executioner, he surveyed the room with glittering eyes.

Unmoving, he waited. Beyond this room, the sounds of polite revelry began to die. The gala was ending. Attendants were going from room to room, shutting off the lights.

Hefting his double-bladed broad axe over one burly shoulder, the tall figure found the light switch governing this room and turned off all lights in advance of the ritual taking place in all the rooms.

Thin moonlight filtered down through the high windows and he again retreated to the shadows, waiting patiently.

When at last the museum had gone silent, he stirred again. Walking over to the glass display case exhibiting the helmet of ebony steel, he raised the axe high over his head, brought it down once sharply, employing the flat of the blade instead of its edge.

The glass shattered. He dropped the weapon to the floor, then pulled off the leather helmet that covered his head. In the wan moonlight, his features could not be discerned.

Two black-gloved hands grasped the helmet, lifted the heavy object and set it upon his broad shoulders. The flange fit perfectly.

For the first time in nearly twenty years, human eyes stared out of the great helm of Stahlmaske....

"Gut!" he intoned. "At last I am ready."

Turning heavily, he moved through the museum's darkened rooms with the heavy tread of his elevator boots.

After he had slipped out the back entrance, the faceless metal head rotated in all directions. And when they spied the emerald radiance bathing Central Park, his glittering eyes took on a keen new light... a greenish glow like the unholy light of avarice....

Chapter 6

THE WITCHING HOUR

NITA VAN SLOAN crouched amid sheltering bushes as she trailed the man who resembled a more flamboyant yet twisted version of The Spider.

Her ebon witch's robes, combined with the broad circular brim of her conical hat, provided perfect concealment… at least for as long as she did not move.

It was no accident that she had accosted Mrs. McAllister shortly after she noticed the false "Spider" slipping out of the Metropolitan Museum of Art. In her doeskin Maid Marian costume, she would be too conspicuous shadowing the mystery man. On the other hand, black witch's robes are not far removed from the true Spider's dark cloak and fedora.

It had taken less than a minute to convince the woman to switch costumes. Nita had been persuasive. Artfully, she had told the woman that they were nearly the same size. That was being generous. Nita's form was much slimmer. But Mrs. McAllister had accepted the compliment.

Slipping out the back way, Nita failed to catch sight of "The Spider" who was not. Richard Wentworth had taught her the stealthy art of trailing, and it had included reading of natural signs, including partial footprints in soil, as well as the telltale signs of shoe-crushed grass.

Cautiously, Nita followed the signs into the park.

The chilly green glow coming from the Ramble puzzled her. But her violet eyes searched only for the black-cloaked imposter.

She spied no sign of Richard Wentworth, who had gone before.

But Nita had not expected to. Even dressed in green, Dick understood the arcane skill that enabled him to blend with the shifting night shadows when he wore The Spider's dark habiliments. The greenish foliage of Central Park in late evening provided perfect concealment.

Nita was unarmed. This did not faze her in the slightest. Dick's instructions were to keep an eye on the fanciful "Spider." It was not yet clear if he was friend, foe or otherwise.

Hunkering down in the concealment of ornamental bushes allowed Nita to peer in all directions without being seen. Brilliant moonlight mixed with the unsteady radiance of the fallen meteor made the surroundings uncanny. The green light was a peculiar shade. With a woman's eye for such things, Nita decided it was not quite emerald, nor was it exactly jade. It was no hue of green to which she could put a name. The realization made her shiver a little in spine of the warmish Indian summer night. This particular green struck her as… unearthly.

Nita shook off the uncomfortable feeling. From her vantage point, she spied a man walking a dog along the winding bridle path encircling the Reservoir, which looked as if it had acquired a scum of algae, except that it glowed….

There was nothing unusual about the man, and the dog was a Collie.

Nita considered rising from her shelter to ask the dog walker if he had spied a fellow dressed as The Spider. But she decided not to. Better to let the man pass by and so continue with her shadowing, unsuspected. The crisp night air carried the sound of voices and she did not want "The Spider" to know that he was being tracked.

The dog walker disappeared along the path. Nita rose from concealment and began slipping toward the pulsing green glow. She knew that was where Dick was bound. Therefore, the pseudo-Spider would not be far behind him.

Among the footprints Nita spied amid the grass were those of Dick Wentworth. They showed less often. For the Master of Men was skilled in concealing his trail. Not so the mystery man garbed as The Spider. He appeared to be unconcerned about his footprints. Where the ground was soft, they showed clearly. Nita judged the man to wear a size eleven shoe. She made a mental note of that fact, knowing it might come in handy in the future.

Dick taught her to notice and retain such apparent trifles.

There came a point where it appeared that the imposter was no longer following Wentworth. Or perhaps he was shifting around to intercept his path from another and unexpected direction. The pseudo-Spider's footprints showed signs of haste, and increased pace.

Nita wondered if Dick knew he was being followed. She shook the worry from her mind. Even if not, he knew how to protect himself.

She was deep in the park now, where the oaks and black locust trees were the thickest. She floated through the spaces between the dark tree boles silvered with moonlight, and eerie green where they faced the meteorite....

UNEXPECTEDLY, NITA came across the dark figure hunched beside a spreading oak tree which cast a formidable monster of a shadow.

It was the man who dared impersonate The Spider. There was no mistaking his twisted figure.

The lurker was staring in the direction of the green glow, and the night breeze played at the muslin skirt falling below the velvet domino mask.

A spectral figure in black, Nita slipped toward the watcher, flitting from tree trunk to tree trunk, pausing often and keeping to the dark patches of shadow, which were fewer now that she had drifted into the pulsing zone created by the Green Meteorite.

Now she crouched three tree trunks over from him. Watching carefully from under the wide circular brim of the witch's hat, she was no longer Nita van Sloan. She was The Spider's mate.

With careful movements, violet eyes watching her feet so she did not snap a twig underfoot, Nita van Sloan managed to creep within one tree of her quarry.

If she could only snatch that mask away....

Suddenly, a woman's scream pierced the night air.

"Oh, God! I'm on fire. I'm burning. *Burning alive!"*

Her screams were so piteous, Nita forgot herself for a moment. She stepped out of concealment, seeking the source of the distressed woman's cries.

And in doing so, caught the attention of the false Spider....

Nita saw him react out of the tail of her eye and realized that the jig was up. She attempted to cover for herself.

"Did you hear that?" she called over. Why should she not? She was not Nita van Sloan, fiancée of Richard Wentworth. She was a woman walking through Central Park on Halloween Eve dressed as a witch. Nothing unusual about that on such a night.

The false Spider's voice was thin. "Probably a Halloween prank," he said dismissively.

"That is no prank," said Nita. "Listen to her voice. Her shrieks bespeak agony."

The woman cried out again. Now her voice soared to a dog-like howling. Pain lashed her. It distorted every syllable.

"Well, if you're not going to do anything about it, I will," Nita said firmly.

But before she could take three steps, "The Spider" was upon her!

They grappled. Nita drove one heel hard into the top of his right foot, where the toe bones were sensitive. The man had not expected it. He let out a curse, and slapped Nita on the side of her head with such force that her witch hat went tumbling away.

In the mixture of silver moonlight and green radiation, the tumbling chestnut curls of Nita van Sloan stood out distinctly.

Another curse erupted from the man. And Nita realized that she had been recognized.

"I'll fix you!" he snarled.

One fist lifted. Nita's left hand swept out, grasping the skirt of the black velvet mask. The mask held, but the skirts tore free.

The lower part of the face was square and brutish. The nose had been hammered to one side. It was the face of a man who had taken considerable punishment to his features.

Nita gasped. She did not recognize the face, had never seen it before. But the viciousness of the man's countenance could not be denied.

That viciousness was proven by his next act. Both hands reached out, seized Nita by her plentiful locks, and pivoted with all his might.

Nita's skull went slamming into the side of a tree. She crumpled. There she lay, a disorderly pile of black crêpe....

Reaching into his shirt front, the false Spider produced a .45-caliber automatic that gleamed in the moonlight with the sheen of blued steel.

Jacking a round into the chamber, he pointed the weapon at the top of Nita's head and prepared to squeeze the trigger.

But the agonizing screams of the woman brought him up short. Perhaps he thought that someone would come rushing to the woman's rescue and witness his cold-blooded act of murder. Or perhaps his nerve simply broke. The screams were that terrible.

Clutching the unfired weapon, he turned and vanished into the night, his black cloak floating behind him as if alive in its own way....

Chapter 7

THE HUMAN JUGGERNAUT

GRIM-FACED, RICHARD WENTWORTH exited the Metropolitan Museum of Art on the Fifth Avenue side, via the main entrance.

Stepping out to the curb, he pulled a silver whistle from a concealed pocket and blew three times shrilly.

Two blocks north, powerful headlamps blazed to life. An equally powerful engine roared. And down the street came at a brisk pace a sleek Daimler limousine. Swiftly, it pulled over and the man in the crisp grey livery of a chauffeur stepped out from behind the wheel. He all but saluted when his dark-brown eyes came to rest upon Richard Wentworth in his forest-green Robin Hood attire.

This was Ronald Jackson, Wentworth's trusted aide. The wide-faced man had been Major Wentworth's top sergeant during their days in France, when both were with the Allied Expeditionary Force. Jackson had declined a well-deserved commission to remain at Wentworth's side. Their bond of loyalty had only strengthened since the Great War some twenty years before, for unhesitatingly Jackson followed Wentworth into civilian life....

"Begging your pardon, Major," Jackson volunteered. "But when I saw the building lights going out with no sign of you or Miss Nita I began to worry."

"Jackson—take me into Central Park. Make it snappy!"

Wentworth dived into the rear compartment and clapped the passenger door shut while Jackson put the powerful machine in motion.

The Daimler whirled through the late-night traffic, and Wentworth rapidly recited the facts of this new threat confronting Manhattan.

"I heard the sound of the meteor striking, sir," Jackson responded. "And I've been following the news reports on the dash radio. But I knew better than to leave my post in case you required a fast exit."

"Good man. It is clear to me that Miss Nita trailed the false Spider from the museum. The fact that she has not returned is alarming. Our first job is to hunt her."

"What if we find this funny 'Spider?'"

Wentworth frowned. "Only notables were invited to this gala. Yet anyone can purloin an invitation. Since this was a costume ball, it would be quite possible for an interloper to crash it undetected."

"If he took a shot at the police commissioner, as you say, he's a no-good."

"Undoubtedly. But this impersonator may have fled the park after his failed attempt. It is Miss Nita that we must locate. Kirkpatrick is well protected."

The Daimler was hurtling along one of the transverse roads now.

The eyes of both men were alert. The greenish glow, combined with the cold effulgence of moonlight, made the park look enchanted in a malevolent way.

Behind the wheel, Jackson remarked, "We can't very well canvass the entire park from an automobile."

"Make a circuit of the park, Jackson. The northern portion has been cordoned off by the police. You will have to avoid that sector. I will reconnoiter on foot. Rendezvous by the Great Lawn in a quarter hour if you find nothing."

"Yes, sir," Jackson said smartly.

He slowed slightly and Wentworth was out the door, stepping

off the running board and moving into the greenery. Watching the flitting figure of his boss in the rear-vision mirror, Jackson soon lost sight of Richard Wentworth. The way that man could move combined the speed of a cheetah with the camouflage skills of a chameleon….

As he accelerated, Jackson reflected that this was one of the few times he saw the Major go into action dressed in green. It was an eerie coincidence, given the emerald glow that illuminated Central Park's northern reaches.

WENTWORTH SHIFTED about, not moving in a direct line, pausing often in the eerie shadows of the trees. By the marble obelisk known as Cleopatra's Needle, he halted. He still carried the longbow of Robin Hood, and the quiver at his back was heavy with hardwood shafts. No time to change clothes. Somehow, he felt that staying in the character of Robin Hood fit the present situation….

Respectful of the uncanny power of the fallen meteor, Wentworth kept a safe distance from the zone that turned ordinary New Yorkers into green-orbed man-monsters.

He repressed a shudder. Bullets, daggers, shot-filled leather saps had all sought his destruction in the past. These were occupational hazards to the one who was in truth The Spider, Master of Men.

But to fall victim to a force from outer space that robbed one of the intellect and turned its victims into robotic motors of mayhem was a fate Richard Wentworth truly abhorred. That poor Nita might have blundered into the zone of doom worried him greatly.

Prowling stealthily, he sought signs of her passing. Soon, he found some. Nita still wore the doeskin shoes of Maid Marian. These prints were distinct. They possessed no heels, being akin to Indian moccasins.

The air was redolent with the comfortable smell of autumn leaves burning. Many of the brushfires had been put out, he saw. But a few still burned.

Amid those shifting odors came a less woodsy one. Relying on his keen sense of smell, Wentworth moved in that direction, gripping his longbow in his strong right hand.

Resting on the grass, he found the forlorn remains of a witch's hat, still burning.

"Nita!" he cried. Reconnoitering, he sought additional footprints, and there were many. Not all of them belonged to Nita van Sloan....

Soon, Wentworth found her. It was unexpected. Entirely a surprise.

The crumpled pile of black crêpe bore little resemblance to a human being, for it sat in a pool of shadow, immobile and unmoving.

Suppressing a cry of concern, Wentworth pelted for the pitiful pile.

Dropping bow and arrow, he fell upon the still form, reached down and turned Nita's face to the pale moonlight. Her face, under his questing fingers, was yet warm. She breathed!

His hands checked the folds of the witch's robes, and came away clean. No blood. There was a bruise on one temple. It told its own tale.

Standing up, Wentworth blew his whistle three times, then lifted Nita and bore her carefully to the side of the road, heedless of his own peril.

"Good man, Jackson," he said as the Daimler slid to the side of the road.

"Hospital?" Jackson asked, pale-faced.

"She does not appear to be seriously injured. Merely knocked out. If I judge that bruise correctly, any concussion would be slight. Keep her here with you. I must find that false Spider and pay him back in full...."

With that, Richard Wentworth melted back into the foliage, a hooded goblin in green.

In the rear seat of the limousine was a hidden compartment, within it all the accoutrements he would need to become The Spider. But with another "Spider" abroad in the night, it would be most unwise to don his sinister raiment....

After Kirkpatrick's near miss, the police would shoot on sight. Not that there was anything unusual in that wise. But Richard Wentworth was not interested in receiving a bullet that another man had earned in full measure.

It was not yet clear that the false Spider had struck down Nita van Sloan. But it was likely. Since her bruise was fresh, Wentworth suspected the assassin was still lurking about the park.

But where?

Returning to the spot where he had discovered the burning witch's hat, he retrieved his bow and arrow and examined the ground with his canny eyes, mentally photographing the footprint of the assailant.

The trail was not difficult to follow, and follow it he did. It wound among the trees, coming to an abrupt stop.

Wentworth circled west, then shifted south, always avoiding the pulsing green glow that lay beyond the farther trees.

COMING TO a halt, he suddenly became still. Some instinct caused him to lie down on the grass and become as immobile as a stone.

For effective camouflage, his Robin Hood outfit could not have been better calculated in advance. Keeping his green cowl snugly on his head to conceal virile black hair that shone of hair oil, Wentworth scanned the surrounding trees.

In one leafy crown, moonlight revealed a flash of black velvet and the silver threads of a spider web that was as untidy as a cobweb left to gather dust....

The imposter!

Wentworth studied him closely. His masked profile was directed toward the park entrance where police phaetons and fire trucks congregated.

With a harsh oath, Wentworth realized that the man had taken up a sniper's position. One thick hand gripped an automatic that gleamed bluely.

Gathering himself up, Wentworth set a sturdy shaft to the catgut bowstring, pulled back and prepared to let fly.

He selected the man's thigh as his target. Its black silhouette showed clearly against the silvery stitching of the cloak fabric.

Grimacing, Wentworth released the missile.

The sound of its passing was less than a whistle. It struck! A snarling cry was wrenched from the figure high in the tree. It twisted and turned, releasing the .45 automatic.

Almost immediately, the figure began scrambling down, the shaft sticking out of the upper portion of his thigh. If the arrowhead had struck the femoral artery, the man would swiftly bleed to death.

But that did not seem to be the case. For no sooner had the sinister figure reached solid ground than he leaned one hand against the sturdy tree bole. His masked face looked anxiously around, then gazed upward.

Chill moonlight painted that face, showing the blunt jaw, a bent nose and other signs that were unhandsome.

Wentworth thought he recognized the brutish line of that jaw. But he had to be certain....

Nocking another arrow, he rushed forward, while the false Spider took hold of the shaft protruding from his thigh, as if to yank it free.

Wentworth warned coldly, "If you extract that arrow, you are almost certain to bleed to death before you can reach a hospital."

Venting a savage snarl, the false Spider whipped his head

around, and saw the figure in green aiming a steel-tipped arrow toward his heart.

"Wentworth!" he cried.

"I prefer to be known by my *nom de guerre,* 'Robin Hood,' " laughed Wentworth. "Now kindly put your hands up, Mr. Party Crasher."

Instead, the man threw himself to the ground and attempted to reach the fallen automatic.

Redirecting his aim downward, Wentworth let fly again.

The fleet arrow struck at the midway point between the man's grasping hand and the blue-steel automatic. The hand was wrenched away. Then it snaked out again.

Before questing fingers could reach it, a second arrow transfixed the black sleeve of the clutching hand, pinning it to the ground. The other fist grasped the hardwood shaft, attempting to yank it out.

Vile curses filled the air.

"Attempting to assassinate a police commissioner is a capital crime," said Wentworth as he strode forward. "I fear that you have a date with the electric chair. I will be happy to drive you to said date...."

Dark eyes looked up and glared venomously. Abruptly, they widened. It was not the figure of Richard Wentworth that caused this sudden wonderment. But something that stepped into view, casting an ominously towering shadow....

Wentworth could not help but notice this change in expression in the suddenly-narrowing eyes of the masked pseudo-Spider. A twig snapped somewhere behind him, then he heard the crunch of heavy boots on dry leaves.

Reaching back to grasp the fletching of another arrow, Wentworth pivoted. And what he saw, shocked him.

It was a tall man. Seven feet encompassed his height. He wore the medieval outfit and boots of an executioner. But instead of a black leather hood with a straight line cut across it to permit vision, the giant wore atop his head a conical helmet. It was black and high, the crown tapering to a point. A sugarloaf helm of medieval German design. There was no doubting it. This was the other mystery man he had encountered at the masked ball.

"Stand back," warned Wentworth, lining up the arrowhead on the man's breast. "Keep your distance, *Herr* von Maur."

The approaching Frankenstein's monster of a man did not halt in his tracks. Nor did he speak. He simply strode on, black-gloved hands making formidable fists. One fist clutched the double-headed headsman's axe. He did not raise it. The giant did not appear ready to wield his weapon.

"For the last time, I warn you," Wentworth bit out.

"I laugh at your warning," grunted the approaching man.

There was challenge in his voice and no fear. Recognizing these two qualities, Wentworth released the fletched end of the arrow.

Unerringly, the fluttering missile flew across the space between them, striking the monster of a man square in the chest.

He staggered backward—one, two, then three paces. His upper body twisted slightly to the left. Then, gathering his strength, he came on, undeterred!

Lifting the broad axe, he held it close to the double blade and calmly knocked the arrow off his chest. No blood flowed. No outward sign showed that his breast had been penetrated by the steel arrowhead....

Still, he came on.

Wentworth faded back and from his lips came the flat mocking laugh of The Spider. There was no longer a need for further pretense. This was a battle to the death.

Dropping the bow, he tore at the leather lashings at the front of his tunic, reached in and pulled out a single black automatic.

He fired once at the man's chest. The apparition staggered

backward. Two more bullets struck. But they had negligible effect. The human juggernaut appeared to be made of metal!

Wentworth shifted his aim upward, between the eyes of the bullet-shaped helmet. Two quick shots came in succession. This time the man's head was rocked backward. He staggered, began weaving in circles.

Two more bullets remained in Wentworth's still-smoking automatic. He was prepared to unleash them when a growling behind him caused him to turn.

The false Spider had slipped free of the down-pinning arrow, and had hold of his own automatic.

Laughing, Wentworth shot it from his hands, mangling the weapon before it could discharge.

One bullet remained....

Pivoting, he looked back at the tall figure. Miraculously, he had held his feet!

Wentworth had, during visits to Europe, become familiar with the legends of the Golem. A monster created out of clay to protect the citizens of Prague. This fearsome monstrosity with the steel helmet reminded him of those ancient tales.

Twisting his head about to face him again, Wentworth saw the hulking fellow resume his juggernaut approach, his looming shadow preceding him.

It was as if he was facing a human locomotive, one that was just picking up steam, one that was determined to run him down.

A strange thought lanced through Richard Wentworth's mind: Could this giant wearing the great helm of the infamous German war-monster be, in truth, the *genuine* Stahlmaske, who was long believed to be dead?

It seemed impossible. Yet there he came. A colossus from twenty years gone by. A human fiend who had wrought havoc upon the Allied forces during the Great War.

"Herr Stahlmaske?"

"At your service," the man replied in a hollow voice.

A grim smile touched Wentworth's lips. "Then permit me to introduce you to my other sparring partner." He gestured toward the false Spider. "He goes by the name Count Calypsa. In recent times he called himself the Dictator. Alas for him, his empire has toppled."

The featureless steel head rotated, propelled by powerful shoulders. "I am pleased to make your acquaintance, *mein Graf.*"

Count Calypsa seemed to lack the urbane polish of Friedrich von Maur. Instead of replying in kind, he snarled, "Don't just stand there! Rip him to pieces with that damned axe!"

"It will be my pleasure. Please accept my tenderest regrets, *Herr* Wentworth."

"Save your regrets for the climax, von Maur."

Wentworth lifted his weapon and attempted to lay his sights upon the eye-slits of the otherwise blank steel mask.

His finger squeezed the trigger slowly, carefully. His gun convulsed in the night. Smoke, fire and a brass cartridge all flew out of it from different directions.

The bullet never found its mark. Instead, the great broad double-bladed axe jerked into line, becoming a shield. The slug clanged off it. The battle-axe—for that was what it was now—slapped Steel Mask's helmet, which rocked backward.

Even with the protective helmet, the man's neck should have been snapped. But—

A hollow laugh boomed forth.

"I have counted your shots, *Herr Spinne.* You have none left. Pity. I will decapitate you now."

Wentworth flung himself to the left, spun about, and the flashing blade began biting the air. Steel Mask was swinging his axe about with a confident double-handed grip.

The big man was powerful. Indomitable. But he could not move at the speed of Richard Wentworth, who was adept with the rapier and knew how to avoid an opponent's slashing attack.

In shifting about, Wentworth was handicapped in one special respect. He had two foes to keep an eye on. Because now the false Spider was on his feet and matching his movements, the blue steel automatic in hand, but reversed. It made an ugly club.

Caught between two circling enemies, Wentworth made a move toward his fallen longbow. But it was not within reach. Reaching back with both hands, he removed two steel-tipped arrows from his quiver, bringing them into view.

Stahlmaske chuckled in hollow derision.

"Do you propose to stab us with those flimsy sticks?"

Wentworth did not reply. He held out the arrows on either side of his body.

His foes closed in!

Wentworth used one arrow to keep the false Spider at bay. That was simple to accomplish. The man was virtually unarmed and furthermore handicapped by the shaft protruding from his right leg.

Steel Mask was another matter. But Wentworth had formulated a plan. If he could drive a bullet into the vision-slits, it might or might not penetrate. Certainly the hot lead would splash upon impact, blinding the towering enemy.

But where a bullet might not penetrate—but only lodge in the thin steel aperture—an arrowhead could easily slip through. It was not a thing Richard Wentworth relished, this idea of blinding a man. He had slain many criminals, true, but it was while trading scorching lead....

Circumstances had put him in a place where all choice had fled.

Perhaps Stahlmaske—if it was indeed he—sensed The Spider's intent. For he stopped dead in his tracks. Again he lifted the broad axe before his featureless steel face.

Wentworth was gauging his chances of success when disorderly shouting rolled from the north. He dared to look in that direction. Through the trees, their badges painted by moonlight as they stood limned in the pulsing green glow of the thing from another sphere, came a cohort of New York's finest!

Count Calypsa sneered, "The police! We must clear out. Before they get here."

"Not before I have his head...."

Wentworth turned, and the monster was coming at him, a looming menace. He understood that his own strength was not equal to that of Stahlmaske. But he also knew he could make a good account of himself in the last measure of life.

It never came to that.

In the confusion, Count Calypsa slipped up and smashed Wentworth on his forest-green hood with the butt of his mangled automatic.

Wentworth went down. Steel Mask loomed up, lifting his executioner's axe high over his head. It poised there, painted silver on one side and green on the other by the opposing light sources.

Suddenly, Count Calypsa stepped in. "No! I have a better idea." Stripping off his web-lined cloak, he threw it over Wentworth's fallen form. Dropping the mangled automatic beside Wentworth, he said, "That should fix it with the cops. They'll hang him for sure. Hang him for that shot I took at the damned commissioner."

"But did this man not stand beside the official when you fired?"

"Doesn't matter. The Spider is suspected of a thousand Underworld killings. When the tabloids get this story, they'll howl for his head!"

The broad-bladed axe came down slowly. The black helmet rotated and behind the matched eye-slots, dark orbs blinked in appreciation.

"You are a fellow who thinks on your feet. I admire that. So many do not. Come. Let us be away from here and leave this unfortunate man to his fate...."

As a last gesture, the erstwhile false Spider placed his hat and black velvet mask on Wentworth's undisguised features.

"Now it is done," he said.

As police flashlights swept about, they melted into the trees, leaving Richard Wentworth to the tender mercies of the New York Police Department....

Chapter 8

DEAD TO RIGHTS

POLICE ELECTRIC torch beams converged on the sprawled figure in the grass.

His head was swallowed by a rustic green hood belonging to another era. Moonlight picked out the blue finish of a heavy automatic sunk in foot-trampled grass. Warmish night breezes made a black cloak flap as the patrolmen approached. Those sinister folds sent chills up their spines. For all police officers knew what a black cloak signified….

"Geez!" hissed one. "Could that be… The Spider?"

Their service weapons drawn, they approached, gun-barrels pointing, flashlights sweeping jerky illumination about.

The sprawled figure on the grass did not move. Only the light breeze toying with his cloak created movement.

Abruptly, a cross breeze caused one wing of the cloak to lift, revealing a moon-touched lining silvered with a disorderly spider web!

"It *is* The Spider!" breathed one thunderstruck officer.

Tense fingers caressing the triggers of their Police Positives, the four officers surrounded the unmoving form, eyes widening with something akin to awe.

One flashlight dashed light into the insensate one's half-turned face.

"He's wearing a mask—a black mask!"

"Well, rip it off. Let's see who he is."

"Not me," grunted the Sergeant. "That's the commissioner's job. Kirkpatrick has the honor of unmasking The Spider. Somebody fetch him."

While one officer pelted away, the Sergeant picketed his men around the helpless fallen man.

The officers talked among themselves, as nervous men will do.

"What a wild night!" exclaimed one.

"Maddest Halloween I ever experienced in all my forty years, man and boy."

"Hey now! What's that he's wearing under that damn cloak?"

The Sergeant shifted his light, and between the moonlight and the green pulsing glow, he had to blink before he was certain.

"Looks like a Robin Hood costume. That goes with the hood covering his head."

"Didn't that millionaire Wentworth wear such a getup when he was talking with the Commissioner earlier?"

The Sergeant frowned. "Yeah, he did. It looks like the jig is up for Wentworth, not to mention The Spider."

"The guy's been rumored for years to be The Spider. Now look at him. Caught dead to rights."

The Sergeant was studying the man's chiseled profile. "What would make a guy swimming in all those bucks turn crook, I wonder?"

"Talk I hear is The Spider is death to crooks. Not a crook himself. Didn't the President pardon The Spider last month?"

"You're such a gullible sap!" the other snorted. "You swallow every kind of tabloid claptrap printed about the damn Spider. Fact is that the Presidential pardon absolved him of all *past* crimes. And The Spider had more capital charges against his name than any fifty hoods you could grab off the streets. But any new charges will stick. If this one's really The Spider, and he took a shot at the commissioner, he's bought a one-way ticket to the death house." *

The scarlet headlamps of the approaching police limousine

* The Spider: *Machine Guns Over the White House.*

made the environs turn gory. Steel doors clapped open and shut. Before long, Commissioner Kirkpatrick put in an appearance.

"It's The Spider, Commissioner," said the Sergeant.

"So I am told," grunted Kirkpatrick.

"He's out cold, sir."

Stanley Kirkpatrick said nothing as he bustled up and knelt beside the fallen man. With a sharp tug, he pulled back the concealing hood. Venting a sharp breath, his eyes registered the crisp black hair. Then they went to the chiseled profile. Those lips could not be mistaken; the firm jut of the jaw was familiar.

Gingerly, but without hesitation, Kirkpatrick lifted the black velvet domino mask off the face of the fallen man.

"My God, Dick!" he whispered to himself.

The Sergeant was studying The Spider's face. "That's Richard Wentworth, all right. He gets his picture in the paper enough, doesn't he?"

Noticing the cobwebbed cloak, Kirkpatrick tore at it savagely, saw that it was not attached to Wentworth's fallen form. He pulled the fabric free.

He stood up, studying the garment with its weird design worked in silver thread. His face was grim. But there was a light in his eyes, a shine that was knowing.

"I have hunted The Spider for some years now. And I have never known him to wear a cloak with such a garish design." He examined the hem of the cloak. And saw that the garment was normally held in place by a cord. The cord was missing, however.

Kneeling again, Kirkpatrick searched Wentworth's throat, and blazed a flashlight to examine the ground. He found nothing.

"See if you can find a cord lying about," he barked. "This cloak was not attached to his neck, was it?"

The curious Sergeant volunteered, "We didn't touch him at all. We even left the mask in place for you."

Kirkpatrick nodded heavily, studying Wentworth's still face.

After fifteen minutes, the officer reported no sign of any cord....

Kirkpatrick frowned. "The man who took a shot at me must have rendered Wentworth unconscious. He threw his cloak upon his body to make us think he was The Spider."

A man removed his police cap, scratched his head. "Are you sure, Commissioner? We thought we had The Spider dead to rights."

"If this were The Spider in truth, the cloak would have been affixed to his neck in such a way as to hold it in place. That cord is probably still around the neck of the real assassin." Turning to the Sergeant, he directed, "Summon an ambulance. Let's get him to a hospital."

THE AMBULANCE turned up with breathless swiftness. It was one of the emergency vehicles that had been parked near the police cordon.

An interne swept in, checked Wentworth's pulse, examined the wound in his head, and gingerly lifted him onto a stretcher, bearing him away.

While this was being done, a familiar Daimler limousine pulled up. Out popped Wentworth's chauffeur, Ronald Jackson.

Seeing the familiar face on the gurney as it was being loaded into the back of the ambulance, he cried, "Major! What happened here?"

The interne clipped, "Knocked out cold. Not in any danger. But we've got to get him to a hospital for observation."

"Is there room in the wagon for a second patient?"

"What second patient?" demanded Kirkpatrick, striding up forcefully.

"I have Nita van Sloan in my back seat. She's unconscious. Mr. Wentworth found her when he was chasing after that damned... Spider."

"That settles the matter," grunted Kirkpatrick. "Wentworth

was chasing The Spider and he turned on him." To the interne, he said, "Take the woman. See that she gets the best treatment."

Nita van Sloan was carried over to the waiting ambulance by Jackson, and tenderly placed in back. The door slammed in the rear and the ambulance took off with a clanging sound.

Kirkpatrick said, "You may follow in a minute, Jackson. First, I would like your statement."

Ronald Jackson gave a forthright recitation of the last hour, carefully leaving out certain incriminating details.

"I don't have all of it," he concluded. "But that's what I do have, Commissioner."

"It is enough," said Kirkpatrick. "I am confident that the person who has been lurking around the park is The Spider, and not Richard Wentworth."

Jackson nodded solemnly. "If Mr. Wentworth were really The Spider, as some people think, he wouldn't have been walking around dressed like Robin Hood an hour after the gala ball concluded."

"That is sound reasoning, Jackson. You may go now. Thank you."

Reclaiming the Daimler, Jackson took off into the night, following the diminishing clangor of the now-distant ambulance.

Before long, a police sergeant strode up to his superior. "Commissioner, begging your pardon, sir. But if that Spider is still prancing about, this isn't a good spot for you to be standing out in the open."

Kirkpatrick nodded. "Sergeant, take your detail further south. See if you can flush The Spider out. He won't be wearing a mask or a cloak. But take anyone you find skulking about into custody. Man, woman or animal. Do you understand me?"

"Perfectly, Commissioner. Come on, you men. Let's beat the bushes and try not to step on any more knocked-out ones."

Returning to his limousine, Kirkpatrick eased into the back, closed the door and told his driver, "Circle Central Park."

"Yes, sir."

The police machine slid over to the curb side, and Kirkpatrick watched for signs of anyone acting suspicious.

A perimeter had been set up. Police-marked sawhorses were set firmly in place. Kegs of barbed wire were being unrolled. And all the while, that infernal pulsing green glow continued to paint the surrounding buildings. It was like a beacon, hypnotic, other-worldly, calling upon the city's night denizens to investigate it.

The police had so far done a fair job of driving away late-night strollers. But what would happen as the evening wore on? And worse, how would the city handle its citizenry once dawn broke and word reached the general population? Crowds were certain to gather. Immense crowds. All pushing close to see what they could only discern by its radiant light.

"Good God," Kirkpatrick muttered to himself. "If we don't control the public, they will be infected in numbers approaching that of a plague."

"Take me to an all-night drugstore, Carter," Kirkpatrick instructed his driver. "I must call His Honor, the Mayor. We must petition the governor to declare martial law. It is the only way to prevent disaster from overtaking the city."

Obediently, the police chauffeur swung the heavy machine around and sought an appropriate pharmacy. Fortunately, the city harbored many that stayed open all night....

Chapter 9

ALLIES WITHOUT FACES

POLICE RADIO patrol cars had been summoned from all over Manhattan to contain the spreading madness created by the fallen meteorite. To cover the city while the N.Y.P.D. stood watch over Central Park, additional forces were called in from the five boroughs.

One midnight blue prowl car scooted over the Queensboro Bridge and slid into Manhattan's wide concrete canyons. Officer Joseph Lerch radioed dispatch that he was on patrol in lower Manhattan. Then he began to canvass the area.

It was well past midnight, and the greater portion of the city had gone to sleep. Sometimes that was when New York was most dangerous. For the lawless denizens of the night were out on the prowl....

Officer Lerch was not an especially curious individual. But even he could not help but be intrigued by the weird dome of greenish light that made Central Park shine brighter than the moon.

Human nature being what it is, Lerch wheeled his patrol car closer and closer to Central Park. Knowing from radio reports that the northernmost portion was choked with emergency vehicles, he slithered toward Columbus Circle, and the southern end of the park.

While he conscientiously avoided riding close enough to spy the meteorite itself, there was something about that preternatural shining that drew one... even an uncurious fellow like Officer Lerch.

The reports coming over the shortwave made it sound as though Hell itself had opened up under the mile-long oasis of greenery in the heart of the city. The meteorite story was fantastic enough. And the glow that lit up the night sky and turned the surrounding buildings chartreuse was something that the human eyeball rejected at first sight.

But the other reports! Men and women turned into walking automatons, mindless, brainless—eerie green radiation pouring out of their eyes and setting fire to everything from dry leaves to their fellow man. It was like something out of a crazy pseudoscience magazine.

Lerch cruised slowly past the southern verge, brown eyes under his visor cap watchful, expectant of danger.

A man stepped out of the shadows, emerging from a stand of shrubbery. He was shouting something unintelligible and waving his arms frantically over his head.

The man's suit was black, like that of a priest. But this was no priest. He had the burly build and carriage of a prizefighter.

Braking, Officer Lerch popped out from behind the wheel and demanded, "What is it, buddy? What's the trouble here?"

"In the trees, officer. It's… it's awful. You have to see it to believe it. Hurry!"

Drawing his service revolver, Lerch said, "Lead the way."

The police officer didn't know what to expect—a burning body? A green-eyed human monster? Something even worse? Police broadcasts had described both. But Lerch did not hesitate as he plunged after the agitated fellow in black.

"Over here," the man said in a rattled voice. "On the other side of that oak."

The frightened man hesitated, as if fearful to press on. Officer Lerch was neither fearful nor hesitating. He lunged in the direction of the man's pointing finger. That finger shook… shook with fear.

Lerch disappeared around the tree, blazing his flashlight before him.

He never saw the sweeping axe that took off his head at the shoulders. The last sound his ears registered was a short whistle. Soft and breathy. Out of the tail of his eye, he caught a flash of steel.

His head went flying in one direction while his pilotless body hopped in another. The blue uniform body lurched an additional step and then fell, raw neck stump spurting arterial blood....

A seven-foot-tall monster of a man detached himself from an adjoining sycamore tree, shaking a sprinkle of bright blood off his axe's double-bladed head and stooped awkwardly.

Taking firm hold of Officer Lerch's hair, he carried off the man's head, leaving his body to shake and jitter out its last remaining vitality.

"We will take the police car," he told Count Calypsa.

Calypsa stared at the swinging head, which was dripping crimson rain.

"What do you want with that thing?"

"To confound our enemies. To instill fear into their hearts. Nothing more. Now hurry."

Calypsa reached the police machine first, walking with difficulty. The broken shaft of the arrow that had pierced his thigh protruded like a red fragment of bone. He took the wheel. Stahlmaske stepped around and got in the rear. He dropped the head onto the floorboards, kicking it into a corner disdainfully.

Jamming the radio car into gear, Calypsa said tensely, "My hidden headquarters is not far from here."

"Then we will go to your headquarters," said Stahlmaske without concern.

Calypsa piloted the machine with diligent speed, turning corners without running stop lights, thereby attracting no undue attention.

"I commend you," grunted Stahlmaske. "You are able to drive, despite your pain."

"Thanks to you, for chopping off the protruding portion. Wentworth had me convinced that if I touched that damned arrow, I would meet a swift death."

"Wentworth is crafty. He understood that a fugitive walking about transfixed by a feathered shaft would be that much easier to track. Nevertheless, you will have to see a doctor."

"I have one on my secret payroll...."

Presently, he pulled up before a fashionable apartment building nestled between a pair of towering office buildings overlooking the public library. New Yorkers knew this white-stone structure as the Gotham Arms.

Turning in his seat, Calypsa regarded the blank-faced giant.

"You will have to remove that helmet before entering the building."

The black stovepipe helmet rotated from side to side slowly, impelled by powerful shoulders, for it sat on a flange that inhibited the neck from turning freely. "If I remove it, I will be more conspicuous than if I do not."

"Are you wanted?"

The giant hesitated briefly. "Yes, and yet no."

"In that case, we must sneak in the back entrance. We will be less conspicuous."

"It is All Hallows Eve," said the other unconcernedly, popping open the door. "It is to be expected that late night revelers will be returning to their homes curiously attired."

"That may be. But I observed a black steel mask reposing under glass at the Metropolitan Museum of Art. It cannot be a coincidence that you're wearing one just like it. Especially since you were so conspicuous by your height at the gala."

The other rumbled. "I will take my chances. If you will, lead the way."

Abandoning the police machine, Count Calypsa slipped in through an alley to a back door and produced a key. This turned in the lock. The door opened. They entered.

Instead of taking the elevator to a higher floor, the pair descended a stairwell to the basement, passed through storage space where the lights were dim. The same key was used on what appeared to be a closet door. They passed through it and ended up in the basement of an adjoining building. It was a garage. Few vehicles were parked between its support columns, however.

The Count led his hulking companion to a cracked concrete wall that was painted a pale green. Bending, he inserted one finger into a crack and performed a deft manipulation. A concealed doorway broke open, revealing a small private elevator.

"It cost a small fortune to install this secretly," advised the Count. "Follow me. We are almost there."

The automatic car took them to the top floor. Stahlmaske counted the floors and noted that the elevator indicator arrow did not show a thirteenth floor. Disdaining the numbered buttons on the bakelite control panel, the Count had used a brass key to select the floor.

"Peculiar that here in America, the folk are so superstitious as to avoid the number thirteen," Stahlmaske rumbled.

Count Calypsa smiled harshly. "This works to our advantage, wouldn't you agree? Officially, there is no thirteenth floor. When, in fact, the top floor is the non-existent one."

The door rolled open and they stepped out into a sumptuous hallway. When the elevator door closed shut, there was no sign of it. Only a blank wall. They followed the shining parquet floor to a windowless door that was without number or other designation.

AGAIN, THAT universal key was inserted and they entered. Indirect lights came on automatically. They revealed a room that belonged more to the castles of Europe than the canyons of New York, one with a high, vaulted ceiling. Cloth-of-gold draperies covered the walls. They masked a door on the inner side so that once they entered, the hanging fell back into place. There was no sign of any other exit.

Under their feet, the deep pile of rust-colored carpet absorbed the sound of their tread. The place was furnished with expensive taste, the upholstery of the highest quality.

Opposite a wide window that looked down over the New York Public Library, a massive desk of polished mahogany crouched, waiting for its occupant. Into its front was worked a pair of full-maned lions. The chair behind the sumptuous desk was substantial and boasted a high back in the manner of a throne. Another lion was carved into its back, set high.

Finally, the rich tapestry directly behind the throne-like chair and matching desk bore a heraldic design. The figure of a stately lion seated upon a golden crown. On either side spread the lion's forepaws. One paw held a sword, while the other clutched a mitre.

Observing this, Stahlmaske nodded approvingly as much as his cumbersome helmet would permit.

"You fancy yourself to be royalty," he murmured hollowly.

"I am Count Carmine Calypsa. Perhaps you have heard of me."

The Man in the Steel Mask considered briefly. "A year or so ago, someone by that name was sent to the Devil's Island penal colony, along with a female accomplice. As I recall, they were captured in France. The charge was plotting mass murder. During the prison ship transit across the Azores, they escaped overboard, but were never see again."

Firmly seated upon his mahogany throne, his head beneath the lion rampant, the Count nodded in mute acknowledgement.

"At your service, Mr—?"

"*Herr,* if you would. *Herr* Stahlmaske. You may call me Friedrich von Maur."

"You cannot possibly be the infamous Stahlmaske. He was reported to have been killed near the end of the World War."

"The very same," the other said with well-bred smoothness.

"How is it that you live today?"

A black gloved hand settled over the jerkin's front. "A deep passion burns within my breast. Call it simple revenge, or vengeance. It does not matter. It keeps me alive. It has kept me breathing all these long years during my recuperation from a storm of Allied bullets. Now I am ready to move forward with my new master plan."

"Who is this you hate so much?"

"I do not know the *verdammt* one's actual name. But I despise him as much as you fear The Spider."

"But I do not fear The Spider!" spat Calypsa. "Especially after tonight."

"I have read about you, Count. Months ago, you attempted to seize control of this city, but The Spider defeated you." *

Count Calypsa pounded one fist on his desk. "No, not defeated me! It was merely a setback. My face was exposed, my identity compromised. I prudently retreated. My army of lieutenants is intact. They have burrowed themselves into the fabric of the city. I have agents among police ranks, in the Mayor's office, City Hall, and elsewhere. Furthermore, I have insinuated counterfeit money into the city by way of a modest number of cash advances to my followers. When I am ready to strike anew, I will instruct my men to flood Manhattan with phony ten-dollar bills."

"I see," said Stahlmaske. "And what were you doing at the Halloween gala?"

"I was stalking the man I believe to be The Spider. Richard Wentworth. I almost got him in the park. But my shot went astray."

"Your gun hand shook. You lacked nerve to commit the deed. Do not deny it!"

---

* The Spider: *Dictator of the Damned.*

Again that fist banged down. "My shot went wide. That was all. It was not fear. Wentworth was with the police commissioner. I thought I would down them both. And my aim wavered between them. But it no longer matters. Richard Wentworth is in police handcuffs, accused of being the despicable Spider. All will work out in the end."

"And if it does not?"

A wolfish smile made Calypsa's brutish features writhe. "My master plan is still in place. The modest number of counterfeit bills that I have issued have so far gone undetected. Once I leak word of my false money to the authorities, no one will be able to trust their money. It will create a panic. And during the ensuing confusion, I will make my bold move."

Abruptly, Stahlmaske turned to thrust aside the curtain before the window bank and stare down at the matched white-marble lions guarding the public library. "I think the confusion you plan to sow has already been sown."

"You are referring to that meteorite?"

Stahlmaske nodded heavily. "I am. The police have the park surrounded. There, strange things are transpiring. Things that are beyond understanding."

"Yes, I saw some of them. Unexplained bonfires. Dead bodies ablaze. And worse."

"As I said, things beyond understanding." Suddenly the giant turned and pointed a black-gloved forefinger toward the cabinet radio receiver standing in one corner.

"Perhaps that instrument will shed light on these events. If you will permit me?"

"Feel free."

Stahlmaske strode over to the console, turned it on and waited for the tubes to warm. Soon, he had located a radio broadcast. An excited announcer was speaking.

"Newsflash! A meteor has slammed into Central Park. Police

are asking all citizens to stay clear of the park. It has been cordoned off. They say there is danger, but refused to explain themselves. Reporters have been turned away. A veil of secrecy has descended upon Central Park. One moment."

A rustle of paper came over the air.

"This just in! Ambulances have carried several victims from the park. They are believed to have been burned in the aftermath of the meteor landing. Scientists are saying this is unlike any meteorite ever before seen. Folks, this is something new on the Earth. New and inexplicable."

There was more, but much of it was repetitive. The two conspirators listened to it all intently.

"Bulletin! A noted scientist is claiming that the radiation coming from the meteorite is affecting the human brain. Turning ordinary citizens into something like automatons—destructive, rampaging, mindless beasts. All citizens are strongly advised to avoid the area. There are rumors that the Governor will declare martial law in order to exert control over the worsening situation."

Listening to this excited account, Count Calypsa murmured, "Not only are their brains affected by the meteor rays, their eyes turn green, and I don't mean their iris color. The eyeballs shoot out emerald beams. These rays are deadly—and the source of those wildfires."

Stahlmaske was silent for fully a minute. Finally, he intoned, "Fate has delivered to us a powerful weapon of terror. If we can only seize it."

"But how could we do that? You heard the radio announcer. The rays affect the human brain. To approach the object is to becomes its victim."

Stahlmaske turned, and his metal-framed eyes showed strange red lights. Lifting one black-gloved hand, he laid it against his metallic temple. He tapped it twice, for emphasis.

"This shell encasing my head is forged from precision steel. But it is lined with lead. For in my wartime career, I often worked with radium and other injurious elements. Inset into the eyeholes of my helmet are lenses of leaded glass, which are proof against dangerous rays."

Count Calypsa stood up abruptly. "Are you suggesting that the lead will shield your brain from the green rays?"

"I am virtually certain of it. I, and I alone, may approach the meteorite unscathed. Only I can safely carry it away."

"Carry off a large meteorite? How do you propose to do that? It's audacious. Preposterous."

The answer came in such a way that Count Calypsa knew that Stahlmaske was smiling behind his helmet.

"You should understand now that I am an audacious man. I will find a way." He lifted the double-headed executioner's axe, which he had placed in a corner upon entering the sumptuous room.

"With this, it may be possible to hack the meteorite into smaller fragments, to make them more manageable. And to transport them to a place of safety, from which we can distribute them throughout the city." The slotted eyes looked around the spacious room. "A place such as this…."

Count Calypsa's eyes widened in appreciation.

"You aim to sow fear and confusion?"

"No," said Stahlmaske ominously. "I propose to turn the population of New York City into rampaging monsters. I intend to bring the city to its knees. And while it is begging for mercy—a mercy that does not exist—you and I will loot it with impunity."

"My God! That's brilliant. If only you can pull it off."

"We will await tomorrow's developments. By sunset, the situation at the park will either be calm, and the police off their guard, or it will be out of control due to the pressing in upon all sides by an insatiably curious populace. Either way, we will strike under cover of darkness."

"You are proposing an alliance?"

Stahlmaske inclined his metal head somberly. "You and I are of noble blood, *mein Graf.* We both are Europeans. Who better than us to crush this mongrel city beneath our booted heels?"

"Agreed," said Count Calypsa, returning to his seat. His eyes were filled with avarice. His rugged face twisted with delight. Abruptly, he looked up.

"Why don't you remove your helmet? Make yourself comfortable while we await the break of dawn."

"If I were to lift this shell," said Stahlmaske, "you would no doubt run fleeing from this room. You see, my face was destroyed during the war."

"No plastic surgery could remedy the damage?"

"Plastic surgery kept me from dying of my injuries. Plastic surgeons were able to repair me so that I could heal. But they could not restore what was no longer there...."

With each guttural word, Stahlmaske's voice grew lower in register.

"I understand," murmured the Count. "I, too, have undergone plastic surgery."

Stahlmaske laughed raggedly. "You do not seem to be much improved by it, if you will pardon me for saying so."

Calypsa chuckled like a dry bone breaking. "On the contrary, I was once a handsome man. All of Europe smiled at my face. Men wished to be me. Women desired my company. This was immediately after the war. But after I escaped the prison ship that went aground before reaching Devil's Island, that face became a wanted one. I sought out a plastic surgeon. He turned me into this battered bruiser you see before you. Coming to New York City, I called myself Casey Grogan. No one suspected that the man who had begun operating as the Dictator, and who had once been the infamous Carmine Calypsa, would wear such a disgusting face. For months, I escaped detection. But The Spider changed all that."

"I see," said Stahlmaske slowly. "We are more alike than I at first thought. Both of us have lost forever the faces with which we were born. Both of us have suffered the curse of ugliness in the furtherance of our aims. It is fitting that we should meet. Even more fitting that we should become confederates."

Once more Count Calypsa pounded his fist down on his mahogany desktop. This time with shocking vehemence.

"We are not confederates. We are allies! And before we are finished, we will be co-rulers of the city. This city—and more!"

The hollow laughter emanating from the conical helmet of Stahlmaske boomed out in rising appreciation….

A stabbing pain in his thigh reminded Count Calypsa of the broken arrow lodged there. He reached for a device reposing upon his desk, a boxy instrument known as a "Call-o-phone." Depressing a switch, he began chanting, "Calling Number Twelve. Report to Headquarters A immediately. Bring your black bag. It is urgent…."

Chapter 10

OPERATOR 5 OF THE
INTELLIGENCE SERVICE

ONE OF the last persons to leave the Halloween gala at the Metropolitan Museum of Art was the society photographer, Carleton Victor.

Victor personally carried his photographic equipment and plates to an expensive black roadster parked on Fifth Avenue. It was past midnight now. A waning crescent moon swam uncertainly amid the fast-scudding clouds overhead.

Closing the trunk on his equipment, Victor looked up at the night sky with level blue eyes. He had removed the celluloid skull which concealed his features, revealing the strong, intelligent lines of a youthful face, and prepared to shuck off the crimson robes of the red death.

A strange aura brushed the undersides of the fleeing clouds with a greenish tinge.

Victor's eyebrows crowded together as he pondered the glow. It took only a moment's study to understand that the clouds were reflecting a powerful light source emanating from the ground.

During the gala the society photographer had been exceedingly busy and paid little attention to the comings and goings of people. Victor had only one significant distraction. And that was Richard Wentworth, whom he had been studiously avoiding in the matter of sitting for a portrait.

Carleton Victor had nothing against Wentworth. Not personally. But he had his reasons for avoiding the man. Although a criminologist of note, the man's reputation was clouded by suspicion....

Ripping off his crimson monk's robes, the photographer revealed an elegant tuxedo, the formal evening attire of Carleton Victor. It had been his intention to drive to his luxury apartment in the East Sixties, just a few blocks from here. But the unholy jade glare painting the sky appeared to be a cause for concern.

Victor had good reason to investigate the source of the ghastly illumination. While New York society knew him as the superb Carleton Victor, that was merely a cover—a façade concealing his true name and work.

For the clean-cut young man who wheeled his streamlined black roadster up Fifth Avenue was none other than James Christopher, who was recorded in the annals of the United States Secret Service as Operator 5.

The powerful roadster's diesel engine propelled it along as James Christopher tooled the machine toward North Central Park, his red robes now stuffed under the passenger seat.

Christopher knew of the meteorite's impact. He had felt it shake the substantial Metropolitan Museum building. But he did not dare to abandon his cover and investigate. The sound of sirens that followed did not register as terribly significant, but when their banshee screeching swelled in number, he became alarmed.

Still, he refused to break cover. This was a police matter, not one falling under the jurisdiction of the Intelligence Service.

Once the park came into view, the uncanny glow appeared stronger. It pulsated like a living thing. It dawned on James Christopher that this was no conventional metallic meteor that had fallen.

Braking at the edge of the police cordon, Christopher emerged from behind the wheel and approached a police officer, who shot out his blunt jaw in truculent fashion.

"Hey, you. Haul that fancy heap out of here! The police commissioner has cordoned off the park."

Instead of retreating, Christopher advanced, taking from an

inner pocket of his suit coat a flat silver case. He opened it up. Within the case reposed a letter. It read:

THE WHITE HOUSE

WASHINGTON

To whom it may concern:

The identity of the bearer of this letter must be kept absolutely confidential. He is Operator 5 of the United States Intelligence Service.

The signature was that of the president of the United States of America.

Absorbing this declaration, the police officer stiffened.

"Tell me everything you know about this emergency," Operator 5 requested briskly, his manner direct and self-assured.

The patrolman swallowed hard before he found the words with which to express himself.

"It's like this, you see. The meteor smacked into the park. Luckily, it landed in the Ramble. But it's dangerous. Plenty dangerous. Those green rays get hold of a man, and practically wipe his brain out. But that's not the worst of it. Something gets into the brain, and the eyes start shooting out green rays, just like the meteorite. When these rays touch anything, they burn. Trees. Animals. Even people. I lost count of how many charred corpses they hauled out of the park. Commissioner Kirkpatrick has ordered a quarantine of the area. There's talk the Governor might call in the National Guard if the crowds can't be kept back."

James Christopher nodded. His keen intellect instantly grasped the problem. It was far past midnight. And on a Sunday night. Tomorrow morning would be the first work day of the new week. City streets would fill with rushing pedestrians. Human nature being what it was, and New Yorkers being perhaps the most human of all human beings, common curiosity would bring them to the park. The flimsy sawhorses, even the barbed-wire barricades, would not hold back the press of humanity for long.

"Martial law," he breathed, "is the only solution."

"That's what they say," the officer agreed. "But they got to haul that damn meteorite out of the park somehow. And no one's figured out a way to get near it without going meteor-nuts."

"Thank you," said James. "Tell no one of this conversation. Understand?"

The officer raised his billy club in salute. "Mum's the word."

Returning to his roadster, Operator 5 keyed the ignition and sent the black machine west and then south, toward Columbus Circle. His destination was in Midtown.

But fate had something else in store.

Hurtling down Fifth Avenue, Operator 5 recognized an oncoming car. It was a smart coupé. He knew it by its color, but it was the license plate that identified the owner.

Without pausing to identify the person behind the wheel, James Christopher cut across traffic, swerved to a halt, blocking the oncoming machine. He jumped out. He wore no hat. His firm-featured face was painted by the moonlight.

The coupé had plenty of time to brake, and it did. The driver popped out. It was an attractive young girl, perhaps twenty-six, dressed in a tasteful frock of subdued hue. She rushed up to greet him, eyes sparkling.

"Jimmy! Have you heard?"

"Yes," Christopher replied, stepping up to meet her.

The young woman was Diane Elliot, reporter for the Amalgamated Press. She was one of the few persons outside of the Intelligence Service who knew that James Christopher was the real name of Secret Service Operator 5.

"You must turn back, Diane," he told her sternly. "The police have cordoned off the park. It's too dangerous to approach now."

"That is exactly why I must get as close as I can. This is an incredible story—the public must know about it!"

"I must disagree," returned James. "The meteorite's rays are as lethal as radium. They are affecting ordinary people in extraordinary ways. The police know what they're doing. You must turn around. Stay as far away from the meteorite as you can. Do you understand?"

The young woman's brown eyes were sympathetic. But her voice was pleading. "I have a job to do. You know that. I mustn't let anything get in the way of covering this story."

They stood in the middle of the avenue, blocking traffic. Fortunately there was little.

James continued speaking. "This is no time to tarry. I must report to headquarters. The police have the matter in hand, for now. But the coming morning could be terrible."

"I know," said Diane. "If I can gather facts in time for the morning editions, the public will know to stay away."

James laughed roughly. It was a trace of sardonic humor in his vibrant voice when he continued.

"The sensible portions of the public will stay away, Diane. But there are always those elements which cannot control themselves. Those are the people I worry about most. They will attempt to slip behind police lines in order to take pictures or steal souvenirs. Go back to your office and write that up. You need not witness the meteorite's power to report it accurately."

"All right, then," said Diane reluctantly. "I trust you to tell me the truth. You know that."

"I would never lead you astray." James smiled. "And you know that, Di. Don't you?" His voice softened, acquiring a tenderness that bespoke of his warm feelings for the attractive brunette.

Before Diane Elliot could reply, something stumbled out of the park and lurched toward the avenue.

The thing was tattered. Its clothes were old and soiled. A man in his 40s. He wore no hat, no tie. He was stringy of muscle, and his unkempt hair had not been raked by a comb in weeks. One shoe sole flapped when he walked. But that was not the horrible thing.

The man's face was vacant... yet his eyes glowed with an evil greenish light. As he stepped off the curb and into traffic, that light appeared to intensify. From each individual eyeball, a beam of green extended like questing antennae. They grew brighter.

Seeing this, Diane lifted a hand to her open mouth. "What is wrong with that man?"

"He appears to be a tramp, a hobo," said James tightly. "I recognize him. He panhandles in the park. He must live there. But look at him now. His expression tells me he has no mind of his own. The burning in his eyes is the light of the queer green meteorite. This is what you need to write about, Diane. *That man has been driven meteor-mad!*"

James Christopher pulled Diane back into her coupé, and then turned to intercept the stumbling hobo.

Removing his tuxedo jacket, he was no longer a society photographer but Operator 5. It was his habit to carry a .45-caliber automatic in a shoulder holster, but not when he was in the person of Carleton Victor. Victor would never sully his immaculate hands with such a weapon.

But Operator 5 was not unarmed. Around his waist he wore a leather belt. One hand grasped the complicated buckle—the right. On the back of that hand was a greyish-black scar. It depicted a spread-winged eagle—the American eagle.

With a sweeping motion, James pulled on the buckle. Out sprang a rapier of flexible steel. The belt was its sheath. No one examining him would ever suspect that the well-made belt could contain such a weapon.

Brandishing the rapier, James called over, "You! Turn back; you'll be run over."

The shining-eyed hobo nervously shifted his gaze around like a dazed dog. Upon hearing the ring of Operator 5's clear clarion voice, his attention veered toward the sound.

Unholy green eyes blazed up. James could feel their heat. He stepped back several paces. The cool-looking green rays bathing his body somehow imparted a feverish warmth. James could only imagine what was going on in the man's irradiated brain.

"Back! Back, I say," he ordered.

But the meteor-mad man did not seem to understand, or care. He advanced, his left shoe sole flapping like a macabre desiccated tongue. The hobo spoke no words, made no threat. His posture was poor, his limbs uncoordinated. Nothing in his walk suggested menace.

But that green vacant face and the lambent eyes told otherwise....

Not wishing to engage the other man, James continued his retreat.

This was not cowardice, but prudence. He had heard from the picketed police officer of the terrible burning eyes of the victims of the Green Meteorite. And he accepted that report, fantastic as it sounded. Now he felt the awful beams burning in his direction. Operator 5 fully comprehended the danger. It was mortal....

Diane was backing her automobile away, watching intently.

James continued to retreat. At his back yawned an alley. Not a good place to become trapped. Then he saw something dull gleaming in the moonlight. An ashcan.

Turning, James rushed to it, and saw that it had been placed on the sidewalk for collection. The lid was on firmly. He lifted it up. It was heavy. The galvanized steel would make a serviceable shield—at least until it heated up....

Holding this by the handle, he wielded it in the manner of a knight warding off a charging lance, holding it high to protect face and chest.

Something caused the meteor-addled tramp to charge suddenly. Now James had no choice. Standing his ground, he lifted the shield. Almost instantly, the metal became warm, then warmer. Soon it was hot—searing hot!

Knowing that the lid would quickly become too hot to hold, James took a position, advanced two confident steps. Holding the shield against the strange green beams, he lunged.

The rapier licked in, struck the middle of the starvation-sunken chest, piercing the pounding heart. The transfixed hobo emitted a strange cry. His emaciated arms flew up. James withdrew, taking the ensanguined blade with him.

The unfortunate hobo fell backward, landing on his back. He lay there, unmoving. The back of his head had struck the granite curbing, and the sound of it was final. Where the loose sole hung down, the dirty toes of one foot showed distinctly in the moonlight.

Cautiously, James circled the defeated wretch. Spectral green beams continued shooting up into the sky. But as he watched, these rays grew less intense. They seemed to retreat into the man's head. Soon, the eyes simply shone with a weak emerald light. Finally, the sickly shining subsided.

The atavistic human horror lay dead.

Replacing the ashcan lid, James rushed to Diane's auto. "Return to your office and report everything you saw, Di. Leave me out of it, of course. But what you've witnessed is what the city will face tomorrow morning if the radiation from the Green Meteorite is not brought under absolute control."

"I will!" exclaimed Diane. "What are you going to do? What can *anyone* do?"

"I must return to my headquarters. I can do nothing on my own. You forget that I am only an operative of the United States Intelligence Service. I require orders from my superior. Now go. If you hurry, you can make the morning editions."

Without another word, Diane Elliot turned her moaning machine around and raced toward the offices of the Amalgamated Wire Service. They were open all night, of course.

BACK BEHIND the wheel of his roadster, James continued south, then turned toward the white stone tower that was the famed Vertex Building, one of Manhattan's newest and tallest skyscrapers.

Parking within sight of the towering Art Deco-style building near Fifth Avenue, James exited the automobile, and entered the lobby. It was never locked. But at this hour there was no one at the guard desk.

The elevators ran all night. Christopher took one to a high floor, stepping off on the fifty-sixth floor and then taking the fire stairs down to the fifty-fifth level. It was not that he suspected that he was being followed. This was merely a routine precaution.

Down a blank corridor, he walked until he came to a pebbled glass door on which was outlined in black:

Consolidated Paper Mills

There was no such concern. It was a blind. A month before, the name of the company was different. In another month, the concern might move to another floor in this same skyscraper, or to another building entirely. Always, the cover name changed to foil detection by foreign enemies.

For this was the Intelligence Service's central New York office, designated Secret Headquarters M. It was the nerve center of New York undercover operations. Radiating from it, electronically protected communications went out to the world by radio, teletype, telephone and cable. This station was a subsidiary of Intelligence Central Headquarters in Washington, D.C., code-named WDC-13.

Even though the hour was very late, James found a placid-faced woman seated at a reception desk.

"May I help you?" she enquired.

"Is this the fifty-fifth floor?"

"It is. You are the fifth person to ask that question today."

"I know that I am five hours early, but I have an appointment."

The receptionist consulted her calendar. "Your name?"

"Javier Cinco."

"How odd. Cinco is Spanish for five. No matter. You may enter."

"Thank you," said Operator 5, having successfully code-worded his way in. The fact that the receptionist knew his name well was of no moment. James sometimes arrived in disguise, and there was also the danger of impersonation by an enemy agent.

After being buzzed in, he went through another door. In that room, a dictagraph machine sat uncovered on an otherwise-empty desk. He touched a cam and spoke into the transmitter. "Operator 5 reporting."

A distant voice replied, "Enter, Operator 5."

An electrical latch clicked. James passed through into a sizable office. Behind the fumed oak desk sat a man who was nondescript in general appearance, even to his hair, which was an even brown. This was T-3, in charge of the New York office. He was James's immediate superior.

"I know why you are here," said T-3. "We have been monitoring activities around the Green Zone. The police appear to have the matter under control."

James took a chair and got to the point. His voice was firm.

"The police are doing the best they can," he concurred. "They have cordoned off the zone of contagion. But no one has ever seen anything like it, unless I miss my guess. Who knows how far these rays can travel? The brave officers standing watch tonight may even now be slowly absorbing the power rays, and before long could become afflicted themselves."

T-3's intelligent eyes widened. "I had not thought of that...."

"It is only a supposition on my part," returned Operator 5 urgently. "But with the dawn, New York will awaken. How many hundreds or thousands will be drawn to this horror, compelled by curiosity and even greed? If they are not kept away, many will be transformed into destructive robots. I encountered one such specimen on my way here. Imagine an army of them running amuck, rampaging, and torching everything they encountered in their blind, atavistic confusion!"

"Are they capable of thought, in your estimation?"

James shook his head. "No, they are not. They appear to be completely mindless. But that is what makes them so dangerous. These meteor-crazed madmen cannot be reasoned with. They can only be killed—put down like dogs. Most of them will be ordinary New Yorkers. If there is no way to contain or cure them, who could predict how many people sleeping peacefully in their beds now will be transformed into brainless automatons in the morning?"

"Good grief!" exclaimed T-3. "But this is the jurisdiction of the police and, of course, the Mayor. They will have to make these decisions. This is not our affair. We can only hope and pray they do the correct thing."

A bell sounded. A teletype in the corner of the office began clattering. The two men stood up and went to it. A perforated strip of paper rolled out, capitalized words punched into the thin material.

NEW YORK POLICE ASSERT CENTRAL PARK UNDER QUARANTINE AT THIS HOUR... METEORITE OF UNKNOWN PROPERTIES COR-DONED OFF... ESTIMATED THIRTEEN CASUALTIES AS A RESULT OF DOOM RAYS... GOVERNOR CONSIDERING CALLING ON NATIONAL GUARD... DECISION EXPECTED ON THE MORROW....

"What—tomorrow!" cried T-3. "That decision needs to be handed down tonight. It must be made now. Morning may be too late!"

The teletype resumed clattering.

FLASH! SECOND METEORITE REPORTED DOWN IN LONG ISLAND… REPORTS OF SCATTERED BRUSHFIRES… LOCATION OF SECOND IMPACT CRATER NOT YET ESTABLISHED….

"There were two of them!" groaned T-3. "Could this be a storm of meteors?"

Operator 5 said, "I've made a study of the phenomenon of shooting stars. This is the time of year for the Leonid meteor shower. And it's not unusual for a meteor to break apart while entering the atmosphere and land in separate localities. This could be an example of that phenomenon."

"Let's hope you're right, Operator 5. Because if this is a storm, we will more than have our hands full."

The two men remained by the teletype machine all night. Reports continued to clatter off the wire.

POLICE SAY MOB OF METEOR-MAD MEN APPEARS SUPPRESSED. FINAL VICTIM FOUND NOT A BLOCK AWAY FROM PARK. BELIEVED TO BE NAMELESS HOBO….

"That was the poor wretch I ran through with my blade," explained James. "If this report is accurate, the contagion has been stopped. For now."

Tape continued clattering out.

… FIRST AUTOPSIES SHOW METEOR VICTIMS SUFFERING FROM SEVERE BRAIN LESIONS, EFFECTIVELY ROBBING THEM OF REASON….

T-3 remarked, "Radiation has that effect upon the brain, as you know."

James looked almost relieved. "Evidently, the plague cannot be transmitted from person to person... only from meteorite to victim...."

An hour later brought a flash from Long Island.

WILD ANIMALS INFECTED BY STRANGE GLOWING PHENOMENON... FIRES CONTINUE TO SPREAD... LOCATION OF SECOND METEORITE STILL NOT ESTABLISHED TO SATISFACTION OF AUTHORITIES....

T-3 ventured, "While this is not good news, we are not hearing about a third meteorite. Your theory may be correct, Operator 5."

Two hours along, the teletype awoke from a lengthy period of inactivity.

LONG ISLAND SITUATION APPEARS TO BE CONTAINED....ALL FIRES OUT.... CASUALTIES UNKNOWN... METEORITE APPEARS TO HAVE BEEN DESTROYED BY PERSONS YET TO BE IDENTIFIED....

"Good. I want to know how they accomplished that," muttered T-3.

James Christopher fingered his firm chin thoughtfully. "I want to know who *did* it! Did the reports say nothing about police action?"

"Long Island is pretty wild. Maybe some of the farmers out there took matters into their own hands. We'll know more in the morning."

"Morning," mused James slowly. "Somehow, I dread the dawn more than I have ever dreaded anything in my entire life...."

Chapter 11

AUDACIOUS PLAN

THE RISING morning sun bathed the cold marble lions named "Patience" and "Fortitude" guarding the entrance to the New York Public Library, warming them to a pale semblance of life.

The man who called himself *Herr* Friedrich von Maur, but who was in actuality Stahlmaske, watched the avenue below. It was packed with scurrying early-morning Gothamites. With hands clasped behind his broad back, his posture was thoughtful for a long time. But now he turned to Count Calypsa, sitting behind his mahogany desk set before the cloth-of-gold hangings with their heraldic leonine design.

"I have reconsidered my plan," he announced hollowly.

The radio continually blared warnings to the populace of Manhattan to steer clear of Central Park. Those warnings were escalating. The voice of the radio announcer sounded nervous, fretful.

"The public must keep their distance from the park," the announcer repeated in a strident tone. *"It is vital that they do so."*

Count Calypsa reminded, "I understood that your idea was to wait for human nature to take its inevitable course."

"It was," rumbled Stahlmaske. "But I grow impatient. I see that we cannot count upon the rabble to succumb into the meteorite's uncanny allure. Now I conceive a superior idea."

"I will consider it," allowed Calypsa.

"Instead of waiting for the inevitable outbreak of radiation-maddened citizens to run wild, we will steal the meteorite today."

"Under the noses of the police! How do you propose to pull off that audacious act in broad daylight?"

"By hijacking a common truck. By driving it into the confusion created when the first morning victims manifest themselves— as we both know they surely will. These are Americans, after all. They are like children in that way. They can barely control themselves. You, as a European, know this as well as I."

Count Calypsa nodded his thick-featured head. "I do. But Americans, as you learned during the war, can be exceedingly ingenious, and therefore dangerous."

Stahlmaske seemed unmoved by the reminder. "Where may one acquire a suitable truck?"

Calypsa continued briskly. "The city sanitation yards. I can drive us there. But what about your helmet? Shouldn't you remove it? After all, it is no longer Halloween."

"You think that you are ugly," laughed Stahlmaske. "If I were to lift this helmet, you would see that I am quite hideous. Furthermore, you would violently divulge your breakfast. And you have only just eaten."

"Then it will be wiser if you rode along prone upon the back seat. I will take us where we need to go."

"Very good," said Stahlmaske, striding over to the corner and taking firm hold of his heavy headsman's axe.

It was still early morning, but not so early that taking the public elevator to the basement garage was a smart thing to do.

Count Calypsa pulled from a desk drawer a hood of black silk. It was something he wore when he addressed his underlings during his first battle with The Spider, back when he needed to conceal his true features.

Pressing a button on the desk caused one of the wall hangings to slide aside, revealing an elevator door.

"My private elevator," he said. Pressing another button caused an electric door to open, and the two men crossed the thickly-carpeted room and stepped aboard the car. In silence, it lowered them to the basement garage.

Calypsa walked stiffly. The physician who had been summoned in the middle of the night had done an excellent job of removing the arrow's shaft and binding the wound. He had left behind a cane and sufficient morphine to dull the pain. The Count had disdained the walking stick… but the pain had receded to a dull throbbing of his thigh muscle….

A blue sedan awaited. Stahlmaske slid into the back and hunkered low while his confederate in crime took the wheel. Calypsa laid his silken mask on the seat beside him.

Engaging the powerful engine, he drove to the concrete ramp that led to a loading door. Stepping out, he pressed an electric button. The steel door slid upward slowly.

Reclaiming the wheel, he slid out into traffic, not bothering to close the door. After three minutes, an electric timer would cause it to descend automatically.

Count Calypsa drove through the light traffic. He called into the back seat, "I have operatives stationed throughout the city. I have told you this, von Maur. Some are in high positions. Others are in lowly ones. Sometimes, it is the lowly ones who are the most valuable…."

"What are you suggesting—that you have such a person entrenched in the sanitation department?"

"My man oversees the main yard. Your idea fits perfectly with my organization. He will let us in and so we will have our choice of vehicles."

THE DRIVE to the sanitation yard was not particularly long. The sedan rolled up to the gate and Count Calypsa drew on his black silk hood. There was no one about at this early hour in this corner of the city. He honked the horn three times, then twice more.

A blond-haired man in work clothes appeared at the gate, opened it, and Count Calypsa rolled his machine in, braking sharply.

"I will handle this alone," he told Stahlmaske. "Stay out of sight."

"I have no wish to frighten your underling," said Stahlmaske agreeably.

Count Calypsa emerged from the driver's seat and permitted the man to approach.

"Number Forty-seven, I will require the strongest and latest model sanitation truck at your disposal. Bring it out it once."

"At once, Count. Please park your car wherever you wish."

This was done, and a gleaming sanitation truck came rumbling out of the garage. It was the type that boasted a trio of hatch doors on each side into which refuse was pitched. The machine looked as if it had never been driven. There was no grime, no dust of the city streets upon its blunt cab or bulky rear compartment with its uniform rows of loading hatches.

Examining the machine, Count Calypsa nodded approvingly.

"That will do nicely. Return to your post. Do not look in this direction. And, of course, never speak of this to anyone again. You understand the gravity of these instructions?"

"Never fear, Count. Forty-seven is loyal."

Number Forty-seven turned to walk away. From the back of the blue sedan Stahlmaske stepped out, gripping his double-bladed executioner's axe. Instead of going to the Count's side, he stalked after the departing gate man. The fellow heard something, half-turned—but too late!

Two burly arms lifted the axe, swung it horizontally, and the sanitation man's head went flying off his shoulders in a sudden spray of arterial blood.

The body naturally crumpled. The head bounced twice before rolling to a halt, wide staring eyes looking up at the victim's final dawn.

Count Calypsa's silken hood shook with his intense rage.

"Why did you do such a foolish thing?" he raged. "That man is—was—valuable to me. He has proven it!"

No particular emotion threaded the hulking Stahlmaske's hollow voice; he might have been a machine enunciating methodical words. "I wish no witnesses. Not until I am ready to announce my presence to America. Let us waste no time."

Grinding his teeth wordlessly, Count Calypsa yanked off his hood and climbed into the cab, settling behind the wheel.

Stahlmaske went to one of the hatch doors on the side of the sanitation truck's broad, squat body. He jerked it open, looked inside and saw the interior was spotlessly clean. Conveyor mechanism stood in shadow, smelling of fresh oil. He called out, "I will ride inside. You will drive directly to the meteorite."

"Are you mad? I have no protection against the doom rays. You know that!"

"*Ach,* forgive me. I am so forgetful. Yes, drive me to the southern end of Central Park. I will take the wheel after that. You will stand ready until my return."

Without waiting for an answer, Stahlmaske stepped onto the long running board, put his head and upper body into the gaping hatch door and pulled himself inside. The trap slammed shut.

Count Calypsa ground the starter, then piloted the huge machine out of the sanitation yard.

He drove carefully, unfamiliar with the handling of the monster truck. He encountered no problems. His silken black hood lay on the seat beside him. There were some risks because the battered countenance was known to the police as the face of Count Carmine Calypsa, the Dictator. But he had been lying low for several months, knowing that "Casey Grogan" was a wanted man.

No doubt the police—not to mention Richard Wentworth—had long before this time concluded that he had fled the city, if not the country. This, too, was part of his master plan. To lay low until his enemies believed he was no longer operating. And then to strike!

Now, thanks to a freak of fate he was able to strike in a way that they could never have imagined. Indeed, Count Calypsa could not have conceived his good fortune that began on Halloween night when the strange glowing visitant from the outer reaches of interstellar space slammed like a glowing green fist into Central Park....

Chapter 12

DAWN OF FEAR

INEVITABLY, THE dawn came.

A sliver of hot orange sunlight peeped over the sun-dappled watery horizon of the Atlantic Ocean. The crisp Autumn morning air began to warm as the solar orb struggled to reveal itself. Indian summer appeared to be over.

In the trees of lower Central Park, songbirds twittered. But north of the Sheep's Meadow, no birds sang. All had fled from the interminable emerald glow.

Creeping sunlight began to infiltrate that halo of jade light. The aura lost some of its former strength, faded in intensity, yet continued pulsing intermittently. It was like the beating of a great green heart—the heart of a fallen monster that refused to die....

As the first morning of the month of November showed itself above Manhattan's steel and stone spires, milk wagons began to appear, city buses resumed running. The clattery banging of the elevated trains increased in tempo, rousing from their night schedule.

Little sunlight penetrated the office of T-3 in the secret headquarters of the United States Intelligence Service in the Vertex spire, facing Fifth Avenue, for it had been constructed with windows of one-way glass. No mutter of traffic, no honking of horns, penetrated those confines. The office was entirely soundproofed by thick paneling.

An electric clock on the wall made a steady grinding noise as the hour struck six a.m. Reflexively, the intelligence chief consulted his wristwatch. It was perfectly synchronized with the wall clock.

Standing by the teletype machine, James Christopher fingered a curious gleaming object affixed to the watch chain of his vest. During the night he had changed out of Carleton Victor's evening clothes and into more appropriate business attire.

Dangling from the links was a small golden skull-and-crossbones. Its eyes were twin rubies. James always carried this. But for dark reasons.

As an operative of the U.S. Intelligence Service, he was eternally at risk of capture by foreign agents. He possessed knowledge that, were it to be extracted by torture or other means, would prove fatal to his fellow agents—and to the security of the Intelligence Service.

James had only to flick a catch at the crown of the golden skull, and the top would pop open. Nestled safely in the hollow brain cavity was a small black sphere. The sphere contained a deadly gas called Diphenochlorasine. Crushing it would release the deadly vapor. Although the sphere contained but a small quantity, there was enough of the devil's brew to instantly kill him if he were to decide death was preferable to disgrace. But more than that, the gas would wipe out any of his captors within a significant radius. For the potency of this lethal stuff was such that were the black sphere to be ground under foot in Madison Square Garden during a public event, all in attendance would perish within minutes.

It was perhaps a subconscious indication of James Christopher's precarious position living under cover and fighting America's enemies in secret that in quiet moments his fingers drifted to the gleaming golden skull and made it dance, its ruby eyes flashing with sinister glints.

"We will know in an hour or so if the police are equal to the challenge," advised T-3.

James replied nothing. He had utmost respect for the New York Police Department. Commissioner Kirkpatrick was an upstanding public servant. He had shepherded the city through many past crises. But while his word was law among his officers, he was not the ultimate authority. Kirkpatrick answered to the Mayor.

But only the Governor in Albany could declare martial law. And the Governor had not been heard from all night....

A knock came at the door and a clerk entered with a morning paper. The headlines were black and terrible:

MONSTER METEOR LANDS IN CENTRAL PARK!

POLICE BARRICADE RAMBLE

All Citizens Advised To Avoid Area

The byline read Diane Elliot.

Operator 5 absorbed her report, his stern expression softening. She described the green-eyed hobo who had to be put down by an unidentified citizen who had encountered it in the hours past midnight.

"This Good Samaritan," Diane had written, "no doubt saved the life of this reporter—and perhaps others—had the creature been allowed to roam free."

There were quotes from Stanley Kirkpatrick as well as the Mayor taken from official statements. One stated:

"In order to safeguard the city, citizens were strongly advised to avoid Central Park until the police can clear it. The emergency is not yet over. It is vital that no further New Yorkers fall victim to the pernicious radiation that robs ordinary persona of their normal thoughts and converts them into walking blowtorches."

Satisfied, James handed the paper to his superior. T-3 read it swiftly and remarked, "This could go a long way toward curbing any further problems."

James shook his head. "Not everyone reads this newspaper. Too many take the tabloids. No doubt they are playing this up for all its sensational value. My fear is the public appetite for rubbernecking will not be whetted."

"Well, we'll know soon," grunted T-3.

James consulted his wristwatch again. "Let me suggest that you contact Z-7 once he reaches his office."

Z-7 was the Washington Chief of the Intelligence Service—the chief of chiefs. T-3 and all other branch heads reported directly to him. James had worked under Z-7 on many important espionage cases.

T-3 shook his head. "As the matter stands at present, this is a New York City administration problem."

"True," agreed James. "But if the meteor-mad contagion spreads to adjoining states, it could become a national emergency."

"You're right." Reaching for his desk dictaphone, he keyed it and said, "Call Z-7 in Washington."

A connection was established and the desk telephone rang back. T-3 picked it up and began his report without any formalities. The telephone was fitted with a frequency-distorter that electronically garbled the transmission of his voice, which was decoded at the other end of the direct wire to WDC-13.

When T-3 concluded, he added, "Operator 5 is here with me. I am inclined to send him over to Central Park to keep a close eye on the developing situation."

The strong, chesty voice of Z-7 vibrated over the wire.

"Operator 5 is our best man. You have my permission to do exactly that. Stay in close contact. The Intelligence Service will not interfere unless the matter rises to the level of national import. That is all."

Hanging up, T-3 said crisply, "Z-7 agrees with me that we should monitor the meteorite. You're the right man for this. Establish a watch post overlooking the Green Zone. Report all unusual activities to me. And good luck, Operator 5."

"Thank you, sir."

EXITING THE building, James found his black roadster and it was soon nosing through traffic headed north toward Central Park. He possessed no illusions about the difficulty of the task before him. The police cordon would be tight. Standing watch from the ground would be all but impossible. So James drove to a staid hotel overlooking Central Park, the Collier.

"I wish a room facing Central Park," he told the desk clerk. "One no lower than the fifth floor, but no higher than the fifteenth."

The desk clerk smiled thinly. "You're not the only one looking for a bird's-eye view of that meteorite that fell."

James frowned. He had been afraid of that.

"A lot of them are reporters, of course," advised the desk man. "They can't get near the park. But they and their photographers have a ringside seat to whatever happens."

"Thank you," said James, signing the desk register with a flourish. He used the name Morton Clegg, one of his cover identities. He rarely used it except in situations such as this. There was no such person. It was simply a name on the door of a certain Manhattan apartment situated not far from this hotel.

James carried a leather valise to the elevator and, when he entered his room, he unpacked it. This valise included a pair of binoculars as well as other equipment.

Going to the window, he pulled the curtains aside and studied Central Park. Christoper gave particular attention to the sprawling woodsy Ramble.

There, no fires burned. They had been extinguished somehow. The stone from space sat in a earthen crater of its own making. It seemed small, somehow. Yet it was substantial in size. The luminosity of the meteorite had abated dramatically. Cleansing sunshine had done that.

From his coign of vantage, Operator 5 saw that the police cordon remained in place. Patrol cars circled the park, intercepting the curious. The Metropolitan police were functioning like the well-oiled civic machine that they were.

But James felt a vague unease. Morning was still dawning. Only the early risers were about. In another hour, their numbers would swell. Then the avenues and sidewalks would be thick with teeming, jostling humanity.

Absentmindedly fingering the golden death's head dangling from his watch chain, he turned on the console radio and found a news announcer expostulating.

"Manhattan is holding its breath this morning as it awaits the disposition of the strange meteorite that fell in Central Park on Halloween evening. Police are urging all citizens to remain away from a ten-square-block zone around upper Central Park, the so-called Green Zone. The transverse streets have been closed off. Lower Central Park is also off-limits to all but officials.

"The Mayor is promising that the meteorite will be conveyed out of the city, where it can do no further harm, but at this early hour no one seems to know how that will be accomplished.

"In a bit of good news, a second meteor that landed in Long Island last night appears to have been destroyed. Details are sketchy at this hour. However, this radio station has it on good authority that the threat to Long Island is over."

As he listened to the broadcast, James watched the police hold their lines.

Time passed. The morning grew long. The shadows became shorter.

Little by little, people were creeping toward the park. The uncanny glow was not sufficiently strong to attract them now. But newspaper hawkers were doing a brisk business, no doubt feeding the public curiosity as much as quelling nervous fears.

James noticed two individuals attempt to sneak through police lines. Both were intercepted. One was turned away. But the other was hauled off in handcuffs, then stuffed into the back of a Black Mariah, which soon took off for the Tombs.

It was to be expected. There were always elements who flouted the law....

More time passed. The police lines appeared to hold.

Then something unexpected happened.

James missed the start of it. His binoculars were sweeping east and west when the radio behind him suddenly broke in with the bulletin.

"Flash! Just this minute, a shooting erupted in the vicinity of the fallen meteor. One of our roving reporters in the Hotel Collier has called in the news. We are waiting for the report. Stand by."

James's striking blue eyes swept about, soon located a commotion. Focusing, they darkened, clouding over. Even from this height he could make out the blue uniforms of the New York Police Force. Several had drawn their Police Positives. They were shooting at something.

James swept his binoculars about until he found the thing they were aiming at.

To his horror, he realized it was a fellow policeman!

"Good Lord!" he cried.

Under a hammering fusillade of bullets, the hapless officer staggered about, then collapsed into a pile of leaves. They soon caught flame, blazed up. Fiery tongues started eating at the fallen man....

Through the binocular lenses, Operator 5 could see the jade-green gleam in the burning man's eyes. It faded as his life did. The body twisted in final death throes, then became still.

A lump rose in James's throat, but more than that, fear dawned in his brain.

"What if," he whispered, "prolonged exposure to the rays has infiltrated the unprotected brains of the picketed police?"

Raising the binoculars to his eyes again, Operator 5 began

searching the milling bluecoats for any signs that the owners were about to go meteor-mad....

He was about to release a sigh of relief when a second officer began lurching about drunkenly. This was noticed. Attempts were made to talk to the stricken officer. They did no good.

One patrolman, approaching his comrade, suddenly yanked his cap off and flung it away. It had caught fire—caught fire simply by being stared at by another glowing-eyed policeman!

Again, revolvers were drawn, gun smoke puffed out—and again another man in blue crumpled, never to rise again.

It did not require a third such incident to convince the police to pull back from their established lines. James spied a tall, fault-lessly-attired figure stepping out of a police limousine to direct the retreat.

Commissioner Kirkpatrick! There was no mistaking him strid-ing about, imposing, decisive and commanding. But was he too late?

As James followed the shifting of police lines, he noticed some-thing that stood out.

A sanitation truck came trundling up Fifth Avenue. There is nothing unusual about it. Refuse trucks could be seen on Man-hattan streets almost every day of the week.

This one, however, was moving in the direction of the quar-antine zone. It was not stopping to empty garbage cans. Nor was it trash day in this part of town.

These trivial things were enough to raise the suspicions of Operator 5. He tracked the garbage truck as it approached the barbed-wire and sawhorse perimeter.

Startled police officers noted it, of course. They waved at it, encouraging the driver to turn around.

Instead, the huge truck took a sudden lurch toward the park. It picked up speed. A juggernaut of steel and rubber tires, it smashed through the sawhorses, trampled the barbed-wire entanglement, and raced along the browning sward, hurtling toward the Ramble!

James Christopher did not need to witness any more. Dropping the binoculars, he rushed for the door.

Behind his departing form, the hotel-room radio was blaring:

"Folks! Something strange is going on down by the Green Zone. A large truck has smashed through police lines. It is charging for the crater where the meteorite lies. What could this development possibly mean?"

Chapter 13

THE BATTLE AT THE CRATER

HERR STAHLMASKE crouched on his haunches like a dog as the sanitation truck trundled through early morning traffic. He did not move. Only the rising and falling of his great chest suggested that vitality resided in the muscular hulk that was his body.

Not even the conical head turned visibly from side to side. The heavy steel helmet sat upon his shoulders on a flaring flange that held it firmly in place. Stahlmaske could not rotate his head without also turning his entire upper body.

In that regard, he was a prisoner of the ugly black shell.

As the rumble of traffic and the honking of horns penetrated the absolute darkness of the sanitation-truck body, black-gloved hands lifted and took hold of the conical shell. With an effort, he removed it. Stahlmaske laid it down beside him, threw his head back and inhaled a long draught of unobstructed air.

In the nearly absolute darkness, nothing could be seen of the revealed head. The leather-gloved hand went to the top of his exposed skull. Fragments of greying hair grew there. But only fragments. He touched a few dry strands, as if to make sure they were still present.

Of the ruined features, nothing could be seen.

Patiently, Stahlmaske waited as the trundling truck wended its way through traffic until at last it lurched to a sliding halt.

From the truck cabin, the cultured voice of Count Calypsa resounded.

"We are here."

Stahlmaske called back. "Exit and make yourself scarce. Leave the rest to me."

"Where shall I wait for you?"

Stahlmaske hesitated before answering. Finally, he said, "Perhaps it is better for you to return to your headquarters. What I am about to undertake will be dangerous. And you have no protection, as you have so carefully reminded me. Be prepared to receive me once I have achieved my objective. I will see you anon."

The sound of the cab door opening and slamming shut came. Stahlmaske continued to abide in darkness, as if reluctant to stir back to life.

With a deep sigh, he found his heavy helm and restored it carefully to his shoulders. Coming out of his crouch, he reached for a side hatch and forced it to open, exiting that way.

Strong sunlight struck his eyes as he looked about. The garbage truck was parked on Fifth Avenue, below Columbus Circle. Swiftly, he went to the cab, climbed aboard and engaged the clutch.

As the monster truck pushed north, he trod the accelerator pedal and the steel juggernaut steadily gathered momentum.

It had taken a half-hour to drive this far. Behind his steel helmet, broken white teeth twisted into a snarl.

"No doubt by now the meteorite is working its will on those who were so reckless and foolhardy as to brave the police cordon...."

Onward, through the traffic whirl of Columbus Circle and up Fifth Avenue, the sanitation truck barreled. A few pedestrians spied the black-steel helmet of the driver jerking in unison with the truck's suspension. But he flashed by so fast they blinked and rubbed their eyes in disbelief, not knowing what to make of the apparition.

POLICE COMMISSIONER STANLEY KIRKPATRICK did not know what to make of it, either.

He was pulling up from a morning conference with the Mayor as he emerged from his official limousine. His saturnine face surveyed the crowd. He had exhorted the Mayor to call the Governor and have martial law declared. Stubbornly, the Mayor had refused, not wishing to relinquish control of the situation. Foolishly, he believed that he could manage the day ahead.

The fact that Election Day lay just around the corner no doubt figured in his thinking....

A police lieutenant rushed up to meet Kirkpatrick, his face red as a McIntosh apple.

"Commissioner!" he shouted.

"What is it?"

"Two of our men had to be shot. Their faces started to go blank and their eyes took on a green shimmer. There was no reasoning with either of them. We had to put both down like damned rabid dogs...."

"Good God!" thundered Kirkpatrick. "Who let them get close to the Green Zone? My orders were crystal clear."

"That's the hell of it, sir. They didn't. Everyone has kept a safe distance. Or so we thought."

"Man, are you saying—!"

The Lieutenant threw up helpless hands. "I think there might not be such a thing as a safe distance. All of us who stood outside of the danger zone were being bombarded by the doom rays. They were weaker, but they were still acting on us. They—they must have got to Santos and poor O'Malley."

Kirkpatrick's brows crowded together, and he reached for one wing of his military mustache as if to give the waxed point an annoyed tug. He never completed the gesture.

Two hundred yards away, a commotion started, followed by frantic shouting. Then a man screamed. Another one joined in.

"Musto has turned into a Meteor Maniac!"

Gunfire broke out. It was brief. The thud of a falling body could be heard through the shifting and milling police lines.

"Musto...." Kirkpatrick groaned. "I know that name."

The Lieutenant turned. "Sir, we have to pull back. We can't hold these lines if it means that we're all—"

"Afflicted," said Kirkpatrick heavily. "I am forced to agree. Relay the order. Retreat one block. Leave the sawhorses and wire in place. We will police as best we can."

The order had no sooner been given than the uniformed police stirred into action. Then a garbage truck came racing up the avenue. With a screeching of tires, it swerved into the park, jumped over grass after crushing sawhorses and barbed wire entanglement, and braked to a halt close to the disturbed crater of upflung earth surrounding the meteorite.

"What the hell!" yelled the Lieutenant.

"Stop him!" Kirkpatrick roared. "By any means at your disposal."

The police put forth a valiant effort. But they knew better than to rush into the danger zone. Especially as they had been pulling back.

Police Positives barked spitefully in rock-steady hands. There was no return fire.

Kirkpatrick took a pair of binoculars from his lieutenant, and clamped them to his narrowing eyes.

The sanitation truck had braked askew, its side loading doors standing open.

A towering man marched fearlessly toward the meteorite, which bulked up like an automobile that had been flattened. He looked too tall to be human. His head was entirely encased in a black form like a howitzer shell with a blunt bullet-shaped top.

As Kirkpatrick watched, the giant lifted a double-bladed axe and began hacking away at the meteorite with the fury of a lumberjack attempting to demolish a stubborn tree stump.

The flashing blade bit down time and again, fracturing the unearthly mass and breaking off pieces from the faintly glowing substance. With each blow of the axe came a brittle sound, like dense crystal shattering….

The giant paused only to throw bits and shards into the body of the sanitation truck, whose interior shimmered an eerie green. He worked with a single-minded determination that combined speed and deliberation. He was like a machine. Controlled. Tireless. Unstoppable.

Singing bullets were directed toward him. He simply shifted his position, letting the steel-sided sanitation truck absorb the punishing police slugs.

One struck him in the shoulder, staggering him. But only for a moment. Another seemed to bounce off the bullet-shaped helmet. Again, the owner staggered. The helmet stayed in place. It was too heavy to be dislodged. The impact should have broken the man's neck, steel shell notwithstanding. But the helmet was anchored in such a way that no regulation bullet could accomplish that feat.

Faced with the choice between sending his officers to their doom and continuing the retreat, Stanley Kirkpatrick made the only choice he could. He ordered retreat.

"The longer he keeps at that, the sooner he will succumb to the meteorite's rays," Kirkpatrick told his lieutenant. "That fellow is doomed, whoever he is."

The officer nodded somberly. But deep in his eyes lurked a dark gleam of doubt.

Under his breath, he muttered to himself, "Sure doesn't seem to be fazed by the stuff so far."

The police started moving their machines, creating fresh roadblocks in order to seal off all escape routes from Upper Central Park. Kirkpatrick had ordered that done.

Retreating to his own limousine, he was driven one block east. There he got out.

Again, the binoculars were brought up. But the angle was not favorable. He could not see the refuse truck or its driver. He could only hear the monotonous fury of the steel blade chipping, chipping, chipping away at the shimmering meteorite....

Of that, Stanley Kirkpatrick was certain.

"What kind of monster desires control of such a foul thing?"

Chapter 14

ENTER CAPTAIN GATE

A FLASHY roadster coasted to a stop at the main gate to Mitchel Field, and the driver handed over an official card that identified him as Captain George Gate, United States Army Air Corps.

The sentry on duty studied the picture on the identification card. It showed a mature man of perhaps forty, one who still retained many of his youthful characteristics. His frank grey eyes belied his age. The muscular planes of his face were lean and firm, the mouth mobile and slightly humorous. Every exposed inch of his epidermis was wind-burned to a pleasantly outdoorsy reddish-tan.

"You may pass, Captain," the guard said, returning the card.

"Thanks," clipped Gate. He drove on.

Once he found a parking spot, an orderly rushed up to him, shouting, "Captain Gate! Colonel Pinch-face wants to see you in his office. Pronto!"

"I was just on my way to see Colonel Jasper," returned Gate good-naturedly.

Sunken-cheeked Colonel Jasper was pacing the floor when Gate entered his office, snapping a crisp salute. The seasoned officer swung over and said gruffly, "At ease, Captain."

Captain Gate relaxed. There was an easy familiarity about the way they stood in one another's presence, indicating that they had worked together a long time.

"No doubt you heard about the meteorite," Jasper began.

Gate nodded. "It was all over the morning radio broadcasts. It sounds like a big deal, Colonel."

"If you saw the morning paper, you might have noticed something interesting on an inner page. Something that has nothing to do with the meteorite landing in Central Park."

The Captain waited patiently for the Colonel to resume speaking.

Striding over to his desk, Colonel Jasper unwrapped a folded newspaper. "As you know, the army loaned a certain steel helmet to the Metropolitan Museum of Art for their Art of War exhibit. It was being displayed under lock and key."

"It was all anyone ever found of *Herr* Stahlmaske after our last skirmish. No one's heard anything of him in almost twenty years. It's a cinch that he's long dead."

"You might reconsider your opinion after you read this."

Captain Gate accepted the folded newspaper. His eyes fell upon the headline. It read:

HELMET OF STAHLMASKE STOLEN

Gate scanned the story below swiftly. Colonel Jasper filled him in as he did so.

"It happened not long after the meteor landed. The revelers had been cleared out of the museum, and the lights were doused. Everything seemed as it should be. But when they opened the museum in the morning, the glass case lay shattered and the helmet was gone."

"There are many people who collect war souvenirs," murmured Captain Gate. "Not all of them are honest."

"That may be, Gate. But the thief left one clue: a leather hood. A man had arrived in the costume of a medieval executioner wearing the identical hood. A large man. No one is quite sure who he was. But he wielded a headsman's axe that witnesses described as formidable and very sharp."

A flicker of interest came into Gate's humorous grey eyes. "Go on, Colonel."

"A police officer was beheaded late last night in Central Park, and his police cruiser stolen. Sounds like the work of the same man. You should look into this mystery."

"Only you and I know that I'm attached to Mitchel Field as an agent of Military Intelligence. Poking my nose into a civilian matter could get dicey… for both of us."

"I know that," said Jasper sharply. "But I also know that if there's a chance in hell that Stahlmaske has come back from the dead, you're the man to look into it."

"All right, I will. How do you want me to handle this?"

"I'll place a call to the head of the Intelligence Service. We'll let them know of your interest. Steer clear of the police. But if necessary, you'll work with the Secret Service. I'll make the call now."

"I'll have to brave Central Park. I heard they quarantined it pretty tight."

"I hope they have," said Colonel Jasper, picking up the telephone handset. "But it's the logical place to start digging. And that's where you will begin your investigation, Captain. Dismissed!"

Returning the officer's sharp salute, Captain Gate turned on his heel and left the office.

MINUTES LATER, Gate appeared in a small hangar in a remote corner of Mitchel Field.

Slipping in via the side door, he encountered a mechanic.

"Ricks, is the *Hummingbird* fueled up?"

"She's ready to rip, Cap'n. All yours."

"Thanks," said Gate. He went over to the streamlined aircraft while the mechanic opened the electric doors.

The *Hummingbird* was a stub-winged experimental gyroplane. More advanced than an autogyro, but not quite a helicopter, the spindly-looking ship possessed a single duralumin propeller in the nose, as well as a pusher in the rear. The overhead rotor wing was three-bladed. These vanes drooped, as if wilting.

She was a cabin job. Captain Gate climbed aboard, sealed her up, and started flipping switches. The nose propeller commenced dragging the sleek ship forward. Then the pusher started up, boosting her along smartly. She bounded on her fat hydraulic tires.

When the throttle was fully open, the gyroplane scooted upward swiftly, but it eschewed the runway. The rotor blade was engaged. It began turning furiously, kicking up dust and stray leaves.

Abruptly, the *Hummingbird* leaped into the air almost straight up, canted, seeking altitude. Landing wheels toiled up into their recessed compartments and were soon concealed by closing doors. The smooth undercarriage had something of the look of a broad pontoon, indicating that it could alight on calm water, if necessary.

Once it reached three thousand feet, the silvery super-gyro started in the direction of Manhattan, winging straight for the Vertex Building's landmark spire, riding the bumpy downdrafts like a proud, plunging horse.

There was a commercial radio built in the cockpit and Captain Gate switched it on. Fishing around on the dial, he found a news broadcast.

An excited broadcaster was saying:

"This just in! The police have fallen back from the dangerous meteorite. No reason has been given as to why. But a city sanitation truck just smashed through the police roadblock, traveling in the direction of the impact crater. It is not clear if this is a police operation, or something else."

Captain Gate swung the *Hummingbird* around as he listened, enjoying her sweet handling.

A moment passed, and the broadcaster was back on the air. His excitement was mounting.

"Flash! Something strange is transpiring within the forbidden Green Zone. Not only are the Metropolitan Police withdrawing with haste, there are reports of shots being fired. Police officers have been killed. It is not immediately clear who the perpetrators are, but eyewitness reports claim that the sanitation truck that invaded the exclusion zone around the strange meteorite was driven by a man wearing a black helmet like that of a knight of old. Rumors are circulating that this is a special helmet constructed to protect the city workers assigned the task of relocating the meteorite out of city boundaries, but this has not been confirmed...."

Hearing these words, Captain Gate grated his strong white teeth and hissed out a single word:

"Stahlmaske...."

Chapter 15

THE INVULNERABLE COLOSSUS

JAMES CHRISTOPHER, Operator 5 of the United States Intelligence Service, jumped off the halted elevator car in the vestibule of the Hotel Collier.

The Art Nouveau lobby was jammed with newspaper reporters, from the disreputable look of some of them. He recognized Diane Elliot, attired in a fresh frock. But there was no time to speak with her. He had to reach the Man in the Steel Mask before he got away with the pieces of the terrible meteorite that had turned central Manhattan upside down.

Exiting the building, he raced for his black roadster, sent it squealing into traffic. It was a short drive to the Ramble, but every moment counted.

The police had pulled back entirely from their barricade and were setting up vehicle roadblocks. James encountered one, stepped out, and displayed his official letter from the President of the United States.

The officer said, "I'm sorry, but no one is allowed beyond this point."

James's voice was commanding, imperative. "I have instructions from my superiors to do everything in my power to prevent that meteorite from being carried off by criminals. I must pass. You will pass me."

Plainly, the patrolman did not know what to do. He had his orders. A signed letter from the President of United States was not a document to scoff at. But nothing in his instructions allowed him to pass anyone without strict instructions from the Commissioner, or someone higher up in the city chain of command.

"I will have to radio headquarters," he said at last.

James returned harshly, "By the time you're done, that meteorite will be gone."

"We have the area blocked on every approach," the bluecoat said stiffly. "No one will get through."

The patrolman got into his radio car and called his precinct dispatcher.

While he was doing so, James jumped the barricade and raced for the park.

The officer craned his head out, yelling, "Are you crazy? It's certain death to go in there. Do you hear me? *Certain death!*"

Christopher heard, but he did not care. He had his duty. In one hand he gripped a .45-caliber automatic, its safety off. And he was prepared to use it.

Reaching the edge of the park, he slowed, switched to creeping carefully along.

The gritty hacking of a battle-axe came to his ears. Inching forward, he began to feel strange.

It was a difficult sensation to describe. There was a pulsing pressure on his forehead. His brow dripped sudden sweat. He felt feverish, but only slightly. The sensation was queer... indefinable....

It was a cool morning, so Operator 5 knew this was not the action of morning sunlight on his face.

The deeper into the park he went, the more feverish he felt. His brain began to throb. It was no good. He was forced to retreat.

Circling at a wide distance, Christopher attempted to stalk the Man in the Steel Mask. The big garbage truck was blocking his view. But as he shifted about, sometimes advancing, but often retreating, he worked his way through shrubbery until he caught sight of the man-mountain.

The green glowing meteorite lay upon the disturbed ground in broken shards. A great deal of it had already been thrown into the open side hatches of the gleaming sanitation truck. The silent colossus dropped his great axe. With his black-gloved hands, he picked up loose pieces and flung them into the broad body of the truck, where they made a clatter.

Despite the size of these pieces, and their deadly rays, he did this almost without effort.

Operator 5 raised his voice. "You there—in the helmet. Stop what you're doing. Throw up your hands!"

The brawny giant did stop. He turned his entire body about until the slits in his high-crowned steel helmet were facing James. The black shell was entirely featureless. The eyes could not be clearly seen clearly. They were in shadow.

In a loud Teutonic voice, he cried out, "Behold! I throw up my hands. Now I drop them again. You can do nothing to me."

So saying, the man did exactly what he promised. Both burly arms went up, then came down again. With calm indifference to Operator 5's steady gun muzzle, he resumed his work.

James warned, "Don't force me to shoot."

"Go ahead and shoot," the hollow voice returned carelessly. "See what good it does you."

Lining his gun sights on the man's broad back, Operator 5 squeezed the trigger. The weapon jumped, its mechanism ejecting a smoking shell casing.

The bullet forced out of the barrel struck the man's back while he was bending over. It jolted him. Then he reached behind him and rubbed the spot where a bullet had seemingly lodged.

He dug around for a moment, then seemed to throw something away that annoyed him. The clink of metal against stone came distinctly.

"Try again," sneered the giant in the black helmet. "That one only stung, like a hornet."

Angered more than surprised, James fired again. This time at the helmet. And this time he accomplished something.

The scorching slug caught the helmet at the correct angle, for the man was sent stumbling forward. The heavy black shell did not come off. As if sledge-hammered, the man was struck down by the irresistible power of the bullet. He lay there amid the scattered shards of the shimmering green meteorite.

James let out a breath of relief. He had succeeded!

CAREFULLY RETREATING, he kept his eyes on the fallen giant, ready to shoot again. Then something happened that was unexpected.

The giant reared up into a sitting position, shaking his head from side to side. His entire upper body moved with that shaking. He appeared to have been stunned, or perhaps simply disoriented.

Bellowing in anger, he climbed to his feet, clutching a broken shard of meteorite. Yelling something inarticulate, he threw it in James's direction. It traveled far.

James knew that proximity to the radioactive substance would start in motion something he could not call back. So he did the only thing he could sensibly do. He turned about and dashed away. He was not ashamed about it. He had a job to do. It was a job he could not accomplish if transformed into a mindless meteor-mad monster.

The giant's strength was formidable. The rock flew far, sailed over James's head and landed in front of him, a stony green obstacle... seemingly alive with lambent light....

James was forced to retreat from it, turning back toward the meteorite crater. Another shard came whipping in his direction. James dodged it, flung about, then took quick aim. He shot yet another shard in midair just as it left the giant's gloved hands. The steel helmet tipped back and a dreadful, booming laugh roared out.

"You have only puny bullets. I have something mightier. Run away, American. Run away or become a brainless automaton of death and destruction!"

Operator 5 didn't run away. He shifted south, found shelter in a copse of black locust trees, then began working his way back toward police lines.

Once more, he turned and fired a bullet in the direction of the laughing colossus.

But the range was too great. He merely clipped one steel side of the garbage truck, accomplishing less than nothing.

As he stumbled through the park, seeking a safe exit, he heard a rustle in nearby shrubbery, and turned to see who else was sneaking about the park.

James Christopher halted. He spied the blue uniform of a policeman. The man was walking about aimlessly, often stumbling as if palsied. His uniform cap was cocked back on his head, and he searched the vicinity with eyes that seemed to shimmer with a weak green light.

James froze. He did not want to attract attention. If all reports were true, to get too close to that meteorite-made living dead man would be to invite the blazing glare of his eyes and to go up in flames like a living torch.

Crouching down, James watched carefully.

If it came to it, he would have to shoot the officer. Not only to save himself, but to put the poor unfortunate patrolman out of his misery. For he knew there would be no reclaiming him once the meteorite fever seized his brain.

But Operator 5 never had to face that awful choice. The stricken police officer wandered about, seemed unsteady on his feet, and without warning simply collapsed.

He lay in the grass, breathing his last. The green light of his eyes was weak and steadily grew weaker. Finally, it faded….

Cautiously, James crept up to the man and laid a hand over

his uniform tunic, above the heart. He felt no beating. He placed the back of his right hand, where the tattoo-like birthmark scar of an American eagle was spread, over the officer's still nostrils.

No feeling of air, no moisture of respiration touched his skin.

The patrol officer was dead. James examined him quickly for any signs of injuries. He found none.

There was no obvious explanation for why the stricken man had expired. Yet expired he had.

Silently, James walked up to the man's fallen uniform cap. He placed it carefully over his face in a solemn gesture of respect. The police could claim the body later. Right now, it was imperative that Operator 5 leave the park and prepare to intercept the refuse truck filled with meteorite fragments before it could leave the vicinity.

Chapter 16

FRESH HORROR

RICHARD WENTWORTH lay in a hospital bed, mouthing words that could not be understood. He had slept all night. His head was bandaged. Outside the door, faithful Ronald Jackson stood guard, along with a turbaned Sikh with a bushy beard, the latter resplendent in the colorful native costume of his mountainous homeland.

"Did you hear something?" Jackson asked the bushy-bearded man.

"*Wah!* It sounds like the master. He rouses from sleep."

He turned to open the door. Jackson laid a hand on the Sikh's tunic sleeve, arresting him.

"One second there, you heathen. The doc said Mr. Wentworth was not to be disturbed."

The other growled, "The doctor is not my master. Richard Wentworth is my master. Yours as well. The city is in peril. The *Sahib* would want to be told."

"Suit yourself, Ram Singh," said Jackson, shrugging negligently. "But if his condition worsens, it'll be on your conscience."

Ram Singh shook off Jackson's heavy hand. "I look to *Sahib* Wentworth to be the judge of my conscience. Enter—or stay outside, as you will."

Both men barged in, came up short. They spied Richard Wentworth in bed, his eyes closed. But his lips were moving. They drew to the bedside and bent their heads to listen.

The utterances were unintelligible. They drew nearer.

"Perhaps you are correct," whispered Ram Singh. "That is the voice of delirium, not wakefulness."

Quietly, they turned to go—when suddenly a strong hand shot up, grasped Jackson by the uniform sleeve, and stayed him!

Grey-blue eyes snapped open, blazing with energy. "Miss Nita?" he croaked out.

"Sleeping peacefully. Her injuries are minor compared to yours."

"Thank God," breathed Wentworth. "What of the city? The false Spider?"

Ram Singh reported, "There was no sign of the false one. But the police have the meteor stone from space surrounded and are keeping all others out."

"Is there a radio?"

Jackson said, "You bet. This is a private room."

It was a tabletop model, a so-called "midget" radio. Jackson switched it on and almost immediately a news broadcaster was chattering away.

"*—shooting in Central Park. Many police officers involved. An unknown man wearing a black metal shell has smashed a sanitation truck through the police barricades and by all accounts is shattering the meteor into pieces like a convict on a chain gang wielding a sledgehammer. Increasingly, it does not appear that this is a city worker, but some madman determined to carry off the deadly meteorite in pieces.*"

Wentworth suddenly sat up, eyes aflame.

"The city needs me! Jackson, my clothes. Hurry!"

Ronald Jackson knew better than to disobey. He drew Wentworth's impeccable attire from the drawer and placed it on the bed.

"Are you sure you're up to this, Major?"

Stripping off his hospital pajamas and climbing into street clothes, Richard Wentworth bit out pungent words.

"I do not know who this Man in the Steel Mask may be, but he must be stopped at all costs. Jackson, lead me to the limousine.

Ram Singh, you will remain here and safeguard Miss Nita. Count Calypsa is back! No doubt he has assumed that I am The Spider and may strike at this hospital. Guard Miss Nita well, my warrior."

"*Han, sahib.* It will be as you say."

Wentworth was dressed now, and Jackson led him out to the elevator bank. In the white-walled corridor, they encountered a young physician who took one look at Wentworth and objected strenuously. "Here, now, you belong in bed." Then he swallowed his next words.

For the blazing force in Richard Wentworth's steely eyes checked him, stopped him in his tracks. He could not have accounted for why he took an involuntary step backward and uttered no further objection. He simply stood passively aside and let his patient lurch onto the elevator and vanish from view....

THE DAIMLER was soon charging in the direction of Central Park. Owing to the fact that the police were rerouting all vehicles around the park and the immediate environs, traffic was heavy.

Soon, vehicular movement ground to a standstill. Car horns blared and beeped. But nothing on wheels moved.

Jackson had turned on the dashboard radio receiver, and both men listened closely.

"*Witnesses at the Hotel Collier are reporting that the fleeing sanitation truck is now backing out of the park. The police are fortifying the roadblocks, but concern mounts that the force is stretched too thin to accomplish the job.*"

Wentworth bit out, "I must go now, Jackson. Catch up to me when you are able."

"Right, Major."

Richard Wentworth switched the controls of the hidden compartment containing his Spider robes. A portion of the rear seat rolled out and revolved, displaying his black cloak and hat. He left his assortment of masks and other tools, taking only a pair of heavy automatics. Loading them, he checked the action. After restoring the weapons to their holsters, he swung out.

It would have been foolhardy to don on the ominous regalia of The Spider, especially in broad daylight. Richard Wentworth had sometimes been accused of being extremely foolhardy. But not on this morning. On this morning, he was intent upon stopping a sanitation truck that contained enough meteor matter to doom the city to a mad carnival of death and destruction. Nothing reckless in that mission....

Racing along the sidewalk, he cut across a side street and hailed a cab. Climbing in, he said, "Central Park—snappy!"

"Are you nuts, Bo? Police got it roped off!"

The cold steel muzzle of a .45 automatic was suddenly laid across top of the front passenger seat. It did not point directly at the cabbie. But its meaning was clear.

"If you are afraid to drive to the park," grated Wentworth, "I will take the wheel in your stead."

"Tell you what," the driver said shakily. "I'll take you as far as we can go. After that, you're on your own."

"Fair enough," said Wentworth, falling back onto the cushions but holding onto the automatic in his strong right fist.

It was a beautiful November morning as the taxicab jockeyed about the streets, inching closer and closer to Central Park and its splendid riot of turning leaves.

Such a wonderful time of year, thought Richard Wentworth. The Fall had always been his favorite season of the year. The smell of burning leaves was an aroma that took him back to his youth and happier days.

The fact that the sun went down earlier meant that The Spider could prowl sooner. But dusk was far off now. The Spider must not sleep—sleep the restorative sleep that belonged only to

Richard Wentworth. But neither personality could rest until he had taken a hand in the game, whatever it might be.

Ultimately, the cab slipped up to a police roadblock. Throwing a twenty-dollar bill onto the front seat, Wentworth exited and walked up to the officer standing before his radio car. The .45 automatic was out of view, snug in its shoulder holster.

Wentworth offered the officer a friendly smile.

"I imagine you recognize me. Wentworth. I'm a friend of the commissioner's."

"Yes, sir. I do," the patrolman said respectfully.

"Where can I find Kirkpatrick?"

"North end of the park. But you can't go up there, sir. Strict orders to keep all civilians out. You know how it is."

"I understand perfectly," returned Wentworth, still smiling in a friendly manner. Then his cultured voice hardened. "What is being done to stop the sanitation truck from absconding with the remnants of the fallen meteorite?"

"Barricades, just like this one here."

"Do you think one radio car is enough to block the road?"

The officer shrugged. "It's all we have, so it will have to be."

"Can you raise Kirkpatrick on your shortwave? It is urgent that I speak with him. I have information essential to this present crisis."

The bluecoat tipped back his cap visor. "It's highly irregular, Mr. Wentworth. But seeing as how you rate with the commissioner, it won't hurt to try."

Wentworth stood patiently while the officer worked his shortwave radio and requested to be cut into the police commissioner's limousine two-way radio.

Transmission was naturally handled through the dispatch office at the precinct headquarters and took a few minutes. Finally, the officer got through.

"This is Patrolman Chauncey at the southern end of Central

Park. Mr. Richard Wentworth just showed up. He wants to talk to the commissioner P.D.Q. Says he has important information."

The call was taken by Sergeant Carter, the commissioner's driver. Wentworth recognized his voice.

"Hold on. I'll ask Commissioner Kirkpatrick."

There was a pause. Then a great deal of background noise. It could be heard not only over the dashboard radio grille, but it was in the air, far away and indistinct.

Mixed in with it was the spiteful snap of revolvers.

Hearing those familiar sounds, Wentworth leaned into the patrol car and demanded, "What is going on up there?"

"Sounds like shooting!" replied the patrolman. He called into the microphone, "What's happening?"

"No time to talk!" yelled Sergeant Carter. *"I've got to get the Commissioner out of here—fast."*

Once again, Wentworth snagged the microphone. "Is Kirkpatrick in danger?"

The voice coming back sent chills up and down their spines.

"The whole damned city's in danger! Nobody suspected how strong the meteorite rays were. They've gotten to the ones who stood guard all night. They look drunk—drunk as sailors. They're milling about aimlessly. Their eyes! My God, their eyes are turning… green!"

Chapter 17

THE POLICE FALL

JAMES CHRISTOPHER heard the bark of revolvers and understood that new danger threatened.

Rushing from the park, he gained the sidewalk and flung his gaze in all directions. What he beheld sent a thrill of horror coursing through his veins.

It was the sight of the Metropolitan Police, walking about in a blank-faced daze, their eyes as luminous as if green fireflies had hatched in each eyeball....

The beams that shot out from those eyes were not fully visible in the climbing sunlight. But whatever they touched, then melted, curled, bubbled or blackened, depending upon the substance affected. Police sawhorses were smoldering, and not a few were blazing angrily.

Some of the unaffected officers recoiled in horror, but when they saw their brothers in blue become walking engines of destruction, they manfully did their duty. Bullets flew. Skulls split open. Brains and gore splattered.

Blue-clad bodies dropped everywhere.

Those officers who could manage it piled into their cruisers, retreating even further.

"Good Lord!" groaned Operator 5. "That is the end of the police cordon."

It was undeniable. Police lines that had held all night, could hold no more. Fully a third of the picketed officers had stood watch for too long, their unprotected brains exposed to the dangerous radiant power of the meteor from beyond the Earth. No doubt serious lesions had opened up in the wrinkles and folds of their living brains....

Keenly aware of the danger, James rushed across the street, desperate to put distance between himself and the powerful doom-rays which were now emanating from the sanitation truck.

The engine had been idling all this time. Now it roared into throaty life.

James turned, and his sharpening eyes went hard.

The truck was backing up, crushing foliage, undeterred by obstacles. Steadily, remorselessly, it reversed until its tires were up on the sidewalk—and then the lumbering machine jumped onto the avenue.

James went down to a crouch and laid the muzzle of his automatic across one raised forearm. He aimed for the turning tires.

Before he could fire, the fever came upon him again. Perspiration broke out on his high forehead. His brain throbbed. He realized the steel body of the sanitation truck offered no barrier to the glowing fragments of an unknown substance.

Operator 5 fired one shot and hastily retreated. The bullet struck a tire, but the monster machine traveled on. It was pointing south now—south toward the light roadblock at the far end of Central Park, just short of Columbus Circle.

James looked around for a vehicle with which to give chase. He saw only police machines, and these were in retreat....

Gritting his teeth in frustration, he raced in the opposite direction, toward his Diesel-powered roadster, still parked at the park's northernmost end. He jumped behind the wheel and flung the powerful machine around—around and in hot pursuit of the refuse truck laden with glowing doom....

RICHARD WENTWORTH saw the sanitation truck barreling down the avenue. His keen brain realized at once the danger. A single patrol car would not stand up to the monstrous truck.

And if it carried the broken detritus of the meteorite, they would be subjected to its harsh radium-like rays if they stood their ground....

Fiercely, Wentworth told the officer behind the wheel, "Clear out of the way! You cannot stop it. Your machine will be destroyed. And so will you."

Stubbornly, the officer hurled back, "I have my orders. I cannot do otherwise."

Seeing the bravery of the officer, Richard Wentworth hesitated. The hurtling snout of the four-ton garbage truck was only two hundred yards away now. Through the windshield, he could see the black, featureless shell of the Man in the Steel Mask, the perpetrator of the theft—one of the most brazen thefts in all the history of New York City.

Other men had stolen gold, robbed banks and kidnapped the innocent for profit. This unknown monster was trying to get away with a substance so destructive that it could turn the entire population of Manhattan into crazed human blowtorches!

Knowing this, Richard Wentworth slammed his body into the police car, pushing the officer into the passenger seat. The man struck his head against the door post, was dazed.

"It's just as well," bit out Wentworth. "I would not like to have to knock out such a brave man."

He got the car started, backing out just in time. He slipped up onto the sidewalk, and the strange driver, seeing the radio car retreat, deliberately swerved and clipped the nose of the police machine.

Wentworth was jolted, and the police car rocked on its springs as the truck blundered past. He knew that if he followed too closely, he was subject to the deadly rays. He clutched the steering wheel tightly as he counted to sixty, then 120... 280....

After the second equivalent to three minutes passed, he turned the police phaeton into traffic and set out to pursue the sanitation truck. He knew he could not stop the machine, juggernaut that it was. Wentworth also knew that he dared not try. For if he did, if he caused an accident, and the garbage truck broke open, several square blocks of innocent civilians would be subject to terrible rays from which there seemed to be no reliable protection.

As he swung into traffic, powering toward Columbus Circle, a gleaming black roadster came shooting down the avenue and began to pace him.

Wentworth glanced over at the driver. Grey-blue eyes reflected recognition when he saw the clean-cut profile of the young man. He knew the fellow. Had met him once, a few short years ago. A Secret Service man. Last name of Christopher. He could not recall the first name, indeed could not remember if he had been introduced formally. It was during the reign of the Egyptian Death Madness.*

Wentworth did not know that Christopher was not in fact an ordinary agent of the Secret Service, but belonged to the branch of that service dedicated to intelligence. Nor did it matter. No doubt the man was bent on stopping the sanitation truck by whatever means possible.

The other's window was down. Wentworth called over in a loud voice:

"Agent Christopher! If you attempt to sideswipe that truck, you risk subjecting the citizens to unnecessary destruction. A better course of action would be to follow it to its destination. Contain it there. Together, we can overmaster this steel-headed monster."

Christopher's crystal-clear blue eyes glanced over, but he said nothing in return. He was intent upon pursuit. The man might have been a machine made of flesh and blood. Nothing would stop him.

Shrugging, Wentworth turned his attention back to the road

---

* The Spider: *Master of the Death-Madness.*

ahead. Together, the two automobiles dogged the lumbering sanitation truck as it worked its way through midtown Manhattan toward an unknown destination….

Chapter 18

CONFLICT

RICHARD WENTWORTH paced the black roadster driven by Secret Service Agent Christopher in his purloined radio patrol car.

It was a damnable situation in which he found himself. To trail this hurtling sanitation truck too closely would be to invite the meteor madness into his own brain. But if Wentworth hung back too far, he risked losing it in Manhattan's busy, maze-like thoroughfares.

Losing sight of the sanitation truck was unlikely, he knew. But the city was a witch's brew of traffic, for it was the Monday morning rush hour.

Wentworth recalled that it was All Saints' Day. A holy day. It was madness to be spending such a fine morning in pursuit of an apparent madman bent upon a murderous mission. For there was no doubt in his mind that the steel-helmeted giant was intent upon some monumental devilry.

Wentworth longed to cut in front of the sanitation truck, step out and disable its tires with well-placed shots. That would not do. If the lumbering machine idled in any one spot for very long, pedestrians and motorists would swiftly succumb to the strange radiation....

The best course of action, he knew, was to follow it to the steely one's headquarters, wherever that was. He strongly suspected that this headquarters would also be the hidden sanctuary of Count Calypsa....

But Agent Christopher knew nothing about Count Calypsa. He was after the Man in the Steel Mask.

Glancing over, Wentworth again studied the determined young man. Did he not understand the risks involved? Could he glean the importance of an intelligent objective?

Perhaps more importantly, would he accept or reject the advice of Richard Wentworth? Advice that the police commissioner often took to heart might have no impact upon the thinking of a Secret Service agent. Wentworth had worked with the Secret Service in the past, but it had always been an uneasy alliance….

Up ahead the light turned red, and traffic flowed in from the cross street.

Suppressing an oath, Wentworth watched, knowing what would happen before it did.

The hurtling sanitation truck did not slow down. Indeed, failed to brake at all. It accelerated, smashing through the intersection like a steel fist knocking aside taxis, roadsters and other lesser machines.

"That driver cares nothing for human life!" Wentworth snapped.

In the other lane, Agent Christopher surged forward, and Wentworth, fearful of the recklessness of youth, swerved sharply and all but cut him off.

Christopher recovered by riding up on the curb on two wheels, charging forward several dozen yards and slamming back onto the avenue. He shot an angry glance in Wentworth's direction.

The Master of Men ignored him.

The cars ahead had braked for the red light, so they were forced to do the same.

Agent Christopher called over sternly, "Do not interfere again! As an official agent of the United States government, I so order you."

Wentworth bit back, "We cannot hope to stop the truck—nor should we. If we tail it to its destination, we can avoid civilian casualties and possibly contain the threat."

"Stay out of this. It is no affair of yours. You are subject to arrest if you do not comply."

The damnable fool! Wentworth thought hotly. Christopher did not know that he was speaking to The Spider, who had fought hundreds of battles in defense of this very city. Who had suffered wounds unimaginable—in the body as well as of the spirit. Why, the sacrifices he had made so that New Yorkers could breathe free and live their lives according to the laws of man and God were incalculable.

But it was no use thinking such bitter thoughts. Wentworth would no sooner admit his identity than he could shoot a police officer in cold blood. That way lay ruination. And the destruction of all that he held dear....

So Wentworth held his tongue. The Spider did not laugh back. He simply turned his attention to the stop light, waiting for it to change. And change it did.

The double line of cars jostled forward, and as they plowed through the intersection, he saw the carnage wrought by the indifferent sanitation truck. One man had been thrown clear of his door-sprung automobile. Another machine had turned turtle. Its tires were still spinning futilely in empty air....

PICKING UP the radio microphone, Wentworth called the accident in to headquarters. He disconnected when the dispatcher questioned his identity. There was no time for such niceties. The Spider was on the trail!

He caught sight of the sanitation truck again. It was barreling south, as before. It appeared to be heading in the general direction of Bryant Park. But there was no telling its true destination. No guessing the intent of the driver, only that he could not hope to elude police pursuit for long.

Police pursuit....

Suddenly, Wentworth realized that there was no pursuer other than himself and Christopher. Surely Kirkpatrick had dispatched additional radio cars. But none appeared. Wentworth expected them to come shooting down the cross streets. But there was no sign of the police.

Peculiar….

An ominous feeling came over Wentworth at that moment. But he shook it off. There was no point in calling for assistance; the police would only attempt to stop the runaway sanitation truck. That was the thing Wentworth most feared. That, and the meteorite fragments rattling in the back of the steel body….

At least Agent Christopher was showing good sense now. He did not attempt to weave in and out of traffic, nor did he show any inclination to overhaul the sanitation truck. That much was a relief.

Then something happened to change the game.

Wentworth caught the glimmer of stubby silver wings flashing in the early morning sun. Craning his head, he spotted a streamlined autogyro of a new type descending at a steep angle. He did not recognize the design.

Doubtful that it was a police airplane. Perhaps it was a government ship. There were no markings on it… another oddity.

As he watched, it crossed a cluster of buildings and made a beeline for the fleeing truck.

"What in God's name is that pilot intending?" Wentworth exclaimed.

The answer soon came.

Up ahead, the mystery pilot executed a nimble maneuver, and the whirling ship slowed. It settled in place, hovering above an intersection, its myriad blades creating countervailing vortices.

At the exact moment that the light changed, there was a pause in cross traffic and the autogyro flopped down into the center of the intersection before any traffic could flow, its fore-and-aft propellers jerking to a halt.

"What is that pilot doing?" Wentworth raged. His complaint was directed to Agent Christopher, who suddenly swerved onto the sidewalk and began racing along it, honking his horn repeatedly, and scattering frightened pedestrians in his path.

Jerking his wheel to the right, Wentworth leapt in pursuit, motor buzzing like an angry hornet.

Frantic pedestrians dodged out of the way. The sidewalk was thus cleared.

But what would happen when the sanitation truck encountered the settling autogyro? The duralumin-skinned ship was too frail a craft to serve as an effective roadblock.

Straining to see through his windscreen, Wentworth saw a cabin door pop open in the side of the landed aircraft. Out stepped a man wearing the leather jacket and flying helmet of a military pilot, his eyes masked by regulation aviator goggles that reflected the shifting shadows of the still-turning rotor wing.

In his arms, he cradled a Thompson submachine gun. He directed its steel snout toward the sanitation truck and its faceless fiend of a driver....

Chapter 19

STEELY STALEMATE

CAPTAIN GATE of G-2 buzzed the city for several minutes before he caught a glimpse of the sanitation truck he sought.

There was no mistaking it for any other. Racing down Park Avenue, the oversized machine recklessly weaved through traffic, shouldering smaller vehicles out of the way, caroming violently off others, knocking loose bumpers and crumpling fenders, before tearing through an intersection without regard for cross traffic. These reckless acts proclaimed the fleeing vehicle's identity clearly.

Pushing the control wheel forward, Gate began his descent on spinning rotor wings. The blades turned the air madly, acting as a brake for his landing, much in the manner of a conventional autogyro, whose blades turn freely and not under power.

This ultramodern gyroplane was capable of hovering in place and landing without benefit of runway. The *Hummingbird* was about to prove its mettle.

Flashing ahead of the fugitive truck, the gyroplane pilot spied the perfect spot to put down. An intersection. The much-dented sanitation truck was barreling toward it. There appeared to be time to beat it, but that depended upon the red light not changing to green.

Fluttering and dipping, the streamlined aircraft slanted toward the spot, a block shy of Grand Central Station.

Then the light turned green. One direction of traffic halted, while the other prepared to resume.

In that split-second, Captain Gate placed the *Hummingbird*

super-gyro in the square of blacktop before the oncoming auto-mobile traffic.

Chopping the power to the nose and tail propellers and twirling rotor wing, Gate pulled down the goggles of his flying helmet to conceal his features. Then he lifted from an open crate behind the pilot's seat a ponderous Thompson submachine gun. Charging it, he kicked open the door and stepped out.

There he took a position of challenge, oblivious to the honking and blaring of car horns all around him.

The refuse truck was visible three car lengths back of the blocked intersection. It rode higher than any surrounding vehi-cle. The morning sun streamed through the windshield glass and made the head of the driver clear.

The driver had no face! It was a blank black curve of precision steel, coming to a conical point at the top of the skull. Two slits permitted vision, but nothing of the head encased in the helmet could be discerned.

Recognizing the severe lines of this helmet, Captain Gate uttered a single sibilant word, *"Stahlmaske!"*

Cradling the Thompson sub-gun, he advanced three paces, came to a halt and pointed the muzzle at the strange driver.

He lifted his voice commandingly. "Step out of that truck, whoever you are!"

The enshadowed eyes in the featureless steel mask regarded him without concern.

"I warn you! I will riddle you where you sit!"

This time the driver reacted. Not in fear, nor in obedience. Instead, he gunned the engine, slammed into the roadster directly in front of him, pushing it aside and accelerating over its detached rear bumper. The sound of mangled metal came. The impact cracked the engine, whose radiator instantly disgorged clouds of scalding steam!

Not wishing to be demolished by the unstoppable four-ton juggernaut, drivers at the head of the lane gunned their engines as they muscled their stubborn steering wheels, fighting to clear the way.

Seeing the way of things, Captain Gate lifted the submachine gun stock to his shoulder and prepared to squeeze the trigger and empty the heavy drum of .45 caliber bullets.

He never completed the gesture.

Shooting out from the sidewalk came a powerful black roadster, followed by a police radio car. They careened into the intersection, slewed to a halt. Doors popped open.

A young man in a conservative grey suit and matching vest shouted, "Lower your weapon! I am Operator 5 of the Intelligence Service."

A second man rushed up, proclaiming, "Listen to him! That truck contains dangerous meteorite fragments. If it is not moved, its radiations will affect everyone around it—including ourselves!"

Captain Gate hesitated. The lumbering sanitation truck continued bearing down on him. Out from the cabin window, the steel head poked out.

A hollow voice barked gutturally, "Do as they say if you value your life!"

"I know your voice!" Gate cried out. "But I thought you were dead!"

"You know my voice? *I know yours!*"

The smooth black cone withdrew, and the steel-faced driver bore down on the gas pedal.

Once again, the Tommy gun lifted—but not in time.

The well-dressed man stepped up, wrenched it from his hands. When he directed the muzzle skyward, he pulled back on the trigger. The weapon chattered madly, showering the blacktop with smoking brass cartridges. The drum soon ran empty. Then he handed back the smoking submachine gun.

The man's intense grey-blue eyes brooked no defiance. "Climb aboard your plane—or be run over!"

But there was no time to reclaim the gyroplane—only to clear a path for the hurtling sanitation truck!

Captain Gate dashed out of the way before the steaming radiator grille and steel bumper could knock him down.

"Come on!" barked Richard Wentworth. "We are in pursuit."

Picking up his Thompson, Gate followed him into the patrol car and got in back.

Noticing the unconscious patrolman sprawled in the front passenger seat, he frowned.

"What happened to that cop?"

"Injured in the line of duty," Wentworth returned crisply. "I was forced to commandeer his car. He is merely knocked out, by the way."

"The Commissioner will have something to say about a civilian driving an official police vehicle. "

"Kirkpatrick and I have... an understanding," Wentworth said without concern.

The Diesel-powered roadster driven by Operator 5 took off first. The police radio car followed closely, siren screaming.

"Who are you?" demanded Gate.

"Richard Wentworth."

Gate nodded. "The criminologist. I've heard of you. Friend of the police commissioner's, aren't you?"

"Yes."

"And rumored to be the notorious Spider."

Wentworth said nothing; he was focused on his driving. Once more, he was pacing alongside the Diesel-powered roadster. Again they were forced to maintain a safe distance lest the deadly radiation seep into their skulls.

"Not all rumors are to be believed," returned Wentworth tightly.

Captain Gate did not reply. On squalling tires, the two cars wrenched around, finally settling down to a brisk sprint.

CALLING OVER his shoulder, Wentworth declared, "I heard you say that you recognized that voice. And he, yours. Explain yourself."

Captain Gate made his voice casual.

"Who I am is none of your business. I work for G-2—Military Intelligence. That's all you need to know."

"Why don't you lift your goggles?"

"I prefer to keep my face out of public view."

Wentworth nodded. "A wise course of action, especially for an undercover man like yourself. No doubt you are an expert at disguise, when called upon."

Captain Gate did not respond.

Wentworth pressed on, "I judge us to be of similar age. Might you have been in the war?"

"I might've been," Gate returned casually.

"I served as well. Rose to the rank of major. During my wartime service, I encountered many fellow officers. As I listen to you, I can't help but feel that your voice, too, is somehow familiar. Did you serve in France?"

Gate's voice was thin. "Among other spots."

"What did you say your name was?"

"I didn't."

"Is it a secret?"

"Not really. The name is Gate. Captain George Gate."

"Gate," murmured Wentworth. "I do not recall encountering an officer by that name. Still, your voice is familiar to me. Gate…. I wonder if you could be the Army intelligence officer whose code name was once a byword in the trenches?"

"Why do you ask that?" Gate said sharply.

"Perhaps it is the coincidence of your last name, Gate…."

"Bunk! Forget it! Captain Gate is my rank and name. I'm on the trail of a dangerous war criminal long believed dead."

"Stahlmaske! You believe this monster to be him?"

"Who else would go to the trouble of stealing Stahlmaske's helmet? And then go on a murder spree?"

"You make an excellent point," said Wentworth, turning a corner on yipping tires.

They were shooting crosstown toward Bryant Park now, staying close to the fleeing garbage truck.

Captain Gate frowned. "He can't hope to shake us."

"Steel Mask knows we cannot interfere with his escape. But I fail to grasp his immediate intentions..." Wentworth's voice trailed off. A low moan settled in his throat.

"What's wrong?" demanded Gate.

"I hope that I am mistaken in my suspicion. But that truck is headed toward the high school!"

Goggled eyes blinked. "You might be onto something.... But what would be his game?"

"I pray that I am mistaken," Wentworth said slowly. "But if Steel Mask is determined to throw us off his trail—and I do not doubt that he is—his best hope is to force our hand."

The sanitation truck turned two corners in succession, then reversed itself. They lost sight of it rounding the second block, but when they turned the corner in unison—the police machine and the drumming black roadster—an oath was wrenched from Richard Wentworth's throat.

The fugitive truck had pulled over and lurched to a dead halt—stopped directly in front of the asphalt playground of the Steeger School. Came to a dead stop while yellow buses were dropping off students at the beginning of the school day!

Recognizing this, Captain George Gate gritted, "Damn it!"

Wentworth swerved, then braked. The black roadster did likewise. The trio exited their machines.

The door to the refuse truck's cab also popped open. And down climbed a burly colossus of a man whose head was squeezed into a steel stovepipe painted a flat black.

"Welcome!" he boomed out. "Welcome to my little party. Do you see what I have done here?"

Wentworth answered that.

"You madman! You dare subject small children to the meteorite rays?"

"Yes!" thundered Stahlmaske. "Rays to which I am impervious, thanks to my lead-lined helmet. I will make you a proposition. You do not have much time to think it over. I will not repeat myself. Retreat from my sight. Do not attempt further pursuit. Do this immediately, and I will quit the vicinity. Where I go is not for you fine fellows to know. If you attempt to double-cross me, I will simply return to this or some other school. And you will have the opportunity to see the little children turn into green-eyed marauders. I do not think you would like to witness such a sight. So go—*now!*"

The three men exchanged glances, but no words. No words would have helped the situation. They climbed back into their machines. Only this time, Captain Gate got into the black roadster.

Backing up, the two automobiles left the area with nervous speed.

Stahlmaske watched them go. Then, satisfied that his subterfuge had worked, he climbed back behind the wheel of the sanitation truck and got it into operation.

The children playing in the schoolyard remained oblivious to the danger lurking so perilously close.

As the garbage truck lurched into gear, its cracked engine releasing fresh steam, a grim chuckle echoed within the driver's hollow helmet.

"I win this round, *Geh-Acht!* Just as I will win all the rounds that lie ahead."

The much-dented truck trundled about, then headed north. Back in the general direction of Central Park....

Chapter 20

NO STANDING

RICHARD WENTWORTH followed the black roadster closely. He did not know where Christopher was bound, but he intended to confer with the two government agents. There was no question that Steel Mask was up to no good. And it would take the combined efforts of all three to thwart the plan, whatever it might be.

The roadster swiftly returned to the intersection of Park Avenue and East Forty-fourth Street, still partially blocked by Captain Gate's streamlined gyroplane. There he pulled over.

A beat patrolman had come up on the congested spot and was doing his best to unsnarl traffic when they rolled up.

"Is this your contraption, bud?" he demanded of the pilot when the latter paused at the open cabin door.

Gate nodded in a friendly fashion. "Government business. Give me a minute to warm her up."

"I'll give you half a minute."

Operator 5 stepped up, showed his special letter, and the officer became more reasonable.

Noting the bluecoat, Wentworth parked well short of the intersection and hurried up on foot. Even the commissioner's friend would be hard put to explain the commandeering of a police radio car, never mind the unconscious officer, whom Wentworth had carefully placed in the back seat, his cap covering his face so passersby would assume he was napping.

Striding up, he announced, "I have a plan."

Agent Christopher turned and said stiffly, "I take orders only from my superiors."

The gyroplane rotor blades were turning slowly, stirring their hair. The front and rear props spun to life. The silvery fuselage shook under their combined torque.

Wentworth plied his case. "The threat to the city is dire. It will require a concerted effort to suppress it. We three could supply the brain power to defeat Steel Mask!"

Christopher regarded him skeptically. He was unmoved. Undaunted, Wentworth pressed on.

"Did that pilot identify himself to you?"

"He did not," said Christopher.

"I believe I know him from the war. His real name was never disclosed. But he went by the *nom de guerre* of—*G-8!*"

James Christopher looked suitably impressed. He had read the daring accounts of the Flying Spy during the World War.

Sticking his head out of the cockpit cabin, the goggled pilot barked, "G-8 belongs to the past. Captain George Gate is the name I use now."

"You see?" cried Wentworth. "I was correct. Think of it! We could be the modern Musketeers!"

Christopher regarded him coldly, saying, "You have no official standing, Wentworth. A cloud of suspicion hangs over your motives."

Stung, Wentworth returned with equal coldness, "Very well. I will handle this damnable menace in my own fashion."

"As long as you stay out of our way. You may be a personal friend of the police commissioner, but you have no authority otherwise. We are government agents."

Suppressing his anger, Richard Wentworth turned on his heel and walked away. He went directly to a drugstore, there to call for a taxicab.

After he had entered, Operator 5 told the G-2 officer, "That man is rumored to be The Spider."

"I know," said G-8, nodding. "Whoever The Spider is, he's done some good work."

"Outside the law," reminded James Christopher.

"The President himself granted The Spider a pardon last month," reminded the Master Spy. "After that mess down in Washington." *

Christopher was unmoved. "There is no place for vigilante justice in a modern metropolis," he stated crisply. "If he is The Spider, sooner or later he will be exposed."

G-8 nodded. He was ready to take off.

"My superiors instructed me to coordinate with the Intelligence Service. Where is your headquarters?"

"Secret. We should rendezvous in a secure place. I suggest Bryant Park. It's not far from here."

"I'll meet you there," returned G-8, slamming the door shut. The vibrating gyroplane increased its rotation, kicking up dust and city grit.

With astonishing suddenness, the *Hummingbird* vaulted into the air, canted and whirled toward Bryant Park, an ultra-modern marvel of aeronautics.

Operator 5 returned to his roadster and shot into the free flow of traffic. His clear blue eyes were cloudy now....

STAHLMASKE WRESTLED the huge trash-collecting truck through Manhattan's concrete canyons. A common Sanitation Department truck does not ordinarily attract much attention, but this one was different.

All over the city, police radio cars heard the urgent call:

"Signal Thirty. Repeat: Signal Three-zero. Be on the lookout for New York Department of Sanitation truck license plate Six-twenty-two. Truck last seen departing vicinity of Central Park, carrying dangerous cargo. Follow, but do not approach. Repeat: Do not approach. Truck contains meteorite whose emanations

---

* The Spider: *Machine Guns Over the White House.*

cause madness and death. Follow at respectful distance and report progress of truck. That is all."

Officer Maurizio Vitale heard the call, just as the truck in question trundled by him. He shot a practiced eye toward the lumbering machine, checked the license plate and saw it was the wanted vehicle.

Pulling into the main thoroughfare, he fell in behind the truck.

Sticking out of the driver-side door was a mirror. Vitale's eyes went to it. It reflected the face of the truck driver. Or rather, it failed to reflect the fellow's face. All that could be seen was a blank curved sheet of black metal, in which two eyes burned, framed by notches cut in the steel.

"What the hell," he muttered to himself.

He lifted the microphone, then checked himself. Time enough to report once he had an idea of the truck's course....

The steel-faced driver was pushing steadily north. He made no effort to speed up, nor dodge unexpectedly onto the cross streets.

Two burning eyes edged in steel did not blink at noticing the radio car in his rear-vision mirror. Officer Vitale knew this to a certainty. The fugitive did not seem bothered by the fact that he was being tailed by a marked police car.

Vitale considered turning on his siren. He did not think it was a very good idea. So he kept pace with the vehicle, holding to a reasonable distance. Not that the officer had much choice in the matter. Two automobiles, one a taxicab, occupied the moving space between his front bumper and the rear of the battered-looking truck.

Vitale started worrying about the drivers ahead of him. Orders were to keep a fair distance. Frowning, he wondered how that would be measured....

A red light winked on up ahead. Traffic halted. The sanitation truck was the third in line; it lurched to a stop.

Seeing his opportunity, Officer Vitale raised the microphone to his lips and pressed the button.

"Car Fifty-two reporting to headquarters. Sanitation truck tag number Six-twenty-two stopped at red light on Sixth Avenue."

Dispatcher came back instantly. *"Car Fifty-two. Say cross street."*

The officer damned himself mentally for forgetting that simple bit of protocol. "East Forty-seventh Street," he said.

"Stay with the truck. Assistance is on the way."

"Over and out!"

The red light seemed to take forever changing to green. The sanitation truck jerked forward, was moving again. But the taxi directly behind did not follow.

The driver's side door fell open and out tottered the cabbie. He stood up, looked around with a strange dead expression on his face. When his eyes turned in Officer Vitale's direction, they gleamed with the same emerald hue as the traffic light!

"Holy hell!" Vitale shouted. Into the microphone, he barked, "There's a cabbie here who's turned into one of those mete-or-crazed walking dead men! The taxi is blocking the street. I can't pursue the sanitation truck."

The response coming back from dispatch was chilling.

"Car Fifty-two. Shoot the cab driver."

"Shoot—?"

"Repeat: Shoot the cab driver. Kirkpatrick's orders. Meteor Monsters cannot be made normal again. Put the cab driver out of his misery. That is all."

Officer Vitale had fired his weapon in the performance of his duties before. He had several kills to his credit. All hardened criminals. He did not hesitate to shoot then—but he held back now as he emerged from his patrol car.

The cabbie was looking around, as if not comprehending where he stood. In the morning sunlight, the emerald rays emanating from his optic nerves were not visible, except when he turned his weird gaze directly in the officer's direction. Then they resembled a cat's cool, chatoyant orbs....

Everywhere the cabbie stared, automobile paint began to blacken and bubble… and even worse things resulted.

The driver directly behind was furiously honking his horn at the stalled cab. This attracted the attention of the green-eyed cabbie. The latter lurched toward the source of the commotion.

Thinking he was being challenged, the driver stepped out of his machine and began shouting.

"Get that hack moving, you! I'm tryin' to get to work!"

The cabbie started for the shouting man, who quickly closed the distance, putting up his fists in a truculent attitude. He was prepared for an argument, and worse.

Worse is what he got. He saw the green shine in the man's otherwise-dead eyes, demanded, "What's the matter with your eyes?"

Then the cool yet burning gaze fell upon him… and his tie caught fire! Frantically, he yanked it off, singeing his fingers. But it did no good. The front of his coat was soon ablaze.

A bundle of fire, he stumbled toward the sidewalk where a recoiling matron screamed in horror.

Then the blank-faced cab driver noticed the officer's blue uniform. His dead face did not change expression. He simply charged on.

Officer Vitale lifted his Police Positive, lined the gun sight on the man's chest, and fired twice.

The mindless cabbie spun halfway about, then took another quarter turn and began stumbling in a way that was different than before….

The wounded one did not fall at once. He took four stumbling steps, and almost managed a fifth. Then he crumpled.

Gingerly, Officer Vitale approached, saw the dead eyes staring upward, and studied the lingering, fading green shining that was soon no more.

"Dead! Poor guy. It wasn't his fault. Just an ordinary New York cabbie who was on duty on a Monday morning. And look what happened to him...."

Officer Vitale got behind the wheel of the cab, wrestled it up half onto the sidewalk, then ran back to his radio car, getting it into motion as drivers honked impatiently all about him.

"Keep your shirts on, all of you!" he yelled in the face of the intermittent, cacophonous blaring.

Back behind the wheel, Vitale trod the accelerator and attempted to pick up the trail of the wanted sanitation truck.

He frowned severely. There was no sign of it up ahead. He turned on his siren. He jockeyed his machine frantically around the immediate vicinity, crisscrossing several blocks before being forced to give up.

Contacting dispatch, he said, "This is Car Fifty-two. I have lost the sanitation truck. Repeat: Wanted truck has disappeared in the vicinity of Bryant Park."

Dispatch radioed back, *"Keep searching! The matter is urgent. Do not give up."*

Officer Vitale pushed through traffic congestion, but it was to no avail.

Amazingly, the mechanical juggernaut had vanished from sight—vanished hauling a cargo so dangerous that no matter where it had parked, the lives of numerous citizens would be at risk....

Chapter 21

THE DICTATOR COMMANDS

SEATED BEHIND the desk in his ostentatious headquarters overlooking the New York Public Library, Count Carmine Calypsa keyed the Call-o-phone box on his mahogany desk.

A light winked on, then a crisp voice came out of the annunciator.

"This is Number Forty-four. Reporting."

"Continue, Number Forty-four."

"You instructed all Numbers to keep watch for that sanitation truck. It's on Forty-second Street, under the Sixth Avenue Elevated. Coming your way."

"What of police pursuit?

"There is no police pursuit. Cops are tied up in other parts of the city. It's like a carnival of murder and mayhem out there."

"Stand by, Number Forty-four."

Picking up a desk telephone, he called down to the lobby.

Before the desk man could answer, he said, "This is the Dictator."

The Dictator was the cognomen by which Count Calypsa had operated since his advent in Manhattan almost a year ago. It was the title he used to strike fear into his underlings, and also an egotistical expression of his criminal ambitions.

"Yes, sir," quavered the trembling voice at the other end of the wire.

The Count's tone took on a note of forced urgency. "Open the basement garage door! Hold it open until I tell you otherwise. Very soon, a New York City municipal sanitation truck will attempt to enter. When it does, close the doors behind it immediately. Once you do that, leave your post. Evacuate the building instantly! Do you understand?"

"Perfectly." The line went dead.

Leaning back in his throne-like leather chair, Count Calypsa rubbed his heavy features with fingers too refined to go with his brutish face. It was as if they belonged to another man entirely—an individual of far finer qualities.

"Unless I am very mistaken," he murmured to himself, "Stahlmaske cannot escape Manhattan Island unchallenged. He will attempt to return here, as he vowed. It is madness, but he may be crafty and cunning enough to pull it off."

Leaning back even further, Calypsa waited, his cruel countenance settling into lines of grave expectation. Above his head, the symbol of his aspirations glared down—a lion seated upon a crown of gold, holding in its paws an upraised sword and mitre. Its expression was regally malevolent.

Soon enough, the desk telephone rang, and the trembling tones of Number Forty-four made the telephonic diaphragm vibrate uncertainly.

"All transpired as you predicted it would, sir. I have closed the door. The driver of the sanitation truck is on his way up to join you."

"Do you remember your orders?"

"Yes! To evacuate."

"Then why are you dawdling?"

Without another word, the lackey hung up.

Sounds of the secret elevator ascending soon came. The Count drew on his concealing hood. Why he did that, even he could not quite explain. His true features were known to Stahlmaske, although the reverse was not yet true. Perhaps because he felt more intimidating with the hood upon his head....

The elevator jolted to a halt, and the electric door slid noiselessly open.

A BLACK leather glove swept the cloth-of-gold drapery aside, and Stahlmaske entered the room with ponderous tread.

The man was a towering figure of terror. He appeared to be nearly eight feet tall, when in fact he stood just shy of seven.

"I have brought you a present!" he thundered.

"I know. Why do you think my minion opened the garage door for you?"

Stahlmaske essayed a courtly bow. "That was very thoughtful of you, Count. My compliments."

Stahlmaske lowered himself into a leather chair and placed both gloved hands on his knees. Although the giant sat perfectly rigid, Count Calypsa could tell that nervous tension persisted in the other's massive frame.

"Perhaps," suggested the Count, "you might feel better if you took off that helmet and breathed like a normal human being."

Stahlmaske laughed hollowly. "If you think you are ugly, think again. I am hideous to behold. If I were to remove my helmet, you would not sleep this night. Perhaps not sleep for many nights to come. I know that you are curious… but be satisfied to gaze upon my blank steel countenance."

Count Calypsa shrugged. "What do you propose to do now that you have successfully evaded the police?"

"*Ach*. The police are the least of my worries. I have encountered my old enemy, G-8. And others. Including your nemesis, The Spider."

"The Spider was never my nemesis!" snarled Calypsa. "I eluded him. He still hunts for me. After all these months, he has never found this headquarters. Your reckless mad dash here might have betrayed my sanctum to any of them."

Now it was Stahlmaske's turn to shrug giant shoulders.

"What should I do? I had no other place that offered refuge and comparative safety. Now if you are worried that this meteorite lies beneath our feet, sending out its deadly radiations, fear not. Here on the top floor, we are beyond its influence."

"What about the persons working below?"

A shrug lifted the helmet slightly. "Then they are fated to become walking dead men. It is of little moment. In short order, they will pour out into the street—as will others in adjoining buildings. It will create a distraction to confound our enemies. They may or may not suspect that the sanitation truck they seek lies hidden in the garage. And if they do? What of it? They dare not enter this building lest they suffer in kind."

The silken hood quivered. "Then we are trapped here?"

"Temporarily. You are smart, but I am a genius. Between us, we will think of something. Perhaps you will create a diversion and I will drive the truck back into traffic. But that is for later. We are now in possession of a powerful weapon. It is useless sitting in the back of that truck for the moment. But it will be useful if we can find a way to ply those broken elements as individual weapons."

Count Calypsa's body shook with the realization of Stahlmaske's intentions.

"Do you imagine that you can turn those meteorite fragments into weapons?"

"*Ach*! I know that I can. The only question is what type of weapon. I have not yet set my mind to pondering the problem. While I consider it, let our enemies hurl themselves against this building and those around it, like mosquitoes dashing themselves against window screens, unable to penetrate, doomed if they do, and thwarted if they do not." Stahlmaske laughed hollowly.

"I like the way you think, *Herr* Stahlmaske."

"I have been thinking this way for more than twenty years. I have thwarted my enemies, and they vexed me in turn. But now I hold the upper hand. Fate has handed us a weapon by which we will conquer this city. I told you that before. Now you can see the truth of my claim."

Stahlmaske's burly shoulders shook with half-suppressed mirth. Count Calypsa was on the point of joining in when he heard the beating of something mechanical not far away. It came in the wake of the departing rattle of a passing Sixth Avenue Elevated train.

"What is that sound?" asked the Count.

"G-8. He has a new aircraft to play with. I believe they call it an autogyro. No doubt he is hunting me. Let us hope that he has more luck now than he had before."

"Why do you want him to have luck?"

Instead of answering directly, Stahlmaske intoned, "The most appropriate place to land such an aircraft would be in Bryant Park, behind the Library. I do not know if he is on my trail or merely searching. But once he investigates this building, his eyes will turn green as an animal's, and his true features, which are to this day unknown to me, will disintegrate into the idiotic madness of a meteor-born imbecile."

Only then did Count Calypsa join in the Man in the Steel Mask's laughter.

"What is true for my enemy, applies to The Spider as well," Stahlmaske offered. "We can only wish them great success in their quest. For the closer they get to us, the sooner they perish."

The autogyro rotor beating lessened, and then became still. It signified that the gyroplane had landed. And landed very close.

Stahlmaske did not rise and pull aside one of the cloth-of-gold window curtains, for he did not care to show his metallic countenance. Not just yet. But when he desired to lure the hated G-8, presenting his featureless mask at any window would prove to be nothing less than a lighthouse beacon guiding the Master Spy to his doom....

Chapter 22

TRIBULATION

RICHARD WENTWORTH flung himself into the back seat of the taxicab when it edged over to the curb.

Slamming the door shut, he barked at the hackman, "Drive!"

"Sure, buddy. Where to?"

"Just drive. Steer where I tell you!"

The cabbie was a seasoned New Yorker. He turned in his seat and said, "Look! If you have a destination, kindly state it. I don't drive in circles for nobody. Can't ever tell what might happen. I hear stories of cabbies who have been hijacked and robbed, some of 'em left for dead. I'm too savvy to fall into that kinda trap."

The driver was forceful in his refusal. Then he looked into the grey-blue eyes of his passenger. Eyes many a criminal had beheld during his last moments on Earth. Compelling eyes. Commanding eyes. Eyes that permitted no refusal.

The taxi man did not know it, but this was the dominating gaze of the Master of Men!

The next words were clipped, almost savage in their restraint. "My name is Richard Wentworth. Perhaps you have heard of me. I have the reputation of being a criminologist of the first rank."

The driver's face seemed to fracture. "That ain't all you've got a reputation for being. Rumor is you're The Spider!"

No use in denying it. There was no time to waste. Instead, Wentworth said coolly, "Believe what you will. I am on the hunt for the arch-criminal who stole the deadly meteorite from Central Park. We are seeking a city sanitation truck. Now get in gear."

Despite himself, the driver obeyed.

"Got fat chance of findin' one garbage truck in a city this size...."

"This particular truck is battered, yet immaculately shiny, as if new," Wentworth related. "It will stand out for that reason. I also have the tag number."

The driver had muscled his hack into the flow of traffic now. Wentworth directed, "Turn left here."

"You got it! But why here?"

Even Richard Wentworth did not know. Sometimes he felt himself possessed of an inner sense that guided him through danger....

"Left, I say!"

With a shrill squealing, the cab wheels wrenched left. The hack shot up cross streets.

In the back, Wentworth watched the close-packed building fronts flash by. Pedestrians were sparse. There was already a nervousness to the city. No doubt word of the maniac outbreak had spread....

Wentworth saw no sign of police radio cars. That in and of itself was a troubling sign. It suggested that the police were concentrated on other parts of the city and could not lend a hand in this particular endeavor.

Suddenly, a thought struck his brain.

"Driver, radio your dispatcher. Inform him that the police are looking for a city sanitation truck in midtown Manhattan. Have all cab drivers be on the lookout for this truck. Instruct him to radio the central dispatcher, and for the dispatcher to contact us."

"I'll do it," said the hackman. "But I don't want to get into any trouble I can't climb out of."

"Once we locate that truck, I will release you. You have my solemn word on that. Now seize your microphone!"

The frowning driver obeyed as he piloted his car around city traffic.

The shortwave exchange was short, terse. Before long, Lady Luck brought favorable news.

Over the dashboard radio came the dispatcher's gruff voice.

"Such a truck was spotted trundling south under the Sixth Avenue Elevated, heading toward Bryant Park."

Wentworth leaned forward, his voice becoming urgent. "Tell the dispatcher to order the driver to follow that truck at a respectable distance. It is too dangerous to approach any closer than three car lengths."

"What if the guy's got a fare?"

Richard Wentworth's voice became hoarse. "The fate of the entire city is at stake, man. What is one fare against that? Do as I say!"

The shaken driver did. He had heard the radio reports, yet did not know what to make of them. But he was a good citizen. New York City was his home. His foot fell heavily on the accelerator.

The driver scurried in the direction of Bryant Park, backtracking when he encountered clogged traffic, and showing a driving skill that Richard Wentworth inwardly admired.

Wentworth declared, "There is no more skilled class of driver in the world," he remarked, "than the New York City cab driver."

"If you're tryin' to butter me up, it only goes so far with me, see? Once we find the truck, I'm dumpin' you. You're on your own. Understand?"

"Perfectly," said Wentworth without concern. Reaching into his tailored suit, he extracted a pair of .45-caliber automatics, checked their action, and restored one to its underarm holster. The other he gripped firmly out of sight.

A TENSION came over his lean body. His expression was set while his posture became keyed up with nervous excitement. On his right temple a thin white battle-scar sprang into life, smoldering like scarlet lightning….

Wentworth did not know how he would deal with the sanitation truck, only that he would. It was imperative to bring it to a stop, have it cordoned off, and, if necessary, torn to bits with dynamite.

But even as he considered that possibility, Wentworth was forced to reject it. To dynamite the sanitation truck would be to blow the insidious green visitant to smithereens. Particles would be dispersed, and possibly carried up in the air. Wentworth shook his head. No, there must be some other way to quarantine the ugly thing. Breaking it apart would only multiply its menace.

The skilled driver jockeyed his cab until he found a clear shot toward Bryant Park. The rattle of the Elevated came clearly to their ears. The Forty-second Street stop loomed ahead. The El was slated to be demolished in another year or so. It had blighted the area for so long the park had fallen into weedy disrepair.

The neighborhood might be a good one to attempt to slip along out of sight, he reasoned. Driving under cover of the Elevated was a smart move. But Richard Wentworth was smarter.

Then came the voice of the dispatcher, warning, *"He lost the truck!"*

"Hand me that microphone!" Wentworth insisted.

Seizing the device, he demanded, "How could you lose something that large?"

"It vanished after turning a corner—just up and vanished. The driver is circling the block, but there's no sign of it."

"What block?"

The dispatcher named the block. Wentworth knew it well.

Handing back the microphone, he told the driver, "Hurry, man. Time is of the essence!"

"You don't have to tell me twice!" hurled back the driver, tromping hard on the gas-feed pedal.

The taxi made good time. They were soon upon the spot where the other hack idled, waiting.

Stepping out, Wentworth accosted the other driver and demanded, "Point out the spot where the truck turned the corner."

"This very one," said the shaken cab driver. "I don't see how it could've vanished so quick!"

"How many car lengths were you behind him?" pressed Wentworth.

"Five."

"Five car lengths would have given him time to run the length of this block and turn either left or right...."

Wentworth looked around. This was an area of office buildings and apartment houses, some large and others less imposing. The New York Public Library stood across the street.

"Unless...."

"Unless what?" This came from the second cabbie, who was an anxious listener.

"Unless the driver managed to slip into one of the basement garages!"

The hackman scratched under his tilted cap. "I don't see how he could, but I suppose it's possible...."

"If that is the case," said Wentworth slowly, "the truck may be within mere yards. Sitting unseen, its deadly cargo sending out pernicious radiation. It is too dangerous to tarry here. We must retreat! Retreat to a safe distance—otherwise we, too, will become stricken by the meteorite madness."

The first cabbie got the idea before the second one registered it.

"Like I told you before," he drawled, "you don't have to tell me twice. Hop in!"

Wentworth handed the second driver a ten-dollar bill for his assistance. It was a Silver Certificate. Before he could depart, the driver glanced down and handed it back, snapping, "Counterfeit!"

Frowning, Wentworth took back the bill, demanding, "What makes you say that?"

"I got one of these before. Read this."

He placed a finger on the face of the bill.

This certifies that there is on deposit in the treasury of

The United States of America

Ten Dollars

In sliver payable on demand

Wentworth saw immediately that the word "silver" was misspelled!

Pocketing the phony bill, he murmured, "My apologies. Here is one that is genuine, I trust."

The hackie's grin showed that it was. They parted company.

The two taxicabs retreated several blocks. While they were in motion, Wentworth instructed his driver to inform his dispatcher that the police were needed in the vicinity surrounding Bryant Park.

"Tell them to expect an imminent outbreak of meteor-created zombies," he bit out.

"Did you say *zombies?*"

Wentworth nodded, grim-faced. "There is no better word to describe them. These are not the newly-dead who have been dug up from their graves and reanimated by black necromancy. These are living-dead humans. Doomed to die in an orgy of destruction not of their conscious making."

"I'll try to remember all that," grunted the cabbie, wrestling the wheel with one hand and bringing his microphone to his lips with the other. The back of his neck was red from long hours sitting behind the wheel with the sun beating down on it. Now it was several shades paler. The flesh was pink. A pallor of pink that suggested that the blood had drained from the man's frightened head....

Chapter 23

THE ELECTRIC BUILDING

CAPTAIN GEORGE GATE piloted his nimble *Hummingbird* gyroplane at a low altitude, threading between buildings, attempting to conceal his aircraft from sky gazers and the inevitable New York rubberneckers.

With no clear idea where the sanitation truck driven by Stahlmaske had gone, he dared not risk being seen as pursuing the fugitive vehicle. But winging for Bryant Park was a chance he had to take. It was the nearest safe landing spot, given that the once luxurious park had in recent years gone to seed, becoming a haven for the city's less savory citizens. This made it perfect for his purposes.

Descending, he plopped the duralumin ship onto the lawn. The *Hummingbird* settled on its fat hydraulic landing wheels. He cut the power plant, and the churning rotor vanes slowed, then drooped, while the nose and tail props jerked to a halt.

Ducking out of the trim craft, Gate awaited the arrival of Operator 5 and his black roadster. Such citizens who had been loitering around had scattered, thinking the rotorplane was in distress and in the throes of a crash landing. Therefore, Captain Gate had the park to himself. He kept his flying helmet and goggles on, the better to conceal his features….

The streamlined black roadster pulled up and Operator 5 emerged. Amid the fading green-to-brown grass of Autumn, the government agents conferred.

"No sign of that truck," Gate related.

James Christopher declared, "I radioed my chief at

headquarters. He requested that an all-points bulletin be issued. Not that it will do much good. The police seem to have their hands full down by Central Park. The Green Zone is no more, of course. Word is the afflicted citizens are on the march."

Gate nodded. "As an agent of Military Intelligence, I am limited in what I can do."

"That's what I wanted to talk to you about, Captain," said Operator 5. "I radioed my chief, suggesting that we get together on this matter. He is seeking permission from your superior officer. You will have to work under Intelligence Service authority, otherwise G-2 risks violating the Posse Comitatus Act of 1878."

G-8's frank grey eyes sparkled grimly. "Smart. And sound thinking. Military Intelligence is prohibited from interfering in domestic affairs. If I follow your lead, we can skate around those restrictions lawfully."

"Once that's settled, we can work unfettered. Now, you know this Stahlmaske. Where do you think he got to?"

Gate looked thoughtful. "The police have all bridges and tunnels under watch. He can't get the truck off the island. He'll have to transfer the meteorite fragments to another vehicle if he expects to pull off this little heist of his."

Christopher nodded. "He must have a hideout somewhere. Probably confederates, as well."

"It would have to be in a remote spot, like a junkyard. Otherwise the meteorite radiation would create new victims wherever he stopped."

Operator 5 said, "The junkyard sounds like a good bet. But any processing plant, river warehouse or covered wharf are possibilities as well. Only the police have the manpower to search them all. And they've got their hands full. I haven't seen a radio car since we left that intersection."

They were looking around when a buzzing taxicab pulled up rather abruptly two blocks farther away, to join another. A man stepped out. Both agents recognized him by his aristocratic carriage.

"Wentworth again!" Christopher snapped.

G-8 smiled grimly. "He doesn't give up, does he? What brought him to this spot? Hm-m-m…. He's not paying us any attention."

As they watched, the millionaire criminologist engaged in an excited conversation with the two cab drivers. After a few minutes, they rushed back to their respective cabs and suddenly turned about, tires screeching and dry-skidding in their direction.

"Something's up for sure," murmured Gate.

The taxi carrying Richard Wentworth charged in their direction, turned smartly, and seemed to notice the autogyro for the first time. The cab wheeled about before braking to a complete halt. Wentworth popped out, sprinted in the direction of the two government agents.

"Quick! The sanitation truck is somewhere within a radius of six blocks of the Electric Building."

Christopher frowned. "How do you know that, Wentworth?"

"A cab driver trailed the truck, but lost it on that corner. It could not have traveled very far under close pursuit. Therefore, it must be in an underground garage in one of these buildings. There are several such in this vicinity."

Operator 5 started for his roadster, saying, "I'll alert the police. The buildings must be searched thoroughly!"

Wentworth stepped in, blocking his way. "Dammit, man! There's no time to summon the police. Radiations from the meteor are no doubt seeping invisibly from the truck. Any unsuspecting person under its influence is doomed! Doomed to become a living dead man—a maniacal zombie of destruction. Don't you see? These buildings must be evacuated before wholesale slaughter breaks out!"

Operator 5 hesitated, loathe to take orders from this highly excitable civilian. But Wentworth made undeniable sense.

"Very well," said Christopher crisply. "We will evacuate the environs. You call the police. As I said before, you have no official standing. Now, be a good citizen and make the call. We will handle matters from here."

Upon Wentworth's temple, an old battle-scar suddenly flamed into life. A vein in his brow pulsed. It was all the criminologist could do to maintain his self-control. Inclining his aristocratic head, he said tightly, "I will do as you suggest. But for God's sake, get on with the evacuation. Every minute counts!"

Wentworth rushed for a pay telephone. Operator 5 and G-8 put their heads together.

"There is a bullhorn and loudspeaker apparatus in my automobile," declared James Christopher.

"I have something similar in my plane. Let me take to the air."

"Good luck!" said Operator 5, jumping back into his roadster. Keying the ignition, he set it in motion as the gyroplane churned its great rotor blades and bolted into the air.

They took turns calling out instructions to passing New Yorkers.

"Attention all citizens within hearing of my voice!" proclaimed Operator 5 in a ringing tone. *"You are hereby instructed to evacuate this area. Withdraw at once! Grave danger is present!"*

From the circling gyro came the commanding voice of G-8, amplified by a bullhorn.

"This is a military aircraft. I hereby announce an official evacuation order. Civilians are at once directed to pull back from the immediate vicinity of the New York Public Library. Leave at once. By foot or by automobile. Do not hesitate. The danger is growing greater by the minute. That is all!"

Naturally, there was a panic. But a panic was better than a disaster. Pedestrians on the sidewalks began to pick up their pace, some breaking out into dead runs. People lost their shoes in their pell-mell haste. But this panic served them in good stead. Those who fled preserved their lives....

Windows opened in some of the office buildings and heads popped out. G-8 repeated his instructions over the mechanical clatter of his rotor wing.

"Evacuate the area! Evacuate at once. No time for explanations!"

Out of the foyers and lobbies of the buildings, humanity flowed. Some were slow. Others halted on the sidewalk to look around, thinking the city was being bombed from the sky. There was a great deal of rubbernecking. This slowed down the exodus. Despite the confusion written on their faces, New Yorkers began streaming out of the area.

IN THE back of a drugstore, Richard Wentworth was shouting into the pay telephone.

He told Kirkpatrick that the missing sanitation truck was somewhere in the neighborhood of the library. "The area is being evacuated by government agents," he stressed. "But there are certain to be stragglers, and where there are stragglers there will be fresh zombies."

"I am en route," the Commissioner said hoarsely.

Hanging up, Wentworth dashed out into the street, saw that the evacuation had begun. Relief washed his features, but only momentarily. Concern swiftly returned.

He stared up at one specific structure: The Electric Building. Memories came flooding back to him. During his previous encounter with Count Calypsa, the self-styled Dictator, suspicion had fallen upon a man who had an office in that building. An ingenious bit of telephone rewiring made it appear that Count Calypsa had his headquarters in that building. The subterfuge was uncovered and the man exonerated. The Dictator's actual headquarters was never discovered.

The fact that the sanitation truck vanished into this cluster of blocks raised new suspicions in Wentworth's mind.

What if that telephonic subterfuge had been accomplished by agents of Count Calypsa operating from this very building? What if the Dictator's headquarters had been in the same building as the person he was attempting to frame? It was a clever bit of misdirection. If true. No one would suspect Calypsa of operating from a different floor in the same building….

To Richard Wentworth, that made the Electric Building the center of the terror that was unfolding. He knew it had a base-ment garage. Another point in support of his theory. What to do about it? If the sanitation truck and its cargo of radiant pestilence were hiding in the basement garage, to approach the building would be to invite mindless doom….

"Dammit!" he grated savagely. "That Steel Mask is a clever fiend. So long as he remains high above the zone of radiation, his position is impregnable."

As Wentworth's mind raced with chaotic thoughts, the first new victim stumbled into view.

The fellow came, not surprisingly, from the foyer of the Electric Building. He looked like an ordinary office worker, perhaps in his mid-30s. He did not wear a hat. His hair showed like dried corn silk.

But it was his eyes that caught the attention. They were green. Even in broad daylight that greenness possessed a feline chatoy-ancy visible from a block away.

The man walked out normally enough, but then he turned to the right and almost toppled over. Catching himself, he staggered on. It was as if his brain was becoming disconnected from his motor functions. His gait wobbled. Struggling with his balance, he threw out his arms. The staggerer looked comically enough like a man trying to walk along one of the seams in the sidewalk, like a child on a dare.

Crossing the street, he was nearly struck by a fleeing coupé. He slapped the hood of the machine as he jumped back. The driver struck out a head to yell at him. Then the driver saw the luminous *emerald* eyes....

Retreating, he gunned the engine and scooted away, while semi-visible green beams followed him, causing the auto's back window to blacken as if from soot....

Another person left the foyer, and then another. One was a woman. They stumbled around, hands groping about, as if losing their sight. They happened to bump into one another by backing up. When they turned, they started snarling, their eyes glared greenly at each other like those of feral cats.

From a distance, Richard Wentworth could see the horror that next transpired. Greenish rays emanating from one pair of optics, struck the other. Their glances met, clashed luminously... and both parties began screaming as their eerie eye-beams burned the other! Hair burning, *they began smoking like human torches....*

Wrenching cries of pain accompanied their stumbling away. One backed into traffic and was struck. The sound of metal striking flesh was sickening. But it was a mercy.

Stepping behind the steel body of a parked automobile, Wentworth slipped into a crouch, and he silently prayed that the automobile would protect him from whatever unseen radiation was streaming his way.

Cursing in his frustration, Wentworth did the only thing he could. He began shooting at the zombies. Knowing that he had no other choice, knowing that they were foredoomed. And knowing, also, that their deaths would be forever on his soul....

He was no longer Richard Wentworth. Yes, he was still recognizable as the scion of the Wentworth millions. But inwardly, he was The Spider. Cold, ruthless and dedicated to justice.

But also to mercy. As he triggered the automatic in his hand, he took care to put a bullet into the brains of the two zombies staggering about. One slug for each. That was enough. They crumpled to the pavement, their brains dashed out, their doomed dance of death cut short.

It was a form of mercy—*the eerie mercy of The Spider!*

More zombies emerged. Wentworth emptied the magazine into them, holstered his weapon and produced a fresh automatic. He never missed. He shot not to wound, not even to kill. This was something else. Something more righteous.

This was… there was no other word for it but—*euthanasia!*

When he had efficiently emptied both smoking weapons, The Spider doubled back one block west, and then raced south and made his way to Bryant Park.

There, he flagged down Operator 5's black roadster, which had also been forced to retreat.

Stepping out, James Christopher shouted, "Wentworth, it is time for you to evacuate the area. You're not wanted here."

"Steel Mask is holed up in the Electric Building!"

"How do you know that?"

"It would take too long to tell. But Steel Mask is not working alone. He is in league with a European criminal, Count Carmine Calypsa, otherwise known as the Dictator!"

Christopher frowned. "The international criminal who attempted to seize control of this city a few months back?"

"The same scoundrel. It was to Count Calypsa's headquarters that Steel Mask retreated. The first zombies blundered out of the Electric Building. Therefore, we dare not assault it. Not without protection, which we do not have. For the moment, Steel Mask and Calypsa are secure. But the zombies are on the march. And since there is no hope for them, they must be exterminated. Exterminated, do you hear?"

James Christopher had been in the Intelligence Service for several years now. His quick-thinking brain grasped the truth instantly.

"I have but one automatic. There's a shotgun in my trunk."

"It will not be enough!" cried Wentworth. "We will need machine guns. G-8 carries one. Radio him. Have him spray any green-eyed person who walks in the drunken, aimless manner of an automaton. It is the only way to suppress the plague of Meteor Monsters issuing from those buildings."

Operator 5 went to his machine and dialed the military frequency he knew G-2 used. He spoke crisp, succinct words. And soon the rotorplane skidded around the sky and came back to rest on the dying grass of Bryant Park.

Captain Gate ducked out from under the swirling rotor wing, a Thompson submachine gun cradled under one arm. Under the other, he lugged two heavy drums of spare ammunition.

Wentworth strode up to him. "I suggest you unleash short bursts to conserve ammunition. Aim for the brain. The souls of the dead will thank you for it. There is no need to cause them any pain. They are not at fault. All are victims, but they must be put to rest—put down as swiftly as possible. Do you understand?"

G-8 nodded. "I get you. Now stand aside."

The G-2 agent strode over to a corner and took a position. He hesitated only a few moments. Soon, an older man of about fifty came backing out of the Electric Building, clutching his hat in his hand.

Once on the sidewalk, he lifted his hat as if to put it on his head. But when he gazed upon it, it burst into flame. The man let out an animal yell as the burning felt scorched his hand. He dropped the smoldering fedora.

That was enough for G-8.

Lifting the steel muzzle of his Tommy gun, he depressed the trigger, barely tapping it. Mechanically, it began to buck and yammer....

Tac-tac-tac-tac!

A withering stream of bullets chopped the man's head into gory fragments that splashed the building façade behind him.

Knees buckling, body corkscrewing, the now-headless meteor zombie collapsed into an unsightly pile upon the pavement.

He was only the first of many. The Thompson sub-gun held tight in G-8's fists chattered again and again, a ghoulishly prolonged stutter of doom. He fought to keep the upward-bucking steel muzzle in line. Gunsmoke was a bitter cloud about him.

Hunkered down behind the black roadster's steel body, Richard Wentworth and James Christopher shut their eyes and did their best to block the horrible sounds of mayhem from their brains.

"They will pay for this madness," Wentworth said with cold force. "Mark my words. Steel Mask and Calypsa will pay with their lives, just as those unfortunates are now paying in blood for no other reason than they came to work on a holy day…."

James Christopher offered no rejoinder. His youthful, clean-cut face was set. And with every chattering cackle of machine-gun fire, it seemed to age a month….

Chapter 24

ZOMBIE RIOT

POLICE COMMISSIONER Stanley Kirkpatrick heard the ghoulish chatter of the Tommy gun as he approached the New York Public Library. The siren of his official limousine howled angrily. Behind him, four radio cars whimpered in pursuit.

When he rounded the corner, Kirkpatrick beheld a nearly unbelievable sight—a man he did not recognize mowing down a fresh pack of zombies with a Thompson submachine gun, his stance wide-legged. The machine-gunner wore a leather flying jacket and matching helmet. Goggles surrounded his eyes, masking his tense features.

Not far behind his recoil-jittering form, Richard Wentworth and another man were hunkered down behind a black roadster.

"Circle the library!" he told his driver. "Bryant Park. Step on it."

Sergeant Carter wrestled the limousine about, followed by the four trailing radio cars.

The limousine pulled up behind the black roadster. Kirkpatrick emerged, demanding, "I received your summons, Dick. Kindly bring me up to date."

The police official's face was haggard. Kirkpatrick looked as if he had aged three years, and it was not yet the noon hour.

Wentworth joined him in the back of the limousine. His words were clipped.

"Briefly, I managed to trail that sanitation truck to the Electric Building. It's parked in the basement garage. As you can see, its foul, penetrating radiations are creating more meteor-maddened zombies. That man with the Thompson gun is a government agent, with Military Intelligence. He is putting them down before the horror that has befallen them has fully played out."

"Great God!" Kirkpatrick said hoarsely. "This is terrible beyond comprehension. This is horror—madness. It smacks of tribulation straight out of the Book of Revelation."

"Listen to me," said Wentworth urgently. "I have good reason to believe Steel Mask and Count Calypsa are both holed up in the higher floors of the Electric Building. It cannot be assaulted. The radiations will turn any man into a Doom Zombie before he could reach their secret headquarters. For the moment, suppressing the growing zombie menace is the best we can do. I suggest that your men train their riot guns on the emerging wretches until there are no more left. We cannot let them get beyond two square blocks."

"Hand me my microphone, please," Kirkpatrick said dully.

Clearing his throat, the Commissioner rapped out sharp radio orders. Soon, it was done. Police officers stationed themselves at different points, taking appropriate positions behind parked cars and lampposts for their own safety.

Riot guns came up and began hammering. Zombies, resembling marionettes without visible strings, crumbled and fell. Others were slammed about when whistling buckshot perforated their unprotected flesh. It was a slaughter. Controlled, restrained, but a slaughter nonetheless.

Eventually, G-8's Tommy gun was exhausted. The pavement at his feet was littered with empty ammunition drums.

Kirkpatrick stepped from his machine and leveled a finger at the G-2 aviator, who was collecting the discarded drums.

"You there! I understand that you belong to the Intelligence Service. Leave the vicinity immediately. This a police matter. We have the sole jurisdiction."

Wordlessly, the agent from G-2 returned to Operator 5's side. His goggled face was pale, as was Christopher's.

"Military Intelligence has no business operating in this city," said Operator 5, pulling out the case containing his identification. "But my identification letter from the chief executive is a different matter."

G-8 shook his helmeted head, stayed Christopher with a firm hand. "Never mind. Better we preserve our anonymity. The police have things under control. I think we got most of them, anyway. We'll slip away, since the commissioner insists. The zombies don't have the brains to hide. The noise of gunfire is driving them out onto the sidewalks. It's like a turkey shoot—but with human beings."

Operator 5 wiped the perspiration of stress from his high forehead. "The police will cordon off the building. That part of it is in their hands. I suggest that we repair to Intelligence headquarters and report to my superior. This is a law-enforcement operation now."

G-8 nodded. His face was drained. Behind the lenses of his flying goggles, his grey eyes appeared hot, as if feverish.

"No one is getting in or out of that building, that's for sure. But is it smart to leave the situation in police hands?"

"Z-7 must be notified at once!" insisted Christopher. "As a member of the Intelligence Service, I must submit myself to my superior. He will want a timely report, and issue instructions based upon that."

"I don't like leaving Stahlmaske where he might escape capture."

"I understand, Gate. But like you, I am merely a number in the Intelligence Service rolls. I cannot act rashly, or outside of my jurisdiction. The police have the building surrounded. They will hold their positions until we receive clear instructions."

"If you say so," said Gate dubiously.

Abandoning the gyroplane in Bryant Park, they piled into the black roadster and took off.

Staring into his rearview mirror, James Christopher said, "I do not like leaving Richard Wentworth with the commissioner. He has a great deal of influence upon Kirkpatrick. There is no telling what rash moves he might make in our absence."

"Wentworth is the commissioner's worry, not ours," grunted the Master Spy.

RICHARD WENTWORTH'S intense eyes narrowed as they watched the two Intelligence officers depart the area of Bryant Park.

His head swiveled back and his expression flinched at the sight of the dead and dying, lying sprawled on the crimson-stained pavement. The gutters were running red with their evacuated life fluid....

"The Thompson sub-gun is no weapon with which to put down those who were only minutes ago ordinary citizens," he muttered.

Kirkpatrick nodded gravely. "Who were those men?"

"The younger one is a man I met in the course of the depredations of the recent Death-Madness. He identified himself as a Secret Service agent named Christopher. Perhaps he is. The other I did not know by sight, only by voice. I encountered him during the war. His true name is unknown to me. During the World War, he was known under the *nom de guerre... G-8.*"

"Yes, yes," stated Kirkpatrick. "The renowned flying spy of wartime fame. I'm not surprised to see the Secret Service in the picture. The Governor is at present resisting entreaties to call out the National Guard. He does not want to precipitate a panic."

Wentworth spun about, his features hardening. "Panic? This is nothing less than a catastrophe! The police cannot long check this zombie advance. Not so long as that meteorite is exerting its evil will. It must be destroyed at once!"

"But how?" choked out Kirkpatrick. "Anyone approaching the

Electric Building risks becoming one of the green-eyed damned. Dick," he rasped, "the casualties are staggering. I've lost two precincts' worth of my officers to that curse. I cannot afford to lose any more. Nor will I order them to their deaths. You know as well as I that, once their eyes become green, they are lost—lost and irredeemable."

Wentworth frowned. "Steel Mask conveyed the meteorite all the way from Central Park to this spot. He appears to be immune. There is only one reasonable explanation for that fact."

The police commissioner met Wentworth's gaze.

"His helmet," Kirkpatrick said gravely. "Perhaps the radiation will not penetrate solid steel."

Wentworth shook his head vigorously. "Steel is not known to be a protection against such rays. But lead is. Kirk, I will wager any amount of money that Steel Mask's helmet is lined with lead. He experimented with some diabolical forces during the war. No doubt his helm was contrived to protect him from deadly rays."

Kirkpatrick's wintry eyes grew reflective. "Lead," he said dully. "Common lead…."

"Yes, lead. One of the most useful heavy metals in existence. It melts quickly and easily, and blocks X-rays. Perhaps helmets of lead could be fashioned to permit the safe breaching of the Electric Building."

Again, the commissioner shook his head. "I will not experiment with my remaining men. There must be another way."

"There is," Wentworth response crisply. "Keep the barricade intact. I will see what I can do."

Richard Wentworth started away, but the strong hand of the commissioner seized him by one arm, pulled him back.

For Kirkpatrick's eyes were haunted as he examined the face of his longtime friend.

"Dick, Dick. In this hour of desperation, I cannot afford to lose you as well…."

Gently, Wentworth pried Kirkpatrick's fingers off his arm. "Nor will you. I will brave the Electric Building. But first, I must make ready. I am not about to throw my life away. Hold the lines, Kirk. Hold them resolutely. I will return…."

So saying, Richard Wentworth strode off, his chin up, his head held high, a steely determination graven in the lean lines of his face.

Behind him there was a sudden commotion, and a police riot gun belched twice. There followed a short scream and the thud of a body falling. Wentworth did not look back. This was not the time for looking back. Only forward.

It was time for The Spider to walk again….

Chapter 25

WALKING THE WEB

RICHARD WENTWORTH had not gone four blocks in search of a pay telephone when he heard a familiar voice hail him.

"Major!"

It was unmistakable, that voice—the reassuring ring of his old comrade-in-arms, Ronald Jackson.

The Daimler was idling across the street, Jackson behind the wheel. Wentworth sprinted toward it, flung himself into the back seat and said tersely, "Sutton Place."

"Not the hospital, sir?"

"There is no time. Much as I long to look in on Nita, there are urgent matters to attend. Steel Mask and Count Calypsa are barricaded high in the Electric Building. It is impossible to penetrate without special protection—protection I intend to fashion as quickly as Providence will permit."

"Yes, sir." The limousine surged into traffic, motor purring like a stalking tiger.

The Daimler slithered east, soon penetrated Sutton Place amid the slums of the East River. It pulled up to a gate at the end of a dead-end street. Wentworth leaned his head out of the rear compartment and blew on a silver whistle, producing a short, wavering skirl. A concealed mechanism was attuned to that sound. The gate opened smartly through electrical means, each wing sliding to one side.

Rolling in, the Daimler found lodgment in the built-in garage of the fortress-like building Richard Wentworth had caused to be constructed here among the decrepit docks of the East River. Rearing four stories high, it sat between two piers.

By means of a private elevator, Wentworth rushed immediately to his workshop.

"Fire up the metal-working furnace," he instructed Jackson, as he shucked off his evening clothes.

While the loyal chauffeur got busy, Wentworth opened a cabinet and pulled out blocky pigs of lead. These, he used to smelt his own bullets. For had millionaire Richard Wentworth been detected purchasing ammunition wholesale, it would represent a telltale clue as to The Spider's identity—for the Master of Men could be exceedingly liberal with his lead.

"Making bullets, sir?" Jackson wondered. "You must be planning for a war."

"The war has already commenced," Wentworth snapped. "Kirkpatrick tells me that his forces have been decimated. But no, I do not need to increase my supply of bullets. I must fashion a helmet that will be proof against that infernal meteorite's rays."

Jackson looked perplexed. But he tended to his furnace until it was red hot.

Stacking several pigs into a steel container, Wentworth donned thick asbestos gloves and shoved the thing into the hot flames. Jackson closed the grated door with a prod. The door was already red-hot.

The lead soon collapsed and became a slow bubbling pool of thick grey matter, smoking faintly. The bitter stink of hot slag grew annoying.

Wentworth went to a cabinet where were stored the masks of The Spider on shelves. Over the years, he had donned many different contrivances calculated to conceal his striking features.

One was a domino mask with a black silk curtain hanging down to conceal the nose, mouth and chin. There was a hideous countenance cast of steel that showed a hooked nose, vampire fangs and other disagreeable features. That one fit so closely to his features it could not be lined with lead and employed for his purposes. Wentworth laid it aside.

At last, he came to a domino mask that was fashioned from blue steel. He had never worn it. Not once. The contours of the mask were edged with hook-like extensions. These resembled a spider's legs... or perhaps they suggested *fangs*.... This he took down.

There was another object. It bore a general resemblance to a deep-sea diver's helmet but with a square visor of heavy glass. This casque was constructed of steel as well. It was something his late friend Professor Brownlee had been working on before his tragic death—an air-tight head protector meant to be used in conjunction with a small air tank to enable The Spider to brave poisonous atmospheres, whether it was police tear-gas or lethal vapors. Wentworth examined the interior and nodded with satisfaction.

Placing it in an enamel work sink, he upended it, making a kind of bowl.

Wentworth studied this for a few minutes, then nodded approvingly.

"Bring the molten lead," he instructed.

Stolidly, Jackson squared his jaw and complied. He had on his own fire-resistant work gloves. He used a pair of tongs to pull out the fireproof pan. The molten lead was heavy. He took great care carrying it over, and Wentworth took equal care stepping back.

"Set it on the side of the sink, Jackson."

Jackson dropped it as carefully as he could, then stepped away, sweating.

Perspiration shone on Wentworth's features as he maneuvered the container about. A lip-like spout indented one side of the rim. Carefully, he poured the lead into the headpiece, then snapped.

"Cold water! Hurry!"

Reaching around, Jackson opened the tap. Water cascaded down, hissing and sizzling, obscuring their vision.

"That is enough," said Wentworth. Jackson twisted the tap abruptly. He set the lead container aside and stepped back. They both did.

They gave the sink time to cease steaming. Then Wentworth approached.

The lead had formed a thick crust in the bottom of the casque, and it was still semi-molten. Using the tongs, Wentworth lifted the helmet and tipped it this way and that, swirling the hot metal so that a skin formed of the fast-cooling slag, until the interior was coated with lead. The glass visor hung open, keeping it clear of the slag. More cold water was applied. Fresh steam erupted. But not as much as before.

Finally, when the lead was fixed in place and cool to the touch, Wentworth lifted the heavy helmet and upended it. The lead coating remained in place.

First donning the blue-steel mask, Richard Wentworth placed the steel casque over his head. And it fit in a clumsy fashion. He closed the visor over the angular domino mask.

"The lead completely surrounds the top of my skull," he observed.

"Will that be enough?"

"It was enough for Steel Mask. That should suffice for... *The Spider!*"

"Pardon me for saying so, Major," said Jackson. "But you kinda look like a crusading knight of the Twentieth Century."

Wentworth tried nodding. But the confining casque inhibited the natural action. "For Steel Mask rather resembles a medieval Black Knight come to life."

Striding ponderously to another cabinet, he extracted a black cloak. He looked it over. Wentworth decided it was not what he wanted. He took out another. This one had a steely blue lining that matched his mask. It was made of a special silk that had the unique property of being bulletproof.

Thinking of the false Spider traipsing about the city, Wentworth laid the cloak upon a work table, with the blue lining a-shimmer under the lights. Taking a jar and fountain pen from a cabinet, he dipped the nib into the opened jar, and worked the charging lever.

With quick, sure strokes, he inscribed an orb web onto the lining, inscribing it with almost uncanny symmetry… as if he were a human spider spinning its skien.

Jackson looked puzzled. "Radium?"

Wentworth nodded. "It will absorb sunlight, and glow under certain conditions—of my own choosing." He finished off the sinister design with a final stroke.

Throwing this over his shoulders with a flourish, Richard Wentworth closed it by the collar, using a silver clasp on which was stamped a venomous-looking blood-red spider. Thin black gloves went over his fingers. Finally, the ring that was The Spider's signet found its place on one finger.

Checking his guns, he holstered them anew. As a final gesture, he investigated a coat pocket until he felt the cold metal of his platinum cigarette lighter. The device contained the vermilion seals of The Spider that the Underworld dreaded to see upon the foreheads of their slain comrades.

Turning with a swirl of his black cloak, The Spider hissed, "You will convey me to a spot three blocks south of the Electric Building. I will find my way from there."

"In broad daylight?"

"There is no time to lose! Who can divine what deviltry Steel Mask and Count Calypsa are plotting? Should they decide to make a break for it, police riot guns may not be sufficient to halt them."

"You're bound to encounter more Meteorite Maniacs, Major."

"If I must slay more of those wretches, then I will," said Wentworth heavily. "It is my solemn duty to save this city."

From one of the open cabinets, Jackson reached in and pulled out a long black sword cane. "Perhaps you should carry this as well. Silent but efficient."

Wentworth took the stick, exposed the thin blade and examined the tip. It was coated with a combination of unpleasantly lethal natural substances. He had not found a use for it in years. But in times past, it had dispatched many vicious criminals.

"Very good, Jackson. I fear that I will be forced to make effective use of it. But you are correct—entirely correct. With this, I can penetrate the danger zone around the Electric Building and silently deal with any zombies I may encounter without arousing police attention."

Minutes later, the Daimler was sliding out of its garage and coasting through the disreputable slums that surrounded Sutton Place.

In the rear compartment, The Spider sat heavily on the cushions. The weight of the steel casque upon his head was crushing. And yet it was strangely reassuring. Grey-blue eyes looked out from a mask of blued steel… and they no longer held the kind regard of Richard Wentworth. But the sharp, bitter glints of The Spider!

Shortly thereafter, the Daimler coasted to a stop well short of the police cordon. Sawhorses and coiling barbed wire had been set into place. Blue uniforms were everywhere… but their numbers were thin… painfully, distressingly thin….

Preparing to step out, Wentworth hesitated. His fingers went to a pocket and extracted the counterfeit ten-dollar Silver Certificate. He had forgotten about it in the mounting emergency….

"Jackson, take this bill. It is counterfeit. If I do not return, surrender it to Kirkpatrick. He will know what to do."

"Good luck, Major."

The rear door clicked shut, and Richard Wentworth ceased to exist in a way….

FROM A safe distance, The Spider studied the police lines. He knew that with such a barricade hindering all approaches to the block, he could not hope to penetrate far. Not with the afternoon sun shining down on the city. The city! A low laugh escaped his throat. It had been attacked before. Skyscrapers had been razed by evil minds. Innocents had been slaughtered. But this—this Luciferian scourge threatened the magnificent metropolis in a new way.

Master minds of crime had not created the Green Meteorite. They had taken advantage of the foul, shining thing. What evil misfortune had caused the meteoroid to land on the same night that Steel Mask had resurfaced to reclaim his long-lost helmet? And what was the objective of the false Spider who appeared to have been Count Calypsa in disguise? Were these two fiends now joined in common cause? Had the same unholy fate brought them all together on Halloween night—these sworn enemies of mankind, and the one person who could balk them?

These were the troubled thoughts of Richard Wentworth as he flitted through the alleys between buildings that reared up around Bryant Park and the Public Library, his sword cane in one hand, his black cloak flaunting itself with each step.

Even in sunny daylight, there was something uncanny about the way he moved. The Spider stalked in silence, sliding and pausing, at times hunkering down and becoming uncannily immobile, seeming to possess an eerie sixth sense that allowed him to escape notice.

Many species of arachnids boasted eight orbs. The Spider appeared to have eyes in the back of his head....

When he reached the point at which he knew he could no longer operate invisibly, The Spider entered a deserted apartment building, The Gotham Arms, and took the elevator to the top floor. Exiting, he climbed rickety steps until he gained the roof.

A cool November breeze played with the folds of his black

cloak as he stood surveying the Electric Building across the street. His searching eyes were sharp.

Somewhere on those upper floors, no doubt, Steel Mask and his confederate held forth.

But which floor? Which side of the building?

The Spider searched every window. He stood firm, resolute, on feet that were spread slightly apart, lithe muscles poised to spring at a moment's notice in any direction.

A sudden gust caused his cloak to spill open. And the blue-steel lining revealed the ghostly green lines of an orb web. The Spider appeared to be standing in a luminous web of his own making!

Spreading one edge like a wing, he inserted his sword cane into a long narrow pocket stitched into the lining hem, then buttoned it shut. Then he reached into a pocket of a leather tool kit worn girdled about his waist, removing a coiled length of silken cord, no thicker around than a pencil. The police had dubbed this strong line... the Web. That was good enough for Richard Wentworth. The Web it was.

Fashioning a lariat at one terminus, The Spider cast it toward the next rooftop. He snared a vertical standing pipe, then yanked hard, jerking the line tight. The loose loop closed like a hangman's noose.

Tugging until the line was taut, he tied the loose end around a similar pipe at his feet. This created a high wire between the two buildings. But dare he walk it?

It would be safer to do so at dusk, when he was less likely to be seen. But to take up the threat of the two master villains meant that The Spider's safety did not factor into the equation of counter-crime. He would cross the precarious high wire that was not intended to serve as such....

Cautiously, he stepped onto the high parapet surrounding the roof, and then placed the gummed sole of his right shoe along the taut line. The soft gum was perfect for this purpose. It gave sufficiently to create a gripping groove where the line dug in.

Perhaps no other man would have dared such a thing. It was audacious, supremely dangerous. Circus aerialists have been known to cross between two poles in this fashion. But those were barefoot and walked tightropes woven from heavy wire—wire that would not break under the weight of a man.

And while the Web possessed a tensile strength that rivaled steel, it was not steel. Nor wire. But silk. The same grade of silk as his cape lining—the only natural fiber capable of withstanding bullets.

Like his eight-legged namesake, the Master of Men stepped across a strand of Web of his own making. His left sole pressed down, and the Web pushed upward, creating a second groove.

Slowly, carefully, The Spider eased his right foot forward, not lifting it, but sliding it forward, keeping the groove intact. His left foot followed. Then his right advanced. Left, right, left again. Easing forward, sliding carefully, he advanced.

There was no going back now. He could not turn in place. He dared not. He could only slide forward, inches at a time. Right foot. Left foot. Right foot again.

Carefully, he lifted his arms at right angles to his slightly swaying body, providing balance. And in each gloved hand, adding to his balance and weight, was a heavy automatic, laden with lead.

The crossing was slow, painstaking and arduous. Police eyes were focused on the ground, and upon the revolving doors of office buildings where mindless meteor-crazed zombies could be expected to emerge. But none did.

And so, The Spider slid unseen along his Web, unseen, unsuspected and balanced precariously between this world and the next.

And all the while, his steely eyes were fixed upon the windows of the Electric Building, fixed and focused, searching for any sign of his quarry....

Three-quarters of the way along, The Spider paused. It was momentary. A breeze whipped up. Slightly stiff, it caused his black cloak to billow outward, revealing once again the blue-steel lining with its luminous stitchery.

Bright sunlight striking that design caused it to gleam. A canny eye spotted that metallic glint—a lone police officer.

Something flashed in the sky and he looked up. He saw the man in black, his head oversized and steely. But it was the blue lining of the fluttering cloak that captured his attention. The pattern was that of a spider's web. No mistake about it!

Lifting his Police Positive above his head, he fired a single concussive shot into the air—a barking shot of warning. It was not directed at The Spider. Not yet. It was aimed to summon the attention of his fellow officers.

"Look skyward!" he howled. "If that ain't the damn Spider, I'll eat my cap, badge and all."

Fellow officers came running, forming a knot of blue, their shaking fingers pointed toward the man walking between two buildings. From their positions, the Web was not visible. Not visible at all....

"Look at him!" breathed one bluecoat. "Looks like he's walkin' on thin air."

"Mother of mercy! If he ain't the picture of a human spider creeping along his web—a web you can't see with the naked eye."

One shouted, "You up there! Freeze!"

The Spider did not freeze. He inched forward, left foot, right foot, left foot again. He seemed oblivious to the excited shouting of the officers below.

So impressed were the police that they did not have the heart to shoot at the bravest man they ever saw with their own eyes....

"Fetch Kirkpatrick!" one snapped. "Let him give the order."

As The Spider continued his death-defying slide, Stanley Kirkpatrick was alerted. He arrived in his limousine, emerged from the back. Shading his wintry eyes in order to peer upward, a low oath of the amazement escaped his firm lips.

"The damn fool!" he said hoarsely. "He cannot make it all the way across."

A bluecoat so entranced by the sight forgot his manners and remarked, "Well, he's more than half-way across. If I were a betting man, my nickel would be on The Spider."

Kirkpatrick favored the man with a sharp glance but did not rebuke him. He had not the heart.

"Lower your guns," he said heavily. "Let him live. If he survives the crossing, perhaps he deserves to do so. As for me, I will be in my limousine." His voice shook a little. "I cannot bear to watch a brave man commit suicide… inch by agonizing inch…."

Chapter 26

THE SPIDER'S FANG

THE SPIDER did not hear the excited shouts of the policemen gathered below. He could not possibly have heard them standing at the height at which he braved death and tempted fate.

Nor did he dare to glance downward. In truth, he could not look down. The protective casque prevented him from moving his head significantly. And so he plodded on, one agonizing inch at a time, his gummed shoe soles easing their steady, methodical way along the stretched and straining Web....

As The Spider approached the Electric Building roof, his attention fell on the closed loop tied tightly around the far standpipe. It was holding. He had no doubt that it would. The silken line was tremendously strong, the knot of the lariat was time-tested. Western wranglers who throw wild bulls to the ground favored that identical knot.

The line was holding magnificently. But the standpipe began to lean toward him. Its anchoring flange was old. With each careful step that was not a step, he heard a creaking and groaning of the pipe bending, its rusted anchoring screws coming loose.

Recognizing his peril, The Spider increased the speed of his steady progress. But it was still inching, the creeping of an inchworm....

With another creak, the pipe gave slightly more. The tightness of the silken Web slackened ever so slightly. It was that very tautness that permitted this miraculous crossing to take place.

Wentworth slid forward, and in his haste moved an inch too far, too fast. His constricting fingers squeezed his gun butts as he began to waver.

Teeth clenched, lips peeling back from the white enamel, he kept his balance. But the pipe. That damn pipe. It was not strong enough….

Then, with a slow creaking that was like a door falling open, the pipe commenced to bend alarmingly in his direction.

There was nothing left to do but to fall—tumble helplessly to his death.

But The Spider did not fall! He refused death!

Even as the supporting tightness started going out of the silken Web, he reacted. His superb brain, his incredibly coordinated reflexes, kicked into life.

Releasing one of the automatics to drop to the pavement below, Wentworth lowered the other and with one smooth trigger-squeeze, loosed an unerring shot, parting the silken line with a blunt bullet.

It should not have worked. But no other course of action was possible. The Web broke before him. His support was gone!

Falling, The Spider dropped his smoking automatic. His gloved hands dived for the whipping near end. Steel-strong fingers caught! Miraculously, they held.

Twisting the captured line in clenching fists, he let gravity-borne momentum carry him downward. Fortunately, he did not have far to plummet. He jerked to a halt. This was the moment of truth….

The Web's feeble anchorage held! Then Wentworth was swinging on the frayed end of the silk line—swinging toward the stone side of the Electric Building!

To crash against the structure's façade would have knocked the wind out of his lungs and dashed the senses from his brain. But The Spider did not strike the unforgiving side of the structure.

The parabola of his descent brought his soft soles toward clear window glass. This was the next test. The Spider's knees were bent, his legs pulled in. They struck! Glass shattered crazily! He sailed through, his bulletproof cloak protecting him from the razor shards that flew about. But not entirely.

One jagged triangle sliced against his forearm, but he did not feel its sharp bite. He was crashing to the floor—crashing and rolling. And he might have broken his neck except for the lead-lined steel casque that prevented his neck from snapping.

Perhaps that and that alone preserved the life of The Spider, alias Richard Wentworth.

Rolling hard, he crashed against the far wall, lay there stunned for the moment, his astounding reservoir of vitality spent.

When his full senses returned, The Spider sat up carefully, took stock of himself and saw the blood flowing out of his left forearm. No artery had been severed. The sluggish flow told him that. From a pocket of his cloak, he took out a black bandage and made a tourniquet of it. There was no time to do more than that....

Wentworth came heavily to his feet, took stock, experimenting with his mobility. He could walk. But only with a stiffness. His limberness was gone.

Going to the door, he paused, then carefully eased it open a few inches. His sharp ears detected no sounds.

Before stepping out into the corridor, The Spider reached into his cloak for his guns—but then remembered that he had let them plummet to the concrete below.

A low oath escaped his parted lips. There was nothing else to do but draw from a long seam in his cloak... the ebon stick that was a sword cane.

The handle was a smooth tube of amber, perfect for fitting into his palm. Reaching into a pocket, Wentworth removed a small object. A sphere of ivory, carved to resemble a lion's head. He slipped this over the amber handle. Set into the lion's gaping mouth was a small magnifying mirror.

Sticking this out of the open doorjamb, The Spider twisted

the lion's head about, until the mirror showed the hallway to be devoid of traps.

Pocketing the ivory ornament, he gave the amber handle a twist. The barrel fell to the floor. He walked forward, holding a gleaming thin blade ahead of him like a poisonous spider's fang....

The corridor was deserted. But one question remained: Upon what floor and in which suite would his enemies be found?

The Spider decided to take the elevator to the top floor and work his way down. That seemed the most sensible course of action.

Locating the elevator, he pressed the call button. The car soon came to a stop on this floor, and the automatic door slid aside. He stepped aboard and pressed the number corresponding to the topmost floor, which was nineteen.

With a smooth jerk, the cage ascended. As he was conveyed up the shaft, Richard Wentworth studied the panel of buttons and saw that in typical fashion, there was no floor designated thirteen… behind the glass plate of his casque, his eyes narrowed....

THE WHINE of the elevator penetrated the curtained room where Count Calypsa, the self-styled Dictator, presided from his mahogany desk over a medieval chamber rich with cloth-of-gold wall hangings.

Hearing this, Stahlmaske's brawny upper body rotated heavily, and his hollow voice boomed out.

"Who could that be?"

Count Calypsa stood up, one smooth hand going for his silken hood. He drew this on. It was a reflex, nothing more. The act of a guilty man with a troubled conscience....

"It could not be one of the office workers. They would have perished by now, their brains destroyed."

Stahlmaske rumbled, "It cannot be the police."

"Then who?"

Stahlmaske hesitated slightly. "Someone more formidable than the police force, and more dangerous than a meteor-maddened New Yorker."

"The Spider!" Count Calypsa hissed venomously.

Reaching for his headsman's axe, Stahlmaske shrugged despite the weight of his black helmet. "Or G-8. I will deal with whomever it is…."

Going to the curtained door, he threw it open and stepped out into the corridor.

The elevator came to a stop and the door rolled open.

A black tube topped by an ivory lion's head poked out. It rotated, finally showing its face. Stahlmaske saw his black helmet reflected in a tiny mirror held between the lion's jaws….

The tube withdrew. Out stepped a fantastic figure. A man garbed in black habiliments, an ebony cloak concealing most of his lithe form. Upon his head perched a grotesque casque. A domino mask forged from blue steel concealed such features as were visible through its glass plate.

Seeing this contraption, Stahlmaske gave forth a hollow laugh and strode forward.

"Greetings, *Herr Spinne.* I see you brought with you a formidable-looking blade." He laughed again. It was a very hearty laugh. "I have two blades. One with which to split that helmet in two, and the other of which to remove your head from your shoulders. How do you like that?"

The Spider whirled, and his cloak fell open, revealing the shimmering blue-silk lining with its pale, luminous orb web.

"*En guard!*" he cried, stepping forward.

Steel Mask lifted his formidable axe. Ducking low, The Spider lunged forward, aiming not at the man's chest, for he knew chainmail lay beneath the fabric of his tunic. Instead, the tip of The Spider's blade sought the left aperture behind which rolled Steel Mask's eyeball!

Recognizing his peril despite the protective lenses of leaded glass, the lumbering man twisted, and the blade scored the side of his black steel helmet, scraping harmlessly past. But in stepping back, the giant lost his balance—and his advantage. His axe slipped from his clenching fists and slammed resoundingly to the floor.

The Spider whirled, ripped off his cloak, set it sailing over the conical helmet, blinding Steel Mask completely.

He roared. Black-gloved hands clenched at the weird fabric, wrenched and pulled while The Spider drove his blade home again and again, seeking a vulnerable point, endeavoring to penetrate the helmet... but encountering only protective metal.

Hissing tightly through his teeth, Wentworth refused to give up. He slashed about, questing for a soft spot before driving the point home. But there was no soft spot. There was nothing like a soft spot. There was only obdurate and indomitable metal....

Reluctantly recognizing that the blade was not up to the challenge, Wentworth flung it aside and lunged for the haft of the double-headed axe. It was heavy—heavier than he expected. Exerting himself, he lifted it up, swung wide—and the flat of the matched blades made a clanging sound against Steel Mask's helm! The giant toppled over.

Switching the blade to the edge, Wentworth came in and brought it down against the face of the metal, attempting to cleave the front of the helmet between the eye slits.

The blade was sharp, exceedingly so. It bit—but failed to penetrate. Wentworth raised it again and, cursing, brought the cutting metal down.

He did not notice the black leather hand creeping toward his feet until iron-banded fingers found his ankle and wrenched him off his feet.

On the floor, they wrestled, grunting and heaving in their muscular exertions. Wentworth soon realized his strength was insufficient to overcome his overlarge opponent.

Nor could the helmeted colossus prevail against his wiry foeman. In his agitation, Steel Mask floundered about, finding The Spider's poisonous stick, and attempted to wield it.

Unable to reach the axe, Wentworth swept up his discarded cloak and flourished it the way a matador confuses a raging bull. The silken strands of the lining were strong. They caught the blade again and again—but it failed to penetrate. The strands would turn a bullet, and so the thin rapier-like blade could not penetrate the tough silk.

Steel Mask laughed resoundingly. *"Ach!* You appear to be a worthy opponent."

"As do you, *Herr...* von Maur," laughed The Spider.

The laugh was threaded with ironic humor. But then it swelled, became metallic and menacing, a sinister thing to be feared. It was not the laugh of a madman. But rather, the mirth of a fearless man....

"It will interest you to know," The Spider said, "that the tip of the blade is coated with a mixture of curare poison and black-widow spider venom."

"Why would you tell me this?"

"So that you're careful not to cut yourself, *Herr* Steel Mask." Again, The Spider laughed. It was taunting this time.

"All the better to pierce your breast and extinguish your life," returned Steel Mask with a trace of old-world gallantry.

He pushed the blade forward, putting all his burly might into it. But might was not sufficient. Swirling the cape held in both hands, The Spider danced away, only to slip up behind his towering opponent.

One gummed shoe sole lifted and kicked at the small of Steel Mask's back. He stumbled forward. In a panic, the giant released the stick, employing his animated limbs to catch himself. He dared not prick himself with the poisonous blade....

Laughing, The Spider rushed for the open door from which Steel Mask had entered. The opening was concealed by drapery of some kind. He swept this aside, stepped in—and found himself standing in the room whose windows were covered. And staring back at the far end stood the hooded figure of the Dictator, Count Calypsa!

"We meet again," taunted The Spider.

"How did you…?"

"Locate your floor?" The Spider's tone was like the crack of a bullwhip. "This is a twenty-story building. Curiously, there is no floor numbered thirteen, yet nineteen is its highest numbered level. Two floors are missing. That could only mean a private twentieth floor! I employed my lockpick on a rather suspicious keyhole with satisfactory results…."

A Luger automatic was gripped in Calypsa's right hand, its black barrel pointing like a steel finger of death. He lifted it. But The Spider was already moving to the right, ahead of the bullet.

A whistling lead slug jabbed the stuffing out of a heavy chair, Wentworth crouched safely behind it. Laughing wildly, he rushed out, lunging for the mahogany desk with its lion emblazoned on the broad front.

Kicking with his good leg, The Spider cleared the space and vaulted across the desk, his body slamming into that of Count Calypsa! A muffled report told that the automatic had discharged. The Spider felt nothing. Perhaps he had been wounded. He did not know. Nor did he care.

But when The Spider landed on the other side, Count Calypsa and his high-backed throne of a chair sprawled around him. He found himself in another battle to the death.

Fists rained blows in both directions. The Spider's stiffened fingers knocked the smoking Luger from the other's hand. It struck a wall-hanging and slid down with a hissing sound.

The Dictator yelled hurt rage. He was beside himself. The thigh which had been pieced by an arrow and sewn shut, popped several stitches, exacerbating his discomfort.

Fully in control of his passions, The Spider seized the Luger, brought it up and around. He fired once. He meant to burst the heart of his enemy, but Count Calypsa was moving with frantic speed. The bullet lodged in the man's shoulder after first twisting him half around. Calypsa made an ugly sound deep in his throat. And then the pain caused him to become innervated with fury. Fear of death, along with the hatred of a foe he feared more than death itself, combined like volatile chemicals, producing an explosive reaction.

Oblivious to the threat of his captured automatic, the Dictator charged. Spatulate fingers clenching, he clutched for The Spider's armed fist.

Wentworth knocked him back with a sideways blow of the steel-barreled automatic. Then he swept it around again, striking Count Calypsa in the temple. The robed and hooded figure went down without another sound—other than the mushy thud of his falling upon the rust-colored deep-pile rug. He became still.

Grinning fiercely, The Spider rushed out to the corridor to confront Steel Mask with the Luger. His intention was to empty the remaining loaded chambers into the giant's hulking form.

But Steel Mask was nowhere to be found!

The human monster from the past was not in the hallway, nor in any of the office suites surrounding it.

Then Wentworth's attention went to the moving arrow of the elevator indicator that marked the passing floors below.

Steel Mask was riding the elevator car downward. Downward to the basement where the sanitation truck and its glowing load of radiant doom awaited....

Cursing, The Spider found the fire stairs and rushed for the basement garage. But the strain on his tourniquet was too much. He pulled up, checked—came to a halt. Blood was seeping from the bandage. He tightened the tourniquet again. But when he resumed his downward troop, his right leg would not obey him. He was slowed to a virtual crawl... like a spider missing a limb....

Chapter 27

WAR STORY

AN ALARM bell sounded, followed by the chatter of the tele-type spitting out a fresh length of perforated tape.

James Christopher had just introduced Z-7 to Captain Gate of G-2. The three men were standing in the Intelligence officer's windowless office high in the Vertex Building, the secret spot designated as Headquarters M.

Z-7 was the commander in chief of the Intelligence Service. He had flown up from WDC-13 in Washington, to take control of the fast-moving situation from station chief T-3.

He was a mature, hard-faced individual with intensely black eyes, matching thick eyebrows crowding close together. His hair was raven-black, while his suit was a neutral grey. His true name was unknown to the men who served under him; nor would it ever be revealed—not even upon his death.

"One moment," Z-7 said throatily, rushing to the teletype. He lifted the tape as it came spooling out of the mechanism.

Turning, he told the two agents, "This is a report from Long Island. The rampage appears to have subsided over there."

"That is a relief, Chief," said James Christopher. "But New York remains in grave peril."

Nodding grimly, Z-7 returned to his desk and gestured for the two men to take seats. He addressed G-8, who had his flying helmet and goggles in hand, exposing his wind-burned, regular features.

"I have been on the telephone with your superior, Captain Gate. Colonel Jasper has released you temporarily to the Intelligence

Service. You will work with Operator 5 until the present unrest in Manhattan is quelled."

G-8 nodded. "Fine by me."

In a less formal tone, the intelligence chief added, "Of course, I have more than passing familiarity with the exploits of G-8 during the World War. You can be assured that I will strive to protect your identity during the course of our shared mission. Only myself and Operator 5 know your cover identity. And there it will stand."

Captain Gate smiled in a friendly way.

"My chief objective is to hunt down Stahlmaske," he stated. "Securing the city is the joint responsibility of civilian Intelligence, working with the police department."

Z-7 said, "There are unconfirmed reports that the Governor was going to call in the National Guard to quell the spreading zombie riots."

James Christopher interjected, "The destruction of the Green Meteorite is the only thing that will stop this insidious plan in its tracks. If we locate Stahlmaske, the meteorite fragments are sure to fall into our hands."

G-8 reminded, "Once we locate the meteorite, Stahlmaske will not be far away. Catch one and we will have control of the other."

Z-7 invited, "Tell us everything you know about this Stahlmaske fellow."

G-8 settled into his chair, casually lit a cigarette. The others did not join him. "I first encountered him early in the war. He was a German soldier of unknown rank. To this day, his real name is unknown to Allied Intelligence. He was operating an aerial balloon and up to some mischief at the front when I came flying by. I ruptured his balloon with my Vickers guns, and it burst into flames. The man somehow survived the fiery crash, but his face was disfigured in a horrible way. A helmet was forged to conceal the living horror that was his head. Ever since, he has burned with hatred against me—a hatred that extends to all of the Allies of that time."

Z-7 nodded somberly. "I read accounts from the war suggesting that he had a brilliant mind."

G-8 laughed shortly. "A *diabolically* brilliant mind, if I may correct you. The nameless German was a scientist of some sort. Time after time, he devised fiendish death devices, which he turned on our forces. We managed to break every feint he made, and believe me, he made a great many. Stahlmaske was an expert in the science of destructive rays. Once, he had constructed a tank that tore through the trenches, gobbling up living soldiers, grinding them up in a mechanism that converted them into emergency food rations for the starving German foot soldiers."

Z-7 visibly shuddered. "I had not heard that account." *

"Probably it's still a secret," replied Gate. "But you needed to know the depths of Stahlmaske's devilishness."

Operator 5 asked, "Wasn't Stahlmaske believed to be killed near the end of the war?"

"In my last confrontation with him," said G-8 steadily, "he was riddled with bullets and fell from a great height. Only his helmet was ever found. But it was good enough for the brass. The Allied generals believed he was finished. They closed the file on *Herr* Stahlmaske after that." **

"Evidently, he did survive the war," remarked Z-7.

"Obviously," nodded Gate, exhaling a slow plume of smoke. "When I heard that his helmet had been stolen, I felt a little shiver of apprehension. That absence of a body always bothered me. I was never quite convinced that Stahlmaske was dead."

Operator 5 inquired, "Are you certain that this is the same man, and not an imposter?"

* G-8 and His Battle Aces: *Patrol of the Iron Hand.*
** G-8 and His Battle Aces: *Wings of the Death Monster.*

Captain Gate's level grey eyes gleamed before he replied. "I recognized his voice. It's like a hollow death knell. There is no question that Stahlmaske has returned from the dead. None whatsoever."

THE TELETYPE alarm bell rang again and the Intelligence Chief swung over to it. He read aloud the latest flash for the benefit of the two agents under his authority.

"Commissioner Kirkpatrick admits that his department has been decimated by the zombie plague," Z-7 declared. "Police officers are being rushed in from New Jersey to make up for the fallen forces."

Returning to his desk, he added throatily, "We must be ready for anything—any horror. Any attempt to take advantage of the havoc wrought by this meteor from Hell."

"What would be Stahlmaske's game?" asked James Christopher, idly toying with his golden skull watch charm. "It's almost twenty years since the war ended."

Captain Gate fingered his chin thoughtfully. "Stahlmaske would not come all the way to America simply to reclaim his old helmet. No doubt he managed to devise some other means by which he could conceal his ugliness. He has always hated me, but he also learned to fear me. I handed him too many defeats. Near the end of his wartime career, he was practically a nervous wreck. Now, he seems to be back in control of himself."

Z-7 advised, "He has had long enough to get his shattered nerves back in order. But what is his objective? The war is long in the past. Germany is at peace."

"This is just a guess," said the aviator who was once known as G-8. "But I think he stole that helmet to draw me out of the secret ranks of Military Intelligence. There's no question in my mind that Stahlmaske still thirsts for revenge. At the same time, he has had two decades to pursue it. More than revenge is on his mind now. Perhaps he is still under the control of the German government...."

"And has been sent on a secret mission!" James exclaimed.

Eyes sparkling like black diamonds, Z-7 mused, "The United States and Germany are on reasonably good terms at present. If Stahlmaske was dispatched to New York to foment trouble, it is a very serious matter between our two countries."

"A grave matter," agreed Gate. "One that could hurl us back into armed conflict."

James Christopher had been listening intently. Now he offered an opinion of his own.

"The situation in Europe is becoming troubled. Could Stahlmaske have been sent here for the simple purpose of assassinating you in anticipation of the coming war?"

Captain Gate looked thoughtful for a minute. His still-youthful features brightened slightly. The energy of his response was electric.

Snapping his fingers, he exclaimed, "If German Intelligence believes that war is coming, they'd want me out of the picture, all right. And there's no more perfect an assassin than Stahlmaske, who would happily stick a dagger in my ticker on general principles."

Z-7 asked, "Then you don't think that the meteorite and Stahlmaske are connected in this plot?"

Gate answered swiftly, "No, I don't. I think it was just a lucky thing that the meteorite landed where it did when Stahlmaske made his first move."

"Unlucky thing, you mean," countered Operator 5.

G-8 laughed with good humor. "That depends on whose side you're on, I guess. Back to Stahlmaske. Twenty years does not seem to have diminished his strength, nor his drive to conquer. We will have our hands full fighting him. He didn't just chop up that meteor to make it easy to cart away. Now that he has it in pieces, you can be damn sure that he's going to figure out ingenious ways to turn those fragments against us. He was one of the most brilliant war scientists Germany ever had. Mark my words, it won't be long until he shows his hand again."

Z-7 said gravely, "You can be sure we will be ready to meet any contingency. Now, how do you two men propose to apprehend your quarry?"

James Christopher spoke first. "The Metropolitan Police have the Electric Building surrounded, along with the truck containing most of the meteorite fragments. They dare not enter, but neither can Stahlmaske escape."

"Don't bet on it!" G-8 countered. "Stahlmaske isn't dumb enough to get himself into a tight spot out of which he couldn't wriggle. I'm sure he has an escape plan, whether it's by air or sewer pipe."

Z-7 stood up. "You make sense, Gate. The police have every right to arrest Stahlmaske, but in the end they must surrender him to us. Either way, we cannot permit him to get away from us. Operator 5, you will drive around the police cordon, watchful for anything suspicious. While you, Captain Gate, fly low in your gyroplane. Canvass the immediate environs of the Electric Building. One of you is bound to get lucky."

G-8 chuckled grimly. "Not as lucky as Stahlmaske!"

Neither of the other two men laughed in response. The grim jest was not humorous to them.

Again, the teletype alarm sounded. And Z-7 rushed to capture the ticker tape as it slipped out of the mechanism.

"Great Scott!" he cried out. "The missing sanitation truck has broken free of the Electric Building! Reports are that it has been hijacked by no less than the notorious Spider himself!"

"On my way, Chief," said Operator 5, reaching for his hat.

Exiting the building, Christopher told G-8 tight-voiced, "If Richard Wentworth is behind this, he will rue this day...."

"You said it!"

Chapter 28

DESPERATE RACE

IN THE illuminated stairwell of the Electric Building, The Spider managed to limp down two flights down when he realized that he could go no farther.

It would have been a futile effort, this mad dash down flights of stairs in pursuit of Steel Mask. Only the driving passion to capture the faceless fiend had made Wentworth believe it was worth the effort.

Shouldering through the fire door, he found himself on the eighteenth floor corridor. Making his way to the elevator, he saw that the indicator arrow had come to a stop. Not on the lobby level, but below that, in the basement garage.

He depressed the call button. The car was slow to respond. Eventually, the indicator arrow began to crawl backward in its enumerated crescent as the lifting mechanism toiled noisily.

While he waited impatiently, The Spider stiffened, hearing another sound. A soft sighing, mechanical in nature.

It sounded for all the world like another elevator cage descending.

Whirling about, he made for the sound. At a blank wall at the end of the corridor, he felt its vibrations. Pressing one ear to the plaster, he detected a familiar sound.

There was no questioning it! A secret elevator. Nor was there any doubt about its direction. It was descending.

"Count Calypsa!" he hissed.

It seemed impossible. The blackguard had been soundly knocked senseless. And yet—

Perhaps he had only been stunned, after all....

Rushing to the public elevator, Wentworth arrived just as the electric door rolled open. Diving in, he hit the garage button. The cage dropped after the door closed again.

Fierce tension took hold of The Spider's masked face as the car dropped. He had no guns, save for the nearly-empty Luger taken from the Dictator. That, and his sword cane. They would have to suffice.

It was a race now. A race between two elevators. Once again, The Spider understood that he was at a disadvantage while he was prisoner of the elevator car. But once the door rolled open again....

The cage jarred to a halt. Wentworth grabbed the edge of the opening steel door and attempted to force it to open faster. Of course, it could not.

Squeezing out of the growing aperture, he found himself in the gloomy confines of a basement garage. Odors of motor oil came to his sensitive nose.

Seeing nothing, he paused, closed his eyes. Now his ears were listening, listening for any slight sound.

No mechanical noise was discernible. But there was a gentle rustle as of silk or some other soft fabric.... He listened carefully, pinpointed its location and opened his sharp eyes.

There were several cars parked about. The Spider wended his way through them.

Towering over all others was the shiny steel sanitation truck. Its side loading doors were closed, but in the gloom of the garage, the row of hatches stood out distinctly—outlined in a shimmering, luminous green....

This was the source of the uncanny power that transformed ordinary men into emerald-eyed monsters!

Fortunately, his lead-lined casque should shield him from the doom rays....

Threading around parked autos, The Spider swiftly gained the opposite wall. He paused. The rustling was heard no more.

There came a click—distinct and metallic. Moving low, Wentworth slipped in that direction, his black robes fluttering.

A shot rang out. Unseen lead ricocheted off a concrete pillar. Across the gloomy space, there was a flash of fire, brief, but telling.

In the flash, two venomous eyes stared murderously from the silken folds of a black hood. The Dictator!

Snarling, the hooded fiend fired again. The Spider was already moving. Slugs sniped at him, hunting for a vital spot. He dropped into a crouch, firing back unerringly.

Luger-driven hot lead had sped true. A muffled voice made an ugly sound. *"Ugh!"* There was a scramble of frantic feet, followed by the slamming of a door that was not made of wood or steel.

Then there was only silence.

The Spider moved cautiously, found the wall where Count Calypsa had lurked in the framing of a hidden door. There was no sign of that door now. Only cracked concrete. The cracks did not suggest a pattern... except to imply a cobweb.

It was difficult to tell where the door lay with any precision. Peering down at the concrete floor, The Spider spied semicircular scratches indicating a heavy portal had opened at the spot. There were impressions of motor oil. While not recognizable as footprints, it was The Spider's judgment that a man had stepped in a puddle of motor oil and made messy tracks.

If the Dictator had disappeared down this passage, it stood to reason that Steel Mask had preceded him....

Furiously, The Spider attempted to breach the hidden exit, but there was no discoverable catch, nor any indication of how to open the thing. It was so cunningly made it was difficult to discern the seams that should frame a door.

Cursing in temporary defeat, The Spider swirled around and

made for the sanitation truck, his silken cape belling behind him, disclosing its inner web.

Here at least was a measure of victory. Both foes had fled into the catacombs of New York City. But they had left behind their greatest prize. The shattered remnants of the Green Meteorite of Doom....

Rushing to the driver's side, The Spider yanked back the lever that opened one disposal hatch. It had not been fully closed. Now he peered in.

In the darkness of the container portion of the truck, fragments of green material from some other realm of space glowed like emeralds that burned with an unholy yet lambent light. They pulsed, as if somehow alive....

No fear showed on The Spider's face as he stared into that shiny space. Inwardly, he prayed that his lead-lined casque would protect him from the awful radiation. But, of course, that was a mere hope—a calculated risk that it would. Otherwise, Steel Mask could not have driven the truck all the way from Central Park to this hidden spot safely.

Of that, The Spider had no doubt whatsoever.

SLAMMING THE hatch shut and dogging it, The Spider showed sudden determination. His eyes became steely, as steely as the blue-steel mask that half concealed his set features.

Moving painfully, Wentworth climbed behind the wheel and found that the keys were still in the ignition. There he sat, pondering while unearthly death pulsed in the container directly behind his seat.

If he opened the garage door and called to Commissioner Kirkpatrick, he would be exposing the police to grave peril, not to mention all but revealing himself to be The Spider.

That would not do.

Richard Wentworth considered all eventualities. None were pleasant. All were dangerous. And all but one was undeniably fatal....

The tight set of his jaw indicated that he had made up his mind.

Grim-eyed, he went to the electric button that caused the garage door to roll upward on its tracks. Pausing only for a moment, he depressed this. As the machinery whined and toiled ceilingward, he rushed back to the truck.

Pulling the cab door shut, he keyed the ignition and pressed the gas pedal.

Bright sunlight came streaming in through the lifting door edge. He choked the engine. Diesel fumes quickly filled the garage interior.

Hoarse shouting came from the police blockade.

Distinctly, someone yelled, "Here it comes!"

At that moment, the sanitation truck lurched forward, climbed a concrete incline and rolled out onto the sidewalk, tires jarring as they breached the curbstone. From its radiator grille clouds of angry steam billowed!

Wentworth cursed. He had forgotten that the engine had been cracked previously.

Someone spying the steel casque encasing his head jumped to a conclusion, unable to see clearly through the engine steam.

"Look! It's that damn steel-skulled devil!"

The Spider wrenched the wheel to the right, and its front ties rolled over the curb and dropped, jouncing. He was on the empty thoroughfare.

The police had kept a sensible distance. That gave The Spider a clear advantage. He began accelerating while they were still gathering their forces.

No gunfire erupted. Not at first.

Piloting the steaming sanitation truck down deserted Forty-second Street, The Spider abruptly lunged in the direction of the East River. It was the shortest distance across town.

This was a mad, desperate gamble he was taking. Escape from

the law was not uppermost in The Spider's mind. No, he had in mind a higher game, a loftier goal. His intention was to drive the sanitation truck to the East River and send it plunging into its waters, where its radiations could be confined. It would be necessary to evacuate a certain portion of the city, but it could be done.

As the blunt prow of the sanitation truck accelerated, smashing through a line of police sawhorses, well-placed bullets began banging and punching holes in the truck's bulky steel body, adding to its battered exterior.

Naturally, The Spider would not shoot back; he never fired at policemen. But the holes, the damn bullet holes, would cause the radiation to leak out more strongly. He needed to frighten the police into withholding their fire.

And so he did what he needed to do. The only thing he could think to do.

Throwing back his head, he gave forth with the wild, metallic laughter of The Spider. The sinister sound lifted above the truck engine and froze the blood of every man who heard it.

"Holy hell!" a cop yelled. "That's not Stahlmaske! *That's the damn Spider!*"

Stanley Kirkpatrick heard that cry. Hoarsely, he gasped, "The Spider." Under his breath, he added, "Dick. My God, what are you thinking?"

Bluecoats lunged for their radio cars with the clear intent of pursuing the escaping sanitation truck.

Behind the wheel of the police limousine, Sergeant Carter warned, "Looks like he's headed east, Commissioner."

Frowning, Kirkpatrick said tersely, "Yes. To the river!"

"What good is that going to do?"

Kirkpatrick's saturnine features gathered in thought, the action making his military mustache points quirk. "The Spider may be an outlaw, but he is no madman. He dared that building for one purpose and one purpose alone. To rid the city of the Green Meteorite. Unless I miss my guess, The Spider is headed for the East River, determined to drown the insidious meteor and bring its mindless reign of horror to a conclusion."

"Well, if that's his game, he can't get far. Can he? The doom rays will get to him—drill into his brain—just like the others."

"Yes," admitted Kirkpatrick thickly. "Just like the others...."

Chapter 29

THE SPIDER FAILS

DOWN BUSY Sixth Avenue shot the black roadster belonging to James Christopher, known in the archives of the United States Intelligence Service as Operator 5.

Beside him sat G-8, his open, wind-burned features undisguised. It could be seen that the lines of his face were regular, and leanly muscled... a perfect face for a master of disguise....

Both men were grim as they listened to the dashboard short-wave radio. It was tuned to the police frequency band. A dispatcher's voice crackled.

"City sanitation truck heading east on East Forty-second Street. All cars be advised to stay well clear of it. Pursue, but do not attempt to intercept. Danger too great. That is all."

"The Spider must be a madman to think he can get away with that truck!" gritted James Christopher.

G-8 nodded. "The police dare not approach, but neither can it get very far. Drop me off at Bryant Park. I'll reclaim my gyro."

"No time for that!" Operator 5 snapped. "If we hurry, we may head off the truck."

"Sure. But what then?"

A haunted look came into James Christopher's darkening blue eyes. "I do not know," he confessed.

Responding to his foot pressure, the Diesel engine propelled the speedy roadster into a crosstown street. Operator 5 honked his horn at every intersection. It blared as the powerful automobile roared through, for there was no time to waste. Every second counted....

HURTLING DOWN East Forty-second like a careening dread-nought, the battered truck flew. Thus far, the miraculous luck of The Spider was holding out. Traffic ahead was sparse. Police sedans howled their wild cry of pursuit.

No more bullets struck. No doubt Kirkpatrick had warned them against puncturing the sanitation truck. Its steel sides were no protection against the escaping rays. Not the way lead shielded it. But neither was it negligible.

Up ahead loomed Tudor City Place, a luxury apartment build-ing surrounded by thickly-settled tenement buildings. If he could but reach it....

In back, the fragments of meteorite clinked and jostled with each rocking turn. The truck was now on a dead run. The Spider did not stop for the lights. So he blared his horn and crashed on through.

Amazingly, his luck held.

Then—*the unexpected!* From the cross street a black roadster whirled into view. The Spider's eyes narrowed. He eyed the machine, recognized the youthful face of the driver through the windscreen.

"Christopher!" he hissed. "What in heaven's name does he intend to do? Doesn't he grasp the danger?"

Seemingly oblivious to his peril, Operator 5's roaring machine lunged ahead, engine crying out a song of power. Front tires turning sharply, he braked—blocking the way!

Wrenching the wheel with both hands, The Spider threw back his helmeted head, gave out a challenging laugh, then wrestled the steering wheel, sending the sanitation truck climbing onto the sidewalk, smashing through a mailbox and knocking over the iron stanchion of a streetlight standard, further cracking the engine, which vomited more scalding steam, coating the windshield.

Out of the roadster popped two heads. Christopher and G-8!

Christopher lifted an automatic and fired a single warning shot into the air.

G-8 cradled his Tommy gun close to his leather flying jacket. But The Spider merely laughed at that. The Flying Spy had exhausted his ammunition drums back at the Electric Building. Unlikely that he could have acquired additional shells in the interim, but it was not impossible.

"You men keep your distance!" Wentworth yelled through the open window. "You know what cargo I carry!"

Instead of replying, Operator 5 lowered his automatic and took aim, sending a bullet smacking into the sanitation truck's front tire.

The inner tube blew out. The Spider cursed, then jammed the accelerator to the floorboards, producing billows of steam that obscured the way. Its moist heat penetrated the cabin, suffusing it with intolerable warmth.

Struggling, the sanitation truck lumbered on, grinding along in second gear. Another shot came, but it missed the rear tire by the barest margin.

Rounding the blocking roadster, nudging it aside, The Spider gained the street again. The jouncing machine picked up speed, one tire wobbling alarmingly.

It had been Richard Wentworth's plan to push the machine to its upper speed limit once the East River was in sight. That plan was no longer feasible. The ruined engine began laboring, while the struggling tire would retard its forward progress.

Still, he held the road, hunkered down and pushed the truck to its mechanical limits, slapping the horn button frantically to warn drivers coming up the side streets.

One grey-blue eye went to the driver's-door mirror. In its bouncing surface, he spied the black roadster, its doors open. The two men were climbing back aboard. With a surge of Diesel-engine power, they gave chase.

Wentworth cursed anew.

"The fools! The damned fools. Do they want the city to collapse in a carnival of chaos?"

The two men were agents of the United States government. He could not bring harm to them... no more than he could injure a beat cop doing his duty.

Lifting out of the seat, The Spider all but stood on the accelerator pedal as he urged the struggling truck closer and closer to the East River.

It responded with the diminished power of its cracked Diesel engine. The wheel rims were chewing up the tire, and the steering wheel wobbled in his hands. He held it down, keeping it steady... and then he saw the dock.

An ancient wharf, falling into ruin. Its pilings were thick—old but still stable.

Smashing through a chainlink fence, he shot the garbage truck onto the wharf, where it careened along the half-rotted planks.

Holding the vibrating wheel steady was all but impossible. The Spider kicked open the driver's-side door, prepared to leap to safety.

Only after the front wheels jumped off the far end of the dock did he do so.

It was no graceful leap. It was more of the mad plunge of a desperate man.

Splashing awkwardly, Wentworth entered the water. Only a few watery feet away, the sanitation truck lurched over the wooden edge. Lurched—and stuck!

It hung there, radiator grille exhaling hot steam, its rear tires smoking. The stink of rubber filled the air. Momentum had not been enough to throw it out into the water... the engine had finally gasped its last....

As he sank below the surface, Wentworth fought back a choking rage.

He had been so close, so close....

Kicking his feet, he attempted to push himself up, but he was too weak. He found himself sinking. Sinking *headfirst*....

Only then did he realize his predicament.

The lead-lined casque! He was still wearing it. Of course, he needed to. It was indispensable, essential to protect his living brain from the terrible lesions induced by the mind-destroying green radiation. That same metallic helmet was pulling him down... down to a watery grave. He could not fight its weight. Not when it was lined with heavy lead.

As he sank, Richard Wentworth cursed himself for a blind fool. "I failed. Failed...."

Chapter 30

BRINK OF VICTORY

CAPTAIN GEORGE Gate leveled a finger at the tottering sanitation truck, its crushed radiator grille hanging in space.

"It didn't go over!"

"I see that," snapped James Christopher. "And The Spider jumped—jumped for his life."

"At least he's not getting away with that meteor. We saw to that."

James Christopher's crystal-blue eyes narrowed. "What if he wasn't trying to get away? What if his goal was to plunge the meteorite fragments into the river?"

"You mean to get them out of the city safely?"

Christopher nodded firmly. "Or as safely as could be managed. Water isn't going to block the rays, but it might help inhibit them."

"It might at that," agreed G-8.

Tone turning decisive, James Christopher directed, "Step out of the car."

He braked abruptly. The roadster's gleaming grille faced the rotting pilings.

"What are you thinking?" demanded G-8.

"I think," declared Operator 5, "that by God I will finish what The Spider started."

"Good luck!"

G-8 stepped to the side, and James Christopher ran his roadster up onto the dock, picking up speed. There was not much to the dock. A hundred feet or so. But the steel body of the roadster was bulletproof. The hurtling machine was heavy. It slammed into the back of the sanitation truck and knocked it ahead—and over!

The four-ton machine tumbled into the water with a gigantic splashing. It sank. The roadster dry-skidded briefly. Operator 5 jammed it into reverse. He knew he had driven into the zone of danger and was anxious to reverse out of it as quickly as possible.

One arm across the back of his seat, he turned his head around and kept the wheel steady as the roadster ran backward, gears whining.

Dropping back onto land, he threw open the door. G-8 climbed in. They drove away from the vicinity, stopping three blocks north.

Stepping out, they looked out over the water.

G-8 shaded his eyes with one hand.

"No sign of The Spider."

"The damn fool was wearing a helmet when he went into the water. It had to have been constructed of lead, or at least lined with it. Otherwise, he would have turned into a maddened maniac before he got this far."

G-8 nodded. "Makes sense to me."

Suddenly, Operator 5 was shucking off his coat, exposing his vest and the gold chain that draped its front. He stepped out of his shoes, then removed his belt containing the thin, deadly rapier.

Handing his automatic to G-8, he said decisively, "I'm going in—into the water."

The G-2 captain blocked his way, arresting him with his frank gaze.

"For God's sake! You can't do that! He went in too close to the truck. In order to reach him, you'd have to swim through the danger zone. What would be the point? It's death to try—sheer suicide!"

James Christopher's eyes sharpened. His voice when he spoke was torn.

"The Spider may have saved the city from that meteorite. Whatever his crimes, whatever his motivations, he did this city— and the nation—a good turn today. I can't just let him drown."

"You can't throw away your life, either. Think sensibly. The Spider knew the risk he was taking. If he's down there, he's probably dead by now."

Operator 5 went stiff of face, a grey pallor darkening his complexion.

"You're right," he said heavily. "I was too rash." Picking up his coat, he donned it carefully, then reclaimed his belt and shoes.

When he was once more respectably attired, he looked around and saw curious crowds gathering.

"We are going to have to keep these people away from the dock. Come to think of it, this neighborhood must be quarantined. There is no other way. The fate of The Spider can wait."

G-8 nodded in agreement.

"Once we have the situation under control, a towboat can drag that sanitation truck out to sea, where it will only trouble the fish."

Operator 5 nodded somberly. "Maybe The Spider was thinking along those same lines."

With a final backward glance at the heaving water, the two government agents turned to go about their tasks....

ONLY A few hundred yards away, The Spider was working his way along the muddy river bottom, crawling like his namesake, struggling to creep out of range of the insidious radiation.

With every step, blood seeped out from the wound in his right leg and small bubbles escaped his firm lips. When they reached the surface, they popped with tiny sounds. Only the circling seagulls noticed them.

Very soon, the minute bubbles ceased to rise....

Chapter 31

"THE SPIDER IS DEAD!"

WITH A sharp squealing of tires entangled with siren wails, a squad of police radio cars arrived at the East River docks.

Bluecoats emerged, took stock of the scene.

Operator 5 strode up and presented his credentials.

"The Spider drove the sanitation truck into the water," he declared. "Looks like he drowned doing so. We're going to have to evacuate the docks immediately. Quarantine the neighborhood until the truck can be salvaged and hauled out to sea."

The two police officers listening did not know what to do. They did not take orders from the Intelligence Service, but they knew enough to respect an authorized representative of the government.

Their conundrum was solved when the official limousine bearing Commissioner Stanley Kirkpatrick rolled up and he stepped out.

His saturnine face frowning, he accosted James Christopher, saying, "I will not upbraid you for your brave actions in attempting to halt the refuse truck, but once again I must remind you that policing the city falls under my jurisdiction."

"I just informed your men that this neighborhood will require evacuation in advance of quarantining," James Christopher stated, unmoved.

"I'll see that this is done," Kirkpatrick returned brusquely. "Now, did anyone see what befell The Spider?"

"If that really was The Spider..." G-8 mused.

Kirkpatrick glowered. "I have every reason to believe that The

Spider hijacked the truck," he said in a brittle, authoritative tone. "And my question stands unanswered."

"The Spider jumped as the truck tottered on the lip of the dock," Operator 5 reported. "He did not come up for air. In my opinion, he could not. He was wearing a heavy metal helmet. It preserved him from the meteorite's effects, but probably led to his drowning."

Kirkpatrick made futile fists at his sides. "I'll have the river dragged for his body," he said heavily.

"If I were you, Commissioner, I'd wait until the truck and its cargo are hauled outside the three-mile limit. Anyone attempting to salvage that body is subject to the radium-like rays. A dozen inches of water are equivalent to one inch of lead shielding, but we cannot know how much water is proof against those unearthly rays."

Kirkpatrick's white-knuckled fists hardened. He did not care for taking advice from someone so young. But the Intelligence agent made sense. Finally, he nodded silently.

Turning, he began issuing clipped orders.

While James Christopher and Captain Gate returned to the black roadster and wheeled out of the vicinity, the police once again set to work transferring their sawhorse-and-barbed-wire barricades to the streets leading to the dock in question.

The evacuation did not go smoothly, but progress was made through the afternoon.

It was mandatory to stay as far back from the dock as practical. From time to time, Kirkpatrick's gaze swept in the direction of the sparkling water and he winced in pain.

This time, The Spider appeared to be gone for certain.

Wintry eyes hard, Kirkpatrick hoped that this did not mean the end of Richard Wentworth, but he was all but certain that it did. His only hope lay in the fact that a false Spider had figured in the previous night's saturnalia of terror.

Until the body was recovered, there was no knowing for certain who had saved the city from the meteorite menace....

AFTERNOON PAPERS screamed their headlines.

SPIDER DEAD!

Mystery man drowns attempting to steal deadly meteorite pieces!

STEEL MASK SOUGHT

Long-dead war criminal believed to be back from the grave. Authorities dumbfounded. Doubt hovers over the true identity of the helmeted marauder, and confusion reigns over his motives for perpetrating high crimes against the city.

There was no mention of Count Calypsa, the hidden Dictator. He had not figured in the hellish activities that had commenced on Halloween night. Not publicly. Only Stanley Kirkpatrick and a few others knew that he was back on the scene.

Against the threat of the Green Meteorite, Count Calypsa seemed like the least of the city's worries. Even there, Kirkpatrick harbored deep concerns.

The threat of Steel Mask, the Germanic Black Knight long believed to be dead, was terrible enough. But he was only one man. Count Calypsa headed an organization of secret agents that had infiltrated every aspect of New York's civic life.

In the aftermath of Calypsa's first attempt to seize control of Manhattan, Kirkpatrick had uncovered many of these agents. Some even in the Police Department. But not all of them had been rooted out. No doubt many remained in place, unknown and, worse—unsuspected... awaiting whispered word to do the bidding of the would-be Dictator.

The Spider had succeeded in wresting from their evil grasp the power of the Green Meteorite. Count Calypsa and Steel Mask would not be so easily bested.

The Electric Building had been thoroughly searched. No trace of the duo had been found. No doubt they would surface again. And conceivably soon.

That challenge would have to await the cleansing of New York City. The last pockets of zombies were being exterminated. It was a harsh word—extermination—but it fit the situation. The Governor had finally succumbed to reason. Even now, National Guard trucks were en route. The city would be secured. Order would be restored. The dead would be buried and life would go on.

Only after civic normalcy was restored would the hunt for Steel Mask and Count Calypsa resume in earnest. Stanley Kirkpatrick looked forward to that near day.

For he fully intended to avenge his late friend, Richard Wentworth... alias The Spider....

Chapter 32

THE LAST GASP

IN THE sunlight-shot waters of the East River waterfront, flounder and fluke swam away in agitation. A few striped bass investigated the violent splash created by the drowned sanitation truck. The machine's nose had caved in upon itself smashing into the silt of the river bed. That disturbed silt threw up muddy, watery clouds that dispersed specks of buried particulate food, attracting the fish.

They darted through the spreading clouds, biting at morsels, before swimming on.

Here and there, flat eyes took on the radiance of emeralds.... Because they dwelt underwater, the rays emanating from either side of their flat faces caused the chilly water to warm and bubble slightly, but otherwise no significant disturbance resulted.

No harm to anything except the fish themselves, which swam aimlessly, as if blind, and then convulsing, curled up lifelessly, falling to the seabed where they became food for other, uncontaminated fish....

Forty yards or more from the spreading cloud, a desperate man crawled along the silty bottom of the river.

Weighed down by a lead-lined steel helmet that he dared not remove, The Spider crawled like his namesake, dragging along slowly, desperately, for his life. He knew he dared not fling off the heavy headpiece, lest he suffer a fate worse than mere drowning. Yet he refused to drown.

After releasing the last air bubbles from his tortured lungs, he felt a burning deep within him. It rose in his throat. It seemed to strike his brain like a geyser of consuming fire....

Bereft of life-giving oxygen, strength even, The Spider yet crawled. Crawled as far away as he could from the awful influence of the broken meteorite... for he knew that, like lead, water baffled deadly radiations... but he knew not how many feet or yards of water were necessary to shield him safely....

He was like an animal now, crawling, not daring to breathe, his head weighed down, hanging, hanging as if it lacked the strength to hold itself erect.

A roaring came to his ears. His eyes were shut. But even so, the dancing of sunlight on the river surface made dappled light through his closed eyelids.

He was close to death now. Whether Richard Wentworth or The Spider—for the two were hardly separate in spirit, although very different in body—he was down to his last iota of strength.

Breathe! Breathe!

When he was at the ultimate point beyond which his screaming lungs could not refuse to inhale—even though that would mean ingesting seawater and suffering an ignominious death—The Spider threw himself back and balanced on his knees in the muck, flung the helmet off with both hands. Then, with a final, desperate effort, uncoiled his legs, propelling himself toward the surface.

Even as his body shot upward, he wondered if it was too late. Too late to reach reviving oxygen. But his worst fear was hammering at his pounding brain. He had crawled as far as he was able. What if, what if, he had not crawled far *enough*...?

THE POLICE evacuation consisted of going door-to-door and ordering people out of their homes. It was a messy affair, one which required the brandishing threat of police truncheons, if not the occasional application of the same blunt instruments.

Although all did not go smoothly, the operation proceeded with ruthless efficiency, for lives were at stake.

"Come on, come on!" one bluecoat shouted. "Do you want to turn into a green-eyed maniac? And become a threat to your own family? Get a move on!"

In the noisy exodus, one man moved in the opposite direction, a husky man, whose Gascon jaw was set and tight, jaw muscles clenching until they stood out like walnuts.

Ronald Jackson had been waiting for the return of Richard Wentworth scant blocks from the besieged Electric Building. When the sanitation truck had come crashing out of the garage, careening onto the street, he had been among the vehicles trailing the runaway truck.

Forced to keep his distance during the chase, Jackson parked the Daimler as close to the docks as he dared and exited, slipping through alleys and disreputable streets until he reached the waterfront.

Encountering Stanley Kirkpatrick, he loitered around the corner and listened as hard-pressed police officers shouted orders.

One sergeant rushed up, accosted his superior.

"Pardon me, Commissioner. We got a gaggle of reporters pushing at our lines. They want to know what's what. Do you want to talk to them?"

Kirkpatrick drew himself up. "Inform the press that I will have a statement when the evacuation is complete. In the meanwhile, you may confirm that The Spider is dead. Tell them for me that he may have saved the city. That is all."

"Yes, sir," said the sergeant, racing off to convey the sensational news.

Hearing this, and putting the pieces together, Ronald Jackson swallowed a furious oath.

Kirkpatrick studied the docks and the dirty water of the East River. His sharp gaze noticed the blunt snout of the Daimler limousine peeping out from the corner of an old brick building.

Squaring his shoulders, he marched for the machine, his saturnine features working with conflicting emotions.

Stepping out from behind the apartment building where he was lurking, Jackson trooped up to Kirkpatrick, saying, "Beg pardon, Commissioner. I've been looking all over for you. Mr. Wentworth asked me to give you this. Said it was urgent."

Halting, Kirkpatrick accepted the ten-dollar bill, frowning like a storm cloud preparing to unleash a downpour.

Jackson added, "It's funny money—counterfeit. You can see the word 'silver' spelled as 'sliver.' "

The police official studied the bill as if not quite comprehending it.

Without looking up to meet Jackson's frank gaze, he murmured gravely, "I regret to inform you that The Spider is believed drowned...."

Kirkpatrick looked up sharply. He studied the chauffeur's features. They did not alter an iota.

"The Spider is no never-mind to me..." Jackson said casually.

"Where is Wentworth at this moment?"

"Can't say, Commissioner. He sent me on this errand. Imagine he's visiting Miss van Sloan in the hospital."

The two men locked gazes, but neither flinched in his regard. "I see. Thank him for me... if you see him... will you, Jackson?"

"I will, sir."

"Now kindly evacuate the waterfront. It is dangerous to tarry." Kirkpatrick's voice was thick with repressed emotion, verging on hoarseness.

RONALD JACKSON retreated to the Daimler. He drove only a short distance. Parking in another waterfront alley, he exited. Creeping carefully to the docks, he looked out over the waters, but saw nothing. Nothing at all....

The temptation to plunge into the chilly river was more than he could resist. Ronald Jackson and Richard Wentworth had saved one another's lives in No Man's Land long ago. He was not about to leave his former commanding officer to float underwater, whether living or otherwise. It was the least one soldier could do for another....

Jackson was removing his shoes and his grey uniform tunic when a thin sound reached his ears.

It was a whistle. Pitched very low, it was airy and thin. And its thinness was the thinness of a strand of spider silk....

Jackson's heavy chest expanded in surprise. He first heard that sound in the trenches some twenty years ago. It was a sound Major Richard Wentworth made when he wanted to signal without words. These were the same five thin notes The Spider employed when he wished to communicate with his civilian aides.

"He lives!" Jackson gasped. "The Major lives...."

He ran down to one of the docks, the one parallel to the wharf over which the sanitation truck had splashed from view.

The sound came again. Low, thin and weak. It did not have much duration. But as Jackson stood at the dock's edge, sweeping the watery surface with his steady brown eyes, he could hear a whistling gasp, as of a man gulping air—gulping as much oxygen as could be pulled into his struggling lungs.

Jackson whistled back. Loud and sharp.

He waited for a response. It came.

A weak voice croaked out, "Jackson?"

"Major! Where are you?"

The answer was slow in coming. Wentworth sounded as if he were struggling for breath.

"Under your... feet."

Jackson got down on his hands and knees and peered between the weathered planks. Then he saw the dark-haired head bobbing in the water. Not quite bobbing. For Richard Wentworth was clinging to a rotted piling. Clinging weakly. Even now, one hand was slipping.

"Hold on, Major!"

Jackson slid down the piling, dropped into the water and splashed over.

"Rest easy, Major. I've got you. Just hold on. I know you're all but spent. I'll get you to shore."

But the body in his arms was unresponsive. As if lacking neck bones, Wentworth's head rolled over to one side.

Keeping his boss's head out of the water, Ronald Jackson hauled him landward until his feet could touch river bottom. There, he lifted Wentworth into his strong arms and carried him to shore.

The loyal aide did not bother with his shoes. Barefoot, he walked his master back to the waiting Daimler limousine. Carefully, he placed him in the back seat and closed the door.

But not before checking to see that Richard Wentworth's respiration was steady. Steady yes, but not strong....

Slamming the Daimler into gear, Jackson sent it hammering north, speeding up Second Avenue toward Sutton Place. It was fortunate that the police cordon had not yet been put into place along this thoroughfare.

As he raced back home, Ronald Jackson shot anxious glances into the back seat through the rear-vision mirror. Richard Wentworth lay supine—sprawled like a waterlogged spider plucked from a sink.

Jackson soon swerved onto the access road that led to the gates of the Sutton Place redoubt. There, Richard Wentworth would be safe. There, the family physician would be called. There, he could recuperate.

When the limousine's nose approached the gate, Richard Wentworth suddenly spasmed. He sat up as if electrified. His eyes wild, he looked around him. For a moment, he seemed not to understand where he sat. But then recognition dawned.

"Where are we?"

"Almost home, Major," reassured Jackson.

"God in heaven," muttered Wentworth. "It was nearly the end."

"We'll get you fixed up in no time, sir."

The Daimler coasted to a stop and Jackson engaged the whistle that would actuate the electric gates.

The familiar sound seemed to penetrate Richard Wentworth's agonized brain. For a new energy seized him. His eyes were shocked.

"Jackson!"

"Yes, Major?"

"Jackson. I crawled as hard and as fast and as far as I could, but I do not know that I crawled far enough. Do you understand what I am saying?"

"I think I do, Major. The meteorite...."

"Yes, the damned meteorite. I may have been subjected to its accursed rays—subjected without benefit of my lead helmet. Do you understand what that means?"

"You know I do," returned Jackson somberly.

Now Richard Wentworth's tones were urgent and pleading.

"Jackson, I want you to promise me something. I want you to keep close watch on my eyes. Should they show any signs of turning... *green*...."

"Don't you think they would've done that by now?"

"For God's sake, listen to me, Jackson! If my eyes change color, I want you to promise me that you will immediately blow my brains out. Without hesitation. Is that understood, *Sergeant?*"

The emphasis on the final word was like a sting penetrating the former top sergeant's soldierly soul. Although these two men were civilians now, in each man's heart of hearts they remained a superior officer and his loyal aide.

"I shall not fail you, Major Wentworth," promised Jackson in a heavy tone. He again took the silver whistle into his mouth and blew on it shrilly.

The heavy gates of Sutton Place rolled open and the Daimler slipped back into its warren....

Chapter 33

THWARTED PLAN

THE RADIO receiver in the corner was tuned to a news program. The announcer's excited voice literally jumped out of the speaker grille.

"Flash! This just in! The Governor has declared the city rid of the menace created by the Green Meteor that landed in Central Park last night.

"In the last hours, there have been no new reports of stricken citizens. Police Commissioner Kirkpatrick has declared in no uncertain terms that the threat to the city has been all but concluded. The Green Zone is no more. Central Park is once again open to the public.

"The National Guard has cordoned off a stretch of the East River waterfront between Sutton Place and the Queensboro Bridge. Citizens are being kept out of their homes while arrangements are made to tow the sunken sanitation truck containing the broken remnants of the mysterious meteorite out to sea where, it is believed, they will no longer constitute a threat to human life.

"In an ironic note, the notorious individual known only as The Spider is being credited with saving the city from further turmoil. It is not known at this hour if The Spider was acting in good faith or was intent on purloining the meteorite for his own dire purposes. The President of the United States, whose life the mysterious vigilante saved last month, has issued a public statement of condolence.

"The whereabouts of the man the police are calling Stahlmaske, alias Steel Mask, remain unknown. But a police task force

has been formed, and a dragnet has been cast over the city. The police anticipate his apprehension in short order."

Seated in a heavy leather chair, Stahlmaske boomed out a hollow laugh.

"They think they can apprehend me as if I were but a common criminal! Do they not know my reputation? Have the passing years erased my infamy?"

Seated behind his mahogany desk, Count Calypsa, the self-styled Dictator, frowned. He was not wearing his customary hood. A bandage swathed his upper skull. The meaty face of the illusory Casey Grogan looked as if it had just stepped out of the prize-fighting ring. He had acquired one of The Spider's bullets in the shoulder. A second slug had cut a gory groove along his ribs. The stoppered bottle of morphine pills resting on the desk was noticeably diminished....

"Some of the men who patrol the city streets had hardly been born when you were last reported on," grunted Calypsa.

Stahlmaske looked around him, admiring his sumptuous surroundings.

"This is quite remarkable," he amused. "If I did not know any better, I would swear a blood oath that I sat in the same chambers which we formerly occupied. The draperies are identical. Even the desk. I could not point to any detail that was not present in the other one. Only by flinging aside the window curtains would I know that we are now holding forth in the Gotham Arms, and not the Electric Building."

Pressing a cold compress to his forehead, Count Calypsa said smugly, "When I set up my organization months ago, I knew that the risk of The Spider—or for that matter, the police—breaching my hidden headquarters was not inconsiderable. Thus, I had two constructed. The tunnel between this apartment building and the Electric Building was not merely for clandestine comings and goings. It was the escape passage between my two headquarters.

No doubt the police combed every inch of the Electric Building, looking for my original suite of offices. Perhaps they will find it. Perhaps not. But they will not find this one. They have not the imagination to consider its existence. Therefore, we are safe here, you and I."

Stahlmaske chuckled like a discordant chime. "You need no longer live in dread of The Spider. Just as I no longer fear my detested foe, G-8. He vexed me for so many years, thwarting my plans, that I actually grew afraid of him—terribly so. It has taken long years for me to regain my nerve and restore my courage. Now I fear nothing. And no one."

Outside, the weekday hum of traffic was returning. The police had removed their sawhorses and barbed-wire entanglements from the street below, reassembling them by the East River.

Count Calypsa remarked, "You—or should I say we?—are bereft of our most potent weapon. All but the pieces you salvaged from the sanitation truck before we fled the Electric Building."

In one corner of the room, there lay a small pile of lead pipes. They were of short length, but each end was stopped by a threaded lead cap.

Stahlmaske had one of these pipes in hand. It shifted around in his black-gloved paw, a heavy but inert thing.

"Those that I salvaged may prove sufficient to further our plan. Especially now that the city thinks the menace of the Green Meteorite has been abolished."

Calypsa adjusted his ice pack to the other side of his broad head.

"What good are they? Sealed in lead that way."

Stahlmaske shrugged elaborately. It caused his heavy black helmet to shift ponderously on his broad shoulders.

"These caps can be unscrewed, of course." He lifted the object and pointed it in Calypsa's direction. "But with one end open, I could wield this like an electric torch—one whose rays are most pernicious."

"A clumsy weapon," remarked Calypsa. "But I imagine it would be serviceable."

"Serviceable, if unwieldy, as you say," allowed Stahlmaske. "But if I engineer a baffle at one end, and a lever with which to actuate it, it becomes a much more practical weapon. The man carrying it, provided he stays safely behind the open aperture, may wield it with impunity."

Calypsa nodded agreeably. "I have agents who could do that dangerous work for us." He tapped the boxy Call-o-phone at his elbow. "They will do my bidding without question. For I own their lives—never mind the details. But what do you intend to accomplish?"

THE MAN in the Steel Mask steepled his fingers. "What I came to America to accomplish, *mein Graf.* Namely the demise of G-8. But he did not fall. Before, I served the Kaiser of Germany. This was in war. After the war, I required peace and sufficient time to heal. The Kaiser is no more. Now Germany has a chancellor—a great man. Perhaps a man of destiny. He mustered me out of retirement. I do not know if he is contemplating a new war, or what his aims are. But he has charged me with a secret mission, and I intend to carry it out. For it suits me very much. The destruction of G-8 is my only goal in America."

"I see. I believe I understand. Your leader, having been in the war himself, well remembers that G-8 smashed many German military plans almost single-handedly. He wants him out of the picture, should war come again."

"Precisely. You might say that the death of G-8 will mark the first cannon shot of the coming war. I tell you these things because I know you are no lover of America. And the things that we say to one another will remain between us. *Nein?*"

"Understood," agreed Calypsa.

"Good. I know that you desire the death of Commissioner

Kirkpatrick as much as I seek G-8's head. Together, we will spread terror throughout the city and lure both antagonists to their doom. Perhaps they will die the death of mindless meteorite-crazed maniacs. That would be fitting. Do you not think so, my friend?"

The radio had been playing classical music. Now the announcer broke in urgently.

"Flash! This just in! The Office of the Commissioner has announced that counterfeit ten-dollar bills have been discovered circulating in the city. These phonies are easily detected, however. For they are Silver Certificates—and the counterfeiter must have had an off day. The word 'silver' is clearly misspelled. Commissioner Kirkpatrick has asked all citizens to surrender any such counterfeit tens to Centre Street Police Headquarters. That is all."

Count Calypsa leaped to his feet in a rage. He pounded his desk, sending pills scattering in all directions.

"No, no!" he bellowed. "It is too soon! *Too soon!*"

"Calm yourself," encouraged Stahlmaske.

Shaking his fists, the Count raged on. "Kirkpatrick's efforts have thwarted my plan to flood the city with counterfeit money! It was to be the next wave in my conquest of Manhattan. I went to tremendous effort to have quantities of ten-dollar bills printed. My agents planted them throughout the city's agencies, which would have been perfect purveyors of these phony bills. But Kirkpatrick and his accursed bluecoats have discovered the flaw I introduced into my counterfeits!"

Stahlmaske rumbled, "You—*deliberately* misspelled a word?"

Count Calypsa paced, fuming. "Yes, yes! Don't you see? No one reads the fine print on money. Once I flooded the city, I intended to instruct one of my Numbers to pretend to have discovered the flaw. This would enable any citizen to recognize the worthless bills. Financial chaos would have resulted. But no more—no more! Kirkpatrick somehow captured a sample before I could unleash my flood of counterfeits. If I do so now, the bills could be traced back to my agents, thus destroying their usefulness to me. My master plan has once again been balked. I was only in the beginning stages of launching this latest scheme when that meteor landed and you and I made common cause.

"Yes, killing Kirkpatrick is as important to me as destroying G-8 is to you. And with The Spider in a watery grave, once we accomplish our aims, we can marshal another plan, one that will be fruitful."

Still clutching the baton-like lead pipe, Stahlmaske stood up abruptly.

"Then it is agreed. You will have your agents bring me the tools I require to transform these lead pipes into formidable doom-ray projectors. Once I have done so, we will undertake spreading fresh terror. When the new zombies appear, no one will know what to make of it. G-8 will come. As will Kirkpatrick. We will deal with them accordingly. Then no one will stand in our way."

Count Calypsa pressed the key illuminating his Call-o-phone and intoned, "Number Fifty-five. I require your expertise...."

Chapter 34

"STAHLMASKE MUST DIE!"

HIGH ON the fifty-fifth floor of the Vertex Building near Fifth Avenue, James Christopher sat in the windowless office of his chief, Z-7, who was addressing him.

"That was sharp work and swift thinking, Operator 5," Z-7 was saying, his eyes glittering like ebon diamonds. "If you hadn't knocked that damned truck into the water when you did, the East Side would be a devil's playground right now."

"Thank you, Chief," said James modestly. "The real credit goes to The Spider—whoever he might be."

"Or was," interjected G-8. The Flying Spy sat in another chair.

Z-7 went on in his deep, resonant voice. "The identity of The Spider is for the police to determine, once his body has been recovered. Our task is to locate Stahlmaske. As you both know, he is a dangerous foreign agent. No doubt the devil has slipped into this country to do mischief. It's up to us to uncover exactly what that mischief is."

James returned crisply, "Don't worry, Chief. Mr. Steel Mask is as good as captured. Count on it."

G-8 laughed politely. "Don't think, because he stands nearly seven feet tall with his skull encased in a black stovepipe, Stahlmaske can't hide effectively. I chased him all over Europe during the World War; he never stayed captured for long. Finding him in a city of this size won't be easy."

Z-7 eyed the Master Spy frankly.

"You know Stahlmaske better than anyone alive. What do you think his purpose might be?"

G-8 did not have to think very long before replying.

"That meteorite was not something you yank out of the sky at a whim. It was a fluke. Stahlmaske and his partner in crime simply took advantage of it. I'd bet my last dollar on that. The brazen way he sneaked into the museum and reclaimed his old helmet makes me think that in doing so his original objective was to call attention to the theft."

"Why?" demanded Z-7.

G-8 shrugged negligently. "To bait me into showing myself."

James Christopher asked, "So you think he is angling for a showdown?"

G-8 nodded. "I'd bet my second last dollar on that score. Speaking of scores, I think Stahlmaske yearns to settle an old one. And I am the bird he aims to settle the score with."

Z-7's shaggy brows knotted together. "Do you really believe it's as simple as all that?"

"Perhaps not that simple. Maybe there's more to it. Could be Berlin is planning to flex her military muscles again. It's just a hunch. But if the German leader sent Stahlmaske over here, it wasn't to reclaim an old war trophy, but to knock me out of action before the fireworks start."

"You make sense!" exclaimed Z-7. "I've been speaking with your commanding officer, as well as Major-General Falk in Washington. Both agree that you should remain attached to our service until the matter of Stahlmaske is concluded—one way or another."

G-8 grinned infectiously, causing ten years to melt from his rangy face.

"I'm itching to finish the job I started back in the Big Fuss."

Z-7's eyes flashed. "Work closely with Operator 5. Hunt Stahlmaske. Stop him in his tracks. I want that black helmet back in its case at the Metropolitan Museum. Empty or full, you understand?"

G-8 laughed good-naturedly.

"You mean that you want his head, don't you?"

"For the good of the nation, Stahlmaske must die. That is all."

The two agents stood up to go.

Unexpectedly, the teletype in the corner began clacking away noisily.

Z-7 rushed over to it. The two agents loitered a moment.

Face tensing, the Intelligence Chief ripped off the ticker tape. His black eyes grew sharp as he turned to speak.

"According to this," he rasped out harshly, "a zombie was just struck down in Times Square."

"Impossible, Chief!" exploded Operator 5. "We have timed these doomed men. They don't last an hour after being infected. The meteorite is in the river now. How could this have happened?"

G-8 inserted, "I'll tell you what happened! Not every chunk of that meteor went into the East River. There must be a few pieces floating around loose. Probably in the hands of Stahlmaske. He's making himself known again. It's bait, I tell you. Bait for me."

Z-7 said sternly, "Take the bait, G-8. Take that bait and cram it down his throat. That is an order."

G-8 started to salute, but checked himself. Z-7 was not a military man.

"Yes, sir. Count on me."

"And count on me to see this mission through to the bitter end," added Operator 5.

The two men exited the office, moved swiftly through several closely-guarded rooms on their way to the elevator.

"We have no leads to Stahlmaske," said James Christopher tightly. "Nothing to go on, except zombie corpses scattered here and there."

"No leads," agreed G-8. "But plenty of bait! You're looking at him. What do you say we take a spin in my gyroplane? Odds are that Stahlmaske will spot it and make a move."

"All right. But it's not just Stahlmaske I'm after now. It's up to us to recover every shard of that Satan-sent meteorite." Abruptly, James snapped his fingers. "I have an idea! The nature of this meteoric radiation is not known, but if we have a Geiger-Muller tube, it might lead us to any loose fragments."

G-8 exclaimed, "Good thinking! They're like mechanical bloodhounds for detecting radioactive stuff. It might just work; we won't know until we try!"

Turning on his heel, Operator 5 ducked into a room where special equipment was stored. In his hands he carried a rectangular box of black composition material. Two knurled rheostat-style knobs and a simple meter were built into its top surface.

"I have requisitioned this Geiger-Muller tube," he explained as they made their way to the elevator bank. "We'll scout the city by air. Should we pass over any meteoric fragments, the scintillation counter will signal."

"I'm with you!" said G-8 with enthusiasm, his boyish grin once again stripping the maturity from his wind-burned features.

The elevator door opened and the two men stepped aboard. Between them, they stood high among the ranks of the finest Intelligence agents America had ever employed. Dedication was written on their faces. Determination, too. Through long years of service, neither man had ever failed to find his quarry, or run him to earth. In their minds, they shared one certainty.

Stahlmaske was doomed!

POLICE COMMISSIONER STANLEY KIRKPATRICK took the report of the lone zombie terrorizing Times Square in his office.

Sergeant Carter brought in the yellow flimsy on which were pasted a white teletype strip cut into short segments.

"Sir! Maniac reported in Times Square! One of our men gunned him down. But not before he torched two civilians. They're all dead now!"

Glancing over the bulletin, Kirkpatrick crumpled it in one hand. "How could this be?"

"Where there is one, sir, we have to be on the lookout for others. You can never know about these things."

The second report arrived fifteen minutes later.

A green-eyed human monster was seen in the vicinity of the former Knickerbocker Theater on Broadway. He had come up from the subway, emerald eyes blazing. Commuters had been set afire. Thankfully, none died. But many had been carried away in ambulances. Their burns were terrible, disfiguring....

"Bring the car around," Kirkpatrick ordered his aide.

Soon the police limousine was racing up Broadway. Times Square was being cleared. Where there had been one zombie, fear of others had taken hold. No need for a police evacuation. Terror had caused brave New Yorkers to flee the scene.

Sergeant Carter pulled over to the curbing. Kirkpatrick stormed out and sought one of his plainclothes detectives.

"Let me have your report, detective."

"He got away in the crowd, sir. We're trying to find him. If we don't—"

"If you do not," finished Kirkpatrick, "he will burn out like a battery in short order. In the meantime, there's no telling how much havoc he will wreak. My God, where are they coming from?"

"It stands to reason there are fragments of that meteor floating around the city. Small fragments."

Kirkpatrick studied the prospect of Times Square—the Crossroads of the World—deserted in broad daylight! It was an unheard-of sight, staggering.

"I fear you are correct, detective. Otherwise, we would be seeing hordes of these man-monsters. Our job now is damnably difficult. Rather than seeking a large and dangerous meteorite, we may be looking for splinters."

The detective looked around anxiously. "It's like needles and haystacks, sir. Needles and haystacks."

"Carry on, detective," said Kirkpatrick, pivoting to stalk back to his waiting limousine.

BEHIND THE wheel, Sergeant Carter waited patiently. The afternoon was pleasantly warm, and so he had rolled down his window.

Someone walked over to it. Carter looked up. A smile wreathed his face.

"Is that you, Halloran?"

Halloran owned a nearby tavern, one of the city's more popular saloons. It was frequented by politicians and policemen and everyone in between. Halloran had a reputation as a man who could be trusted with a little gossip. He kept any secret that was whispered in his establishment.

Halloran stepped up and asked, "Got a minute, Sarge?"

Carter looked around. "I got until the Commissioner comes back. Spill."

"I found this lying in the street," confided Halloran in a hushed voice. "It looks suspicious. I thought I'd take it to the cops. Then I see you sittin' there."

The man lifted a lead pipe. It appeared to be sealed at both ends. That fact all but made Sergeant Carter's hair stand on end. He had encountered such infernal machines before.

"Holy—! That looks like a pipe bomb," he breathed, eyes going sick.

"Maybe it is. It's got a funny little jigger on the side. It wiggles when I move it with my thumb."

Eyes widening, Carter said, "Whatever you do, don't wiggle it anymore. It might go off!"

"Hell, it would've gone off by now if it was going to go off. See?"

Then to Sergeant Carter's eternal horror, Halloran tripped the little lever, and a baffle opened at the end of the short pipe.

Transfixed, Carter looked down the lead tube. Deep in its shadowy interior gleamed something green. Green and glowing... like a fiery emerald....

Despite his growing apprehension, Sergeant Carter could not take his eyes off the glowing matter. He opened his mouth to speak, but then it simply dropped open as his face went blank and his eyes slowly took on the coloration of the green glowing thing that could not be clearly seen.

Turning abruptly, Halloran melted away. His thumb came off the trigger and the baffle fell back into place, sealing the fragment of interstellar hell.

Commissioner Kirkpatrick strode up to his limousine and threw open the door. He was not the type of official who needed a flunky to open and close it for him. Settling himself into the cushions, he barked, "Back to headquarters, Sergeant."

Sergeant Carter did not immediately turn. His head was wobbling on his shoulders in a queer fashion. Nor did he speak.

"Did you hear me?"

If Carter heard his superior officer, it did not show.

Kirkpatrick reached forward to shake the man, but then froze.

For in the rear-view mirror, he detected a strange reflection. A greenish light. It seemed to have no apparent source.

Then Sergeant Carter slowly rotated his head, and the color of his blank eyes glowed a phosphorescent *green*....

Kirkpatrick's tie caught fire immediately. Strangling an oath, he tore it off and threw himself out of the back of the limousine, stepping onto the sidewalk.

By the time he got clear, the entire rear seat was aflame!

"Carter!" he cried out. "Good God! *Not you!*"

But Sergeant Carter was beyond appeal. His head rotated slowly in the opposite direction and pale beams of eerie green sought Police Commissioner Stanley Kirkpatrick.

Radiating through the open window, they happened to fall on one shoe, and it became immediately warm, then hot.

Stepping back, Kirkpatrick pulled out the long-barreled revolver he always carried with him.

"Stay where you are, Sergeant," he ordered.

If Sergeant Carter heard or understood that order, he did not acknowledge it. Instead, he fumbled for the door latch and threw himself out as the limousine interior turned into a coffin of boiling smoke and leaping flames.

Having no other choice, Kirkpatrick leveled his revolver and, with tears in his eyes, squeezed the trigger twice.

It was one trigger pull too many. The first slug traversed the air between them, and Sergeant Carter's head snapped back on its neck with such force that the sound of the cervical bones breaking came distinctly.

The second slug whistled over and above the body as it collapsed lifelessly to the pavement.

Holding his smoking revolver in his hand, Kirkpatrick ground out, "Dick, Dick. I need you now more than ever before...."

Chapter 35

SINISTER SCHEME

THE STREAMLINED black roadster pulled up before Bryant Park, where James Christopher, Operator 5, accompanied by the G-2 captain code-named G-8, trooped across the grass to the waiting gyroplane, whose still rotor vanes drooped listlessly.

Climbing aboard, Gate took the pilot's seat while Operator 5 settled in beside him.

Operator 5 had the bulky black Geiger-Muller instrument on his lap. He turned this on.

As the rotor wing churned back to life, gleaning blades spinning and lifting over their heads, James suggested, "Crisscross the city. The tube is sure to react sooner or later."

"Right," said G-8. gunning the throttle. With a springy bound, the gyro scrambled into the air, shouldered north, beating its rotor wing madly, gaining altitude.

Neither man noticed that, in an apartment building not far from their takeoff spot, a black-gloved hand pulled aside a cloth-of-gold curtain and a featureless face like a black shield showed briefly in the window pane.

With an angry swipe, the heavy hanging snapped back into place.

And a hollow voice cursed, "The *verdammt* one!"

RIDING A vortex of disturbed air, the rotorplane swung over Central Park, loafed over the northern end, but the tube did not react.

"Steel Mask must have gathered up every last piece of that meteorite," remarked Christopher. "Nothing for us to do here."

Shooting north, they flew as far as Inwood Hill Park. Approaching the northernmost tip of Manhattan Island, G-8 jinked the nimble little ship about, then coursed south, over Riverside Drive.

Reaching Thirty-fifth Street, he turned east, the buzzing nose prop pulling the ship toward the East River, riding the turbulent air with slashing grace.

Stitching a complicated flight path over the city, G-8 gritted his teeth in frustration.

"There must be pieces of that damned meteorite somewhere! These new zombies aren't coming from people's imaginations. They're real!"

James Christopher nodded silently. He kept his eyes on the tube. They were flying low, low enough to pick up any radium-like emanations below. Yet the Geiger-Muller device was unable to register the presence of any such rays.

"I don't get this," complained G-8 as he guided the dragonfly ship up and down. "I know this is like looking for a needle in a haystack, but this mechanical bloodhound should have sniffed out something by now."

"Not if the meteorite fragments are shielded by lead," countered Operator 5. "Lead will block any radiation known to man. If the doom-rays can't leak out, the scintillation counter won't detect it."

"Then we're licked, for now. We might as well set down."

"We can't quit now!" snapped Christopher. "Something is making fresh victims."

"I know it. But we're running low on fuel. I'll have to set this whirligig down anyway. Might as well make the best of it. We can jump back into the air before it gets dark."

Reluctantly, James Christopher agreed. His troubled eyes were fixed upon the Geiger-Muller tube. Such a tiny device for such a monumental task....

AS STAHLMASKE watched the silvery gyro disappear over a forest of skyscrapers, he made hissing sounds inside his cylindrical helmet. His eyes burned to thin slits. Their light was oddly reddish.

"Had I known," he growled, "that the *verdammt* G-8 and his special plane still sat across the street, I would have stormed down there and broken his neck with my bare hands." His gloved fists lifted angrily, clutching as if at an imaginary throat....

Seated at his leonine desk, Count Calypsa intoned calmly, "That would be most unwise, *Herr* Stahlmaske. Caparisoned as you are, you cannot but be recognized on sight. Police riot guns would chop you to pieces. You are doubtless the most wanted man in America at this moment. I would not be surprised if the F.B.I. has honored you with the designation of Public Enemy Number One. Please remain calm. I have come up with a way to increase the reign of terror that has only begun."

Turning from the heavy wall drape as it dropped back into place, Stahlmaske regarded his partner in conspiracy with cold regard. The weird reddish light was fading from his eyes now.

"Speak. I wish to hear your plan."

"My agents have done exemplary work in spreading the new terror. Your monsters are wreaking havoc upon the populace. But we have insufficient numbers to truly terrorize the city. We require more zombies."

Stahlmaske lifted the lead pipe in his fist and rumbled, "Our resources are stretched thin, would you not agree?"

Instead of replying, Count Calypsa smiled in his cruel-lipped way. He was no longer applying the ice pack to his forehead. His battered features were no better than before. One eye was blackened. It was nearly closed.

"I have a man at the General Post Office in Midtown. He works in the basement. He is a supervisor there. If we can pulverize a piece of the meteorite into splinters, these can be sent around the city, where they will be quite destructive. This could be done in such a way that none of my agents are at risk of discovery."

Striding heavily across the carpet on which the lion-seated-on-a-crown emblem was woven, the human hulk approached the massive desk. Cold eyes looked down.

"Tell me more."

Count Calypsa smiled again, more widely. His thick features were no less brutal. "No doubt you are familiar with Berlin, which by reputation is one of the most modern cities in the world. Would it surprise you to learn that, beneath the streets of Manhattan Island, lies a system of tubes some twenty-seven miles long? I'm not referring to the subway system. No, these are much smaller tubes. They are used to transport mail at high speed between government post offices and certain designated buildings."

The steel helmet inclined ponderously in a caricature of a nod.

"You are referring to the pneumatic-tube system."

"Indeed. Bundles of mail are packed into metal capsules and dropped into these tubes and sealed. Air pressure does the rest. It is all very modern and efficient. These capsules whisk along, unseen, at a speed of thirty-five miles an hour. The system reaches as far as Brooklyn. But we are only concerned with Manhattan. Now, are you willing to sacrifice one of your precious fragments for the next phase of our campaign?"

"*Ja.* I am. In order to convince your man to insert these fragments of hell into the tubes, he must not know what they truly are. He will have to remove them from the lead containers by hand. He is certain to succumb to the radiation."

Calypsa nodded. "My agents have all pledged their loyalty to me. And their very lives. They're like dimes, which I spend as I see fit. Take the pipe into another room and do what you need to do. By the time you're finished, Number Seventy-four will be present. I will see that he has clear instructions, so that none of the meteorite splinters are wasted in this new endeavor."

Without saying a word, Stahlmaske turned on his heel, swept aside a heavy wall hanging, exiting the spacious room through a heavy door.

Reaching for his Call-o-phone instrument, Count Calypsa began speaking.

"Number Seventy-four, report to headquarters immediately. Immediately, do you understand?"

"At once, Dictator," replied a crisp voice.

IN THE basement of New York's General Post Office on Eighth Avenue in Midtown, between Thirty-first and Thirty-third Streets, a truncated forest of pneumatic pipes stood in orderly ranks and rows. They came straight up from the floor and then angled noticeably. Each pipe was capped.

Merely by lifting a cap, inserting a sealed capsule, and locking the cap again, a packet of mail would be whisked on its way. It only required that a button be pressed. Compressed air did the rest. Each pipe had a terminus in a different branch of the post office, or some other locality. The speed with which the capsules traveled would have amazed most New Yorkers unfamiliar with the intricacies of the pneumatic system.

Number Seventy-four carried the lead pipe into the basement pneumatic-tube department.

Workers were busily removing the labeled capsules from canvas bins, which were taken up by others. All wore the blue uniforms of postmen. They dropped them into the designated tubes, sealing them, and depressing the buttons that actuated the powerful compressed-air mechanisms.

The speed with which these men worked was impressive. They looked very much like men in a trance. They did not look up when Number Seventy-four entered and began picking through a canvas bin of fresh capsules.

He opened several of these, sprinkling greenish grit from the uncapped lead pipe he had smuggled into the building. Number Seventy-four did not question his orders. They came directly from the Dictator. He only obeyed his hooded master's will.

Number Seventy-four inserted only pinches into each capsule before resealing them. He made sure to insert some of the greenish matter into a capsule intended for Police Headquarters. Another went to Macy's Department Store.

Lastly, he selected one that was designated to go to the Vertex Building. It was one of the few skyscrapers which boasted its own pneumatic tube terminus.

Closing this last capsule, he set the now-empty lead pipe on a work bench.

For a few moments, he watched a man come and take the canvas wheeled cart and, with practiced efficiency, insert each capsule into the appropriate tube and send it whooshing on its way.

Number Seventy-four smiled thinly. The Dictator would be pleased. Every tampered package had been dispatched to different destinations. What would happen when they arrived was not his concern. He was merely a tool, doing what he was instructed to do....

He did not smile for very long. His smile slowly turned downward, as if his lips were rubber bands that had lost their elasticity. His face went blank. He passed a troubled hand over his forehead.

For some strange reason, he noticed a green glow painting the back of his hand. His slowly dulling brain could not understand what was shining so greenly.

Then the emerald eye-beams emanating from his pinpoint pupils began to cook the skin on the back of his hand... and doomed Number Seventy-four let out a horrific shriek....

Chapter 36

THE FALL OF MACY'S

G-8 REFUELED his *Hummingbird* super-gyro at Mitchel Field.

The seasoned Master Spy and the brisk young intelligence agent were discussing their next move when an orderly came into the hangar and shouted, "Captain Gate! The Colonel wants to see you in his office—pronto. All hell is breaking loose in Manhattan!"

The two agents rushed to the office where pinched-faced Colonel Jasper paced.

"You two had better make tracks back to the city as fast as you can!" he ordered. "The Main Post Office is practically a riot situation! Somehow, a zombie got into the basement. Before the police could put him down, he created five human torches. Macy's Department Store had to be evacuated when an employee turned into a Meteor Monster. There's trouble at the Vertex Building as well, but no details as yet."

"The Vertex Building!" rapped Operator 5.

Colonel Jasper nodded vigorously. "Another wave of Meteorite Maniacs has burst into the open. They're popping up all over the city! No one can explain it! But something has to be done about it, and done expeditiously. This is too much—even for the combined city police and National Guard!"

"Yes, sir," snapped G-8, popping a salute.

The two men went swooping through the air once the fuel tanks were topped off. The windmill plane was shooting low toward the downtown sector.

Grim-faced, G-8 gritted, "This is a worse mess than before."

"I'll say," said James Christopher. "These new marauders are scattered all about town. They'll be harder to control."

Unexpectedly, the Geiger-Muller tube showed a reaction—a frying sound like intermittent, stuttering static manifested.

"Swing around!" he told the G-2 officer. "We just passed over something hot."

The Master Spy redirected his ship, and the tube reacted with increased intensity, producing more concentrated static.

"Isn't that Macy's down there?" he asked.

James Christopher nodded. "It is." His brow wrinkled. "I wonder...."

"Wonder what?"

"The buildings that were targeted—all have one thing in common. Either they're connected to the central post office pneumatic-tube mail system, or they have a tube system of their own... or *both!*"

Holding the hovering ship in place, G-8 muttered, "That would be a diabolical way to send small pieces of that meteorite shooting around town. Through the pneumatic tubes!"

James groaned. "How the devil do we contain the spread of that stuff? It's like a plague has been loosed upon the metropolis—a plague from interstellar space!"

"Search me," returned G-8. "But until we figure it out, we're just going to have to shoot as many zombies as we can run down."

Operator 5's voice thickened. "It will be a slaughter."

"It's war," vowed the G-2 officer. "A war for control of the city. And we *must* win, otherwise Manhattan will fall...."

Manipulating the complicated controls, G-8 settled the beating gyroplane down on the flat roof of Macy's Department Store, overlooking Herald Square. Taking up his Tommy gun, he charged it. Operator 5 checked his automatic. Without another word, they stepped out of the gyroplane and prepared to take on come what may....

Christopher forced a roof hatch open; they went down the stairs. Almost at once, the bitter tang of smoke assailed their eyes and noses.

G-8 muttered, "We've got to find that zombie before it burns the building to its bare frame!"

"Don't assume there's only one," warned James.

Swiftly, the two men clattered down the stairs and banged through a fire door on the top floor of the immense, many-storied department store.

The smoke was worse now. But it could be navigated. Handkerchiefs came out, were clapped to mouths and noses. These helped.

This floor, given over to furniture and mattresses, appeared to be empty. At least there was no one in sight. They found the escalator and rode it down. It was still operating, its machinery making a monotonous sound as it moved the wooden cleats along.

The next floor was even more smoky, but likewise it was empty of life. Bakery and Delicatessen were deserted. They pressed on, smarting eyes leaking moisture.

"Look sharp," Operator 5 warned.

The third floor down was stocked with draperies, bedspreads and floor coverings. One corner was blazing. The fire was confined, but would not be for long....

Encumbered by the heavy Thompson submachine gun, G-8 directed, "Look for a fire extinguisher. Let's get that blaze out before we push down any further."

James Christopher ranged around the smoky floor, found a fire extinguisher of the pump type. He lugged it over to a burning display of hope chests, began pumping vigorously. Smoke caused him to cough and hack. But he stayed with it until the fire was snuffed out.

Tossing aside the empty fire extinguisher, he nodded to G-8. Together, they rode the escalator downward, the G-2 agent in the lead.

SOMETHING WAS moving around on the eighth floor. The sound of breaking wood could be heard.

"That's either a bull in a china shop, or a clumsy zombie," quipped G-8 with ironic humor.

It proved to be the latter. It was a man. He was dressed rather primly, with a white carnation in his suit lapel. A floorwalker! But his expression was that of a dead man. He was careening around aimlessly, bumping into display items in Sporting Goods, and acting surprised whenever something caught fire after his flashing green gaze fell upon it.

James Christopher lined up his automatic and clipped briskly, "No sense in wasting bullets. I have him."

He fired once. The weapon jumped in his hands, and a bullet scorched a path toward the zombie's well-tonsured skull.

The .45 slug drilled a clean hole through the zombie's brain, and he jerked around three times, but strangely did not fall. Instead, his flashlight eyeballs swept about, saw the two men and advanced awkwardly.

"He should be dead!" James cried out.

"He *is* dead," grunted G-8. "He just doesn't know it. I fought zombies before, back in the war. Real ones. Believe it or not, there is such a thing." *

"I know," Operator 5 murmured. "I, too, have battled ghastly living dead men...." **

Without another word, G-8 triggered his sub-gun in a short, racketing burst, reducing the oncoming monster's rib cage to a mass of red kindling mixed with well-chewed organ meat.... dyeing the wilted carnation crimson....

The Meteor Monster crumpled. Its fingers continued to twitch. By that time, the two agents were moving for the down escalator.

* G-8 and His Battle Aces: *Flight from the Grave.*
** Operator #5: *The Army of the Dead.*

The firing had attracted attention, and they were met by—not one, but two—dead-faced human corpses. Green eyes flashed at them like hellish torches.

Operator 5 felt his face go warm, then hot, and beat a prudent retreat.

The smell of burning silk told him that his tie was scorched. He wrenched it off, flinging it away. Then he crouched down and triggered once.

His bullet smashed into a zombie shoulder, while G-8 scythed the dead man down with a withering bullet-stream, then did the same with the other.

The two zombies fell, twitching and writhing in their death throes. The green light emanating from their eyes burned upward and scorched the ceiling, darkening it. The bitter smell of plaster being heated came to their nostrils.

Getting a grip on themselves, the government men stepped over the mutilated corpses and reconnoitered the present floor. It was a labyrinth in which musical instruments, radios, cameras and sporting goods were arranged.

A green glow in the far corner warned them that they were not alone….

G-8 elbowed Operator 5 silently, then pointed with his free hand.

James Christopher nodded. He looked around. Pianos clustered in this area. Some were decorated with display mirrors; their reflective surfaces gave him an idea.

Holstering his automatic, he took hold of an oval mirror pinched in a gimbal frame. Carefully, he lifted it, holding it ahead of him so that the mirrored surface faced the green glow.

He gave G-8 a knowing glance, then advanced. Operator 5 made no effort to walk quietly. He stepped smartly and took pains to knock something over. This caught the attention of the fumbling, glowing-eyed creature.

Instantly, the lurking one stepped from behind a pillar, then turned the full fury of his glowing eyes upon the approaching Intelligence officer.

James Christopher swiftly brought the mirror up. The quicksilver surface captured the green glow, reflecting it to one side. Tilting the mirror, James saw that the reflected glow acted with the same combustible power that the direct eye-beams did. Objects bathed in the greenish glow caught fire, smoldered or shriveled, each according to their composition.

Employing the blunt muzzle of his weapon, James tilted the mirror again, this time directly back at its author.

Drenched in the reflected glow, the creature began howling and pawing at his face. His pale features shriveled, then darkened. His hair blazed up. A mad scream of fury was wrenched from his gaping mouth.

In another second, the zombie was a human torch crumbling in on himself!

"Good work, youngster," praised G-8.

Setting the mirror aside, James Christopher found a fire extinguisher and coated the blazing corpse with chemical powder. The fire was soon snuffed out. But the smoke was terrible, a choking, malodorous mass. They were forced to retreat downward, to the next floor.

Here, the worst horror was found. Corpses lay strewn and scattered all about. Ordinary shoppers. They had been transformed into burned-up human torches. The stench of the burning flesh was an assault on their senses.

But there were no more zombies to be found.

James Christopher noticed a half-dismantled display of Halloween costumes in the Games department.

Prominent among them was the regalia of The Spider—a skirted black domino mask and matching hat and cloak, the back of which was clotted with silvery cobwebs.

"I wonder if he's really dead?" Christopher murmured. "The Spider, I mean."

Taking up one of the boxes containing the sinister outfit, G-8 remarked, "It might help our cause if Stahlmaske and Count Calypsa think otherwise." He tucked the box under one arm.

"This is a job for the fire department now," suggested G-8.

"What about the meteorite fragment? If there's one stuck in the store's pneumatic-tube system, we've got to find it."

The Master Spy shook his head vigorously. "No time for that. Besides, we have no protection against the doom-rays. Let's beat it back to the gyro. I can radio the fire department once we're back in the air."

Reluctantly, James Christopher followed G-8 up the wooden escalator, past the smoky disarray of the greatest department store in the world, and back onto the roof.

Once they broke out onto the rooftop, the wail of fire engines lifted to their ears.

"No need to summon the fire department now," said James.

"No, but we've got to let them know that it's dangerous to stay too long. Any firefighter entering that building risks becoming another zombie."

"That means—"

"Yes," said G-8. "They're probably going to have to let the building burn to the ground. Maybe that will quell the danger."

Eyes stinging, faces smudged with soot, they climbed aboard the gyroplane, then leapt up into the air, G-8 at the controls while Operator 5 worked the shortwave radio.

"Calling Cortez Sept. Cortez Sept, come in. No distorter. Repeat, no frequency distorter."

The strained voice of Z-7 came on the air. Cortez Sept was his code name.

"On your wave. Go ahead, Operator 5."

"Chief, Macy's Department Store is on fire! We believe there's a meteorite fragment lodged somewhere in the building's pneumatic-tube mail system. Fire department pump trucks just pulled up. Someone should warn them. They can't enter the building safely. They must let it burn. *Repeat, Macy's must be allowed to burn!"*

"I'll pass along the message. Thanks, Operator 5."

But before James Christopher could sign off, Z-7 directed, "Stand by."

Over the shortwave came a scuffle, some shouting, followed by two pistol shots coming in rapid succession. Then Z-7's voice came back on the frequency.

"Operator 5! It's… T-3! I regret to inform you that the New York station chief is… dead."

"Dead! What just happened?"

Z-7's voice was clogged with congealed emotion.

"I was forced to shoot him! He barged into my office, acting wildly, his eyes as green as emeralds. He had become one of… them…."

James Christopher's blue eyes clouded over. His chiseled face looked ghastly in the dashboard light. He swallowed a rising groan of horror.

"Chief! You must evacuate headquarters! The Vertex Building has its own pneumatic-tube system. One of the meteorite fragments must have penetrated the fifty-fifth floor. Do you understand? *If you don't evacuate, every occupant is at risk of turning into rampaging monsters."*

Chapter 37

CITY IN CHAOS

STANLEY KIRKPATRICK watched in horror as a thick column of black smoke snaked up from Herald Square. He had heard the radio reports. Macy's Department Store was ablaze from ground floor to roof, torched by an unexpected zombie outbreak.

"Great God in Heaven! What is causing this Hell on earth?"

The police commissioner rocked in the back of a careening police radio car driven by a mere patrolman, his limousine having been incinerated until it was but a smoking tangle of steel chassis. His chauffeur was in the morgue... unrecognizable....

The General Post Office had to be evacuated. Fire hoses were being directed to knock down wandering zombies, as well as snuff out the human torches they had blindly created. There were more of the latter than the former.

Racing from scene to scene, Kirkpatrick saw it all. A bacchanal of hellish horrors. A contagion undreamed of by the blackest sorcerers of the Dark Ages.

His police officers worked tirelessly. Each new outbreak was met fearlessly and put down ruthlessly. No one was spared. Not all zombies were working men going about their business. Many were women. Housewives, stenographers, waitresses. A few—fortunately, mercifully, very few—were children....

Gushing fire hoses kept the maniacs flattened against building walls or pushed them caterwauling like the damned into the flooding gutters, until they expired like exhausted dry-cell batteries....

Tear gas was deployed. But this seemed only to worsen the

situation. The gas further maddened the rampaging Meteor Monsters. Madly, they flailed about, howling, burning and killing in their final acts of desperation. The stinging gas meant to shut their eyelids and choke off the preternaturally hot green beams stabbing forth from their leaking pupils, producing little of the desired effect.

Where necessary, police bullets were deciding factors. It was a horror. These were public executions, carried out by the patrolmen themselves. But they were, withal, merciful. Those unfortunates who had been afflicted would never be normal again....

BY THE onset of dusk, miraculously, it was over.

Prowl cars crisscrossed the city, seeking stray zombies, but whatever agency had brought these new afflicted ones to life appeared to have subsided.

Macy's Department Store could not be saved. Streetlights showed it to be a burnt-out shell. One that, no doubt, would be rebuilt in time....

Hearing a newsboy hawking a late edition, Kirkpatrick ordered his driver to cut to the curb.

"Here, boy!" A nickel changed hands and a folded copy was shoved through the open window. "Keep the change," Kirkpatrick told the lad.

The Commissioner read the screaming black headline.

AUTOPSIES OF DEAD REVEAL HORROR!

The City Coroner revealed late today that autopsies conducted upon the brains of victims of what is being called "Meteorite Madness" show a common denominator. Every examined brain displayed deformities in the brain structure caused by numerous brain lesions. Scientists are speculating that the fallen meteor had been emitting lethal gamma rays, and that these rays were responsible for the misbehavior of the so-called Meteor Maniacs, eating away at the soft tissues and making their decaying grey matter radioactive.

No responsible scientist, however, has so far been willing to explain how or why these rays transformed the eyeballs of the afflicted into unearthly blowtorches....

One other paragraph caused Kirkpatrick's wintry eyes to widen.

Sources who wish to remain anonymous strongly suggest that the most recent outbreak means that pieces of the missing meteorite—perhaps as small as pebbles—have been sent through the Postal Service's pneumatic-tube system for the express purpose of broadcasting additional terror and destruction. For every building that has disgorged a fresh crop of maniacs shares a prominent feature—a pneumatic-tube system of its own—and all of them are connected to the central depot in the basement of the General Post Office.

There was more, but it consisted of an account of facts known to the police commissioner—talk of curfews, rumors of wealthier New Yorkers fleeing to New Jersey and Long Island, and an educated guess at the mounting death toll.

The byline, Diane Elliot, registered in Kirkpatrick's brain as a familiar one.

Crumpling up the paper, he tossed it aside and ordered his driver to re-enter the thin traffic of a city whose population was diminishing by the hour....

As the last rays of natural light dwindled in a foreboding dusk, Kirkpatrick returned to his office to oversee police operations and issue general orders.

He was met by a message. The orderly handed it to him, saying, "This just off the teletype, sir."

Kirkpatrick glowered. "Another outbreak?"

"Worse. The Spider is back. Big as life."

"What? Hand me that!"

Kirkpatrick read the perforated words.

SPIDER SIGHTED IN CITY, VICINITY OF MERCY HOSPITAL. DESCRIP-
TION AS FOLLOWS....

Reading the description, Kirkpatrick frowned heavily.

"This is not The Spider!" he bit out fiercely. "It is the impersonator who attempted to gun me down. Cast a city-wide dragnet
He must be apprehended at once. The charge will be attempted
murder of a police official. I want this damned false Spider
apprehended before the night is over! That is all!"

After the orderly shut the door behind him, Kirkpatrick put his
elbows up on his desk and buried his saturnine face in his hands.

"Would to God I never see another Monday as hellish as this
one.... And on All Saints' Day!"

Chapter 38

THE TIDE TURNS...

THE LIGHTS illuminating the heavily-curtained headquarters of Count Carmine Calypsa, the self-styled Dictator, were no different after dark than they were during the day. The indirect bulbs burned incessantly. This was necessary, for every window was shrouded by a cloth-of-gold tapestry emblazoned with the heraldic design depicting a lion rampant.

The console radio tubes were aglow, casting a warm, yellowish light. The Count and his faceless confederate were listening to the latest news broadcast.

"This just in, folks! The Mayor is now asserting that the zombie rampage that has engulfed Manhattan these last twenty-four hours has been broken. The death toll is unknown. But the danger is believed to be past."

Stahlmaske heaved up from his chair, stalked over and angrily turned down the volume on the radio set.

"Something is wrong! The meteor fragments could not have all been confiscated and destroyed. They should be wreaking havoc even as we speak!"

Count Calypsa frowned heavily. "Do you suppose the police have figured out a way to shield their brains with lead?"

"It is possible," rumbled Steel Mask. "But doubtful that they could have confiscated them all. I do not understand why the maniacs are decreasing, not increasing in number. By now, portions of the city should be ablaze."

Calypsa suggested, "Turn up the volume. Perhaps the newscast reports will tell us something more."

"Flash! This just in! The Spider has been sighted. He was seen near Mercy Hospital. His whereabouts are currently unknown. As everyone knows by now, The Spider was believed to have drowned in the East River. But the acute danger of meteorite radiation in the water has so far prevented the police from dragging the river. Stay tuned for further bulletins."

The Count shot up out of his seat, his thick-featured face turning red, angry eyes like boiling water.

"The Spider cannot be alive! It is impossible!"

Stahlmaske grunted dully, "I agree with you that it is unlikely. But impossible to know. Until a body is brought forth, there is no proof of his death. Please calm yourself. We must approach these problems with cool heads."

Calypsa sat down heavily. He banged the mahogany desktop in futile rage. Behind him, the image of a lion seated on a gold crown shook, and if sharing in his anger.

"I must find out the truth! I must know!"

"If the police apprehend The Spider, you will know," Steel Mask reassured him. "Or if he dares come here."

Calypsa shook his head. "The Spider is very clever, but not so clever as I. He may investigate the other headquarters, but not this one. And we dare not repair to our original lair. The police are still combing the Electric Building and will for several days to come. No doubt they will assume that we fled to a far location. We will leave them to believe that folly."

"Gut! I, too, am becoming impatient," declared Stahlmaske. "I wish to lure that *verdammt* G-8 out into the open, where he can be transformed into a brainless, tottering wretch with mere minutes to live. But none of your agents have so far located him."

"Did G-8 not have the reputation of being a master of disguise?"

"Ja. In my day, G-8 could make himself appear to be a German general or a French peasant woman. He possessed extraordinary skills. He could be anyone, anyone at all...."

Count Calypsa looked up, locking gazes with the Man in the Steel Mask.

"Anyone, you say…?"

"*Ja,* G-8 is the greatest disguise artist of all time. Why do you ask?"

"A strange thought has crossed my mind. When I crashed the Halloween ball, I was disguised as The Spider. Do you know where I got my fanciful cloak and hat?"

"Certainly not! I did not know you at that time."

"I had it purchased for me by one of my faithful Numbers. It was a quality costume, manufactured exclusively for Macy's Department Store…."

"I believe that I follow your thinking, Count. Now follow mine. Whether this Spider is G-8, or perhaps another, we must flush him out—learn the truth. Is it not widely suspected that Richard Wentworth is The Spider?"

"This has never been proven. What of it?"

"And did you not put Wentworth's fiancée, Miss Nita van Sloan, into the hospital last night?"

"I did. And she is still there. Number Thirty-two is an orderly at Mercy Hospital. He has reported to me that she is under the protection of Wentworth's personal bodyguard, a fierce Sikh gentleman by the name of Ram Singh."

Steel Mask regarded his leather gauntlet and made a black fist. "Suppose we abduct Miss van Sloan and see *which* Spider comes to her rescue?"

"I fail to perceive your objective…."

"Then permit me to state it baldly," intoned Stahlmaske. "By entrapping Miss van Sloan, we may ensnare G-8, and… another…."

"What other? The Spider is dead."

Steel Mask tapped his helmeted head. "No, The Spider is *believed* dead. Perhaps he is, in truth. If, on the other hand,

Wentworth is also dead, he cannot come. That will tell us that we face one foe, not two. And it may lure Commissioner Kirkpatrick into our trap. For if The Spider is no more, Kirkpatrick and G-8 are our chief opponents."

Calypsa's ugly countenance writhed with ferocious joy. "Clever, clever. That is an excellent idea. I salute you, *Herr* Stahlmaske. You possess a brain—a brain as formidable and as calculating as my own. Yes, we will see to it that Miss van Sloan is removed from the hospital. The best way to do that is to activate one of my Numbers working in the hospital, who will create a suitable diversion."

Stahlmaske asked, "Do you intend to make more meteoric madmen?"

The Count grinned, his brutal features turning wolfish. "I intend to fill that hospital with as many as can be created. They will pour out of its doors like a legion of the doomed and the damned."

An unholy glow made the enshadowed orbs recessed deep in the black steel face shine with an weird reddish light. *"Gut, gut. Do that. I am going to be on hand when that happens. Whoever shows up, I wish to face him myself."*

"It is risky, von Maur. You know that."

Stahlmaske rose heavily. He was pacing the rug. His leather-gloved hands were clasped behind him. And his helmeted head hung heavy, as if the thoughts in his brain were weighing it down. He was like an old bull, pacing with pent-up energy.

"If I should die in this undertaking, I will have no regrets—provided that I take the damned G-8 with me to Hell. For that is where I intend to send him. Even if I have to drag him there personally...."

Chapter 39

TOWER OF TERROR

HUDDLED IN the enclosed cabin of the *Hummingbird* super-gyro, James Christopher radioed frantic instructions to his chief in the Vertex Building, Z-7.

"Evacuation is your only hope!"

"It's no good, my boy!" retorted the Intelligence Chief. *"My men report that the lower floors are crawling with Meteor Maniacs. My God, if they aren't overmastered, this entire skyscraper will go up like a gigantic blazing torch!"*

"In that case," replied James briskly, "barricade yourselves on the fifty-fifth floor. I will join you directly."

"What good can you—one man—do?" Z-7 shot back thickly. *"The situation is beyond hopeless!"*

Operator 5 did not reply directly. His left hand drifted to the golden skull set with the ruby eyes dangling from his watch chain, and his blue eyes clouded up, darkening dramatically.

"I have an idea. A terrible idea. But one that might work in the last ditch."

"But how will you reach us safely? The lobby is choked with marauders!"

"If I can't get in one way," James said resolutely, "I will barge in another way. Over and out."

Replacing the microphone, James turned to G-8. "Can you swing close enough to the tower that I can reach the observation platform?"

G-8 nodded confidently. "This bird can hover in a fixed position exactly like a hummingbird. It's a cinch. But I can't drift too close to the spire without risking the rotor wing coming apart. You'll have to clear the space to the observation platform yourself."

Setting his jaw, Operator 5 said firmly, "Don't worry about that part."

Gunning the engine caused the rear propeller to kick in, adding velocity to the whirligig plane. G-8 sent it barreling toward the Vertex spire, whose lights were beginning to wink on in the gathering dusk.

Dusk! thought James. What a long day it had been! And now night was coming again. Night and the terror that it brought to the city. Less than twenty-four hours had passed since the meteorite had crashed into Central Park. Now Manhattan teetered on the brink of disaster. The police were a shattered force. The populace was streaming out by the hour, the bridges to the five boroughs choked with crawling autos. Only the National Guard was holding Manhattan together. But even they represented an insufficient presence to ensure the survival of the city.

The hop to the Vertex Building was breathlessly brief. Its impressive white tower with its myriad radio antennae lifted far above the sidewalks below.

Manipulating the gyroplane's complicated controls, G-8 brought the dancing ship abreast of the spire.

With astounding air-dexterity, the *Hummingbird* lost all momentum, wallowed briefly, then settled to hover in place, its spinning buzzsaw rotor vanes remaining clear of the gleaming spire.

Like a seasoned boat captain warping his ship dockside, G-8 drifted the nimble craft closer, ever closer....

"Get set," he warned.

"I'm ready."

James opened the starboard-side door, peered downward.

A dizzying prospect lay below. But twelve feet across and ten downward lay the open-air observation platform. It ran around the spire on all four sides.

G-8 called over, "Can you clear it?"

"I can," snapped James. Rising from his seat, he stepped off into space without another word, poised on one stub wing for the briefest of moments, then dropped from view.

The kick of his feet against the *Hummingbird's* dural skin caused her to wobble alarmingly. But she drifted less than three feet—away from the spire!

Carefully, G-8 corrected for that drift, and then began to orbit the skyscraper's spire.

Through one wing of the curved windshield, he caught a glimpse of Operator 5 landing hard. Christopher rolled, then gathered himself together. He leapt to his feet, lunged for the door, sprinting hard.

Under his breath, G-8 murmured, "Good luck, youngster."

Reaching over to pull the passenger door shut, he sent the *Hummingbird* winging south, in the direction of Mercy Hospital....

A SINGLE elevator shaft reached to the observation floor. James Christopher ignored it. Instead, he took the fire stairs, his Colt automatic in hand.

Running hard, he encountered a Meteor Maniac almost immediately.

It was a man—short, portly, and making strange mewling sounds that were not words. He was crawling up the marble steps on his hands and knees. In the weak artificial light of the stairwell, his eyes glowed a lambent green. Fortunately, whatever the beams brushed against did not combust.

At the sound of Operator 5's approach, the inhuman thing looked up. James was forced to duck back.

Twin cones of ghostly emerald light flashed by him, but he was unharmed; his well-trained reflexes had saved him.

Retreating to the next landing above, James lay prone on his stomach and prepared for the crawling zombie's arrival.

A green shining creeping up the walls told him that the creature was drawing closer. He was no longer mewling, but his breathing was heavy and ragged with stress.

Grimly, Operator 5 waited, breathing quietly. When the rising glow had turned the walls chartreuse, he lifted himself with one hand and aimed downward, laying his gunsight on a shock of reddish hair.

A long tongue of saffron flame squirted from the Colt's bucking muzzle. The bullet sped true. It struck the creature near his hairline, literally taking off the top of his skull!

The portly man's death cry was a strangled groan.

Lying prone, James waited. The ghostly green glow on the walls began to fade. When it was completely gone, he stood up and continued down the staircase.

He gave the gory mess that was the portly man the merest glance. James did not need to stare…. That one glance would be burnt into his brain forever….

Further down, he smelled a terrible odor. Human flesh that had been cooked. This warned him what to expect….

Thus, when Operator 5 came upon the well-roasted body of a human being, he was not surprised. The still-smoking corpse was charred black. The smoldering skin lay raw and exposed… for all the clothing had been scorched away.

Stepping carefully around it, James continued on. It was not possible to tell if the blackened remains belonged to a man or a woman….

REACHING THE fifty-fifth floor, James paused at the fire door. It was eerily quiet.

Then came crashing, blundering noises that caused his pounding heart to freeze in his chest. He steeled himself.

Easing open the door, James threw himself into the corridor. At once he saw the office door marked "Consolidated Paper Mills."

The pebbled glass door was shut tight. But beyond the wavy glass panel, yellow-orange flames leapt. There was smoke. It smelled like wood and paper burning, but mixed into it was the faintest hint of cooking flesh....

Operator 5 started for that door, prepared to brave any challenge to reach his beleaguered chief.

Before he cleared half the length, a section of the hallway showed a sudden vertical crack, and two wings of a cunningly-concealed door opened abruptly.

Out of this aperture stepped the black-haired form of Z-7!

"Chief!" blurted James.

"Quiet!" returned Z-7 anxiously, his face haggard. "Follow me."

Wordlessly, Operator 5 followed his superior back to the fire door. Once they were in the stairwell's confines, Z-7 broke the terrible news.

"Headquarters is a total loss! Half of our office has turned into green-eyed marauders! They fell upon the other half. It's a slaughter! I would have stood my ground, but it was no use. The floor is a charnel house of horrors! I employed the secret emergency exit. It was... God help me... the only way out...."

Z-7's black-diamond eyes held terrible glints in their inner depths.

James said nothing. Well he knew the men and women who worked at the station. Brave patriots, all. To think that....

Z-7 started down the stairwell, but before the duo got three stories in the direction of the lobby, they found the stairwell choked with blundering green-eyed zombies!

Blank dumb faces turned upward, angry eyes blazed in the Intelligence agents' direction.

Z-7 was forced to doff his coat, for it started to sprout leaping yellow tongues of fire. He threw this burgeoning bonfire down upon the marauders, who snarled inarticulately and pushed on.

Calmly, James shot one in the temple, whereupon the others recoiled in shock and surprise, emitting inhuman squeals like terrified rats.

"Turn back!" James cried. "Retreat to the observation platform! We will make our stand there."

Z-7 wasted no time. Together, they pounded up the marble steps, gaining ten floors before reaching air clear enough to breathe. Exiting, they made a dash for the special elevator that whisked them upward to the observation platform that buttressed the famed Vertex spire on all four sides.

Both men were breathing hard when they reached the open air. Their faces had acquired a coating of smoke-deposited grime. Perspiration was cutting clear rivulets through the accumulated soot.

"This entire building is infested with the brainless devils!" Z-7 panted.

James glanced at his wristwatch. "The workday is just ending now. There are probably two thousand people in this building— all at risk of being turned into Meteor Maniacs."

Z-7's smoldering eyes grew grave in his careworn face.

"We cannot allow them to escape into the streets, Operator 5. They will run amuck...."

"I know," said James heavily. "For I foresaw this possibility. And I have formulated a solution."

To Z-7's cold horror, Operator 5 yanked the ruby-eyed death's head off his watch chain and held it up in the dying light of sunset.

"Diphenochlorasine!" gasped Z-7.

Operator 5 nodded. "Enough to kill every man and woman in this building."

"But how will you accomplish this? If you break open the

black sphere hidden in the skull's crown, we will die as well. And here in the open air, the gas will blow away!"

"There is no need for both of us to perish," returned James in a resolute tone. "I will take the elevator to the fifty-fifth floor, open the cage door, step out and crush the black sphere underfoot."

Choking on his emotions, the Intelligence official said gently, "My boy, let me do it. I beg you. You have a bright future ahead of you."

"No, sir," insisted James sternly. "You are the supreme chief of U.S. Intelligence. You cannot be spared in the eternal war against America's enemies. I am only a number in the Secret Service. After I am gone, another number will replace me. And should he fall in the performance of his sacred duty, yet another will replace him. We pledged to lay down our lives for our country. I consider that is what I am doing now."

Visibly moved, Z-7 clapped James on the shoulder and said, "I cannot argue with you. But—think this through! Are you prepared to take the lives of your unaffected fellow operators, the ones who are fighting our doomed comrades on the fifty-fifth floor?"

Operator 5's clouded blue eyes verged on turning black. The expression coming over his rugged features indicated that he had not considered this point.

His resolve wavered then. He looked down at the golden skull. With a thumbnail, he tripped the hidden catch. The crown of the skull lifted like a cap. Inside, the top of the deadly sphere showed like a wicked black eyeball... as if staring back with evil intent....

"I—I don't know that I can," James admitted painfully.

"That, my boy, is why this odious duty is my responsibility...."

Wordlessly, the two men stared at one another while the smell of commingled smoke dribbled upward, poisoning the fresh air of the observation platform nearly one hundred dizzying floors above Fifth Avenue.

As they struggled with surging inner emotions, the future of countless lives—not to mention the city of New York—teetered in the balance.

Chapter 40

IMPERTINENT QUESTIONS

DIANE ELLIOT parked her automobile a block away from Mercy Hospital and stepped out into the gathering dusk.

With the possible exception of James Christopher, those who knew her well would not have immediately recognized her. For she wore the crisp white uniform of a registered nurse. A starched cap hat sat perched on her head, half concealing her smart hairdo.

The hospital was one of Manhattan's busiest. Thus, when Diane pushed her way through the revolving door, no one took special note of her. She appeared to be just another nurse arriving for the night shift. There were many such employed by the medical establishment.

Taking the elevator to the seventh floor, Diane stepped off and walked boldly down the corridor, turning her head away as she passed the nurse's station. She was not noticed.

Growing confident that her imposture was succeeding, the newswoman walked down a maze of corridors until she came to a private room, where stood guard a tall man in a native costume and turban, sporting a bushy beard. At his waist, a native knife showed its brassbound hilt. His head turned at her approach and dark, fearsome eyes met her frank and open gaze.

Stepping up to him, Diane said, "I am to look in on Miss van Sloan, please."

The Sikh regarded her suspiciously.

"A different nurse left less than an hour ago," he growled.

"That nurse went home sick. I am replacing her. Please make way."

The dusky-skinned guardian hesitated, then stepped aside to permit her to pass.

"Say nothing to her about Richard Wentworth," he growled.

Nodding mutely, Diane pushed through the door.

The socialite lay on the bed, her chestnut curls spilling over the pale pillow. A tabletop radio was playing classical music.

"Miss van Sloan?"

"Yes, nurse? What is it?" Her voice was distant, almost dreamy.

"I pray that you'll forgive me. But I am not actually a nurse. My name is Diane Elliot. And I—"

Nita van Sloan sat up sharply. Her tone firmed up. "I am familiar with your name. You are with the Amalgamated Press Service, are you not?"

"I am flattered that you recognize my name."

Violet eyes came into sharper focus. "You have a reputation for being resourceful, Miss Elliot—one that you are demonstrating even now. What is it you wish?"

Diane hesitated before speaking. "I assume that you are familiar with the situation facing the city?"

"I've stopped listening to the bulletins. They are… distressing…."

"I wonder if you have some comment about the sighting of The Spider in this neighborhood?"

Nita van Sloan gasped. "The Spider! Here? Impossible!"

"Why do you say that, Miss van Sloan? Is it because you know that The Spider is… deceased?"

The shock of Diane's words made Nita van Sloan recoil. Her face paled, and she turned her profile into her pillow. One hand grasped a handkerchief; she brought it to her mouth.

When she spoke again, her voice was twisted with anguish. "I wish I had never heard of The Spider…."

"Is that because you know who The Spider really is?" pressed Diane. "Perhaps now it is time—time that you told the world the truth…."

Lifting her head, the socialite countered sharply, "Perhaps the day will come when I am not haunted by The Spider, but it is evident that that date has yet to arrive." Her voice turning cold, she added, "I must ask you to leave, Miss Elliot. Or I will have the hospital staff remove you."

"Very well. One last thing. Has Richard Wentworth visited you since The Spider perished?"

"I have it on good authority that Mr. Wentworth is convalescing in his own home. Now good day to you!"

"Goodbye," said Diane, turning to go.

She paced three steps and froze. On the other side of the closed door came a brisk commotion.

The voice of Ram Singh was rising in anger.

"Turn back, thou fiend from Hell!"

STEPPING FORWARD, Diane threw open the door and beheld a stunning tableau.

A man in the hospital whites of an orderly was pointing a tube of some sort at the menacing Sikh warrior. He manipulated it. Instantly, a beam of green light, ghostly and horrible, gushed out at the bearded man.

Lunging forward, Ram Singh grasped the tube and redirected the beam upward, tucking it under the chin of his attacker. Driving him to the floor, he straddled the man, keeping the glaring weapon firmly pressed into the other man's jawbone.

The struggling orderly fought in vain, but his strength was insufficient to the task. Slowly, his hands came away from the tube. The Sikh jumped back, regaining his feet.

As Diane watched in horror, the orderly sat up, and green beams seared from his eyes, scorching the plaster ceiling, which was already beginning to drop hot fragments downward....

Behind her, she heard Nita van Sloan raise her contralto voice in horror.

"What—what is happening out there?"

"It is nothing, Missie Sahib," returned Ram Singh, lifting his knife from his costume tunic and driving it downward, impaling the green-eyed man's liver. He jerked convulsively, then deflated like a human balloon.

Wiping the encrimsoned blade on his defeated foe's hospital whites, the Sikh warrior turned and plunged into the hospital room.

"There are living dead men here, Missie Sahib!" he hissed. "Great danger stalks this hospital. I must whisk you away."

Throwing the covers aside, Nita van Sloan drew on a robe and said, "Let us hurry."

Diane Elliot followed them down the corridor to the elevator, where they halted to press the call button.

Elsewhere on the floor came screams and shouting, intermingled with noisy physical commotion. Feet pounded madly in a crazy tattoo.

"This place is infested with those inhuman horrors," Diane told them urgently.

"Please leave us alone," Nita van Sloan returned firmly. Turning to Ram Singh, she added, "This woman claims that The Spider has been seen in the vicinity."

The Sikh showed great white teeth in a fierce smile. *"Wah!* He lives, then."

"You seem rather interested in The Spider's whereabouts," pressed Diane, "considering that he is believed to be... deceased."

Before either could reply, the elevator arrived, and the stainless-steel door slid aside. All three prepared to step on board, but a hulking form stepped off first.

Ram Singh had been staring suspiciously at Diane Elliot, and so did not notice the lead pipe in the new arrival's upraised hand. With a whisking sound, it came sweeping down.

Reacting to the violent gesture, Ram swiveled—and his dark eyes fell upon the black steel helmet shaped like a stovepipe.

One brown hand flashed to the brass-wire hilt of his hill-knife, but the lead pipe struck first.

The Sikh crumpled to the parquet floor, and black leather fingers reached out to grab Nita van Sloan roughly, pulling her into the elevator car.

The other hand reached for the control lever. But before the door could slide closed, Diane Elliot jumped aboard.

To her surprise, the car jerked upward—*rising, not falling!*

Bravely, Nita demanded, "Am I being kidnapped?"

A booming voice within the steel helmet rang out.

"No, *Fraulein,* we are merely going to the roof to take in the night air. No doubt we will be seen. Perhaps someone will come to your rescue. Perhaps not. But we will see in due course...."

"If you listen to the radio reports or read newspapers, you would know that my fiancé, Richard Wentworth, is a formidable man. He will come for you."

The Man in the Steel Mask gripped her arm more tightly. "I would be interested to see if he does. For I have never met a dead man before. The world knows that Richard Wentworth is The Spider and that The Spider is no more...."

A dreadful laugh emerged from the crude helmet, followed by a fiendish chuckle.

Neither woman joined in that horrid mirth as the elevator climbed to the top floor....

Chapter 41

ROOFTOP RIOT

NO LIGHTS burned on the roof of Mercy Hospital. Night clouds obscured the thin moon and faraway stars. Darkness pressed in, utter and unrelieved.

So it was that, after Steel Mask prodded the two helpless women up the stairs and through the roof hatch, all three had to stand around for some minutes before their eyes adjusted to the dark.

The fires raging in Herald Square and elsewhere were obscured by black smoke whose acrid tang bit into the nostrils and made the tongue taste strange. Here and there, tall buildings were thrown into black relief by a red-orange glow.

While this was transpiring, there was heard a rustle as of silk, or some similar fabric. Soft laugher floated through the night.

Then a commanding voice barked, "Step away from those two women, Stahlmaske. Or I will drill you where you stand!"

For upon the roof loomed a black-cloaked figure, holding a Thompson submachine gun. Under a downturned hat brim, a skirted domino mask of black muslin concealed his features.

"Such a surprise!" thundered Steel Mask. "Whom do I have the honor of addressing?"

Eyes like steel points stared out of the night. "Don't tell me you don't recognize The Spider when you see him in the flesh."

"I see very little flesh. Only fabric. Let me congratulate you on your costume. It appears rather expensive. But I am given to understand that The Spider is no more."

"Enough banter," ground out the other. "This outfit was enough to draw you into the open. Step away from those women. *And do it now!"*

"I am afraid I cannot submit to your instructions," Steel Mask said firmly. "For, if you do not lower your weapon, I will turn them both into beautiful maniacs."

In one hand was clenched a lead pipe. Steel Mask actuated it so that the baffle opened only slightly. A green shine peeped out. It touched the asphalt roof at Nita van Sloan's feet.

"I have only to lift the beam slightly, and the woman will be stricken. Then you will have to shoot her. *Nicht wahr?"*

The cobwebbed challenger was unimpressed. "Think again. At close quarters, I can chop that antique helmet off your shoulders before you can move."

A dry chuckle trailed off. "You may try, my worthy antagonist. We both know that a Thompson submachine gun is difficult to control. No doubt many of your bullets will bounce off my helmet and my chainmail undergarments. The ricochets could fly anywhere. Including into soft, feminine flesh." The giant in the steel mask lifted brawny shoulders and voice resolutely. "Again I say, lower your weapon so that we may discuss this like honorable gentlemen."

The other hesitated. Soft breezes toyed with his ebon cape, revealing glints of silvery threads upon its back. The distant reddish hell-glow brought out the cobweb design, turning the faint silver threads red, like heated electric wires.

Steel Mask's tone darkened. "Do as I say—*Geh-Acht!"*

"Well, you always were the clever devil, Stahlmaske," said G-8, lowering his weapon ever so slightly.

"Danke," returned Steel Mask. His eyes having adjusted to the night, he perceived the streamlined bulk of an autogyro standing on the roof. In the overpowering darkness, he had mistaken it for a squat water tower.

"I see that you kindly brought your sky chariot. Would that

we had such futuristic aircraft in our day, *nein?* Will it seat all four of us?"

Before the G-2 officer could reply, down from the iron ladder of the water tower a ray of light fell. It made a brilliant white disk on the asphalt roof. And in the center of it—*glowed a crimson, hairy-legged spider!*

Seeing this apparition, Nita van Sloan's violet eyes widened, and a sharp gasp escaped her lips.

A laugh broke out, high above their heads—metallic, menacing, troubling the night like a sudden flight of bats.

It was the true laugh of The Spider!

ENCUMBERED BY his heavy, inflexible helmet, Steel Mask struggled to look upward—and the light suddenly found his eyes, blinding him with its reddish-white glare.

Bellowing in anger, he thumbed open the lead pipe's baffle to its full width—and a purling beam jabbed out like emerald lightning. Then he threw his burly arm about, endeavoring to infect everyone within sight.

The beam careened everywhere—*and everyone present knew that the mad green glare spelled instant doom!*

Swinging about his Tommy gun, G-8 ducked back. He did not fire, but refused to release the deadly weapon.

Knowing that they had no recourse, the two women plunged for the roof hatch. Neither were armed....

Clinging to the water tower's ladder by one arm, The Spider attempted to blast the lethal weapon from Steel Mask's waving fist.

Before he could fire, the greenish doom-rays lanced upward, swept him briefly and continued on—but not after bringing to life the spider's web etched in luminous ink that filled the cloak lining. It showed a ghostly radium green....

The automatic in his fist blasted only once—but once was all that was necessary.

The lead slug impacted the pipe, deforming it, knocking it out of the gripping leather glove. Leaping from bullet-stung fingers, the shining contrivance went sliding across the roof, spinning, sweeping the horizon with its brilliant emerald finger of death....

When it clattered to a stop, the weird ray was pointing at the parapet, accomplishing nothing other than to blacken red brick.

Dropping to the rooftop, The Spider stepped up and blasted Steel Mask point-blank in the chest and forehead. Bullets bounced, and the helmet rang like a struck bell. Under the brim of his black hat, The Spider's intense eyes were framed in a domino mask of blued steel. They burned with righteous fury.

Laughing manically, the Master of Men emptied his magazine. Steel Mask staggered about for three halting steps. Like an axed tree, he fell. For half a minute, he lay there, his massive chest rising and falling with his labored breathing. Of blood, there was no sign....

Then, like Frankenstein's monster rising off his bier, the hulking giant struggled to his feet, laughing hollowly, fearlessly, derisively.

"Do you not understand that bullets cannot harm me?" he taunted.

The Spider had drawn a second automatic from beneath his funereal cape and prepared to trigger it.

From the stairwell came the cries of the two women who had reached safety. But they had not reached safety, after all....

"What is it?" demanded The Spider.

Nita van Sloan's horrified voice came back.

"Zombies! The halls are choked with the loathsome creatures. Some of them are—hospital physicians!"

Venting a clipped curse, The Spider turned to G-8, directing curtly, "Hold him here until I am done."

"My pleasure," returned the G-2 agent, grinning.

His ebon cloak whipping behind him like wings, The Spider

drove for the open roof hatch and jumped down, vanishing from view.

Almost immediately, the sound of gunshots came, followed by the howls of the wounded and dying, and then there was smoke and the smell of burning wood mingled with charring human flesh....

Above this hellish cacophony, a resounding laugh thundered out.

It was both dismissive and triumphant at the same time. It was the dreadful, hollow laugh of Stahlmaske....

Chapter 42

ZOMBIE REVELRY

PLUNGING DOWN the roof hatch, The Spider leapt over the stairs and slammed down, his hard heels clicking on the floor like discordant drumbeats.

A second automatic jumped into his hand and he stood for a moment, straddle-legged as he beheld a mad bacchanal of semi-human horrors streaming up the corridor, whose white walls burned greenly.

"The Devil!" he cried out hoarsely,

For blocking the way out were a half-dozen burning-eyed Meteoritic Maniacs, whose blowtorch eyes were searing walls, ceiling and floors. They emitted weird inarticulate cries, like stepped-on rodents, as they jostled one another in their brain-damaged confusion.

Without hesitation, The Spider stood on braced legs and started triggering his weapons in alternation, at the same time placing himself in front of the two women, who were boxed into a corner of the cul-de-sac.

Gun muzzles blasted stabbing tongues of flame. Mortal lead commenced smashing spines, shoulders, obliterating ferocious faces, driving some of the maniacs backward, stumbling into their fellows, creating a hellish maelstrom of blazing human torches, from which horrific shrieks resounded.

The Spider cried out, "Where is Ram Singh?"

Breathlessly, Nita van Sloan answered from behind this elemental human shield, "Struck down while defending me. But he lives."

Diane Elliot added, "An orderly was responsible. He wielded one of the lead pipes that burns with the green light, knocking the other man out. He must have infected those poor people before he attempted to attack Miss van Sloan."

The Spider's hammering guns ran empty. He holstered one, removed the clip from the other, inserted a fresh one, then did the same with his other gun while triggering the first one he had loaded.

Astoundingly accurate lead pummeled the screaming horde, pushing them back with the punishing force of unseen sledge-hammers. Skulls cracked open, disgorging sloppy brain-matter. One howling horror swallowed a burning bullet, snapping back his head. He sprawled back, taking down two of his fellow living dead. Others, unswayed, clambered over them to lurch toward their becaped tormentor.

Well-directed bullets struck them in their breastbones, splintering their rib cages and felling them in mid-stride.

Not all the zombies appeared to comprehend death—or, if they did, feared destruction. For two snarling maniacs came on through the hail of bullets, as their fingers were blasted off straining hands that groped and clawed in The Spider's direction.

When the first automatic ran empty again, Nita cried, "Give that to me! Allow me to help."

The Spider tossed the red-hot weapon to Nita, who caught it in both hands. It was soon followed by a fresh magazine. She jammed it into the grip, raised it fearlessly.

Together, the Master of Men and his mate fired round after smoking round, but it was no good. The zombies who fell did not rise again. But others stepped over them, snarling, directing their burning gaze where it would do the most damage.

Peculiarly, their luminous eyes looked tired, spent, the greenish glow fading by the moment. Even the most vital of them lacked the fiery gaze of those who had caroused destructively only the night before....

Firing his last punishing bullet, The Spider whirled, calling up to the roof hatch.

"Gate! Hand me the Tommy gun! Hurry, man! Time is of the essence."

Down through the open hatch boomed the ribald laughter of Steel Mask.

"If he does as you say, *Herr Spinne,* who will keep me occupied? No, I am afraid that G-8 cannot do for you that little favor."

HOLDING THE Thompson gun level by its fore and rear grips, G-8 wavered. He fully understood then that the situation on the floor below was becoming desperate, may have already deteriorated past that point.

Stahlmaske stood with his arms at his side, showing no attitude of surrender. G-8 had been watching him carefully, while at the same time keeping tabs on the lead pipe that glowed several feet away with a weak green light. He knew that if he surrendered the Tommy gun to The Spider, he would face the Man in the Steel Mask unarmed.

The eyes recessed in the helmet regarded him evilly. They began to glow with a faint reddish radiance. G-8 had known that lurid shine before, years back, during the war. Stahlmaske had learned some mystic art of hypnotism, and his eyes were showing that power coming to the fore once more....

Jerking his gaze away, G-8 avoided the glare that he knew could seize a man's brain and bring it under Stahlmaske's mental control.

His attention naturally went to the lead pipe. He saw that it was cracked and spilling out emerald radiation—doom-rays that were possibly even now seeping into G-8's unprotected brain....

"Oh!" boomed Stahlmaske. "You see your dilemma, do you not? Hold your position—and your poor brain will succumb to the meteorite's influence. Or perhaps my brain-power will take hold of your mind...."

G-8 growled carelessly, "I've killed you before. I can shoot you dead again. It's all in a night's work."

As his finger tightened down on the trigger, Steel Mask put his gloved fists on his hips and issued scorn with his words.

"You will need additional drums, if you wish to kill me. And your friend requires those bullets more than you need to settle our old score, G-8."

It was the truth. There was no denying it.

"Stand aside!" G-8 commanded.

Stahlmaske held his ground. "I refuse."

The red gleam in his eyes resembled burning coals now....

Out in the night, the wailing of police sirens was converging upon the spot.

Over the commotion below, The Spider's strong voice called out again. "What's the devil is keeping you, Captain Gate?"

The Master Spy made his move then. Driving forward, he flipped the Thompson about in his hands, employing the heavy stock to club Steel Mask's chest. Driven by wiry muscles, the blow proved powerful. It caught the helmeted giant by surprise.

He toppled backward, floundering, and G-8 stepped over his massive form, his flying boots crushing the heaving chest and pressing down upon the smooth black helmet.

A guttural oath issued forth from that helm.

Reaching the hatch, G-8 lowered the Thompson, and The Spider's eager hands reached up to claim it.

The interval between the time the weapons changed hands and the strident chatter of the Thompson coming into operation was stunningly brief.

A stream of bullets swept the corridor and turned it into an abattoir—a gore-splatted maelstrom of the dead and the dying, patients, nurses. At least one medico sank into a welter of broken bones and shredded muscle in which individual bodies ceased to appear separate....

Closing their eyes to keep out the horror, the two women turned their faces from the slaughter while The Spider's laugh rose into the air and out through the hatchway and into the night.

It was not the flat mocking laughter that the police and the Underworld alike had come to know and fear. The note was different this time. It was high, wild—perhaps even a little insane.

Its bitter echoes chilled the blood of all who heard it….

Police sirens were winding down as they reached the hospital, skidding and braking as they flung themselves onto the sidewalk before the hospital's main entrance.

Turning from the bloody slaughter he had wrought, The Spider looked up to meet the G-2 captain's horrified domino-masked gaze.

"Can you fly us to safety?"

G-8 nodded grimly. "I can squeeze in four passengers, but what about Stahlmaske? That was my last drum of ammunition you expended."

Handing up the Tommy gun to Gate's waiting hands, The Spider impelled the women up the ladder-steps, then followed. When he reached the top, he said hoarsely, "My guns are empty as well."

G-8 looked down at Steel Mask lying prone on the roof.

"We can't just leave him here. The police won't be able to handle him."

Reaching into his cloak, The Spider removed a coil of line. His infamous Web….

"Get the women into the gyroplane," he rapped out. "I will tie this man up."

G-8 waved to Nita and Diane. "Follow me—hurry!"

As the trio raced for the *Hummingbird* super-gyro, The Spider knelt to truss Steel Mask hand and foot. Grasping one of the leather gloves, he stripped it, and prepared to loop the bare wrist to its mate.

It was evident that the heavy helmet was holding the man's head down. He did not resist.

But the black shell lifted slightly, impelled by bull-strong neck muscles. The hidden eyes came into the light. They were a lurid scarlet, like twin burning coals, and when The Spider's gaze met them, Richard Wentworth could feel the power of the insidious brain behind their uncanny glow.

For several moments, their gazes locked. And the contest of wills began....

THE MENTAL power of Steel Mask radiated outward, and The Spider found his nimble fingers faltering at their task.

"What devilment is this!" he demanded.

In the act of guiding the women into the gyroplane, G-8 turned and barked, "Stahlmaske's some kind of super-hypnotist; don't let him get to you."

Making a fist, The Spider drove his knuckles down, knocking the helmet back, rocking the head encased within. The black shell rang like a dull bell.

With a sudden convulsion, Steel Mask rolled, simultaneously kicking with one booted foot, and struck his opponent's shoulder. The Spider was forced backward. He reached for one of his empty automatics and prepared to use it as a club.

But the Black Knight of modern Germany kept rolling, rolling, rolling toward the cracked lead pipe leaking ugly green radiation....

When he reached it, his bare hand grasped the thing and he jerked it about, pointing it over The Spider's black-hatted head, the doom-rays barely grazing the crown.

"I make you this deal, *Herr Spinne:* leave me your vaunted Web. Go with the others. We will clash again, I promise you. Otherwise, the women will be turned into murderous maniacs."

The lead pipe swept over toward the open hatch of the

gyroplane, filling its interior, making the windscreen turn pale emerald, stopping G-8 and the two women in their tracks, preventing them from boarding.

"Enough!" returned The Spider. "I will take your deal and make you a promise in return. When next we meet, I will see what you look like under that helmet."

"It is a bargain," Steel Mask chucked. "But you would not enjoy the sight."

The weird green beam winked off. But the casing continued leaking where it was cracked.

Depositing his coil of Web on the asphalt, The Spider gained the autogyro in swift bounds. The rotor vanes were already turning, and the nose and tail propellers were also spinning, becoming snarling silvery discs.

When the door clapped shut, the trim little ship jumped like a grasshopper into the sky and began pirouetting about the hospital.

At the controls, G-8 fought to keep the yawing, pitching, overweight ship righted.

"What is he doing?" he demanded.

The Spider replied, "He has tied the Web to a water-tower support and dropped the line over the parapet. He thinks he can climb down it, like a spider...."

"Is it strong enough?"

"That is not the question," returned The Spider. "Is Steel Mask strong enough to make his way down the line without losing his grip?"

Orbiting the hospital, the four passengers watched as the giant without a face laboriously slipped over the parapet and let himself down, hand over hand. The line soon proved sufficiently long to enable him to reach a lower floor, but not the ground.

Watching anxiously, Diane Elliot wondered, "What is he going to do now?"

Steel Mask did the unexpected. He simply let go. Dropping like a stone, he landed on the roof of a police prowl car, denting it significantly.

"Good Lord!" exploded The Spider. "He suicided!"

"Suicide is too good for him," said G-8, flatly "but if that's the way he wanted to go out...."

Before the Master Spy could finish his thought, to their horror, Steel Mask rolled off the police car, strode painfully over to another one that was undamaged, and clubbed the emerging driver to the pavement.

Stepping over the fallen officer, he climbed in and sent the police car scooting away....

"Give chase!" The Spider demanded.

"You don't have to tell me twice!" returned G-8, swinging his buzzing gyroplane about in the night.

Chapter 43

GLOWING GREEN BARRIER

BEHIND THE wheel of the racing police car, Steel Mask cursed gutturally.

With each turn, the pointed crown of his stovepipe helmet violently bumped the car roof. The sight of a black-helmeted giant driving a police radio car would normally have turned heads. Normalcy was not part of this evening, however. Pedestrians were scarce. Automobiles scooted about. It seemed as if the whole city were ablaze. But that was mere appearance.

Mercy Hospital was fully engulfed in flames, many of its windows looking like cut-out jack-o'-lantern eyes with candles flaming behind the window glass. Smoke was starting to dribble out, soon spreading into dark billows. Fire trucks were tearing through the night, racing toward it.

More disturbing perhaps was the site of the uprearing Vertex tower. It, too, was ablaze! But only the upper floors. And while these fires were scattered and fitful, they showed definite signs of spreading.

Taking in these horrific sights, Steel Mask's body shook with dreadful laughter....

AT THE controls of the drumming *Hummingbird* super-gyro, G-8 kept the police car in sight.

"He's heading north!" he told The Spider.

"Stay with him!" urged the Master of Men. "Stay with him if you care to apprehend Steel Mask!"

In an ordinary monoplane aircraft, it would have been all but impossible to chase a single police car through the canyons of the city, but the agile *Hummingbird* could skim between buildings and execute sudden sharp changes in course.

The fleeing machine made several attempts to throw pursuit off the trail, dousing its headlamps, scurrying up side streets and then doubling back, crisscrossing lower Manhattan as if threading a gigantic maze.

Each time, either G-8 or The Spider saw through the subterfuge, and they held to the trail.

Once, the auto ducked into the shadows of the Elevated train tracks, idled there with headlamps dark.

Floodlights mounted on the gyro hull blazed, revealing the lurking machine. The Spider's flashlight painted the midnight-blue vehicle with his scarlet symbol with its eight sprawled limbs....

Roaring from its hiding place, the radio car shot up the streets, headlamps bouncing, careening crazily.

The *Hummingbird* jinked after it, a determined pursuer.

The police had staked out the Electric Building, but with the emergency at Mercy Hospital, radio cars were being summoned from all points to assist in the evacuation. Two squad cars had lately departed the Electric Building vicinity, leaving it unguarded. Citizens had not been allowed to enter since the first skirmish there.

The basement garage door stood invitingly open.

Racing west on East Forty-second Street, Steel Mask suddenly threw the police auto across the sidewalk and, bouncing on its springs, flung the auto into the garage itself.

Buzzing close behind, the G-2 agent spotted the maneuver and pointed with a stiff finger.

"He slipped into the Electric Building!"

"A ruse!" snapped The Spider. "He knows that building harbors a secret escape tunnel to another location. I will brave that tunnel. Drop me off in the street, then take these women to safety!"

Shaking his head stubbornly, G-8 growled, "No dice. Stahlmaske is my assignment. If anyone is taking him in, it'll be me!"

"For God's sake, man! At least let these women off before we plunge into the fray."

There was no denying that necessity. Throttling his trim aircraft, G-8 settled down in grassy Bryant Park. After the props ceased turning and the rotor-wing vanes drooped, hatches were thrown open, and the women stepped out. The Spider directed them to the Bryant Park Elevated station at Sixth and Forty-second Street, unarguably the quickest way out of the neighborhood.

"Be careful... Spider!" implored Nita van Sloan, violent eyes beseeching.

For a moment, it seemed as if The Spider and the beautiful young socialite were about to embrace, but they reasserted control over themselves and went their separate ways.

Alone in the dark, G-8 removed his Spider cloak and other habiliments. He stood revealed in his flying jacket and boots.

"I'm ready if you're ready," he told The Spider.

"Follow me, then."

Gaining the street, passing the silent stone lions guarding the Public Library entrance, G-8 donned his flying helmet and goggles while The Spider drew from his cloak hem his walking stick with the amber handle. He gave it a twist. The barrel dropped free, revealing a slender blade.

"I have no other weapon save this," he said in his harshly metallic tones.

"You've got me beat there," quipped G-8. "I don't even have a pocket knife."

They reached the garage door in quick order. It was now shut.

Slipping around to the main entrance, they made their way down the back stairs. The lights were out in the garage, so they walked carefully by the light of The Spider's flashlight. A crimson spider showed wherever the Master of Men directed his beam.

"Clever," grunted G-8. "You placed your seal on the lens of the electric torch."

The Spider chuckled. "With so many pseudo-Spiders walking around—you among them—I required some way to proclaim my bona fides."

"It's also an excellent way to make yourself a target."

The other shrugged his black-cloaked shoulders indifferently.

"Drawing a foe's fire is a certain way to lure him to his own destruction...."

"If you say so...."

The Spider and the Flying Spy soon found the abandoned police car. They passed to a certain spot in a concrete wall.

The Spider hissed, "Previously, I tracked Count Calypsa to this spot, but could not follow him. If we can locate the switch that opens the concealed door, we will have our trail."

By the light of the electric torch, the Master of Men illuminated a crack in the concrete foundation, found a catch, and managed to trigger it. The crack widened, forming a door which fell open to disclose a narrow dimly-lit tunnel. They entered, walking softly, wary of traps.

They had not progressed very far when they discovered on the concrete floor a sinister object. A short lead pipe such as the one Steel Mask had wielded. It lay on the ground in such a way that the baffle stood open.

Light pouring from the interior was weak, but to their horror, they realized that the greenish glare was pointing deeper into the tunnel, *bathing the way ahead in its unholy glow!*

Chapter 44

LAST STAND

THE SMOKE of scattered fires coming from Intelligence Service headquarters on the fifty-fifth floor of the towering Vertex Building boiled up through the stairwells and the solitary elevator shaft to the observation platform surrounding the Art Deco spire itself.

Coughing, Z-7 said, "The upper floors are ablaze!"

James Christopher cursed under his breath. "I was a fool to hesitate. I waited too long! I should have gone below. I should have—" His voice trailed off into a spasm of coughing.

"Gone below to snuff out the lives of your fellow Intelligence operatives," finished Z-7. "Could you have done that? Perhaps now we will never know...."

James's eyes were strange. "All those good patriotic men down there... facing suffocation if they do not roast alive."

"I have no doubt on that score," said Z-7 in a thick, horror-suffused voice. His black eyes veered to the gold skull on Operator 5's watch chain.

"It may not be too late. If all are doomed to perish, better that they perish quickly, mercifully, not choking and burning, surrendering their lives in a hellish cyclone of destruction."

"I have an idea," said James suddenly, pulling a handkerchief from his breast pocket. "One that might work."

"What is it?"

Instead of replying, Operator 5 covered his nose and mouth with the silk—which was chemically treated to block fumes—and raced toward the elevator car. He stabbed the call button. The cage waited at this level. The grilled door slid aside.

Stepping in, he thumbed a tiny catch on the ruby-eyed golden skull, revealing a black ball of doom no larger than a pea.

Gingerly, Operator 5 held the skull steady as he knelt on the stainless-steel floor. Ever so carefully, he tilted it, slipping the black sphere onto the bundled handkerchief, which he laid at his feet. After it was nestled in the linen folds, he pressed the button marked *55* and swiftly stepped off the elevator.

Door closing, the cage sank, and the instrument of destruction was carried down to its destination.

Z-7 had been standing with horror-stricken eyes, half-expecting that James Christopher had gone manfully to his own destruction, when the latter batted his way out of the growing grey smoke.

"James, my boy! Did your courage fail you? Could you not go through with it?"

"On the contrary," said Operator 5 in a decisive voice. "I sent the sphere of Diphenochlorasine gas down to the fifty-fifth floor. If anyone there is still fighting to escape, no doubt they will take advantage of the arriving elevator. Once a crowd steps on board, someone will almost certainly crush the black pellet underfoot, releasing the deadly gas."

Z-7 swallowed hard. "That—that means—"

"That means virtually everyone still trapped in this building will be dead within minutes, if not seconds. Everyone—" he met Z-7's black eyes with his own blue orbs, "everyone including... *ourselves*...."

"I see what you have done. You could not bring yourself to kill your fellow operators by direct action. So you formulated a means by which someone other than yourself did the terrible deed."

James squared his husky shoulders. "My conscience may not be entirely absolved, but my duty was clear. And I executed it. That is what is of utmost importance."

Operator 5's forceful words struck home. The two men locked eyes, and for fully a minute, neither spoke.

Finally, Z-7 cleared his throat and offered his right hand in a firm handclasp.

"In these last precious moments of life, I want to express my heartfelt appreciation to you, Operator 5. We have worked together but five years, yet I feel like a father toward you. I had hoped that one day you would rise in the organization and perhaps take my place long after I was—gone!" His emotion-thickened voice broke at the last.

James returned the handshake with an iron grip and a dry palm.

"I could not imagine a finer leader than you, sir. You have been an inspiration to me. An inspiration and yet—I still do not know your real name."

Choking back his emotions, the Intelligence Chief said thickly, "I imagine at this ultimate juncture that it would not be a betrayal of my oath of secrecy to reveal my first name, although my sense of duty constrains me from divulging my paternal name."

They released one another's hands.

"I appreciate that, sir," returned James. "But let us not deviate from our duty, even in the face of death. Let us go out, not as men, but loyal and faithful numbers in the Intelligence Service of the United States of America...."

"I bow to your superior sentiment, Operator 5," breathed Z-7.

The smoke was coiling up more strongly, now turning from grey to black. As it stung their nostrils, clogging their windpipes, they wondered if it was yet carrying the deadly chemical gas....

The two men stood staring at one another for agonizingly long minutes. Without another word, they turned and looked out upon the evening horizon of New York City, mutually choosing to be alone with their final thoughts and to gaze upon the lights of the great city that they had long struggled to protect from enemies, foreign and otherwise.

James's thoughts flashed back to his first important assignment, to smash the foreign power that had been terrorizing Manhattan with a diabolic device that killed all electricity in the city. He had traced the attacks to this very building, smashing the espionage ring behind it all... ironic that headquarters would be set up here... even more ironic that the Vertex spire would prove to be the spot where he and Z-7 made their last stand....*

Up from the stairwell, malevolent black smoke squirmed like monster dragons, their rolling coils seemingly endless... and pregnant with poison....

* Operator 5: *The Masked Invasion.*

Chapter 45

BALKED

STANDING ROOTED, momentarily paralyzed by sight of the pulsing greenish glow blocking their path, The Spider and G-8 stared at the lead pipe bathing the narrow tunnel confines with deadly radiation.

"We'll have to turn back," the Flying Spy gasped. "There's no way around it."

Beneath his blue-steel mask, The Spider's teeth clenched. Anguish twisted his rasping voice, "But we are close, so close to running those two monsters to earth...."

"We won't do anybody any good if we turn into brainless zombies, will we?"

"No doubt you are correct," admitted The Spider, turning to point his sword back toward the basement garage. "You may lead the way."

G-8 wasted no time. He sprinted down the passageway, turned a corner, where the green glow no longer painted the cracked concrete walls. The soft footsteps of The Spider echoed behind him. After a minute, he paid them no more heed....

The Master Spy failed to notice that The Spider had not followed him all the way until he was back in the basement garage, all alone....

Had The Spider succumbed to the doom-rays? To turn back and investigate would be to fall victim to the same dire fate.... The prospect sent chills running along G-8's spine. His scalp prickled with growing horror....

FOR HIS part, The Spider trailed Captain George Gate only a few dozen yards and then he abruptly turned about, dashing past the lead pipe, webbed cape flying, sword cane lifted, intent on running his quarry to earth.

The fact that he had rushed through the zone of radiation caused the Master of Men to hesitate not a moment. His grey-blue eyes were ablaze, his mouth a tight slash. Half under his breath, the laughter of The Spider began to rise from his throat—and there was a tinge of madness in its rollicking cadences....

UNDER THE malevolent regard of the proud lion seated upon a crown of gold, Count Calypsa squatted impatiently behind his magnificent desk, the corner radio receiver blasting out the latest bulletins.

"Mercy Hospital is ablaze. Fire engines are converging on the spot. Exact details of this disaster are not yet known... wait! Newsflash! A fire has broken out high in the Vertex tower! It is not certain what has caused this latest blaze, but the conflagration is reported to be spreading. It can only be hoped that the building's sprinkler systems will work to suppress the flames, inasmuch as fire hoses cannot be dragged up to the uppermost floors...."

The hidden elevator car arrived and from behind a heavy wall curtain, Steel Mask stepped out, looking somewhat the worse for wear. His executioner's outfit was torn and tattered. One of his gloves was missing. He walked ponderously in his heavy boots, limping noticeably.

Rising from his high-back chair, Count Calypsa demanded, "You succeeded?"

"Nein," he said wearily, tones heavy. "I failed. I confronted the hated G-8 but failed to crush him. For The Spider lives. I beheld him with my own eyes."

"How do you know that it was the actual article?"

"I know the voice of this one. There is no mistaking it. The Spider lives. I do not understand how. But both he and G-8 have attempted to follow me to this spot."

"Wait! You led them here? You imbecile!"

The Man in the Steel Mask's guttural tones grew surly. "Do not be rash in your accusations, *mein Graf.* For I prepared a trap. I parked in the Electric Building and took the passageway to this place. I left in the tunnel one of the lead pipes, its baffle wide open, but pointing away from any invader. If they see it—and they cannot avoid doing so—they will either turn around in terror or seek to brave it. If they do the latter, they will surely succumb to meteoric doom-rays before they realize that the tunnel leads to the Gotham Arms. Do not exert yourself, Count. We are perfectly safe here."

So saying, Steel Mask walked heavily to one of the massive leather chairs and lowered his imposing bulk into it, clasping the armrest with his heavy hands. He proceeded to remove the remaining glove, and from the steel shell encasing his head, the sound of his breathing came... heavy and ragged.

"What of your scheme to capture Nita van Sloan?" asked Calypsa.

"I succeeded. Temporarily. I also managed to lure G-8 out into the open. But alas, we had a stalemate. But take heart. I do not doubt but that we will clash again."

Lowering himself back into his throne-like chair, Count Calypsa laid his palms down on the mahogany tabletop. He tapped the Call-o-phone instrument with one blunt finger, illuminating it.

"My Numbers are reporting that the city is in confusion again. But not so great an uproar as I had expected. Number Thirty-six successfully distributed fragments of the meteorite to all points in and about the city. But other than the fires engulfing Mercy Hospital and the Vertex spire, there does not seem to be a great deal of chaos generated for all of our efforts."

"Tut-tut," said Steel Mask, waving those concerns away. "The evening is yet young. We will celebrate our zombie saturnalia. Do not doubt it. When the dawn arrives, if the city is not prostrate before us, we have more pieces of meteorite to distribute."

Count Calypsa seemed to relax, but not fully. His hands fidgeted, and he grabbed for the stoppered medicine bottle, swallowing two morphine pills dry. He did not bother with water. He experienced some difficulty swallowing, but finally got the pills down.

Steel Mask inquired, "Your wounds still trouble you?"

"They do. Are you injured?"

"I took a nasty fall. It was rather steep. Fortunately, my armor prevented any breakage of bone, although I would expect that I am bruised most thoroughly."

The two men fell into an uncomfortable silence. They felt a disturbing sense of being under siege—even if they could not see those besieging them.

The radio blared out another imperative bulletin.

"At this hour, the Vertex tower is virtually a firebrand lighting the night sky. Citizens are cautioned to avoid the area, just as Mercy Hospital is being cordoned off to all but lawful authorities."

Just then, the sound of the elevator descending came distinctly to their ears.

Count Calypsa jerked to his feet. "Did you hear that? Someone just summoned the secret elevator, called it downward!"

Steel Mask did not rise from his chair. He did not move a muscle. He seemed sunk in thought.

Slowly, he rasped, "Yes, I heard the sound. It is most interesting. I wonder... who it could be?"

Calypsa trembled. "Do you think it is... The Spider?"

The heavy black helm struggled to nod. "Perhaps only The Spider is foolhardy enough to brave the meteorite radiation. On the other hand, G-8 no doubt burns to drive a bullet into my poor brain at his earliest opportunity. Our mysterious visitor could be either man."

"I would rather face G-8 than The Spider… now."

"I, too, would prefer the despised G-8. But I am willing to confront either gentleman. Or even both. Count, my bones are weary. Would you be kind enough to fetch me one of the remaining lead pipes? I do not think I can move very easily, bruised as I am. With an appropriate weapon in hand, I may not need to."

From a desk drawer, Count Calypsa hastily withdrew one of the lead pipes and carried it over to Steel Mask's side.

"You are very cool for a man about to confront one of his mortal enemies," Calypsa remarked.

"I am resigned to the fact that I will not be getting any well-deserved rest this evening. My entire body aches. I would prefer to put this off. But destiny has cooked for us another dish, no? You might take in hand a suitable weapon for yourself."

From under his robes, Calypsa pulled out a bulldogged .38-caliber revolver.

Steel Mask's slotted eyes noted it. "Such a pitiful weapon for such a momentous occasion. If The Spider shows his masked face, feel free to fill him full of bullets. But if it is G-8 who arrives, kindly leave him to me. For I have been waiting for this hour a very long time…."

The elevator car was returning now. It halted. Beyond the concealing wall hanging came the hum of the automatic door sliding open.

Both men stared at the heavy cloth-of-gold drape, narrowing eyes glittering with interest.

Then, wild laughter filled the room as the heavy curtain was suddenly swept aside—disclosing the steely blue mask of The Spider!

But that chilling sight was not what drew gasps of shock from the lips of Steel Mask and Count Calypsa.

It was the weird greenish glow emanating from the eyeholes of The Spider's metallic mask....

Chapter 46

FEAR'S FACE-OFF

THE LAUGHTER of The Spider was a mad thing; it filled the luxurious room like the mockery of all the devils and imps immured in Hell, a cacophony calculated to stop a man in his tracks, congealing his very soul.

For a moment, the two conspirators froze in place, stunned by the blood-curdling sound—and the sight of those burning green domino-masked eyes....

"Mein Gott!" muttered Steel Mask. "My weapon is of no use now."

Turning his shoulder so that his eye slits faced his confederate, he added, "I am too weak to lift my axe. You must use your pistol. Otherwise, he will torch this room and everything in it. We will burn...."

The Spider stood poised on the threshold, one hand gripping the glittering sword cane tipped with curare poison and black-widow spider venom. The other held a flashlight. He snapped it on, directing the dazzling beam at Count Calypsa, producing a splash of red on the man's meaty, unpleasant countenance, momentarily blinding him before he could tug on the trigger of his revolver.

Recoiling in shock, Calypsa gave an anguished cry and attempted to direct the blunt barrel at his foe.

Dropping the flashlight, The Spider lifted his cape, revealing its shimmering steel-blue lining with its ghostly green stitchery. For a moment, he stood immobile, like an ebony, elongated arachnid suspended in its symmetrical web....

The revolver muzzle shook as its confused owner yanked wildly at the trigger. The gun blasted, its cylinder jerking in its mechanical revolutions.

Turning sideways, The Spider swept the cloak before him. Hot lead plucked at the silken fabric, but failed to penetrate the twitching, bullet-resistant stuff. One silk-arrested slug punched him in the chest, knocking the Master of Men against the elevator's stainless-steel back wall. But he kept his feet, recovering swiftly.

"Two can wear bulletproof garments!" The Spider cried out.

The smoking revolver clicked emptily. Furiously, Calypsa flung it away and attempted retreat.

"Ach, you disappoint me, *mein Graf,"* murmured Steel Mask. Lifting the lead tube, he depressed the button that caused the baffle to pop open. A rush of green light flowed out, pale and ghostly.

Directing this at his cowering confederate, Steel Mask bathed him in its unholy glow, chuckling dryly.

"Now, perhaps, you will be motivated to fight back with all your fury."

Eyes still shocked sightless, Count Calypsa had no inkling of what was happening. He stumbled back against his desk, clutched at it, attempted to fumble his way around its hard edges, finally reaching a drawer, from which he extracted a spike-snouted Luger automatic. This he lifted into view.

Abruptly, he lost interest. His unseeing eyes took on an emerald shine… and when they shot greenish beams downward at the lion-emblazoned carpet, the deep fibers began smoldering….

Laughing, The Spider crossed the room in four swift strides, his rapier carried high, wicked tip pointing ahead. With an arm-straightening lunge, he impaled his confused foe directly in the center of his chest!

The double dose of poison and venom took hold, paralyzing

the beating heart. As The Spider drew back the wetly crimson blade, Calypsa clutched at his chest as he fell to the floor, his weapon discharging once. The slug burned past The Spider's hat brim, nicking it, but otherwise causing no harm except to a concealed ceiling light, which shattered. Sparks flew, spilling upon the carpet.

Sight of his co-conspirator in crime crumpling to the floor caused Steel Mask to lift his heavy body off the chair, crying, *"Gott im Himmel!"*

Turning, The Spider's glittering green eyes fell upon Steel Mask. His maniacal laughter faded, and he declared, "No—Steel Mask in Hell! *Which is where I am sending you!"*

And the rapier-like blade lunged again.

One great beam of an arm came up heavily, and the lead pipe intercepted the glittering blade, knocking it aside.

"You still possess your wits!" Steel Mask cried out. "How?"

"Never mind that now! *En garde!"*

"Very well. Have it your way." Steel Mask raised the pipe, thumbing open the baffle. Pale green light oozed out. It splashed The Spider's face, turning the blue-steel mask an unlovely shade of green.

"You must cower," insisted a guttural voice.

The Spider lunged again, attempting to insert the tip of the blade into one of Steel Mask's eye slots, but he encountered an obstacle.

"Did you forget my leaded glass lenses, *Herr Spinne?"* taunted Stahlmaske. "It helps protect my brain from the meteorite rays. But what protects *you?"*

The Spider only laughed. His blade leapt out, probing and darting, but finding no entry.

The hulking giant did not attempt to dodge any of these feints. He simply stood his ground, holding the heavy pipe steady, keeping its unholy radiance fixed upon The Spider.

For his part, the Master of Men seemed uncaring. His laugh was that of a genuinely brave man, not a foolhardy one.

Steel Mask demanded, "Why do you not fall!"

"I do not care to," returned The Spider coolly.

Stepping back, he swept the blade around, caught the trigger guard of the fallen revolver, flicking it upward. The weapon spun into the air. The Spider's hand snapped out, caught it perfectly. Impaling the carpet with his quivering blade, he slipped two .38-caliber slugs—kept ready in a pocket for exactly such emergencies—into the open cylinder.

Lifting the weapon, The Spider directed the barrel toward the Man in the Steel Mask.

Now it was Stahlmaske's turn to laugh.

"You cannot expect that puny pistol to penetrate my garments when higher-caliber lead could not?"

Shrugging nonchalantly, The Spider said, "It never hurts to try."

The slug slammed into Steel Mask's chest, piercing the protective leather jerkin, but lodging in the chainmail, whose shiny links showed beneath. Directing the muzzle upward, The Spider bounced another slug off the giant's metal forehead. The upper body rocked back, but Steel Mask held his ground, his footing firm.

The green glare of the ray projector was knocked aside. It fell upon Count Calypsa, lying on the carpet. Lying, not dead, but dying. His eyes were squeezed shut in pain, but now they snapped open.

His mouth parted and he shrieked, "Am I dead? Am I dying? God in Heaven—*am I already in Hell?*"

THE SPIDER'S voice rang out, bitterly cold with pitiless judgment.

"*Sic Semper Tyrannis*—Count Dictator... thus always to tyrants...."

Inclining his helmeted skull toward his former partner, Steel Mask suggested deferentially, *"Herr Spinne,* why you do not put him out of his misery?"

"The web of crime is exceedingly sticky," intoned The Spider. "Count Calypsa has earned his misery. Just as you have earned yours!"

With a thin wail, Carmine Calypsa, the would-be Dictator of New York, exhaled his last. Hot yellow flames crept along the carpet toward his body, but he was beyond all fear now... and all harm....

Ignoring his foe as well as the green beam that bathed his cloak, igniting the luminous orb web design of the inner lining, The Spider bent over his newly-dead foe. Extracting his platinum cigarette lighter, he pressed the base, placing the crimson seal of The Spider upon the dead man's meaty brow....

That done, he stood up, recovered his still-upright blade by grasping the amber handle, and turned to face the Man in the Steel Mask.

"Now it is your turn," he said with firm resolve.

"I doubt that you can remove this helmet. But my curiosity remains. Why are you not a raving maniac? Your eyes glittered greenly."

The Spider's lips warped in a bitter smile.

"An illusion. Green contact lenses reflecting the ceiling lights...."

"Yet you stand up to the meteorite's radiation."

"Look at the beam again."

Steel Mask's eyes flicked downward. He grunted. It appeared exceedingly pale now.

"The lead pipe you left in the tunnel shed light that was even paler," explained The Spider. "Perhaps it never occurred to you that the energy radiating from the meteor fragments weakens by the hour. The phenomenon is what is known as nuclear decay.

And now the last fragments are fading in strength. Calypsa succumbed only because he stood closer to you than did I."

Stahlmaske inclined his shell-shaped head deferentially.

"Thank you for explaining why so few doomed zombies walk upon this night. I should have thought of this possibility. All radioactive materials decay over time. This meteorite is no different. That is too bad. I have lost my most powerful weapon."

So saying, Steel Mask closed the baffle. But he did not throw away his weapon. Instead, he advanced, lifting the thing as a club. His intention became clear. It was to dash out The Spider's brains.

Keeping his guard up, The Spider faded backward, his lethal blade dancing before him.

"That will do you no good," remarked Steel Mask.

The Spider lifted his electric torch, turned it on. His flashlight sprayed searing red light in Steel Mask's eyes as he stepped to one side.

The lumbering giant reeled blindly, his uplifted fist attempting to swing downward, but his arms were aching from his terrific fall onto the steel roof of the police car and, while his strength was still potent, his ability to control his brawny muscles was lacking.

Waving blunt fingers before his blank face, Steel Mask temporized, seeking to buy time until his vision returned to normal. Each time, The Spider's flash beam placed the red symbol of The Spider on his helmeted face, blinding him anew.

Several minutes of this produced nothing—except Steel Mask's blundering about brought him to the burning carpet. Feeling the flames caused him to jerk away and crash into one of the sumptuous wall hangings, which dropped free, covering him briefly. With a roar of rage, he swept this away, whereby it nearly knocked over The Spider.

Finally, the two men stood facing one another, neither able to achieve an advantage over his enemy.

Steel Mask panted, "Would you to call this a stalemate?"

"It is more on the order of a Mexican standoff," returned The Spider, his tone edged and steely. "Perhaps you should simply surrender, and I will turn you over to military Intelligence, or the Intelligence Service, if you prefer."

"Thank you, no. I prefer my freedom."

"I prefer your death," said The Spider coolly. "It is just a matter of arranging it."

Steel Mask whipped up both hands. "How do you propose to work your will upon me? I am invulnerable to your blade and your fists—and even your guns, if you only had them."

The Spider's intense eyes went to Steel Mask's ungloved hands.

"One scratch across the back of your hand and you will know exquisite agony," he warned crisply. "Surrender now, if you please."

Clasping both hands behind his back, Steel Mask struck an attitude, proud, inflexible, unafraid.

"I do not please. Did your worst, *Herr... Wentworth!*"

The two foes stared at one another, and then something unexpected transpired.

Through the exposed windowpane from which the heavy drape had fallen, a silvery gyroplane rose into view, catching the attention of both men, its rotor wing churning the night air, nose propeller blasting air into the room with the force of a gathering hurricane. And in the center of the prop's spinner, an ominous steel-rimmed orifice turned....

"*Ach!* I believe we have a visitor." Turning his blank face to the window, Steel Mask shouted, "Welcome, G-8! I see you are well. Is that a thirty-caliber machine gun barrel mounted in the nose of your propeller? Do you propose to shoot me with it? Would you do such a thing?" He lifted his arms and dropped his useless lead-pipe ray projector to the burning carpet.

"As you can see, I am unarmed. I do not think you would shoot an unarmed man. For this is no longer wartime, *nein?*"

Behind the curved gyro windscreen, the grim grey eyes of G-8 peered through his aviator goggles. There was no emotion in them. Only fixity of purpose.

Without warning, the nose propeller gun barrel began vomiting fire and fury, shattering the window pane and casing into flying fragments!

Chapter 47

PAROXYSM OF VIOLENCE

THE HELLISH storm of .30-caliber lead slugs hurled Steel Mask helplessly across the room and into the open elevator cage, where one flailing arm struck the control lever. The car went plummeting downward.

The fury of the screaming lead shattered recessed ceiling fixtures and brought down heavy tapestries, one of which struck The Spider, carrying him to the floor and out of the path of the teeth of ricocheting bullets.

The vicious storm abated almost as quickly as it had erupted.

Struggling to throw off the enveloping tapestry, The Spider found his feet and rushed to the broken window, squeezing his eyes in the teeth of the prop-driven gale.

"Steel Mask is escaping by the elevator!" he warned. "Attempt to head him off!"

G-8 stuck his helmeted head out the open gyroplane cabin window.

"Hop aboard! We'll hunt him together!"

Waving one arm energetically, The Spider called back, "Never mind about me! There is no time! You must land and intercept the blackguard."

Recognizing the steely resolve in the Master of Men's eyes, the G-2 agent executed a snappy salute and flung the rotorplane around, dropping from view.

Withdrawing from the shattered window bank, Richard Wentworth swept the room with anxious eyes. Ignoring the corpse of the dead Dictator, Count Calypsa, he saw the smoldering rug and the flames rapidly consuming a pile of fallen tapestry and knew he must escape the room before the billowing smoke overcame him.

His agile mind recognized that this room was an exact duplicate of the one he had first penetrated in the Electric Building, a short distance away. Until the elevator was again free to be recalled, he could not depart by that route. But he knew there was a secret entrance, and he rushed to the inner wall where he expected it to be.

Sweeping the cloth-of-gold drapery aside, Wentworth revealed—a blank wall!

Cursing in frustration, he brought the hem of his silken cloak up to his mouth and nostrils, seeking to hold back the deepening smoke from penetrating his lungs. Wentworth began to hack and cough distressingly.

"There must be another exit!" he ground out. "There must be!"

As crackling flames crept higher and the room filled with a smothering miasma, The Spider wrenched down the remaining wall hangings with a strength that came from his indomitable will and no other place, finally pulling free the tapestry depicting the arrogant symbol of the Dictator's ruthless ambitions—a lion athwart a crown of gold.

But no tapestry revealed another escape route.

Returning to the window, he hung his head out and peered below. The gyroplane had landed in the street, its rotor wing still spinning in place. He saw the leather-clad figure of Captain George Gate leap from the aircraft and disappear in the direction of the building entrance.

To the north, Wentworth spied the Vertex Building, its upper floors orange with terrible flames. There was smoke there, too, a mounting column of it....

Drawing in great sobbing lungfuls of air, The Spider plunged back into the room, leaping gingerly over the growing flames. The carpet was now almost completely involved....

The Spider's shoes were made of a fireproof material. He kept his bulletproof cloak close about him protectively. But such protections would not long forestall fiery destruction.

Ducking behind the massive mahogany desk, Wentworth fumbled at the broad desktop, feeling around its hard edges, seeking hidden catches or concealed studs.

To his horror, he found none.

Gritting his teeth, he threw open the top drawers on either side and found a small lever. This he threw.

Where a blank cream wall showed opposite the window bank, a cunningly concealed door cracked apart. "At last!" Wentworth crowed. "Succor!"

But escape was not as simple as bounding across the room. For the rug was now entirely ablaze!

Sweeping from the swivel chair to the desktop, The Spider set himself, gathering his cloak protectively about him. The desktop was broad, but not very deep. There was only space sufficient to take two quick steps. With a contemptuous foot, he first kicked away the useless Call-o-phone device.

Bracing himself, Wentworth threw his lithe form across the room, landing short of the open door. He rolled the rest of the way, smothering the burning carpet flames as he sought the relative safety of the open passage.

By this time his silken cloak was trailing fire. He threw the disintegrating garment back into the conflagration, then turned and raced down a corridor to the public elevator.

Miraculously, The Spider had retained his sword cane. His hat sat crazily upon his head, the brim singed and smelling bitterly of smoke. One hand reached up to the blue-steel domino mask that concealed his aristocratic features. It had remained in place—the one certain thing that identified him as the Master of Men!

Stabbing the button, The Spider sent the cage hissing downward. It dropped with agonizing slowness to deposit him in the gloomy basement. As he did so, he removed the green-colored contact lenses that had convinced his enemies that he had succumbed to the emerald doom rays.

Rushing to the secret passage, he plunged in, and instantly smelled smoke, a certain indication that Steel Mask had already passed this way!

"Dammit!" cursed Wentworth.

Turning, he made for the garage entrance door, pressing the button.

It felt warm to his touch!

"Good God! Could Steel Mask have already escaped?"

A fresh trail of motor oil at his feet suggested that the hulking giant had appropriated an automobile and made his escape.

As the electrical machinery actuated, causing the toiling garage door to lift, The Spider waited impatiently, gripping his sword cane.

Ducking under the lifting gate, he stepped out into the street. Night had fully fallen over the city....

There, in the middle of the street, sat the *Hummingbird* gyroplane.

And walking toward him, fists clenched, was the goggled and helmeted Captain Gate!

"Did you see him?" Wentworth demanded. "Which way did the devil go?"

G-8 continued advancing.

"Answer me, man!" raged Wentworth. "Did you see Steel Mask? He must have come this way! Why are you not speaking?"

And then Wentworth noticed the glazed look in G-8's clear eyes, and the cloudy and doubtful expression upon the Master Spy's regular features.

He searched those goggled eyes for signs of greenish light... but they appeared to be an ordinary grey....

And Wentworth knew!

"Great God in Heaven! The steel-faced devil has hypnotized you, hasn't he?"

REGISTERING THOSE words, G-8 lifted his fists and lunged for The Spider!

Tossing aside his sword cane as useless—for he could not impale his fellow crusader with its poisoned tip—The Spider stepped forward, landing the first punch. It rocked G-8 backward, staggering him.

For fully a minute the two men traded blows, The Spider attempting to penetrate the man's dazed mental machinery.

"Throw off your confusion!" he exploded. "Snap out of it! Steel Mask is escaping!"

Gate merely threw another punch, clipping Wentworth on the side of his metallic mask, thereby skinning his own knuckles.

Stepping back four paces, The Spider extracted his platinum cigarette lighter and snapped it alight. Waving the flame before him, he caught G-8's attention and began exerting his own will.

"You possess no mind of your own," he said steadily. "You have no fight left in you. Your mind is an empty vessel—a bowl which I fill with my own will. The dominating power of The Spider, who is correctly called... Master of Men!"

G-8 resembled a prizefighter out on his feet, struggling with his mental focus. Confused ripples crossed his face like a freshening wind troubling a sail.

"When I snap my fingers," intoned The Spider, "you will break free of the spell of Steel Mask!"

So saying, Wentworth snapped his fingers once, sharply.

As if stung, G-8's expression flinched. Twitching, he took a step backward. The confusion twisting his features seemed to ebb away, as if a cloud had been lifted.

Peering about, eyes clearing, the Flying Spy demanded, "Where is he? Where did that damned Stahlmaske get to?"

Speaking breathlessly, The Spider regained his sword cane and rasped, "The coward made his escape by automobile. He must have paused long enough to exert his hypnotic powers upon you. You succumbed, I regret to say. And now he is out in the night, making his getaway."

Balling his fists in frustration, G-8 gritted, "It's coming back to me now. He tore out of the garage, driving a blue sedan like he was on fire."

"Then we must hurry!"

The two men jumped into the gyroplane. G-8 frantically spun the rotor wing, simultaneously engaging fore and aft propellers. The silvery ship jerked on its fat tires, as if eager to take to the sky.

Turning on the dash radio, The Spider fished around the commercial dial, seeking a station known for broadcasting news bulletins. He found one without difficulty.

"At this hour, the fire at Mercy Hospital has been quenched and the dead are being carried out. The casualty count is said to be horrific. More urgently for the city, one of its greatest landmarks, the Vertex Building, is a giant burning candle. There are reports of persons trapped on the observation tower platform, but there is no way of reaching them...."

Their eyes met, those of The Spider and the unknown military Intelligence officer code-named G-8. Not a word passed between them. They simply nodded.

G-8 said tightly, "Those people trapped on the observation platform matter more than capturing Stahlmaske now."

"Agreed. Besides, Steel Mask's power is broken. For the present, at least."

"I dropped Operator 5 onto the platform. That makes it my job to get him off there—before he's roasted alive!"

"In that case," said The Spider, throwing open the cabin door, "I will only be an encumbrance. Perhaps I can pick up Steel Mask's trail alone."

"It's worth a try," said the Master Spy, grinning. "Good luck!"

"Good luck to us both," returned The Spider, clapping the rotorplane hatch shut and ducking under the twirling vanes, then disappearing into the open garage of the Gotham Arms apartment building.

While the churning gyro lifted off, a dark sedan slid out of the garage, crossed the sidewalk, and gained the deserted street.

On snarling tires, jaw set in determined lines, The Spider raced east.

Floating from the front seat came the metallic, disturbing laughter of The Spider!

Turning east was merely a hunch, a wild guess, an act of blind desperation.

But it paid off!

The Spider soon overhauled the careening sedan, thanks to the fact that Steel Mask had paused in his flight to hypnotize G-8. Wentworth could see through the rear window a shapeless dark form—a head, enveloped in some dark material.

Face turning fierce under his metallic mask, The Spider tramped the accelerator and, with motor howling to a crescendo, sent his own machine racing alongside the other.

As he pulled up to pace his quarry, the other turned his gigantic head, and it was with a sudden shock that The Spider saw, not the black helmet of Steel Mask, *but the silken hood of Count Calypsa, the failed Dictator of Crime!*

The shock was momentary. Yet it was enough to throw off his mental balance. The unexpected sight wrung a wild laugh from The Spider's twisted lips.

A hearty laugh came back, booming and derisive.

"I will live to see the day I brand you with your own sigil, *Herr Spinne!*"

"That day will never arrive, von Maur!"

The masked driver threw his wheel to the left, causing fenders to bang and scrape, throwing The Spider's machine up onto the sidewalk and into a lamppost.

The hood had crumpled, the cracked radiator spilling hot steam.

The Master of Men sat stunned as the hurtling machine turned a corner and disappeared from sight. Brushing glass from his lap, he saw that the two wings of the windscreen had ended up in the front seat. Struggling to open the front door, he laboriously hurled glass and bent frame out onto the sidewalk. Then he stepped out unarmed, eyes blazing.

Racing down the side street, The Spider found a passing taxi-cab and flagged it down. By this time, his blue-steel domino mask was in a secret pocket of his jacket. Ducking in, he threw this carelessly onto the seat beside him.

"There's a blue sedan racing south on East Forty-first Street. Pursue it!"

"Are you a detective?"

"Friend of Commissioner Kirkpatrick. Now get into gear!"

For the rest of his natural life, the cabbie never understood why he obeyed—only that the dominating voice carried with it a strange compulsive urgency, one that motivated him to swing around on screeching tires and race headlong for East Forty-first Street.

They soon found the fleeing machine. It had gone out of control turning a corner at high speed.

Exiting, The Spider raced toward it on foot, but when he got to the front seat, he saw that the door was open and there was no one behind the wheel....

On the passenger seat, eye-slits staring mockingly upward, lay the black helmet of Steel Mask. It was empty.

Retrieving it, The Spider realized the damnable truth....

"STEEL MASK got away in Count Calypsa's sedan," Wentworth

explained to Commissioner Kirkpatrick, who pulled up not very many minutes later in response to an urgent telephone call.

Kirkpatrick accepted the dented black shell and said, "When I heard the news that you lived—" His voice trailed off and was lost in an embarrassed rumble of phlegm.

"I had my reasons for staying out of sight."

"I am quite sure that you did," returned Kirkpatrick thinly.

"With The Spider believed dead," continued Wentworth, "I thought by staying under cover, it would lull Steel Mask and his confederate into becoming careless. Which they did. The attempt to get at me through Nita at Mercy Hospital was something I half-expected."

"Dick," Kirkpatrick said firmly. "The Spider was seen at Mercy Hospital."

Wentworth shook his head vigorously. "Not The Spider, but Captain George Gate, whom we now know to be the storied G-8. I'm sure he will confirm his role in the evening's strenuous activities. You have but to ask him."

Regarding the steel helmet again, Kirkpatrick said, "We will leave the matter at that. I will not press you on that point, for The Spider is not currently wanted by the law." He knuckled the waxed points of his mustaches thoughtfully. "You say that Count Calypsa is dead?"

Taking out his platinum cigarette lighter and igniting a cigarette, Wentworth nodded affirmatively. He paused to inhale and blew out a plume of smoke that resembled a dense cloud of ever-shifting cobwebs... but perhaps that was only an illusion of the evening light.

"During my convalescence," he said evenly, "I reasoned that neither confederate could have gotten very far through the secret passageway and that a second headquarters must exist within the radius of a block or two, at most. To excavate a longer escape route would have been too costly an engineering feat. It turns out there was a second lair in the Gotham Arms. I fear it is on fire and whatever evidence remained is going up in smoke even now. Count Calypsa's corpse can be found roasting on the floor. He is no longer a menace to the city. Without their Dictator, his minions will dissolve as a threat. No doubt some future criminal master mind will recruit some of them."

"But Steel Mask has escaped justice?"

"For the moment," said Wentworth, blowing out another plume of webby vapor. His eyes went to the smoldering top of the Vertex Building visible to the northeast and the silvery gyroplane orbiting its Art Deco spire, swooping in and then detaching from it, beating away into the night.

The rescue appeared to have gone well....

"Unless I am very much mistaken," said Wentworth confidently. "Steel Mask will not remain at large for very long. For the combined Metropolitan Police Force, the Intelligence Service and military Intelligence will run him down sooner than later. His hood may conceal his ugliness, but it also forces him to remain in hiding. I do not see how he can evade capture for more than a week...."

"As the ancient Arabian proverb states, from your lips to God's ears," murmured Stanley Kirkpatrick heavily. He scrutinized the hellish skyline of Manhattan. Mercy Hospital was a smoking shell. As was Macy's Department Store. The Vertex spire likewise. Somehow, by some miracle, the upper-story blaze had been quenched by the fire-control sprinkler system.

"Providence be thanked," murmured Wentworth.

Kirkpatrick sighed. "Well, it is over now. The entire ordeal. All that remains is to bury our dead, and to rebuild what we can...."

Wentworth clapped the police official on his broad back. "Tomorrow, Kirk. Tomorrow is soon enough."

Kirkpatrick's bleak eyes reflected the pain of losing so many of New York's finest.

"Yes, tomorrow will come soon enough. Do you realize that it will be All Souls' Day?"

Richard Wentworth's lips drew into a tight, ironic smile. "The day of remembrance of the faithful departed," he murmured. "A fitting day for the horrors that commenced on Halloween, wouldn't you say?"

His whispered laugh was nothing like that of The Spider's....

Chapter 48

MISTER WENTWORTH
COMES CALLING

THE MANHUNT for Steel Mask soon spread statewide, then nationwide. Although the search continued intensively through the month of November, no trace of him was ever discovered. A stolen coupé marked with Steel Mask's fingerprints was discovered in an isolated finger of land on the East River, in an area of factories, warehouses and apartment buildings, abandoned. There the trail ended....

By Thanksgiving, the horrific events that followed the Halloween carnival of horrors had started to fade from the public mind, along with the blaring headlines, *Steel Mask Still Sought!*

On the Friday after Thanksgiving, snappy in a Chesterfield coat and brown Borsalino felt hat, clutching a slim cane, Richard Wentworth presented himself to the elegant Fifth Avenue photographic studio of the renowned Carleton Victor. The reception room was hung with rare and expensive paintings by Picasso, Renoir and Cézanne.

As Wentworth paused to admire the owner's taste, a smiling secretary inquired, "Have you an appointment?"

"I do not," Wentworth returned crisply. "But I am sure that your employer will see me. Please give Mr. Victor my card."

The secretary took the card into the inner chamber and it was several minutes before Wentworth was invited into the studio itself.

Raising the silver knob of his jaunty walking stick in salute, Wentworth greeted, "I am pleased to meet you under less confusing circumstances, Victor—*or do you prefer to be addressed as James Christopher?*"

The face of Carleton Victor stiffened. For it was identical to that of James Christopher, secretly American Intelligence Service Operator 5. The crystal blue eyes were unmistakable.

Producing a silver case, Wentworth snapped it open. He selected a slim cigarette from within and placed it between his lips, offered the exposed array of imported tobacco to the other man.

Waving it away, Christopher asked, "What is the purpose of your visit, Wentworth?"

Firing his cigarette with a platinum lighter, Wentworth remarked, "Tying up loose ends. Nothing more. Consider it a courtesy call. I read in the papers about the horrors of the Vertex Building. Beastly business, that. Except for yourself and another unidentified man who were plucked off the observation platform by a certain mysterious Captain Gate, there were no survivors. Pity."

"It was a terrible tragedy," agreed Christopher briskly. "But it might have been worse."

"I understand that one of the zombie rabble accidentally released a deadly gas, which wiped out everyone who worked on the fifty-fifth floor."

Carleton Victor said nothing. His level eyes were now almost black.

"The strange part of it," continued Wentworth with studied nonchalance, "is that no one seems to know much about Consolidated Paper Mills, the enterprise that formerly operated on that floor. The dead were whisked away and interred in a mass grave without the formality of autopsy. It was all terribly secretive. Especially the part about the lethal gas… Diphenochlorasine, wasn't it? Odd ingredient for a paper manufacturing concern to have in its inventory…." Wentworth exhaled a greyish cloud of tobacco. "Particularly since no manufacturing appears to have been conducted on the premises...."

Christopher's features remained as stiff as a mask. "I am sure that organization—whatever it was—will be reconstituted at another address, if it hasn't already done so. Modern enterprises usually survive the deaths of their officers."

"Quite so." Looking about the extensive studio hung with framed portraits of many notables, including Commissioner Kirkpatrick and the President of the United States, Wentworth added, "Let me get to the point. I know your secret. But it is safe with me, rest assured. My lips are forever sealed."

"If you think that will save you from just punishment if my future duties should bring us into conflict," Christopher said in a brittle voice, "I must remind you that I am obliged by solemn oath to follow the orders of my superiors to the letter."

WENTWORTH'S POLITE smile was careless and unconcerned.

"I would expect no less of the individual designated as... Operator 5."

"How did you know to come here?" inquired Christopher tensely.

A knowing light leapt into Wentworth's grey-blue gaze. "Surely, my reputation as a criminologist precedes me. You will recall that we previously met when you were passing yourself off as a Secret Service agent."

"I happen to be affiliated with both organizations," Christopher said stiffly.

Wentworth continued in a cool tone. "I recalled that Carleton Victor had been present at the Halloween ball, and I have since attempted to make an appointment for my fiancée to have her portrait taken, but without success. So I looked you up in the social register. I will confess that I was not entirely shocked to discover that the picture of Carleton Victor bore the face of the

Secret Service agent I met last year. The rest was simple deduction. The celebrated Mr. Victor was a sham, a necessary pose."

Christopher said nothing.

Leaning on his sword cane, Wentworth asked, "I understand you are quite an accomplished foilist?"

"I studied at the salle d'armes under Scherevesky and am proficient with the foil, epee and saber."

Wentworth laughed lightly and took another puff of his cigarette. "Excellent! My swordsmanship is known throughout the Continent. Perhaps we might engage in a friendly duel one day. I have a fencing room in my Sutton Place townhouse."

James Christopher paused before replying, then stated with an edge in his voice: "I am quite certain that we will cross swords again in the future, one way or another... Wentworth."

Richard Wentworth's laugh grew rich and resonant. After it had trailed off, he added, "I, for one, would prefer to enter into a friendlier contest. I think we could be comrades, Christopher. I understand that my fiancée and Miss Diane Elliot have become rather... chummy."

A brittle flicker came into the eyes of Carleton Victor. He paused before answering. "I am a number in the Intelligence Service of this nation, and The Spider is a notorious vigilante. Such diametrically different personalities could never associate in a respectable manner."

Contemplatively, Wentworth exhaled a gossamer cloud of smoke redolent with expensive imported tobacco. "I see by the papers that Commissioner Kirkpatrick in a rare moment credited The Spider with saving the city from the main body of Green Meteorite. Quite an admission for him. And virtually another pardon for the infamous arachnid."

Christopher paused, and his expression was unreadable.

"The Commissioner is almost certainly correct," he allowed.

For long moments, a strained silence hung between the two men.

Finishing his cigarette, Wentworth shrugged negligently and returned his Borsalino to the top of his head, setting it in place with faultless perfection.

"Well, no matter," he returned casually. "The Spider is no more. He hasn't been heard of since he went into the East River."

"I suspect he won't remain there," replied Christopher, eyes flinty.

Pausing at the door to flash a friendly smile, Richard Wentworth remarked, "I imagine you may be correct. His Presidential pardon remains intact, so he is at liberty to strike at the Underworld with impunity. But until Steel Mask is captured, none of us should rest easy...."

With those words, he closed the door, gently but firmly. His hard-heeled footsteps retreated from the studio of Carleton Victor, whom the world did not suspect to be Operator 5.

As a parting gesture, Richard Wentworth paused at the outer door, and regarded the lettering on the door.

CARLETON VICTOR

PORTRAITIST

Lifting his platinum cigarette lighter, he opened a concealed aperture in its heel and pressed this firmly against the legend. When it came away, it left a red mark, burning like a drop of fresh blood.

But it was no such thing. *For this was the scarlet symbol of The Spider!*

Richard Wentworth exited the building whistling a thin, eerie string of notes....

About the Author

WILL MURRAY

WILL MURRAY first became intrigued by The Spider when he saw a creepy still from the 1938 Columbia serial, *The Spider's Web,* in an issue of *Castle of Frankenstein* back in 1963.

He did not encounter the character for another six years. Murray turned 16 years old in 1969. He picked up his first Doc Savage novel in January and by the summer, Bantam Books added The Shadow to their line of pulp-hero reprints. That November, Berkeley Books released The Spider with a strange promotion where the first two novels in the series were packaged together with a paper band that read: buy one book, get the second one free.

It was probably not the best way to sell paperback books in those days of spinner racks in drugstores and newsstands. Booksellers didn't know what to make of it.

Murray didn't care. He enjoyed *The Spider Strikes* and its sequel, *The Wheel of Death.* When the second and third releases came out, they were not by R.T.M. Scott, but bylined Grant Stockbridge, a house name concealing the unique style of Norvell W. Page.

Wings of the Black Death and *City of Flaming Shadows* made Murray a fan of both The Spider and his greatest author at the same time. Alas, the promised next novel, *Empire of Doom,* was never released in paperback.

Undaunted, Murray eventually came to collect The Spider pulp magazines and got to read that story, as well as many dozens of others.

During the decade when he ghostwrote the Destroyer paper-back series, Murray liked to relax between novels by reading Spider stories. The wild inattention to detail, frenetic plots and high-voltage storytelling were a nice change of pace from having to write stories that made logical sense.

At one point, he became friends with one of Norvell Page's descendants, and he learned a great deal about the remarkable man behind The Spider, who passed away in 1961.

Years later, Murray had the opportunity to write Spider short stories for various Moonstone anthologies, but writing a novel featuring the Master of Men eluded him until recently.

During the period when Radio Archives was releasing the Will Murray Pulp Classics line of pulp audiobooks, Murray success-fully lobbied for The Spider. Dozens of Spider audiobooks have been released since.

In the world of strange synchronicities, the only other person to write a Spider novel in the 21st Century was the late C.J. Henderson. Henderson's daughter Erica went on to fame drawing Squirrel Girl for Marvel Comics—a character created by Will Murray, along with artist Steve Ditko, co-creator of Spider-Man.

It's a small world... full of spiders... and squirrels....

About the Artist

JOE DeVITO

JOE DeVITO was born on March 16, 1957, in New York City. He graduated with honors from Parsons School of Design in 1981 and studied at the Art Students League in New York City. Joe is the founder of DeVito ArtWorks, LLC, an artist-driven transmedia studio dedicated to the creation and development of multi-faceted properties including Skull Island, War Eagles, and the Primordials. DeVito ArtWorks is exclusively represented by Festa Entertainment and Dimensional Branding Group.

Over the years, DeVito has painted many of the most recognizable Pop Culture and pulp icons, including King Kong, Tarzan, Doc Savage, Superman, Batman, Wonder Woman, Spider-Man, *MAD* magazine's Alfred E. Neuman and various characters in World of Warcraft, with a decided emphasis in his illustration on dinosaurs, Action Adventure, SF and Fantasy. He has illustrated hundreds of book and magazine covers, painted several notable posters and numerous trading cards for the major comic book and gaming houses, and created concept and character design for the film and television industries.

In 3-D, DeVito sculpted the official 100th Anniversary statue of *Tarzan of the Apes* for the Edgar Rice Burroughs Estate, *The Cooper Kong* for the Merian C. Cooper Estate, Superman, Wonder Woman and Batman for Chronicle Books' Masterpiece Editions, and several other notable characters.

An avid writer, Joe is also the co-author (with Brad Strickland) of three novels, which he illustrated as well. The first, based on Joe's original *Skull Island* prequel/sequel, was *KONG: King of Skull Island* (DH Press), published in 2004. The second book, *Merian C. Cooper's KING KONG,* was published by St. Martin's Griffin in 2005. In 2017, DeVito ArtWorks published the third book (the first under its own imprint), *King Kong of Skull Island,* the most comprehensive Kong history to date. *King Kong of Skull Island* chronicles the origins of the Kongs and the human civilization on Skull Island, the building of the great Wall, and the prequel/sequel story of King Kong himself. Joe has also contributed essays and articles to such collected works as *Kong Unbound: The Cultural Impact, Pop Mythos, and Scientific Plausibility of a Cinematic Legend* and "Do Android Artists Paint in Oils When They Dream?" in *Pixel or Paint: The Digital Divide in Illustration Art.*

The year 2018 saw the further exploration of DeVito's Kong prequel/sequel series in the BOOM! Studios' highly successful comic book series *Kong of Skull Island,* various special issues delving into events along the Kong timeline, culminating with the six-issue *Kong on the Planet of the Apes* in association with 20th Century Fox. The property is also in full development as a TV series. DeVito continues painting covers for the Wild Adventures sagas (written by Will Murray), featuring Doc Savage, Pat Savage, The Shadow, Tarzan and King Kong—including *King Kong vs. Tarzan,* the first-ever authorized meeting of these iconic characters—and The Spider. DeVito is also developing his newest creation in words and images, a faction world of truly epic proportions titled *The Primordials.*

Regarding *The Doom Legion,* Joe writes:

There is nothing quite like the visceral feel of painting classic pulps: The over-the-top characters, the titles of the stories, the lighting and color schemes—it's all just plain *fun!* This is the first time I have ever worked with The Spider and other associated characters such as Operator 5 and Stahlmaske, and they proved no exception to the rule. And a very special thanks to David Smith for the commission that made it all possible.

What made this cover more challenging than the norm, though, was the number of personalities I was asked to cram into one painting. Will's story had so many cool characters that we didn't want to leave anything out. It was a challenge to narrow it down to the multiple elements that still remained: The Spider and Operator 5 standing back-to- back, wielding two .45s and a rapier respectively. Stahlmaske carrying the woman, zombies and a green meteor. To think we tried to cram in even more!

Once David, Will and I had all the concepts and details on the table, it was up to me to figure out how to put everything together into a painting that worked visually, which is often a lot harder than it looks. A finished painting is much more than the sum of its parts; it is a result of how and where those parts are combined into a coordinated picture that comfortably leads the eye throughout the composition and its oft competing details. To do this requires a balancing of draftsmanship, value (light and dark), color intensity, edge work (hard/soft), size relationships, action vs. non-action, and more.

This is accomplished through a series of graphite sketches, very loose at first, to establish the big picture (which is actually done using the smallest sketches called "thumbnails" in reference to their size). Once the basics are set, then it's on to a more refined version to lock in the details and, finally, the color sketch. I usually paint the color sketch in acrylic due to that medium's quick drying time and good opacity, which come in handy as I make various changes during my search for the right balance of all the aforementioned elements.

One of the more enjoyable aspects of pulp-oriented covers is the color. My color palate is generally more subdued, but a good pulp cover is usually anything but. On the contrary, it is a chromatic riot! Balancing out all of that out requires going back and forth multiple times on the color sketch until I hit the sweet spot. When I felt I had hit that point on *The Doom Legion*, I ran it by Will and Dave to make sure they liked it, too. As always, they were various details that needed to be tweaked. In this case, Will pointed out nuances on the skull keychain, details on Stahlmaske, and on The Spider's mask itself to stay in keeping with recent changes he made to the look of the characters.

When all was said and done, we were all very happy with the result and hope that fans everywhere are as well. The Spider is a very welcome, thrilling new addition to Will's ever-expanding publishing oeuvre. May there be many more to come!

www.jdevito.com
www.kongskullisland.com
FB: Kong of Skull Island
FB: DeVito ArtWorks

About the Patron

DAVE SMITH

AT THE age of 14, I started working for the late John McLaughlin at The Book Sail in old downtown Anaheim. It was here that I was first exposed to the likes of classic comic books from the 1940s, pulp magazines, vintage magic books signed by Harry Houdini, and lots of old and rare books.

I worked there on and off from 1969 to 1979 and then left to open my own store, Fantasy Illustrated, about 1.5 miles from Disneyland. From inception until I sold the store (keeping the name) in 1994, I maintained one of the largest selections of vintage comic book and pulp magazines in the Orange County area.

Wanting a change of pace, I moved out of California in late 1994. On January 1, 1995, I became owner of Rocket Comics of Seattle, Washington. In 1998, I found what would become the famous Yakima Pedigree collection of ultra-high grade pulps. These are considered some of the finest condition pulp magazines known to exist.

Around 9/11, I closed down Rocket Comics as a brick and mortar store and continued dealing full time as Fantasy Illustrated, doing mail order out of my house near Mill Creek, Washington. In 2016, my wife Kelli and I sold the house and moved north to the Silvana area where we have five acres and a 1900 square foot stand-alone building for my pulp, book and comic business.

A few years ago, I decided that I wanted to start sharing my pulp and retailer knowledge, so I began writing for PEAPS *(Pulp Era Amateur Press Society)*. My articles have also appeared in

The Pulpster, Blood 'N' Thunder Magazine, and my own fanzine, *Dave's Clubhouse.*

Both as a dealer and collector, my main emphasis these days is pulp magazines. From there, it was an easy step into collecting associated art. Some time ago, I connected with Will Murray and Joe DeVito and started sponsoring cover art for some of the books Will was writing and Joe was illustrating.

I'm really excited to be involved in this latest exploit resurrecting three pulp heroes into the Wild Adventures series. There is a lot going on here. So how do you do a cover justice with three heroes, a major villain and possibly a damsel in distress?

While in the early stages of throwing ideas around, we thought that if we put all the elements into the cover painting that we wanted, it would most likely come off as very crowded and thus detrimental to the aesthetics of the image. It was decided that only two heroes would be shown on the cover: The Spider and either G-8 or Operator 5. But which one?

Will came up with the great idea to represent G-8 on the cover by using the villain from this series, Stahlmaske. In his arms is Nita van Sloan, Richard (The Spider) Wentworth's fiancée. Lots of ideas were thrown around, even down to should we show shoes on Nita's feet, which Joe decided to hide in the mist instead. Placement of everyone was critical. I love that Joe came up with positioning the characters on the cover in a classic "triangle" arrangement which is very aesthetically pleasing.

Joe did an amazing job on the finished painting. You have the green meteor in the background with Stahlmaske and Nita mid-range and Operator 5 and The Spider front and center. I especially like Op 5's rapier contrasting to The Spider's .45 automatics. I've had a great time working with Will and Joe once more and hope to do so again in the near future.

rocketbat@msn.com

www.fantasyillustrated.net

THE SPIDER

MASTER OF MEN!

The original adventures
of the Master of Men:
coming this Spring
in affordable, mass
market editions, deluxe
hardcovers, and ebooks.

Brought to you by
Altus Press, the leader
in Pulp Fiction.

THE ARGOSY™ LIBRARY

SERIES 4 INCLUDES:

* TUTTLE * ENGLAND * FARLEY *
* BRAND * BRENT * ROSCOE *
* GIESY & SMITH *
* RUD * PETTEE *
* CUNNINGHAM *

THE BEST FICTION
FROM THE FRANK
A. MUNSEY LINE

THE ARGOSY LIBRARY

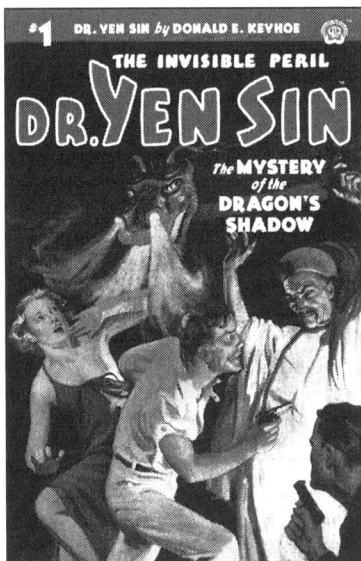

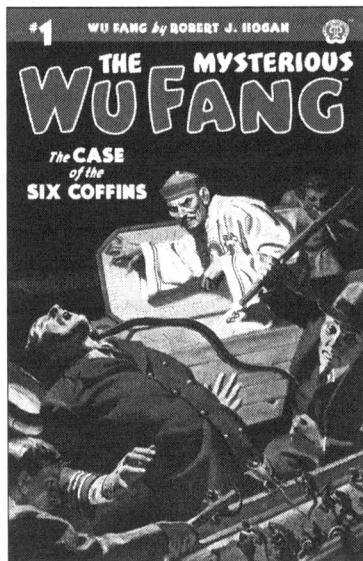

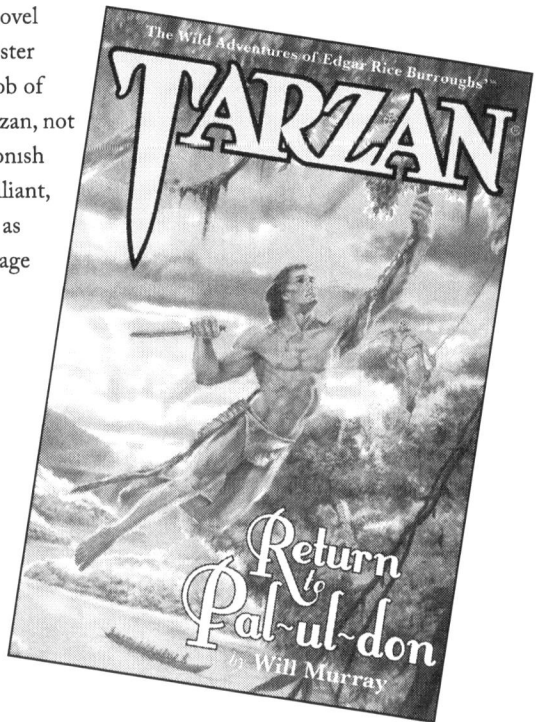

WORDSLINGERS

AN EPITAPH FOR THE WESTERN

☞ WILL MURRAY ☜

Will Murray's Wordslingers is not only the first in-depth history of the Western pulps, it's one of the best and most important books on the pulps ever written, perfectly capturing the era, the magazines, and the writers, editors, and agents who helped fill their pages. Pulp fans will be fascinated by the rich background provided by hundreds of quotes from the people involved in producing the Western pulps, while writers will benefit from the discussions of characterization and storytelling that prove to be both universal and timeless.

—*James Reasoner*

$29.95 softcover
$39.95 hardcover
$8.99 ebook

JOIN THE PREMIER EDGAR RICE BURROUGHS FAN ORGANIZATION

Edgar Rice Burroughs in 1916

In 1947, Edgar Rice Burroughs personally approved the creation of a fan club and fanzine. The fanzine was first published that year as *The Burroughs Bulletin*, and is the longest-running ERB fanzine still being published. The fan club was founded in 1960 as The Burroughs Bibliophiles, which adopted the *Bulletin* as its journal. The Bibliophiles also issues a monthly newsletter, *The Gridley Wave*, and other special publications.

Today, The Burroughs Bibliophiles remains the largest ERB fan organization in the world, with members from around the globe and with local chapters across the United States and in England. Besides publishing its journal and newsletter, the Bibliophiles sponsors the annual convention called the "Dum-Dum," named for ceremonial gatherings of the Great Apes in the Tarzan novels. Members continue to be influential in all aspects of Burroughs, from publishing critical analyses to writing new authorized fiction, including novels in *The Wild Adventures of Edgar Rice Burroughs Series*.

For more information about the society and membership, visit the Bibliophiles' website at www.BurroughsBibliophiles.com or The Burroughs Bibliophiles Facebook page. You can also e-mail the Editor at BurroughsBibliophiles@gmail.com, call (573) 647-0225, or mail 318 Patriot Way, Yorktown, Virginia 23693-4639, USA.

KING KONG VS. TARZAN

THE SPIDER®

Now you can own an authorized cold-cast bronze bust of the dreaded Master of Men as he appears in the Wild Adventures of The Spider.

Sculpted by Lawrence Elig.

Contact: ljelig03@aol.com

Note: image shown is a prototype. The finished sculpture will have a metallic surface. Price not yet set.

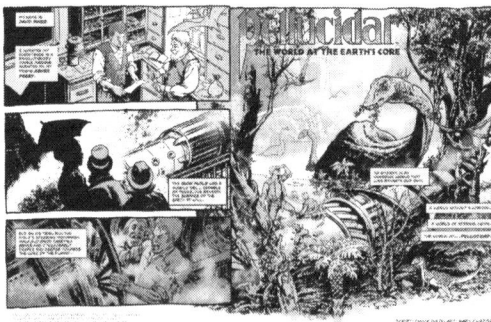

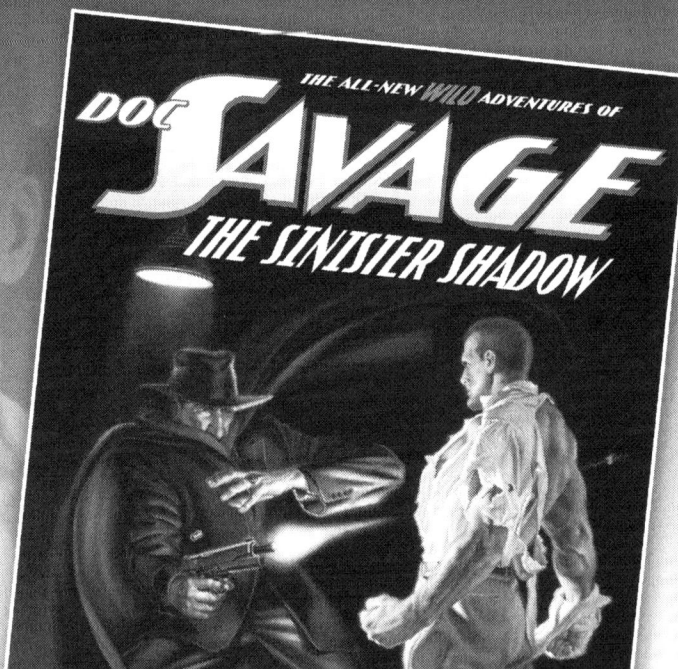

THE LEGENDARY ADVENTURES CONTINUE!

Printed in Great Britain
by Amazon